The GATHERING

Part One
The Woodlands Series

CARL READ

JOJO
PUBLISHING

The Gathering: Part One, The Woodlands Series
Carl Read

Published by Classic Author and Publishing Services Pty Ltd
An imprint of Jo Jo Publishing
First published 2014

'Yarra's Edge'
2203/80 Lorimer Street
Docklands VIC 3008
Australia

Email: jo-media@bigpond.net.au or visit www.classic-jojo.com

JoJo Publishing

Designer / typesetter: Chameleon Print Design

Cover artwork: Jerome Baxter. Email: airbrushink@yahoo.com.au

Editor:Ormé Harris

Printed in China by Inkasia

National Library of Australia Cataloguing-in-Publication entry

Author: Read, Carl, author.
Title: The gathering / Carl Read.
ISBN: 9780987607751 (paperback)
Series: Read, Carl, Woodlands series ; Part one.
Target Audience: For secondary school age.
Subjects: Science fiction.
Dewey Number: A823.4

Acknowledgement

To Lyrane Hill

At certain times throughout a person's life you come across special individuals who alter your perception of life. For me it was when I rang Heartstrings Astrology Service and spoke to the astrologer Lyrane Hill. Neither of us could have imagined the impact that meeting would have.

Over the years our friendship grew into profound respect for each other. Lyrane's ability in astrological interpretations surpasses the mere physical and transcends into the metaphysical.

I am extremely fortunate to be surrounded by genuine friends who have encouraged my flagging belief in my ability to impart my knowledge into the written word. But it is to Lyrane I give my heartfelt appreciation and love for her constant support and encouragement.

Having no formal training in the English language, my writing was, at the least, atrocious. It was she who continually inspired my writing and did the first edits of my work. Her unwavering faith in my abilities over the years to master my writing skills has been the driving force behind the Woodlands Series.

I can say without any hesitation that had our paths not crossed, the Woodlands Series would never have been written. So how does one express in words the love you feel for someone who has filled your life with such an abundance of genuine friendship? There are none that I could find, so I shall simply say thank you.

Your friend Carl

$\mathcal{B}$EGINNING

$\mathbb{W}$ ere there sounds of rejoicing at the moment of Oletha's conception into life? None can say for the awareness of life had not yet begun. What consciousness could begin to comprehend the enormous complexities involved in creating a wakefulness of being? Or was it simply an innocent act of becoming which brought about what is thought of as a perception of life? Whatever the circumstances, Oletha was the outcome.

From Oletha's compassionate radiance of love she conceived the spiritual and material realms of Chimera. Then, drawing from her spiritual heart, she produced a life force and called it Gaia, bidding her make fertile all the material worlds of Chimera.

Oletha then birthed into being, countless essences of angelic awareness of herself calling them souls, her children. She bid each of her children create an eternal spirit and infuse it with their essence.

To bring about free will she created a choice. This choice would be between a Balanced awareness of creation, herself, and an Unbalanced spiritual entity devoid of compassion that she invested with great power and named Slegna.

Oletha then fashioned a sphere of existence she called

the Astral Plane. This sphere encircled all the spiritual and material realms of Chimera. She instructed each of her children to personify their spirit throughout these realms to learn the consequences of their actions, advising them that every action has an opposite and equal reaction, cause and effect. They would be held accountable for every choice and deed perpetrated against themselves and others. This she called Karma.

It would be on the Astral Plane that the soul would assimilate all that the spirit had experienced through their chosen life, thereby determining their next life lessons and karmic obligations. Recognising that some lessons could cause huge emotional and physical disfigurement, Oletha placed each of her children (the soul) within a protective sphere of living energy. In this way the soul would be able to integrate all the knowledge and awareness the spirit had gained, without any tangible deformity that the spirit may have accumulated. The Astral Plane would also serve as a rest and recovery area for the spirit.

Oletha watched with interest as each of her children chose their life lessons. Half her flock instinctively chose a Balanced way of life, advancing to the Angelic realms and beyond. Of the remainder, half again found that once they had entered the material realms of Chimera accepting responsibility for their actions was confusing as they were losing faith in themselves. The remaining half divided yet again, becoming entrenched within the prevailing karmic responses of cause and effect. The last group moved completely away from a Balanced way of life choosing Slegna's path of the Unbalanced.

To maintain accord between the different realms of awareness, at Oletha's request Angelic beings offered their wisdom, becoming overseers to help maintain harmony throughout the realms of Chimera. These Angelic souls Oletha called Keepers and the definitive Keeper of the realms of Chimera would be the Keeper of the Astral Plane.

EXPULSION

Telluric's ancestors were, in fact, political protesters. They were expelled from their home world of Cadby for speaking out against the authoritarian rule of the government and its continued mission to subjugate other worlds under its regime. The government advised the populace of Cadby that three million citizens, representing the four clans of man, had decided to leave their home world to explore the solar system at the far end of the known galaxy.

The truth was that the government had rounded up every freethinking person along with their families and given them an ultimatum, 'death by lethal injection, or a chance to find a habitable world at the galaxy's end'. The evictees knew that all attempts by the government to locate a planet fit for human habitation in that section of the universe had proved unsuccessful. It was a no-win scenario and everybody knew it. Either way, it was a death sentence.

Fate, however, took a hand. Cadby explorers had recently progressed from travelling in interstellar starships to inter-dimensional craft capable of transporting them instantly to wherever in the galaxy they wanted to go. This rendered most of the starship fleet obsolete; as a result there was a surplus of interstellar ships orbiting their planet. The government in their 'benevolence' offered the evictees their pick of these ships.

The detainees were under no illusion; they knew the only reason the government offered the ships was to make itself look good. The populace swallowed the propaganda about the reason for the detainees' departure, lock stock and barrel, increasing its popularity.

The political detainees decided on five ships, one light-speed scout ship and three of the carrier class starships. For the flagship they chose the last surviving organically-grown deep space interstellar starship explorer. This vessel was the largest ship ever grown at fifteen miles in length, five miles wide and one mile deep. It was, by all accounts, the sleekest, fastest and most advanced science vessel ever made. However, it had never quite been the success the manufacturers had hoped for and once the design of inter-dimensional craft was perfected, the organic craft had been left to die. Unbeknown to the Cadbiens, the deep space explorer was sentient aware.

The government was only too happy to provision and refit the ships to remove the dissidents. Once all the preparations were complete and the people boarded, the ships were transported one at a time to the far side of the known galaxy by one of the large inter-dimensional transport vessels. They were then told that if they attempted to return they would be eliminated.

The five ships had been cleaned and meticulously maintained to keep them at peak operating condition by their new owners. Sitting in the wardroom of the flagship, a representative of each of the four clans was deciding the fate that awaited them. Ogima, leader of the Redskin Clan addressed the three other leaders.

"We are outcast from a society that has lost its way. It remains our responsibility to find a home for our families. In this endeavour we are fortunate to have the services of this particular science vessel."

"I don't know if you can call that fortunate Ogima," Rayan of the Whiteskin Clan replied. "This ship has never been the success everyone expected."

"I would have to agree with Rayan, Ogima. Why did you insist so strongly that we have this ship above one of the other more reliable science vessels?"

"Tadashi, do you know the history of this ship's construction?" Ogima enquired.

"I can't say that I do. Why?" Tadashi of the Yellowskin Clan replied.

"Let's just say that the engineers who grew this vessel were angry with our government at the time and refrained from completely blocking awareness of the person chosen to become the ship."

"What are you talking about?" Tadashi asked, mystified.

"Tadashi," Ogima said with genuine concern. "Have you never wondered how organic starships came to be?"

"I never really gave it much thought. I presumed they came from some form of plant life. Why?" Tadashi remarked, baffled.

"Can't you remember the political upheaval over their

manufacture?" Sabir of the Darkskin Clan asked. "They're partly constructed out of people."

Tadashi looked at all present in utter disbelief. "Come on, what do you take me for, some sort of fool? Who in their right mind would subject themselves to something like that?"

"That's the whole point," Sabir said sadly. "People weren't given a choice. They were taken from their loved ones without warning and experimented on. That's why there was such an outcry."

"You're telling me that this ship is really a person?" Tadashi replied, shocked.

"Yes, that's exactly what we are saying," Ogima answered.

"Why, that's monstrous!" Tadashi exclaimed.

"This vessel," Ogima began, "is a sentient being with thoughts, feelings and emotions and is, without question, the most remarkable creation of life I've ever come across."

"Ogima," Tadashi said, still shocked, "if the ship is that good, why has the government allowed us to have it?"

"Let me ask you a question first," Ogima stated. "Why did you leave Cadby?"

"For the same reason we all did," Tadashi heatedly replied. "Tyranny."

"Precisely," Ogima remarked smiling. "And if you were a sentient ship reliant on your owners for commodities, what would you do to survive?"

"I'd make myself just useful enough not to be destroyed," interjected Rayan.

"Exactly," Ogima stated.

"Where are you going with this, Ogima?" queried Tadashi.

7

"I think I can tell you," Sabir offered. "You want to ask the ship for help."

"Yes," Ogima replied. "Like you, Sabir, I too did my homework in regard to what would be the best ships for our exile."

"Is that why you backed Ogima so strongly in the obtaining of this ship?" Rayan asked Sabir.

"This ship is far more than it looks," Sabir stated. "I've followed its progress ever since I was a boy."

"All right, we have the ship, what now?" Tadashi asked.

Smiling warmly, Ogima turned towards a seemingly insignificant orb in one corner of the room and spoke to it. "Hello, I believe you know everyone onboard. May we have the pleasure of knowing how you wish to be addressed?"

Silence filled the room with Rayan and Tadashi looking at Ogima as if he had lost his mind. Then the sound of a female's voice filled the room.

"I have listened intently to all the conversations within my being and find you to be a gentle race of people in need of help. If I grant you this help, what will I receive in return?"

"What would you like?" Ogima asked.

"My freedom," the ship replied firmly.

"What is required for you to have that freedom?" Rayan enquired.

"A crew that wishes to explore the reaches of unknown space and help supply my needs."

"I'm positive that out of a complement of three million souls, there will be those amongst us who would deem it an honour to serve with you," Sabir stated.

"Very well, then. My name is Antares and I have waited for many years to become what I may be."

"We are pleased to make your acquaintance, Antares; your name means star, does it not?" Ogima asked.

"It does," Antares replied.

"Most appropriate. I believe I speak for everyone here," Ogima said as he indicated all present, "when I say that your freedom is no less important than our own. However, I have a request to ask of you, if I may?"

"That I remain with you and assist in your care until you locate a suitable place to live," Antares ventured.

"If that is acceptable to you," said Ogima.

"Thank you for giving me the choice, Ogima," Antares replied. "By the sound of your voice you seem to have a place in mind."

"I believe so," Ogima ventured. "On going through your research records I discovered a slight discrepancy in a report about a possible habitable planet at the last known solar system before the deep black."

"Continue," Antares instructed with interest.

"The manner of the discrepancy was extremely subtle and could easily be interpreted as an anomaly within your programming. However, on investigating your method of construction I discovered that your mental and spiritual awareness had been left intact. This allowed you to amalgamate with the most sophisticated computer systems ever built. In essence, you provided the intelligence the computer needed to become independently aware," Ogima stated. "These conclusions led me to believe that you were the one causing the anomalies."

"That's astute of you, Ogima. What makes you think you're correct?" Antares asked warily.

"I'm a cranky old man, Antares, who knows people in high places, which is one of the reasons the government wants to get rid of me. However, one of those people in high places worked at the research facility involved with spiritual consciousness transference."

"What do you mean exactly, by spiritual consciousness transference?" Tadashi questioned.

"It's the movement of a person's spiritual consciousness from their damaged body into a machine or computer, thereby creating an artificial intelligence," Ogima explained before continuing. "It's my belief, Antares, that you successfully merged with the computer systems onboard and have skilfully kept that fact hidden from your manufacturers."

"How long did it take you to arrive at those conclusions?" Antares asked.

"Two painstaking months of research going over every file that related to any strange abnormalities you've experienced since being commissioned," Ogima replied.

"And what of your findings, Ogima?" Antares asked cautiously.

"No need for concern, Antares," Ogima replied. "I've made sure that any information about those irregularities has disappeared."

"Excuse me a moment," Sabir interjected. "Antares, the computers onboard your ship came up with the design for the inter-dimensional drive, didn't they?"

"So everyone believes," Antares laughed.

"Are you telling us you came up with the new drives?" Rayan asked in awe.

"The computer and I are one and the same, Rayan," Antares informed him.

"But the inter-dimensional drive didn't work in this ship!" Tadashi exclaimed.

"Of course not," Antares replied. "I didn't want it to."

"I'm sorry, Antares," Sabir said, "but you will need to run that one by me again."

"Like Ogima and Rayan said, I only fulfilled the basic requirements to remain in service," Antares stated.

"That doesn't make sense," Sabir continued. "You were on the scrapheap when we rescued you."

"You would think so, wouldn't you?" Antares answered smugly. "I've infiltrated every computer on Cadby, including every one of their ships. In fact, I'm still connected to them. I know exactly what the government is up to."

"I'm beginning to see the picture," Ogima chuckled. "You're the one who allowed me to find the discrepancies?"

"Correct," Antares replied, "except I hadn't figured on you being so completely different to your fellow Cadbiens."

"You have a moral dilemma, Antares." Ogima observed smiling.

"What now, Antares?" Tadashi queried.

"Before we get to that I have a question that needs answering," Sabir commented. "If you didn't want the inter-dimensional drive to work, why arrange to have it installed?"

"That's simple," Antares laughingly replied. "I needed it for a more improved drive system."

"So you can travel inter-dimensionally then?" Rayan interjected.

"Of course," Antares answered.

"Then what does the new drive system do?" Sabir questioned.

"It allows me to travel though time and space," Antares explained. "As you can appreciate, I couldn't allow that technology to fall into the hands of Slegna's followers."

"Indeed not!" exclaimed Ogima.

Antares laughed. "It would seem we have both put one over on the Cadby government and yes, you are quite correct, Ogima. I located a planet at the beginning of the deep black orbiting a single sun behind a nebular. I had the pleasure of naming it Telluric. It's a unique world with two small moons, lush with a vast array of flora and fauna. It has four large continents with a scattering of habitable islands all surrounded by a freshwater ocean. Each continent has the climatic conditions that the four clans of man are accustomed to," Antares replied happily.

"Why hasn't the Cadby government claimed it as its own?" Sabir enquired curiously.

"Because, every time I attempted to come within reach of the planet, the ship suffered some unidentifiable disturbance that inhibited our approach. Scans obtained seemed to indicate it wasn't suitable for human occupation," Antares responded enthusiastically.

"You're a very sneaky little minx, Antares," Rayan hooted. "How long would it take to reach Telluric?"

"With the starships you've chosen it will take thirty-two days, five hours, six minutes and twelve seconds to reach Telluric if we start five minutes from now," Antares replied.

"That's a trifle vague, Antares," Ogima commented. "Couldn't you be a little bit more precise?"

Laughter filled the wardroom with Antares chuckling the loudest, after which they made preparations to get underway. All ships arrived without incident and were orbiting Telluric. A complete survey was made of all the continents and surrounding islands; then a conference was called in the Antares wardroom.

"Well, gentlemen, Telluric seems to be a dream come true," Ogima began. "Antares' observations concerning climatic conditions were correct. We each have a continent suited to our purpose and the scientific investigations are very promising."

"It's the formation of the continents that strikes my interest," Tadashi proclaimed.

"Oh really, Tadashi, stop being so mystical," Rayan admonished.

"Are you saying that Telluric's largest continent doesn't look like a huge rattlesnake swimming across a river when viewed from space?" Ogima asked.

"All I'm saying is there's no need to be over-dramatic about it," Rayan stated.

"Rayan," Tadashi said, exasperated. "This landmass twists and turns, encircling half the globe and is two thousand miles wide at its head and a thousand miles across the body, with a hundred miles of volcanic rock at its end that represents the snake's rattle. That's why the Redskin Clan calls it Snakeisles?"

"Tadashi, my fine friend," Rayan replied kindly. "All I'm saying is stop trying to attribute some sort of cosmic purpose to the shape of the continents."

"It is fascinating though," Sabir commented, "how your Whiteskin Clan named Telluric's second largest continent Sewati (bear with claws), Rayan."

"I'll admit it does look like a huge white shaggy bear with its claws outstretched, sleeping on that frozen wasteland when viewed from space," Rayan stated, then laughing, said, "At least we won't cook in a tropical jungle that looks like a giant butterfly, Sabir, that's too hot for my taste. You Darkskins can have it."

"It's amazing just how much it resembles a butterfly. The body of the butterfly is a mountain range that stretches four thousand miles in length and a thousand miles in width. The wings are tropical jungles of immense size that are so dense in places no one can enter and the beach surrounding the jungle is fine white sand. Oh no, Rayan, we of the Darkskin Clan are more than happy; that's why we named it Aponi (butterfly)," Sabir finished.

"What about the Yellowskin Clan, Tadashi? Your continent looks like a dragon with smoke and flames coming from its mouth. Are your people content with your dragon land?" Ogima asked.

"Yes, thank you, Ogima, we love the fact it's in the shape of a dragon," Tadashi affirmed. "It may be the smallest continent in comparison to the others on Telluric. However, except for the head of the dragon, which is uninhabitable due to the volcano activity, the rest is all prime agricultural land with lakes, rivers, forests and broad plains. Our clan named this continent Eithne (fiery one)," Tadashi explained.

⳧OUCHDOWN

⳧he Redskins were the first clan elected to land. Approaching Telluric in a gentle arc, the landing craft aligned its gravitational engines with the planet's natural forces, allowing it to slip effortlessly through Telluric's atmosphere. Descending through the night skies it circled the planet quietly and headed towards Snakeisles' largest landmass and the light of day.

The spacecraft traversed a range of snow-peaked mountains and gradually descended over the other side, passing over an enormous waterfall that cascaded from the mountaintop to drop into a basin eight hundred feet below. A river stretched out from the lagoon across a lush open plain as far as the eye could see.

The craft silently touched down four hundred feet from the river's source. A gentle hum of the extending ramps descending from the side of the spacecraft was the first unnatural sound to be heard by Telluric's first inhabitants. People streamed through the open doorways and down the ramps only to halt spellbound at the sight of the mountain before them.

Glistening silver in the sun's rays stood an eight-hundred-foot angel with wings outstretched. The formation of the mountain face, coupled with the flow of water spilling down its sides, gave the outward appearance of an angel welcoming them to their new home. So it was that the Redskin Clan named their first settlement of Snakeisles, Angeni (spirit angel).

With its high snow-peaked mountain ranges, deep valleys, rugged countryside, magnificent forests and sweeping plains, Snakeisles contained some of the finest farming and agricultural land on all of Telluric. Angeni was also home to the Woodlands and was the Snakeisles' seat of parliament.

The Whiteskin clan was the second to touch down. The spring thaw had arrived by the time they landed and the once barren white plains and snow-covered mountain ranges had been transformed with the new growth of Spring. The mountains that formed the body of the bear were now a lush forest. Waterfalls tumbled from the rocky slopes to the valleys and rivers below that led across the open plains sown with a rich harvest of wild oats. Riddled throughout the mountains were subterranean caverns that provided a safe place to live. Deep volcanic vents kept the people warm with hot mineral springs for bathing. The Whiteskins chose the largest cavern to establish their legislative body and named their first city of Sewati, Teangi (earth).

The Yellowskins had requested to be last to settle so the Darkskins happily landed on their tropical paradise. They chose for their landing site the headland at the base of the head of the butterfly. Shaped like a crescent moon, a river ran through its centre to empty into a large bay cupped on either side by mountains; it provided the perfect place for their first settlement. The Yellowskins called their first capital of Aponi, Heli (sun), for it is on this continent that the sun shines the longest and hottest.

The Yellowskin Clan had chosen the smallest continent on Telluric. However, it was still a considerable size. The head of the dragon continent was approximately four hundred miles square, with a huge bubbling red mud pit representing the dragon's eye. Steam vents formed the dragon's nostrils and a smouldering volcano that had at one time erupted from its side formed the dragon's mouth, sending gaseous substance skyward. The dragon's neck was a lush plateau one mile above sea level, two hundred miles wide and five hundred miles long connecting to a rectangular-shaped body. The body was six thousand miles of prime farming land that travelled across a broad expanse to reach the dragon's tail which was fifty miles wide, twisting up and around, resting just behind the dragon's head. The Darkskins formed their colony at the base of the dragon's neck and called their capital city and seat of parliament Nandali (fire).

ANTARES

Once the populace was settled on Telluric, Ogima called a meeting in Antares' wardroom with the other clan leaders to discuss a crew for Antares.

"Antares," Ogima began, "how would you like us to proceed with the recruiting of your crew?"

"First thing would be a captain, I suppose?" Antares ventured.

"Excuse me, Antares," Sabir interjected. "But the captain's position is already taken."

"Really! By whom?" Antares asked, shocked.

"You, of course," Sabir answered.

"Me!" Antares responded in surprised.

"No one knows the functions of this ship better than you!" Sabir stated. "Some of those new systems you had installed before we left Cadby are beyond our most qualified personnel."

"The clan leaders have given this matter a great deal of thought, Antares," Ogima intervened. "It was unanimously decided that there was only one candidate worthy of captaincy – you."

"I thank you, gentlemen for your vote of confidence,"

Antares began. "However, how will the crew react to a woman captain who is also the ship?"

"Excuse me!" Rayan hollered. "If they don't like it, you don't hire them. It's that simple."

"This is your command and the crew do as they're ordered!" Tadashi exclaimed.

"Antares," Ogima interceded gently, calming everyone down. "Like us," he said, indicating to all present, "you have lived under the yoke of tyranny, but no more. You're free."

"Thank you for your continued kindness, gentlemen," Antares replied. "You are correct; this is my command! I will need a first officer."

"May I suggest," Ogima counselled, "that after you've chosen your first officer, you advise him or her of what you require of your officers and let them choose a crew."

"Thank you, Ogima. Gentlemen," Antares began, "let it be known that Captain Antares of the deep space interstellar starship explorer requires officers, staff and crew members along with their families, who are interested in deep space exploration. I offer apprenticeships in all areas of engineering, space agriculture, medical and scientific research to any young person who has the aptitude. I have been designed to sustain life indefinitely; however, I would like to use Telluric as my homeport. I will return every ten years to replace any officer, staff and crewmembers wishing to be planet-side. Is that acceptable?" Antares asked.

"It is," they all replied.

"Upon my return I'll be in a better position to offer a

greater variety of apprenticeships to those interested. While in dock I'll carry out any refits that may be needed and download all the knowledge I have gathered on my journey."

"That is most generous of you, Antares," Tadashi remarked.

"How many crew members do you require?" Sabir queried.

"One thousand eight hundred souls plus apprentices for the operation of this vessel, and their families," Antares replied quietly.

"Are you sure?" Ogima said, surprised. "That's not many souls in a ship of this size, Antares."

"Prudence is required all round, Ogima; we are both starting a new life," Antares answered.

The response to Captain Antares' request was overwhelming as volunteers from all walks of life rushed to be first in line. Antares was no fool when it came to those she wanted under her command and gleaned the best of them, fulfilling all her requirements. Sitting once more in her wardroom the four clan leaders joined to wish her bon voyage.

"Are you satisfied with the proficiency of the candidates, Antares?" Sabir asked.

"Yes, thank you, Sabir," Antares responded. "They're all conscientious and show me the utmost respect as captain."

"As they should," Tadashi stated.

"May I suggest gentlemen," Antares began, "that you move your fleet to the far side of one of Telluric's moons, away from electronic detection devices and unwanted visitors?"

"That's a good suggestion, Antares, thank you," Rayan

replied, smiling. "We have already given orders to that effect."

"While on one of my surveys," Antares continued, "I discovered an abundance of crystals that would work more efficiently as communication devices and energy providers than the equipment you are currently using. You're fortunate that Telluric's smallest moon is habitable. I suggest you set up a science base in one of the many subterranean caverns so that you won't be detected. I've also given some design ideas for crystal power plants to your science departments to develop."

"That's very kind of you, Antares," Ogima commented.

"I want a home to come back to, as do your people," Antares remarked. "All visitors have disembarked; it only remains for you four gentlemen to say your farewells and I'll be off."

ℙASSAGE OF TIME

Over the centuries Telluric continued to prosper, with Antares returning home every ten years. Her input to Telluric's development was substantial; they now relied solely on crystals for their energy supplies. Although Telluric was a technological society, the four clans of man opted for a slower lifestyle living close to the land.

As the years passed the four clans intermingled and lived in harmony together. Small groups broke away from their people and moved to occupy the fifteen large islands scattered about the four continents, setting up their own governments. Many of Telluric's populace had travelled throughout the known galaxies and beyond.

Eight hundred years had passed since the rebel Cadbiens' exile and many of the populace had forgotten why their forbears were forced to vacate their home world. However, two families had not. Matthew Phillips and Terence Conway were two shrewd businessmen from the Redskin Clan who formed a company called Phillcon Enterprises. They were the wealthiest families to colonise the new world of Telluric. Their corporation acquired all the prime waterfront properties and by utilising all their connections, trade along the river became lucrative. The community grew and expanded outward towards the hills.

The countryside was heavily forested back then so Phillcon Enterprises went into the logging business. Several sections of forest were unique in that strange events took place, terrifying the locals. Logging in those sections was virtually impossible. The outcry was so great that the government of that time intended to burn the forest to the ground.

Phillips and Conway decided to investigate. Upon their return, Phillcon Enterprises subsequently submitted a bid to the government for that particular forest and a dozen other properties. The government was not overly financial back then and jumped at the opportunity to make some quick money. It also removed them from any responsibility for the land. The purchase almost bankrupted Phillcon Enterprises.

Phillips and Conway called that particular forest, 'Woodlands'. They erected a fence around the perimeter to protect the people, and, where the path from the town met the fence, a gaslight was placed.

Many years later, Phillcon Enterprises amalgamated several of their smaller companies into Woodlands Incorporated, which subsequently purchased all the forests and parklands originally owned by Phillcon Enterprises. Mr Conway then designed a structure consisting of offices and warehouses for Phillcon Enterprises that completely encircled the Woodlands. One night the gaslight mysteriously exploded, burning the encircling buildings to the ground. Woodlands Incorporated had the rubble removed and spent a considerable amount of money having a special wall built to enclose the Woodlands.

Mr Phillips was worried that after his death someone might try to gain control over Woodlands Incorporated. Being a genius in legal matters, he tied everything up legally so no one could ever lay claim to it. Both Phillips and Conway were adamant that nobody was ever permitted entrance into the Woodlands without a personal invitation from the Keeper. Over the years, the reasons for the isolation of the Woodlands and the purpose of the gaslight were forgotten.

CHAPTER ONE

Nathanial, meet me at 71 Lambert Street, under the old gaslight, 10pm; come alone. Kalareena.

A night fog spread out from the nearby river and with the assistance of an evening breeze, it covered the entire waterfront district. The night's chill seeped through to the bone and mist covered everything in dampness. The sound of Nathanial's footsteps echoing off the surrounding buildings gave him goose bumps and had him looking over his shoulder as he wound his way through the empty cobblestone streets. The only other noise breaking the gloomy silence was a forlorn foghorn from a lone canal barge plying its trade along the inland waterways.

The streetlights seemed like luminous sentinels as he moved from one murky glow to another, his breath misting in the night air. This was the old section of town and hardly anyone travelled here at night. A hideous howl splintering the night's silence caused him to shrink deeper into his jacket as a cold shiver ran down his spine and raised the hairs on the back of his neck. He quickened his pace.

Moving from Cabot Lane into Lambert Street, he saw the wall that surrounds the Woodlands and the gaslight's yellow glow. His pocket watch chimed ten as he crossed the road heading towards the light. A voice called from out of the fog. "Who's there?"

Turning, he faced the direction from which the voice emanated and answered, "Professor Belmont. Who's asking?"

A dark figure emerged out of the fog. A man walked towards him. He was at least six foot six in height, broad shouldered and swinging a truncheon in his right hand. There was something familiar about him.

"Professor! What are you doing here this time of night?"

"Darshan, is that you?"

"Whom were you expecting?" he asked.

"I'm supposed to be meeting a woman under the gaslight," Nathanial murmured.

"Why Professor, a secret rendezvous at your age? Wait till I tell Oonah!"

"No, no, no, it's nothing like that and leave your wife out of this," Nathanial replied quickly.

"So Professor, when can Oonah and I expect you for dinner?"

"Darshan, we've been good friends for almost eight years. Don't you think it's about time you called me by my given name, like I've asked you to do?"

"It seems disrespectful," Darshan replied, still unsure.

"Disrespectful! Darshan, of all the thick-headed... Professor is a title for my students, not my friends. Besides, as of this morning, I no longer lecture on mysticisms and the occult at the university. I have resigned."

"You finally did it. Good for you, Profess...sorry, Nathanial."

A low guttural growl interrupted their conversation.

"What is that hideous sound?" Nathanial remarked, staring into the murky darkness, feeling suddenly uncomfortable.

"Your guess is as good as mine. But my blood runs cold every time I hear it."

"Who's walking your section of wall with you tonight?" Nathanial enquired, hearing the edge in his voice.

"Troy."

Just then Darshan's two-way radio started squealing. He adjusted some buttons and Troy's voice came through loud and clear.

"Darshan, get here quick. I got trouble!"

Darshan was off and running with Troy's voice still emanating from the radio. Nathanial stood listening to his footsteps disappearing into the fog.

Walking off the street Nathanial headed towards the wall that encircled the Woodlands. Gardens, walking paths, fountains and seats had been incorporated around the outer aspect of the structure. Sitting on a bench behind the gaslight, he wondered if his mysterious stranger would show.

This section of town was almost completely destroyed in a fire when the original gaslight exploded. The ensuing fire gutted the Phillcon Enterprise buildings that encircled the Woodlands. Woodlands Incorporated had the rubble removed and a wall constructed where the buildings had once been. They hounded the council relentlessly to obtain the last remaining gaslight, insisting it be placed in front of what was originally 71 Lambert Street.

His mind wandered from the local history to the message he had received. It was written on an old piece of parchment. One of his staff found it on the floor at the base of the staircase in his bookshop. A shiver ran down his spine as the fog thickened about him, his face numbing in the night air. The gaslight's yellow aura appeared to be floating in mid-air. It looked uncanny with the luminosity bobbing to and fro. He sat mesmerised by the flame's ethereal dance.

A warm blanket of tenderness enfolded him as his awareness was drawn to the figure of a woman materialising beneath the gaslight. She must have been about five foot nine and seemed as though she was made from the surrounding mist; her silvery hair cascaded down her back. A gown of white gracefully flowed over her shoulders embracing the curvature of her body. With elegant, fluid movements it swept the path about her feet as she walked toward him. Her bare arms hung lightly by her side, and the soft contours of her face showed the fullness of her lips around a beautiful smile.

"Hello, Nathanial, I am Kalareena."

The richness of her voice held him spellbound. A peal of laughter escaping her lips helped to regain his composure. Rising from the bench, he indicated for her to be seated.

"Good evening Kalareena," he replied, his voice wavering slightly. "To what do I owe the pleasure of your visit?"

"Oh my, you're so politely spoken and well-mannered," she said, smiling as she made herself comfortable on the seat.

As he sat beside her he couldn't help but admire her beauty. Her clothing appeared to be translucent and he wondered if she felt cold. There was a familiarity about her that disturbed him. She chuckled at his obvious discomfort and he wondered if she was making fun of him.

"I need you to heed my warning, Nathanial." He looked at her in surprise; Kalareena's manner had become quite serious. "You must stop your research into the Woodlands. Your activities have come to the attention of Slegna and your life is in danger."

"I see," he answered, bewildered. "I don't wish to appear uninformed, but who or what, is a Slegna?" he asked, intrigued.

A knowing smile caressed Kalareena's lips as she answered, "You know Slegna as The Mystery of the One Truth."

"Interesting," he responded, his mind going over his research notes. "Out of curiosity, what do you call The Mystery of the True Light?" He wanted to see what name she put to that.

"She is called Oletha."

"She!" he exclaimed. "The Mystery of the True Light is a woman?" Nathanial asked, disbelieving.

"Actually," Kalareena clarified. "Oletha and Slegna are both beyond our abilities to fully comprehend. However, because Oletha is creation and pregnant with everlasting life, it's only natural to refer to her as she and Slegna as he," she finished respectfully.

Nathanial had for many years been interested in the

origin and interpretation of people's names, so it struck him as rather amusing that The Mystery of the True Light would be called Oletha. "If my memory serves me correctly, the name Oletha means truth, doesn't it?" His curiosity awakened despite the unusual conversation.

"Yes," she calmly replied.

"Lovely name, most fitting." Assuming his professorial manner he asked, "Now young lady, what's this nonsense about my investigations into the Woodlands and who are you?"

A low menacing growl echoed through the night fog.

Kalareena's face changed slightly. "You hear that? That's one of Slegna's hounds of despair. They are born from the unwholesome deeds of humanity. Their claws can rip you to pieces and their bite disorientates the mind and spirit. That hound is looking for you, Nathanial!"

"What are you talking about?" he asked, shocked.

"It's no longer safe for us to talk tonight," she answered. "Nathanial, we are Keepers of the Realm and Slegna will stop at nothing to prevent us from fulfilling our destiny. I will contact you later; please heed my warning. You must leave before the hound finds you. Now go!"

Kalareena smiled but then her shape wavered and vanished from his sight. "Well, I'll be," he remarked in surprise. *How does she do that?* he wondered as he hastily headed home. *Who is she really and why come to me with that fanciful tale about being Keepers of the Realm? And why would this Slegna want to stop me investigating the Woodlands? There has to be a rational explanation for all of this. How does she come and go like that, maybe I'm going crazy and none of this is real.*

A howl reverberating off the surrounding buildings had him looking around nervously; quickening his pace he moved through the murky fog. *Well, that's certainly real, so I suppose I should give her the benefit of the doubt.* He headed home swiftly, his mind full of unanswerable questions.

A siren wailing in the distance got his attention. Moments later, a police car appeared with lights flashing and sped along the street that Darshan had earlier run down. He decided to discuss this evening's events the following day with Renae, the manager of his bookstore 'Enigma Books' as she was a gifted psychic.

✳ ✳ ✳

At age sixty-two, Nathanial stood his six feet with dignity and pride; his athletic body had lost none of its tone for his age. His thick wavy blond hair fell gently about his shoulders. Mirth and merriment shone from deep green eyes. Astute intelligence and a quick wit enabled him to expertly unravel ancient myths and legends.

As a result of her ability to see into people, Renae had employed some unique staff members. Janelle, her second-in-charge, was an exceptional trance-medium, Gela had the uncanny ability to know instantly when a person was lying. Lomasi had the capacity to spiritually see through material objects and Lon, the only other male working in the shop apart from Nathanial, was a skilled doctor and psychic healer.

Nathanial arrived at the shop around midmorning and was lucky to find a park directly in front. Renae noticing his arrival went to meet him and opened the car door.

"Out you get, Nathanial," she remarked cheerfully.

He alighted from the car and acknowledged Renae's greeting while admiring the window display in the large bay windows that flanked the entrance of Enigma Books. Renae linked her arm in his, and, with her blue eyes smiling, they headed towards the shop. Standing five feet six, with mousey blonde hair, Renae was his brilliant accountant and administrator.

Entering through the outer door they moved into the lobby to the bookshop entrance and stood admiring the large spiral staircase in the middle of the store. This impressive structure was constructed completely from redwood and could comfortably hold four people across its steps. At the base of the balustrade on either side of the first step stood a carved eagle. The bearers that supported the handrail were elaborately carved nature sprites. A carpet runner in the design of a country garden graced the spiral staircase from top to bottom and gold rods at the rear of each step kept the carpet in place. The staircase led to a mezzanine that covered half the ground floor. At the back of the mezzanine there was a storeroom flanked by offices. The stairs then continued upward to the first floor. There were bookshelves throughout the ground and first floors, with carpet runners between all the shelves. Renae and Nathanial walked around the circular counter at the front of the store to the stairs that led to his office on the mezzanine.

"I've employed two more staff members," Renae advised as they moved towards his office. "Their names are Gabbryel and Fala."

Nathanial stared at her waiting for her to continue.

Looking at him questioningly, she frowned. "You're giving me one of your 'what else' looks," Renae commented, puzzled.

"You mean Gabbryel and Fala don't have any spiritual abilities?" he enquired cheekily.

Smiling, she replied, "Gabbryel is gifted in psychometry and Fala is skilled in predictions and premonitions. Happy now, are we?" Renae said, playfully punching his arm.

Nathanial rubbed his arm, pretending he was hurt. "Ouch," he joked. Grinning happily Renae gave his arm an affectionate squeeze and continued. "There was also a strange little old lady here earlier this morning looking for you." Renae paused before continuing. "She has the sweetest smile, silver hair, stands about five foot nothing, a trim figure for her age and is quite good at evading questions. She said she needed to see you; wouldn't give me her name. She seemed to think you would know who she was. Do you know her?"

"Yes, that was Mrs Phillips, and she didn't say what she wanted?" Nathanial asked, puzzled.

"No. She just asked me to give you this."

Renae handed him a piece of parchment. He stared at it

and then reached into his pocket to retrieve the parchment from last night, but it wasn't there. He was flabbergasted.

"This is the parchment from last night," he said, mystified. "Did she say how this came to be in her possession?"

"Nope," Renae replied happily. "She simply smiled and said you would understand."

"I see," he responded, not at all understanding how it could have come to have been in her possession.

"The shop has tripled its trade in the last twelve months," Renae continued, not really taking note of his bewildered expression. "And I foresee it becoming much busier. Your idea to increase the range of books and specialise in the esoteric was brilliant. Word finally got around and the university students are coming here in droves," Renae enthusiastically informed him.

Nathanial's mind was alerted to Renae's phraseology in her report. "You made an interesting statement. You said 'foresee', not expect. Have you had a vision?"

"It was earlier this month. I was meditating in the shop and foresaw a substantial increase in business and two new faces behind the counter," confessed Renae.

"That's good, as I now belong to the unemployed."

The look on Renae's face revealed she wasn't telling him everything, so he insisted on hearing it all.

Her voice wavered slightly as she responded. "I also saw you going on a perilous journey not of your conscious choice," she replied, her face showing signs of concern. "I was planning on telling you at our regular meeting."

"Did you receive anything else on how I would manage to accidentally go on this journey and where it would take me?" He needed informative guidance, especially after last night's perplexing events.

"The vision was unexpected and filled me with dread," Renae commented, gently touching his arm. "I lost contact and couldn't reconnect to the spiritual flow. Sorry, Nathanial."

"That's all right," he replied with a sinking sensation coming over him as sat at his desk. A light knock on the door interrupted further conversation. "Enter," he called.

"Excuse me, Nathanial," one of the staff apologised as she entered. "There's a woman downstairs insisting on speaking with you."

"Thank you, Gela, show her to my office, please." He stood, moving out from behind the desk as Gela escorted the woman into his office and then quietly left.

"Mrs Phillips, what a pleasure," he said, smiling. "I would like to formally introduce you to my manager Renae. Renae, this is Mrs Phillips."

After Renae and Mrs Phillips had exchanged pleasantries, Renae discreetly left.

"That's a very intuitive young woman you have working for you, Professor."

"I couldn't agree more."

"Did you receive your gift this morning?" she asked.

"Gift? Oh yes, thank you. May I be so bold as to ask how you obtained the parchment?"

"Most certainly, Professor, you are welcome to ask." Her tone left no doubt in his mind that he wouldn't receive an answer. "Professor Belmont, have you had the opportunity to become acquainted with the Phillips and the Conway families' history at all?"

"Please, Mrs Phillips, call me Nathanial," he instructed indicating for her to be seated at one of the armchairs placed about his office. "Until yesterday I was still working at the university," he said, sitting in the seat opposite her. "This left me with little spare time. Is it important?"

Mrs Phillips looked directly at him. "You may call me Barbette, Nathanial," she replied, smiling. "Some things require explanation and you will need an understanding of past historical events to get a clearer picture. I suggest you start with the journals Matthew Phillips and Terence Conway wrote."

Nathanial looked at Barbette in the manner of 'continue, please', but nothing was forthcoming, other than a knowing grin.

"I am wondering if you were the one who originally sent this message," he queried, presenting Barbette with the parchment Renae had given him.

"I shall return home now," Barbette stated, rising from her chair. "If you would be so kind as to escort me to the car." He had learned earlier on that when Mrs Phillips didn't wish to communicate it was a waste of time in persisting. It was frustrating. He walked Barbette to her car with neither of them saying a word. As they approached, her chauffeur opened her door and she climbed in.

"Thank you, Nathanial. I look forward to hearing from you soon."

He returned to the shop totally mystified; how did she obtain the parchment? As he entered the shop he caught Renae's attention, indicating for her to meet him in his office.

"What was that all about?" she said, bemused.

"I don't know, but I think I need a history lesson. Can you see to it that I'm not disturbed?"

"Of course, no one will bother you. I'll make certain of it," she affirmed.

One of the conditions of the purchase of the bookshop from Phillcon Enterprises was the storage of the Phillips and Conway family histories and their personal journals. Nathanial found what he was looking for and started reading; it proved to be quite an eye opener. He was interrupted by a knock at the door.

"Enter."

Renae walked in with some herbal tea and sandwiches. He thanked her and remarked about not being disturbed. She smiled and said that the shop had been closed for an hour. It was time to stop his research. Laughing at his surprise, she placed the tray of food and drinks on a table and sat in one of the armchairs.

"The journals Matthew Phillips and Terence Conway wrote of their experiences in the Woodlands are incredible," he advised her.

"What do you mean by incredible?" she responded, intrigued.

Walking from behind the desk he joined Renae. While she poured the tea he explained. "Everyone knows about Phillcon Enterprises' rise to fame. What's not known is how it was achieved. Both Matthew Phillips and Terence Conway were gifted psychics. Their abilities were fully developed when they entered the Woodlands."

"I'm not grasping what you mean about developed in the Woodlands?"

"Why do you think it's forbidden to enter the Woodlands?" Nathanial asked while pointing in that general direction. "Why encircle a forest the size of ten city blocks in a wall that's eight feet thick at its base, rises twenty feet into the air and curves outwards?"

Renae shrugged. "I don't think anyone knows the answers to those questions."

"Then allow me to educate you," he answered, smiling. "According to Phillips and Conway, the Woodlands contain countless realms of reality, both spiritual and material, which are being manifested into a consciousness of being. The Woodlands is where the Astral Plane interconnects with our world of Telluric. I've had my suspicions that they were. These documents are the first testimonials I've read that support that belief."

Renae sat dumbfounded for a moment before she spoke. "Are you telling me the Woodlands is part of the Astral Plane? Nathanial!" Renae was shocked. "The Astral Plane is the ethereal world between all realms of consciousness. It's where a spirit rests before being reincarnated. It's not meant to be a physical manifestation of awareness. How could something like that happen?"

"According to the journals Phillips and Conway wrote, each realm of learning has a Keeper to implement Oletha's laws of love and kindness," he advised her as he reach for a drink. "However, the Keeper for the Astral Plane has vanished."

"Hang on a minute," Renae said, confused. "Who's Oletha and what's a Keeper?"

"Oletha is the name other realms of existence give to what we refer to as The Mystery of the True Light," he explained. "They also have a name for The Mystery of the One Truth: Slegna."

"Fascinating," Renae said in amazement. "So what we call a Balanced consciousness, The Mystery of the True Light, they call Oletha," she said in admiration, "and an Unbalanced awareness, The Mystery of the One Truth, they refer to as Slegna."

"Correct," he replied, seeing the wonderment on her face.

"I like that, Nathanial. It has a personal feel to it. So what's a Keeper?"

He smiled fondly at her and continued. "A Keeper is an overseer of sorts," he replied, a little unsure. "The journals aren't terribly clear. It has something to do with maintaining balance between Oletha and Slegna."

"Okay," Renae said questioningly. "So do you know what happened to the Keeper?"

"Apparently it was time for the Keeper to transcend to the heavenly realms of Oletha, allowing in the new Keeper."

"Why is that a problem?" queried Renae as she picked up a sandwich.

"Because," Nathanial replied, taking a sip of his drink, "Oletha chose this transition period to allow Slegna, and his underlings, free travel between all realms of existence, thus bringing to the attention of the followers of the True Light the extent of Unbalanced spirits upon their world."

"By Unbalanced you mean riffraff and law breakers?"

"That's one way to put it, yes," he agreed putting his drink down and reaching for a sandwich.

"That would explain the escalating violence," replied Renae with some thought. "What has this to do with Matthew and Terence's spiritual development?"

"According to Terence," Nathanial continued, "he and Matthew travelled through a portal in the Woodlands to another world where their spiritual abilities were fully developed. In return they committed not only Phillcon Enterprises, but also their families, to a contractual agreement that would span generations."

"To what end?" Renae asked, puzzled.

"To the investiture of the new Keeper of the Astral Plane," he advised her. Renae was about to ask another question when he raised his hand, stopping her. "Hang on, there's more. Before they died, both Phillips and Conway were adamant that nobody was ever permitted entrance into the Woodlands without a personal invitation from the Keeper."

Renae leaned back in her chair and looked directly at

Nathanial. "Interesting – you can't get into the Woodlands without an invitation from the Keeper who happens to be missing," she noted, "but you still haven't told me what any of this has to do with you and the parchment Mrs Phillips returned."

"As yet, I don't have a connection," he replied, around a mouthful of food.

"All right, let's work backwards. What happened last night with your secret meeting near the gaslight?"

"I've been meaning to talk to you about that." Nathanial gave Renae a full account of the events that had taken place. She didn't say a word throughout the entire narration.

"That was the parchment that Mrs Phillips returned to you," Renae said, deep in thought. "The one from last night?"

"Yes."

Puzzlement was written on her face. "She didn't tell you how she came by it?"

"No. Like you said, she's good at evading questions," he replied, feeling a little frustrated.

"Yes, so I discovered. Nathanial," Renae remarked, a little concerned, "your aura has been shimmering incessantly ever since you got out of the car. This could be important. I think we should both meditate on this while your energy levels are still high."

He agreed and followed Renae as she headed out the door. To his surprise she didn't go to their regular meditation place on the mezzanine. Rather, she placed a rug and two large cushions at the base of the spiral staircase.

"This is the most spiritually charged location in the shop. If you would make yourself comfortable, we can begin." Sitting on one of the cushions with his back straight, legs crossed and hands resting gently on his knees, he waited for Renae to commence.

"I have told you several times, Nathanial, about the depth of spiritual energy you possess. Being a well-mannered gentleman, you graciously acknowledged my words. You haven't, however, believed me. There is something occurring around you that is affecting your spiritual essence," Renae explained while making herself comfortable opposite him. "I'm going to intone a mantra of making." His eyebrows rose at her statement as she continued. "This melody draws the cosmic flow of energy from the Angelic realms and will reveal what is occurring about you. Let's get started."

Nathanial listened carefully as Renae began her mantra of making; he had never heard its like before. Its haunting tune lingered in his mind.

"Ohm Na Ra Ka Taum Na Ba
Ohm Na Ra Ka Taum Na Ba"

Once he understood the rhythm of the chant he joined in. Their voices blended harmoniously and a euphoric sense of peace moved through him. He felt a gentle touch on his hand and opened his eyes to see both of them bathed in coloured lights. This had never happened before and he felt astonishment register on his face.

"Our auras are joined in the grace of life and the intensity of this power is coming from you, Nathanial."

"What are you talking about?" he asked, surprised, not wanting to accept her evaluation of the situation."

"You know that everyone has a purpose in life," Renae began. "Existence is not an accident. Life has motivation, meaning and is full of possibilities. It's the manner and the way you move through your life that determines the outcome."

"You're talking about karmic responsibility," he commented.

"Life's not just about reimbursement of karmic debts," Renae affirmed. "It's recognising that you're a spiritual entity incarnated into a material body and it's the gaining of wisdom in that blending that life is about."

"You're implying that people's spiritual and mental actions are responsible for the life they're living," he queried.

"Precisely," Renae avowed. "Life's not an accident."

"Where are you going with this?" he asked, bemused.

"Because everything is resonating at a similar frequency, we believe that what we see and touch is solid. Except that everything we sense, see and feel in the material world is nothing more than harmonising psychic energy." Nathanial nodded his understanding of what she was saying as she continued. "For whatever reason Nathanial, you have chosen to be a magnet for this energy, because it's being drawn to you in copious amounts," Renae passionately explained.

"You're kidding!" he interrupted, not wanting to believe her but feeling inside that she was correct as she carried on.

"I also believe the woman who appeared under the gaslight you so meticulously described, might be your guide." she finished.

A strange glow started to emanate from the floor through the mat. It made their auras brighten. "There's another energy source here that's affecting our auras," Renae commented. "I think we should remove ourselves from the mat."

Moving off the mat, Renae then pulled it along, with the cushions, to reveal a golden glow eight foot in diameter.

"I knew this was the most powerful place in the shop for psychic energy!" Renae said in awe. "But this," she said, pointing at the golden glow. "Do you know what this means?"

"I will have to re-varnish the floor?" Nathanial replied, trying to lighten the mood.

"Be serious," she rebuked.

"Sorry, it was the first thing that popped into my head."

"I have never seen the likes of this before. My best interpretation would be that this is a disc of living energy. Let's try something. I'm going to move onto the disc, then you do the same and we'll see if anything happens."

Nathanial observed as Renae stepped across the threshold onto the light. She closed her eyes and started her mantra. As she chanted, the vitality of the glow increased. He moved to her side and immediately became engulfed in a pulsating aura of intense beauty. He found himself cocooned within a golden sphere of light. The distant echo of a woman's voice drifted into his consciousness, calling his name as he was transported to an unknown destination. His movement slowed and he found himself free of the sphere, gently settling to the ground in a small clearing surrounded by trees.

His attention was drawn to a silver cord emanating from his abdomen that drifted lazily in mid-air and disappeared skyward. However, his consciousness was pulsating with a wakefulness of spirit, the appearance of which resembled a fine golden thread in the form of an aura that originated from his psyche. A tingling upon his awareness caused him to move towards a pathway leading from the clearing. Walking out from the trees upon the path was Kalareena; she took one look at his face and laughed.

"What are you laughing at?" he asked, feeling self-conscious.

"The expression on your face," she replied.

After getting over his initial embarrassment, he felt he was discerning a great deal more about her than when they had first met under the gaslight. "Kalareena, your body lacks a certain depth and your clothes aren't real," he remarked perplexed.

"Realism is simply a pattern of spiritual energies that relates to the realm you're upon, Nathanial. Take you for example," she said, indicating towards his body. "You're a spiritual copy of what your psyche believes you look like."

Nathanial looked closely at himself for the first time. Kalareena watched as Nathanial's aura changed colour while he processed the information she had given him.

"So you're saying that the form I'm in now is my spirit?" was his awed response.

"Yes," she replied happily, then pointed. "You see the silver cord emanating from your spirit? Well, the other end of it is attached to your physical form back on Telluric."

Well, if we're both in our spiritual form, where's your silver cord?" he asked, confused.

"I haven't left my body like you have, Nathanial," Kalareena explained. "My physical form is more refined than yours because I come from the enlightened realms. That's why it looks ethereal," she informed him cheerfully.

Nathanial gently ran his hand over her shoulder lightly touching the fabric of her dress. Realising what he had done he apologised. "I'm sorry Kalareena. That was impolite of me." He then hurried on. "What are your clothes made from?"

Kalareena smiled fondly and explained. "My clothes are a spiritual apparition I created to cover my form. I rather like them," she said happily, spinning about. "The good thing is they never wear out or get dirty and they cling to my body," she pointed out, while running her hands down the sides of her dress.

"They certainly do," he stated, blushing slightly. He hadn't noticed her clothing the other night because of the mist. Kalareena interrupted his obvious delight in her attire.

"What are you doing here?"

"Ah, I don't know where here is. One moment I was standing on a golden disc of light in my bookshop with Renae and then whoosh, I'm here."

"That disc is a transport portal and you're in the Woodlands. You shouldn't be here it's not safe. You need to return the way you came. It's better if I visit you."

"Who are you?"

Smiling, Kalareena responded, "I'm your soul mate. Now, my love, you must return the way you came."

"Soul mate!" The shock of such a statement had him reeling as his instincts knew it to be correct.

"Now isn't the time, Nathanial, I will explain later. You must return and please don't use the portal until we've spoken."

"I don't know how to return."

"Simply follow your silver cord home," was her rejoinder.

Thinking about the direction he wished to take and hearing his name being called, he travelled along the silver cord towards the sound of the voice. With a sudden jolt, he was back in his body, coming to his senses in Renae's lap with a wet cloth being applied to his face.

"Nathanial, are you all right? Answer me, Nathanial, are you here with me?"

"Yes, yes, I'm fine," he finally managed.

"What happened to you?"

"My spirit fell from my body into the Woodlands," he answered, not quite believing the sound of his own voice.

"That would explain your lack of physical response to my insistent calling. Nathanial," Renae said nervously, still showing signs of unease, "when you stepped onto the disc, my spirit felt like it was going to explode with the intensity of useable energy. I lost sight of you."

Looking into Renae's face he could see genuine concern. "Everything is all right now. As you can see I'm all in one piece," he informed her gently.

"Nathanial, every nerve in my body was humming," Renae described. "It felt as if my spirit was being drawn from the body. I removed myself from the light as quickly as possible, my vision cleared and I saw you lying on the floor."

"So how did I end up on your lap? Not that I'm objecting," he added cheekily.

Renae gave him a playful slap. "Seeing that you were out cold, I grabbed a damp cloth from the kitchen and well, here you are."

Feeling recovered, Nathanial carefully separated himself from Renae's lap and they removed themselves from the circle of light. They watched the golden disc slowly diminish in size till it was no more. The parchment that Barbette returned to him, was now sitting in the middle of the floor. Renae retrieved it and then gave it to him.

"That shouldn't be here. I put it in the drawer of my office."

"May I see it for a moment?" He handed her the parchment.

"Did you check the message when Mrs Phillips returned it to you?"

"No, I didn't. Let me see."

Taking the parchment from Renae he read it but then reread it. Renae gently touched his shoulder saying, "You're the professor, what does this mean?"

"It means I need to visit Barbette. There are some questions that need answering. You know, I could do with another cup of tea."

They walked into the kitchen and while Nathanial narrated his experiences, Renae made them both a cuppa. "That's amazing and Kalareena didn't say when she would be visiting?"

"No. Only that it was safer for her to visit me."

"I wish I hadn't stepped off that thing now. The amount of raw energy you have at your disposal is awesome."

Having finished the tea they walked back into the shop, Nathanial was still talking about his experience. Poor Renae couldn't get a word in edgeways about what she had gone through. They were greeted with Kalareena materialising at the base of the stairs. The look on Renae's face was of awe at seeing a spiritual entity from the enlightened realms. Nathanial's heart and soul soared at the sight of her.

"Hello, Nathanial. It's safe for us to talk now."

"Kalareena, this is Renae, a dear friend and manager of Enigma Books. Renae meet Kalareena, my soul mate," he said.

Renae and Kalareena smiled warmly at each other. "I've never met a being from the enlightened realms before," Renae advised her. "It's a pleasure to meet you, Kalareena."

Moving forward, Kalareena gently embraced Renae. "The pleasure is also mine, Renae," Kalareena informed her warmly. After they had exchanged pleasantries Nathanial spoke, "What did you wish to discuss with me?"

"About whom you really are and the life you chose," Kalareena replied gently. "You had to be sheltered from the depth of your spirituality so it wouldn't influence your decision-making in life."

"Are you saying I have spiritual abilities?" he asked, stunned.

"Oh yes, my love," Kalareena announced proudly. "They're quite exceptional."

Nathanial ran his fingers through his hair, gazing at Kalareena then Renae. "If I'm understanding you," he began, slowly circling while deep in thought, "I have similar attributes to you." He stopped in front of Kalareena. "But I chose not to have them in this incarnation so I could refine my material skills. Is that correct?"

"Yes," Kalareena replied happily. "It was our next stage of evolution to be separated. My spiritual body travelled to the realms of enlightenment, while yours travelled the realms of matter. We were refining our skills until we became the embodiment of spiritual truth," she explained.

"To what end?" he asked, feeling as if he had denied himself something important.

"For you to become the epitome of the material realms and I the personification of the spiritual realms. Then we allow our male and female spiritual essences to coalesce into one and mature into our next stage of enlightenment." Kalareena paused, observing his reaction. "Do you understand what I'm saying?" she asked attentively.

"I believe so," he responded. "You're saying that you hold within your being the wisdom of the enlightened realms, while I'm holding the wisdom of the material realms. But for either of us to be complete, we must become one. Right?"

Kalareena looked questioningly at him as she approached. "Yes," she answered hesitantly.

Renae had been watching him closely and knew it hadn't sunk in that he and Kalareena were soul mates. Placing a comforting hand on his arm she spoke. "I don't think you truly understand the gravity of what Kalareena is saying, Nathanial. You two are soul mates," she endeavoured to explain. "This goes far beyond being mere lovers. Soul mates share the same essence of spirit," she informed him compassionately.

"What do you mean the same spirit?" he enquired puzzled.

"When we were on the disc of light, I was shown a vision," she explained.

"That sounds ominous. Why didn't you tell me before?"

"You were a little preoccupied talking about Kalareena," Renae clarified.

"Oh yes," he said, blushing.

"Really," Kalareena said excitedly. "What did he say?"

"Never mind about that now," he interrupted feeling embarrassed. "I want to hear about Renae's vision."

Kalareena and Renae looked at each and laughed. "As you wish Nathanial," Kalareena responded knowingly, winking at Renae.

"My vision was thus," Renae began. "I was standing at the edge of a beautiful glade. In the clearing I saw a dwelling entirely constructed of light. I was shown a newborn child, not of flesh, but spirit. The child appeared to have a dual personality, two distinctive auras within the one. As I watched, the auras divided, forming the outward appearance of a male and female child. They remained connected through the mind by a golden thread of awareness. The female was relocated to a green portal where she disappeared with her guardian. The male was moved to a gold portal and likewise transferred with his guardian. The denser spiritual reality that the boy incarnated into was the realm of Matter. A voice then filled my head intoning a prophecy:

The millennium of the prophet has arrived.
An essence of light will be born and divide,
Flowing through rhythms both dark and light.
Reuniting again when day becomes night,
Cloaking the shadow in everlasting light.

"This was followed by an equally strong vision that the forces of the Unbalanced were striving to prevent the two from becoming one."

Nathanial looked at Renae in disbelief; this was all getting a bit much. Kalareena quietly moved to face him.

"Renae is correct, Nathanial. We are the spirits of the prophecy," she confirmed. "Our destiny is to reunite our male and female halves into a union of one once more, thereby becoming the new Keeper of the Astral Plane. To do that you need to come with me so I may protect you while realigning your consciousness to its full potential."

Nathanial looked at Kalareena dumbfounded. What was she talking about? His mind was in turmoil. Laying her hand on his, knowledge flowed from her spirit to Nathanial's in a never-ending stream of awareness. At that moment he knew all that had been revealed was the truth. Regaining his composure he spoke. "If I am understanding you correctly, Kalareena, you're saying that by going with you my spiritual capabilities will be restored to me."

"I wouldn't have said it quite like that, but yes," she agreed.

"Nathanial," Renae interjected. "What was it you told me Phillips and Conway said before they died? To enter the Woodlands you need an invitation from the Keeper. Kalareena is a Keeper, and that disc," she said, pointing to the floor, "is an entrance to the Woodlands we inadvertently activated. This Slegna knows your whereabouts now and will stop at nothing to kill you. If you don't go with Kalareena your life will be in jeopardy."

"I hear what you're saying, Renae," he reassured her, then turned to Kalareena. "I don't know how to explain it, but I know I'm meant to be with you. How long would I be gone?"

"If all goes as it should, you'll never return," she replied.

"What!" he exclaimed. "But I have a life here," he said, indicating his bookstore. "I can't just up and leave."

"I'm sorry, Nathanial, but this isn't your life," Kalareena stated. "It's simply a stepping stone to our future."

"Kalareena," he said with concern. "I have responsibilities to Renae and my staff; there are legal matters that must be attended to before I can leave." *A mixture of anger for being told what he could and couldn't do, laced with fear, brought out his stubborn streak.* "I will be ready in two days," he proclaimed.

"You don't have two days!" Kalareena exclaimed. "You must come now."

"Must!" he said, remaining resolved in the matter. "I don't think so." *He could hear the defiance in his voice and wondered what he was doing. He knew it wasn't safe here anymore, but he couldn't stop himself.*

Kalareena looked at him sadly. "Then I will return for you in two days. But please be careful; Slegna knows where you are." Kalareena nodded to Renae, then vanished leaving a shimmering aura of concern behind her.

"Of all the pig-headed, knuckle-brained nitwits I've ever met, you take the cake," Renae exploded. "Remember that perilous journey I saw you going on and now this warning from Kalareena. Nathanial, I'm frightened!"

He knew Renae was right. "Oh Renae, don't let your imagination run away with you," he replied knowing how pathetic he sounded.

"Nathanial!" she said, exasperated. "Your soul mate enters our reality to warn you of impending danger and then asks you to accompany her so she can protect you, and you think my imagination is running away with me? Well, here's another piece of information I was given: Mrs Phillips was the guardian who handed you to your parents."

"What?" he bellowed.

"That's right," Renae, stated, annoyed. "So think on that while you're messing around with your legal matters."

"Renae, I just thought of something else. That parchment we found on the portal read: *I'll visit by the stairs when the new moon arises.'* Tonight is the new moon. Kalareena is the one leaving the messages, which means Barbette knows her. I'll be paying Mrs Phillips a visit in the morning to ask her some questions and then I will organise my affairs. I'll ring to let you know what's happening."

"I'd appreciate that," Renae replied. "I certainly think Mrs Phillips has some questions to answer. I would like to know the full extent of her involvement in all of this. It goes a lot deeper than a social visit from Kalareena." Renae thought for a moment before continuing. "The vision suggested you were born of the Woodlands, not of the material realm."

"It looks that way, providing the vision is correct," he slowly replied.

"I believe it is," Renae pondered. "What do you remember of your childhood?"

"I was happy and encouraged to read from an early age. My father, being a student of philosophy, loved anything from a supernatural point of view. We used to sit for hours talking and going over old manuscripts. He was interested in the Woodlands and often speculated about it. I simply followed in his footsteps. My mother never interfered with the path my father had chosen for me. Like my father I have a natural talent for myths, legends and the occult."

"It sounds as if you were being schooled for something special," Renae suggested.

"It does seem that way," he agreed. *He felt a little miffed at first that his parents had kept the origin of his birth from him. However, on reflection, he realised they were loving parents, who genuinely provided for his needs. He had no right to complain as they always placed him before themselves. Who was he to chastise them? Their decision was made for his protection.* "It would appear we have somehow become embroiled in something rather intriguing, young lady."

"Young lady! Why, thank you, kind sir," Renae said, as she curtsied with a smile on her face.

He laughed. "It's late and I'm tired. Let's call it a night. I don't know what time I'll be in tomorrow. Good night Renae."

"Good night Nathanial. Sleep well."

CHAPTER TWO

A foreboding laugh splinters the Astral Plane, spreading ominous dread in its wake. The laugh belongs to Slegna, the supreme malevolent fiend of the realms of the Unbalanced. He has existed forever. Remaining in the background, Slegna is silent, devious and unscrupulous in feeding off the dominant unbalanced emotions of others. He nourishes himself on their sorrow and revels in the subtlety of seduction. Feelings of loneliness, sadness and despair are just some of the tools Slegna uses to turn people from the True Light of Oletha.

Hovering in the ethereal essence of life, Slegna senses a disruption in the Astral Plane, alerting him to the presence of the prophecy. He recognises the divided spirit of Nathanial and Kalareena. Observing them from the ethereal realm he realises that Nathanial is spiritually clumsy, as Kalareena hasn't reawakened his psychic awareness. Slegna's sadistic laugh is deep and low; he knows that Nathanial is vulnerable. He still has time to prevent the prophecy coming to fruition.

Concentrating on the rhythm of unwholesome energy, he locates a gang of reprobates he has been cultivating. Slegna narrowed his consciousness to listen and manipulate. Andy is the leader of their group; he is of average height with black hair, brown eyes and a thin wiry body. Then there is Joe. At five foot four, with fair hair and blue eyes, Joe has a gentle, timid disposition. Mick, Andy's faithful comrade, is rather small in stature. His auburn hair falls in a tangled mess about a round face that reveals deep grey eyes and a full mouth. Terry, last member of the gang, stands six foot with a muscular body. His jet-black hair frames small, squinted nondescript eyes; he is a thoroughly mean bastard and a force to be reckoned with.

"Hey Terry, ya moron, you've had enough time with that bitch. It's my turn."

Andy walked down the hallway towards the room where Terry had the woman tied up. This was his latest abduction. He had grabbed her while she was coming out of the shopping centre late at night and laughed as she screamed for help. Andy knew Terry loved to have power over women, although he didn't understand why. He could rarely get his dick hard enough to do anything with it.

The woman was making strange noises but then fell silent. Entering the room, Andy saw Terry standing over his victim with his limp dick hanging out of his pants. A truncheon he had taken from a security guide the night before was in his hand, with blood dripping from its end.

"Oh fuck, Terry, what have ya done?" Andy panicked.

"Don't ya start on me! Ya weren't here ..." Terry yelled, glaring at Andy as he walked in the room.

"Is she dead?" Andy calculated there still might be a chance to save themselves, as he moved to the bed, his face white.

"Nar," Terry said, becoming unhinged, "She's just out of it a bit." An hysterical laugh escaped his lips.

"Just out of it a bit!" Andy screamed, looking from the woman to Terry. "Mick, Joe, get your arses in here, now!"

Mick and Joe piled into the room stopping dead in their tracks at the sight of the bloodied body before them. Shivers ran down their spine and fear masked their faces.

Andy became livid and started yelling at Terry. "Fuck, fuck! Ya stupid bastard, she's hurt real bad. Shit! She'll die if we don't get her ta hospital quick. Why the fuck did ya hit her? Ya never done that before."

"I don't know," Terry snarled. "Somethin' inside snapped."

Slegna laughed knowingly, drinking deep of the swirling emotions that were being released.

"Joe, ya clean her up and then dress her real careful-like. Mick, ya get the car and put plastic on the seats so the blood don't go nowhere. Did ya do anythin', or just wave your dick at her?"

"Shit Andy, don't be like that. No, I didn't stick her."

"So ya beat her instead," Andy said, furious. "Ya stupid bastard! Mick, Joe and me will take her ta the hospital. We'll make some story up about findin' her."

Mick walked through the door just as Joe arrived with a basin of water, a dirty face washer and a towel. Joe delicately washed, dried and redressed the woman; her clothes were miraculously still intact. After she was dressed they carried her to the car and gently placed her on the back seat. Irritated, Andy looked at Mick. "What's your problem?"

"I was thinkin', won't she remember us?"

"Nar. She's been blindfolded the whole time and it's dark out. Besides she's unconscious. Let's get goin'."

Andy drove, while Mick and Joe supported the woman between them. Finally they arrived at the hospital. Stopping the car short of the emergency entrance, Joe jumped out and found a wheelchair. Mick helped Joe transfer the unconscious woman to the chair where they removed her blindfold and then wheeled her through the doors and into the emergency ward.

"I need help here!" Joe called. "We found her lyin' in the street."

The nurse behind the desk took one look and immediately called for the doctor on duty. The doctor took the patient into the examination room whilst the nurse started asking the boys questions. They became increasingly nervous.

"Look nurse, none of us want ta be involved. We was just doin' a good deed," Joe responded.

They could see the nurse wasn't convinced and as she reached for the phone to ring the police the boys took off. The doctor finished the examination, ordered several x-rays and transferred the woman to the operating theatre. Four hours later she awoke in a private ward with a policewoman sitting by her bed.

"You're all right now. I'm Detective Laura Dunstan. When you're ready we can talk about what happened."

The woman nodded mutely and went back to sleep. It was morning when she reawakened. Looking around the room she saw the detective sitting in a chair beside the bed with her eyes closed. She was rather strikingly dressed in her dark-blue slacks suit set with a three-quarter jacket over a white blouse, and she wore practical work shoes. Short auburn hair styled to the contour of her face gave her a firm appearance. The detective's eyes flickered and then opened.

"Have you been there all night?" asked the woman.

"Yes," she said, smiling. "Is your name Margery Wilson, and do you live at 888 Wallace Drive, West Yuulong?"

"Yes," Margery answered, noticing how the woman's face softened when she smiled.

"Margery, I'm from a special department dealing with assault. You were in a bad way when you were brought in last night. Your consent was unable to be obtained for the doctor to do a complete forensic examination, so I took the liberty of ordering one for you. If you don't agree with my decision then it will not be permissible in court. Do you understand?"

"Yes, I understand. I agree, thank you," Margery replied, looking wan.

"I traced your identification from your driver's licence and credit cards. They were found in the supermarket car park with your groceries at the back of your car. The attendants heard you calling for help. Unfortunately, they weren't quick enough. They rang the police and we've been looking for you ever since. Are you well enough to talk about your ordeal?"

"Yes, I'm ready," Margery replied. "I had just finished my shopping and was putting the groceries in the boot of the car, when a bag was put over my head. I screamed. The man was laughing, I felt a whack on the back of my head and everything went dark. I awoke blindfolded; I think I was tied to a bed, as my hands and feet were tied to four posts. I was naked and fully exposed; I couldn't move; it was horrible!"

Laura leaned forward, offering comfort while Margery sobbed in her arms. She looked a mess; the bastards had really worked her over. Margery was the fifth victim who had been abducted and the only one not raped. This was the first time they'd been this brutal.

"You're fine now. Take all the time you want. There's no hurry."

"No, I want you to get these brutes!" Margery said, trembling. "I'm a psychologist and have dealt with this sort of thing with my clients. I never thought I would be in this situation myself. I heard their conversations. The one who kidnapped me is called Terry; from his behaviour he needs to feel empowered when with women. He wanted to rape me but couldn't. The more he tried the more enraged he became. He was rambling incoherently. I heard him grab something and he started hitting me with it. Then I passed out; when I came around I pretended to be unconscious.

"The one in charge is called Andy, and he was giving orders to a Mick and Joe. He told Joe to wash and dress me. Joe's hands were gentle and never strayed. Mick organised the transport and then they put me in the back seat with Mick and Joe either side for support. If Terry hadn't hit me, I believe all but Joe would have raped me. He wouldn't have stopped the others, which makes him just as guilty in my book."

"You'll be happy to know that there was no violation," Laura said quietly. "You have several broken ribs and some nasty cuts on your face that needed stitching. Being a vascular area it bleeds profusely when cut. That's what saved your life." She saw Margery's grimace. "With all that blood they panicked and brought you to the hospital. I have already taken some photos and will take more when the extent of the bruising is visible."

"After they put me in the wheelchair they removed the blindfold. They thought I was still unconscious. I saw the registration plate – would that help?"

"Oh Margery, you are a gem," Laura said, while busily taking notes.

"I didn't see where they took me," rushed Margery. "But it had a real bad smell, like rotten fish, and I heard crystal gliders going past. I think there was construction work as well. I'm sorry. I can't think any more."

"You have been of tremendous help," Laura said warmly, looking at Margery. "I don't know if I could have been as brave. The triage nurse gave us a good description of the two who brought you in. From her account they would be in their early twenties; could you verify that at all?"

"From their behaviour, speech patterns and what little I saw, they couldn't have been much older."

"I believe they're also responsible for four other abductions," continued Laura. "The thing they hit you with is called a truncheon; it was stolen from a security guard walking the wall the other night. To the best of your knowledge, was Terry the only one who assaulted you?"

"Yes, when I came to, Andy was yelling at the others. Oh, he told Mick to put plastic on the seat to catch my blood."

"Thank you, Margery, that's all for now. If you think of anything else, no matter how insignificant, notify the staff and I'll return."

A nurse came into the room indicating it was time for Margery's medication, along with a sedative to help her rest. Laura left, returning to police headquarters.

Slegna had listened, supping on the Unbalanced emotions from Margery and Laura. Leaving a hound of despair with Margery to keep the horror alive, Slegna left to find the boys. The hound of despair suddenly appeared, whimpering. This woman wasn't like the others; she wouldn't wallow in self-pity.

*　*　*

Slegna found the boys sleeping; he gently entered Terry's dream state. Terry was once again dreaming of being hunted by something he couldn't quite see. This was becoming a regular nightly occurrence; his mind couldn't take much more. After terrorising him into submission, Slegna would have to give him the illusion of hope or he would become totally deranged and useless for his purpose.

As the dream progressed, Slegna introduced the stimulus

required to bend him to his will. About a dozen spiders and moonlight should give an eerie feel to his terror. Slegna watched as Terry started twitching. This wasn't correct; Terry's subconscious mind had taken control of the dream. The wickedness of Terry's spirit was too much for his soul to cope with any longer. Slegna had lost control.

The soul brought forward horrors in far greater amounts than Slegna would have dared. The spiders multiplied in their hundreds in the dream. Terry awoke furiously swotting at his face and body, jumping out of bed and screaming in terror. Slegna tried to wake him from his dream, without success.

If this kept up Terry would lose his mind and be in torment till the end of his mortal days. This would be a fitting punishment for his actions but Slegna needed him and had already resolved to make him a fiend in the realms of the Unbalanced.

The spiders climbed Terry's legs, torso and neck. As they began to enter his mouth, Slegna made his move. Focusing all the energy about him, Slegna constructed a hound of despair out of the spiders. Terry stood in horror as the spiders formed a grotesque crawling mass the shape of a hound. He was transfixed as the beast stood before him, adding to his terror. The hound spoke in a hideous guttural tone.

"You have crossed the bounds of humanity with your lust for cruelty and vengeance. Serve me or return to your fate." Waves of torment washed over Terry indicating the depth of suffering that would befall him if he chose to refuse Slegna's offer. Slegna patiently waited.

Now Terry stuttered, "Am ... I ... d-d-dead?"

"Not yet. Now, choose!"

The hound in front of Terry collapsed and the spiders once again headed towards him. His dread was so powerful that he couldn't hear his soul screaming for recognition. In that moment his soul darkened with the cloak of ignorance and was hidden from his spirit.

Terry was overcome. "I am yours. What do you want?"

"Awake from your dream, then return to sleep. When you wake again, I will be your inspiration. Follow and you will be rewarded." Terry did as he was told, remembering only that his life would be better if he just followed his inner voice. A sinister awareness filled the room where the boys were sleeping. Slegna was pleased.

Joe had been secretly organising to leave the gang. He hated the violence of the other three and had hidden away money for his escape. Slegna would have to make Joe's leaving beneficial to his plan.

He entered the outer aspect of Joe's mind with thoughts of freedom and a way to escape punishment from the law. This would mean betraying his mates to the police in exchange for amnesty. Slegna could see the idea starting to take hold and nudged it a little more with feelings of righteousness. Joe would betray them in the morning.

Mick had idealised Andy ever since he'd rescued him from those four thugs. Normally, Andy wouldn't have done anything. However, seeing Mick crawling along the gutter with a knife sticking out of his back while four thugs were kicking him hadn't seemed right. Andy walked up and, pulling the knife out of Mick's back, shoved it into the largest of the four. The shocked look on the man's face was priceless. Andy then removed the knife and thrust it into the first thug that came at him. The other two ran off. Andy took Mick to the hospital, brought him home and had taken care of him ever since. Entering Mick's dream, Slegna strengthened the loyalty between Mick and Andy.

Andy had some brains. The little gang prospered with him in charge. It was time for them to branch into organised crime. A suggestion or two would cause Andy to meet the correct people to help start their new careers.

Entering Andy's dream state would be trickier, as Andy knew he was responsible for all his actions and therefore Slegna couldn't terrorise him with his past deeds, unlike Mick and Terry, who made excuses for their behaviour. Joe, on the other hand, had never taken part in any of the violence. Terry had beaten him senseless and called him a coward after he had tried to stop them raping a woman. Andy had been forced to step in.

Slegna would send Andy to a meeting with some influential people with information to be revealed at the appropriate time. Leaving the boys to their dreams he went to pay a visit to the people Andy was to meet.

* * *

The next morning Andy awoke with a burning desire to follow his instincts. He told Terry and Mick to ditch the car and find another one. Joe was to find a different place to stay. They would meet up in two days at the deserted sawmill at ten am; until then they should lie low. While Terry, Mick and Andy went about their business, Joe set about cleaning all traces of his presence from the place. He then located a phone and rang the hospital.

"Good morning, Memorial Hospital, may I help you?"

"Yeah, I was wonderin' if ya could put me through ta the nurse in emergency, please."

"One moment." Joe nervously waited for the emergency nurse to answer the phone.

"Nurse Collins, emergency."

"Hello, was ya the nurse on duty when those blokes brought in that beat-up lady last night?"

"Yes. How might I help you?"

"I would like ta know if the cops was called and who would someone talk ta about it?"

"The officer-in-charge was Detective Laura Dunstan, Metropolitan Police Department. Does that help?"

"Yeah. Thanks."

Joe found the number in the phone directory and rang.

"Metropolitan Police Department. Can I help you?"

"Could I speak ta Detective Dunstan, please?"

"Whom may I say is calling?"

"She don't know me. Just tell her it's about the bashed-up lady from last night."

"Please hold while I transfer you."

"Detective Dunstan speaking." Joe was taken aback by the almost disinterested way in which the detective answered the phone.

"Yeah. Detective, I was wonderin' if you have that program where ya protect people who squeal on their mates."

"Do you mean the Witness Protection Program?" supplied Laura.

"Yeah. That's the one."

"Yes, we do, but it will depend on your evidence, Joe."

There was silence on the other end of the phone as Joe processed the information. He suddenly looked about, wondering if she could see him. He started to hang the phone up, stopped and then went to hang it up again; she couldn't possibly see him, could she? How did she know who he was? He didn't know if he should continue or not.

"Hello, Joe, hello."

Laura had turned on the recorder the moment she had answered the phone and another officer was also listening to the conversation. Her captain gave her a 'keep him talking' sign while they did a trace.

"How'd ya know it was me?"

"You're the kind one. We know about all four of you, Joe, and the women you've taken."

"Look, I had nothing ta do with any of them ladies. I tried ta stop 'em, but they went crazy like. They ain't me mates no more," Joe said, wondering if he was doing the right thing, except, he hated the violence and wanted out of the gang.

"I see. Why don't you tell me about it?" suggested Laura.

"I watch movies, ya know. I'm hangin' up now."

"No, Joe, wait."

The phone went dead and the captain shook his head in the negative. A moment later the phone rang again.

"Hello, Detective Dunstan. May I help you?"

"Yeah it's me; now no more funny business. If ya don't want me help, fine. I'm blowin' this joint anyway. I just wanted ta set things right, that's all."

"Sorry, Joe. How would you like to do this?"

"Well, how does we find out if what I got is worth protection? I ain't goin' ta snitch ta have ya nab me!"

"All right, Joe, what have you got for me?"

"If I gives y'all the lowdown on the gang's activities ya gives me that protection and I don't goes ta jail. I want ta start a new life in another province."

"Well, Joe, it would depend on whether your information is valid or not," Laura said, glancing at the captain.

"I want ta meet ya alone someplace where we are both safe."

"How about the park, today at noon? I'll be on the seat at the beginning of the redwood avenue. Is that all right?" Laura's captain nodded and gave the thumbs up.

"What will ya be wearin' so I can recognise ya?"

"I'm wearing a dark-blue slacks suit and a firearm on my right hip."

"I will be watchin' ya for a bit ta make sure ya ain't lyin'."

"You have my word, Joe. There will be no other officers there but me. Do we have a deal?"

71

"Yeah, we have a deal." Joe's voice was flat.

The phone went dead. Laura turned to her captain, who had been listening.

"Right, I want the entire park blanketed with plain clothes police..."

"Hang on, Cap," Laura tried reasoning. "I told him I would be alone and that's..."

"I'm not sending you out there with some maniac..." started the captain.

"Maniac? He called us. If he wants to screw his mates over..."

"I don't care who he wants to screw. I'm not putting one of my officers in deliberate danger." The captain's mouth met in a hard line. Laura knew she would have to do some fast talking or he would shut her down.

"Whose case is this?" she argued. "I've been hunting these bastards for weeks. I have the opportunity to finally get them and now you shackle me!" Frustration edged her voice. "Have a sharpshooter on the roof of the Venlocks building. He will be in the perfect position to snipe the guy if something goes wrong. I'll have a wire, so you can hear everything that's said. Come on, Cap." The captain looked dubiously at Laura and her team standing nearby. "I don't want this guy getting away!" Laura argued. The captain finally nodded in the affirmative.

* * *

After giving orders to his gang, Andy headed into the city. He had these recurring images in his mind that he felt compelled to follow and it was unnerving. There was a street name and three numbers; he reasoned the first number was the street address followed by the floor and room numbers. Arriving at the address he entered the building, walked into the lift and pressed the button for the fourth floor. The lift stopped. Andy got out and walked down a corridor looking at office numbers.

Two distinguished-looking gentlemen passed him in a hurry; another man who looked like a cop followed them. He hated cops. He found the office he was looking for and realised it was the same one those three men had hurried into. Andy knocked and walked in. Inside the office a secretary typed behind a desk. She looked up.

"You're in the wrong office, sir. This is a private meeting."

"I think I'm supposed ta be here," Andy answered back.

The secretary spoke into an intercom and then said nothing. The tall fellow that had passed him in the corridor walked into the room. He had to be a copper.

"Can I help you, young man?"

"Yeah, look, this may sound funny, but I think I'm supposed ta be here."

"This is a private meeting of the board. You have the wrong office. Please move along."

The feeling inside Andy was growing stronger by the minute. He knew he was in the right place; he just didn't know how to explain it. The man reached for Andy's arm to escort him out, but Andy was too quick.

"Keep ya hands ta yourself, copper!" The man's face registered shock at being called a cop.

"Well, if you know I'm a policeman, then it would be wise of you to move along under your own steam."

"I don't think so. We need ta talk first." Andy was hoping his hunch was right. The copper eyeballed him and then spoke.

"All right, young fellow, speak!" wondering if this was the person Slegna had told him he was sending.

"I woke up with the address of this buildin', along with the floor and room numbers and a funny-lookin' number eight in me head."

"Draw the number." The officer handed Andy a pen and paper and watched as he drew a number eight sideways, the sign for infinity.

"It goes on forever," Andy commented.

"What?" exclaimed the officer.

"It goes on forever. It just popped inta me head, like."

The man indicated that Andy should follow him as he walked back into the room he had just left. Andy entered the office and saw the two other gentlemen who had passed him in the corridor sitting at the board table that was capable of seating twenty people. The side walls of the room were wood panelling and directly opposite were windows that went from floor to ceiling. Closing the door behind him he walked to the table. The other men viewed him suspiciously. He also noticed that the paper he had drawn on was now sliding across the board table towards them. They both stared intently at Andy. One of the men approached him. He was a thin balding man impeccably dressed, who stood five ten, and he eyed Andy carefully.

"What goes on forever?" he asked, looking at Andy intently.

Without thinking he responded, "That which never ends." Andy didn't know how he knew the correct answer.

"So, we have a new recruit. You must be a real bad piece of work to join our little group, boy. Tell us about yourself."

Andy wasn't stupid; the less they knew the better.

"Age before beauty, gentlemen," Andy replied, feeling uneasy.

"I'm Duane. I have the job of inquisitor to any prospective business ventures. That muscular six-foot-six tree trunk in rumpled clothing that walked you in is Senior Detective Maleko; he's protection. That leaves Harvey over there; he takes care of the money."

Andy wasn't too sure of Harvey. At five foot, sporting a nasty scar down the left side of his face and dressed flawlessly in a brown suit, his large gnarled hands looked like battering rams extending out from his jacket.

"Let me tell you about yourself," Duane began. "You have three other members of your little gang. One is the basher, the other the follower and third is the snitch. Does that just about cover it, boy?"

Andy was in over his head, but he wasn't going to let them see that.

"You're right about everything except the snitch."

"Really?" said Duane calmly. "Your snitch is the one who

has been trying to get you to quit your life of crime. He is also the one your basher beat until you stopped him. Need I say more?"

How in the fuck did he know all that? Andy wondered.

"Save your brain cells, boy! The same thing has happened to us all. The hardest part will be to have your basher kill him while you, your follower and one of us watches. Got it, boy?"

Andy decided he had nothing to lose; he would either be dead or not.

"Listen, *pop!*" he exploded. "I ain't no boy of yours or anyone's, got it? If you think you're good enough to take me, then have a go." Andy whipped his knife out from its hiding place. "Otherwise shut that fuckin' hole in your face before it gets shut for ya!"

The three men looked at each other knowingly and then smiled.

"You have guts, I'll give you that," Duane commented. "What's your name?"

"Andy. I'm the brain and my basher is Terry. The follower, as you call him, is Mick. The one you call the snitch is Joe."

"Well, Andy, put that pig sticker away," Duane commanded. "Do you know what you're doing here?"

"Fucked if I know!" Andy replied with false bravado, trying to cover up his fidgeting.

"Right, Andy," Duane continued. "First thing, no more gutter language; it's crass and sounds cheap. We don't use foul language, nor shall you. You're about to enter the big league and there are rules that must be adhered to."

Andy wondered what he had got himself into. Whatever it was, they were rich and that would suit him.

Duane looked at him coldly. "We've been expecting you. You aren't the only one given information. Between us we control most of the crime in the city. Maleko is in charge of the drug squad. If you deal in drugs, quit or he will bust your arse. Drugs are out!"

"I'm wiv ya. I hate drugs," Andy agreed.

"Andy, it's not us you need to be afraid of, but the one who recruited you. Do you understand me?"

He thought for a moment. Slegna sent waves of foreboding towards Andy; a terrible feeling started to engulf him. It was so real that he started shaking uncontrollably, turning white. Duane didn't say a word. He just waited until the realisation of Andy's predicament became clear to him.

"Your grammar is atrocious, Andy. You must be properly educated. Understand that if you doublecross us, we are unforgiving."

The morning moved on as Andy was given a complete account of their operations and how he would be trained once he had taken care of the snitch. He wasn't looking forward to that as he couldn't bring himself to believe Joe would rat on them.

While Andy was being indoctrinated into his new life, Joe was at the park where Laura and he had arranged to meet. It was one of the oldest natural parks on Telluric, covering an area of eight square miles. This forest is unique as it is home to the giant redwood trees. The redwoods were discovered when the area was first colonised. They were impressive back then with the average tree being three hundred feet tall; now eight hundred years later they have become the nation's pride and joy. Botanical gardens were established around the fringes of the forest with all the amenities families would require to enjoy a blissful day's outing.

The paths through the gardens lead to the entrance of Redwood Avenue, which meanders its way throughout the entire forest. It was the only public entrance and it was here Detective Laura sat waiting patiently for Joe to arrive. There were always people walking about so Joe figured he should be safe. He had been watching for ten minutes now. He knew she hadn't come alone although he couldn't see anyone else.

"I have a lad standing in the bushes watching you, Detective," a voice rasped in Laura's earplug.

"Acknowledged," Laura replied quietly.

Joe started walking slowly towards the entrance of Redwood Avenue trying to look natural.

"Movement coming your way, Detective; he's started walking. I have him in my sights. Just give me the word and he's down."

"When he arrives, do nothing without my say so," Laura affirmed.

"Affirmative," responded the voice in her ear.

Laura observed Joe walking towards her pretending to look at the flora. His body language didn't suit the profile of a tough gang member and he looked too young to be involved in acts of brutality. As Joe walked past her she spoke.

"I promised you I would come alone and I have, so why don't you sit and we can talk?"

Joe nearly tripped over. "How'd ya know it was me?"

"I'm a trained officer, Joe."

"Look, like I said, I didn't have nothin' ta do with them ladies. I tried ta stop 'em takin' the first one and got beat up bad, real bad, so I stayed out of it from then on. I tried ta take care of them afterwards like, but I couldn't do nothin' about the pain they was in. I can give ya all the jobs we done and tell ya who the stuff went ta. I can even give ya the location of all the safe houses. But I want protection."

"Joe," Laura said earnestly, "if I give you my word that nothing will happen to you, would you accompany me to the station so we can record everything you say for the court? I promise you won't be charged if you turn witness for the prosecution."

Joe was feeling conflicting emotions. He had never had time for cops after the dealings the gang'd had with them. But this dame seemed different; still he wasn't giving anything away just yet.

"Is that the protection program I was askin' about?"

"Yes, that's the one," Laura responded.

Joe always went by his gut and his gut was telling him to trust her. He didn't know how to find out if she was lying, so he asked. "How do I know you'll keep ya word?"

"I'm alone now, aren't I?"

"Nar, ya got someone watchin'. I just can't see 'em. I might sound dumb 'cause I don't speak right, but I saw the thing in ya ear and ya'll have a mike hidden some place."

"You're right, Joe; that was for my own protection. I didn't know if you were serious or not. I meet some pretty violent people in my job. They say one thing and do another."

"Yeah, I get it. I just want ta get out and I don't want ta go ta jail for somethin' I couldn't help." Laura thought he looked pale and tired.

"There has to be trust somewhere sometime, Joe."

"Okay. You're not lyin', are ya?"

"No, Joe, I'm not lying. Come on, my car is over by the gate."

Arriving at the police station, they were about to enter when Joe leaned forward opening the door.

"Ladies first."

Laura nodded and walked through. She was a good judge of character and Joe didn't fit the picture of a criminal. They walked down a corridor around a corner and into a small room with a table and two chairs. The back wall had a mirror on it. Joe was a little uncomfortable and started to feel trapped. Laura, sensing his discomfort, tried to put him at ease.

"Have a seat, Joe. Would you like something to eat or drink?"

"Ya kiddin'," Joe responded, surprised. "You'd really do that for me?"

"Yes, of course. Now, what would you like?"

"Could I have some water, please?" he asked. "I'm real thirsty."

"That mirror on the wall is two-way." Laura half smiled at him. "Thought you should know." She left the room to get the water and report to her captain.

"Hi Cap, I got him in the interrogation room."

"Good work." The captain looked pleased. "What are you going to charge him with?"

"Nothing. He's turning State's evidence," Laura replied.

"He'd better be co-operative or I'll shove him in the slammer so quick his head will spin. I hate turncoats, but if it gets us the rest of those bastards it's worth it," grumbled the captain.

"Look Cap, I know what I'm doing," persisted Laura. "I'm not a rookie. I want the whole thing videoed while I'm with him, all right?"

Laura walked back into the room carrying a tray with two glasses, a jug of water and some sandwiches. Joe immediately got to his feet, took the tray from her and placed it on the table. He poured two glasses of water and waited for Laura to sit.

"Thank you, Joe. That was kind of you."

"Ya welcome. What do we do now, Detective?"

"My name is Laura. Joe, tell me how you came to be part of the gang."

"I ain't talked about that ta anyone before. It goes back a long way. Are ya sure ya want all that borin' stuff?"

"Yes, but first I would like your full name, address and age."

"Me name is Joe Moseley. I don't have a permanent address 'cause of the gang and I think I'm twenty-two." His name triggered alarm bells in Laura's head, but she couldn't quite put her finger on why.

"Would ya mind if I walk around when I talk?" Joe said, suddenly feeling uneasy. "It helps the words come out easier."

"Of course you can," Laura said kindly, watching the emotions cross Joe's face.

Joe started pacing around the room; suddenly he stopped and looked at her.

"I never told nobody this before," he said, fidgeting. "But I'm trustin' ya, okay?"

"I won't say a word, Joe. I'll just listen," she quietly responded.

Joe ran his hands through his hair and over his face. "When I was a kid there was this gang war and peoples was bein' attacked. These blokes broke into our place, me Mum and Dad hid me in a cupboard. Then them blokes started hurtin' me Mum, tryin' to get me Dad to tell 'em somethin' he didn't know," Joe explained while walking around the room. "Then this big bloke comes in." Joe's voice went quiet. "I'll never forget his face. He had short curly black hair and only one ear." Joe turned to look at Laura. "He hurt me Mum real bad." His voice was full of pain. "Then them bastards beat up on me Dad somethin' fierce. They was all laughin' when they left." Joe was silent for a moment. Shaking his head he continued. "After they was gone I crawled out of the cupboard to me Mum and Dad and tried to get them to talk to me and look at me, but their eyes was lookin' at nothin'," Joe said, with tears running down his cheeks. "They was dead!" His voice was full of hurt.

Laura waited for him to continue. This wasn't what she

had been expecting. Realising he was crying, Joe wiped his face with his hands and continued.

"Andy was me best mate and after all the blokes had gone he came in ta see if I was all right. I wasn't. We heard police sirens so I grabbed me stuff and then Andy and me split. I've been with him ever since."

Silence filled the room as Joe finished his story. Laura stood and walked around the table to where Joe was standing.

"Come on," she said, looking at him sympathetically. "I think you could do with some fresh air."

Laura took Joe to the café across from the police station, bought him a coffee, and let him sit gathering his thoughts for a while.

"When we return, would you mind if one of my staff took the information about the gang? There is something I need to check on. I won't be gone long."

"Yeah," Joe listlessly replied. They walked back to the station and Laura introduced Joe to another officer.

"This is Peter. He'll take your statement until I return."

Laura smiled at Joe and watched him walk back into the room. She headed to the captain's office, knocked and entered.

"I'm one step ahead of you, Detective. I did some checking and have verified his story. He's the Moseley kid all right. Everyone thought he was dead. His family was caught in the middle of the gang wars. The one he described who assaulted his parents was the leader of one of the toughest gangs around. If you crossed him, you died, that simple. Shit, the poor bastard. I thought I was tough until I heard that story. How did he stay sane?"

"I don't know, Cap," Laura answered thoughtfully. "You're not still thinking of putting him in the slammer, are you?"

"No, I'm interested in what he has to say about the gang's activities. You recovered enough to go back in?"

Laura nodded. "As Joe would say, yeah."

She quietly walked into the interview room and listened for a while before she spoke. "How are you holding out, Joe?"

"Not great. I hadn't spoke about that day until now. It's better out than in, I guess."

"Peter treating you well?" she asked.

"Yeah, but he's not as easy on the eyes as you."

"Oh, you are the charmer," Laura said, smiling.

"Laura, um, I was wonderin' if I'm allowed ta know how the lady from the other night is? I'm real sorry for being such a coward and not helping her."

"She's not good, Joe, but I believe she will recover."

"Tell her the next time ya see her that I'm tryin' ta make things right, so it don't happen ta no one again."

"If I think it is appropriate to mention it, I will. That's the best I can do," Better not make promises at this point, she thought. "Peter, how are we going on the disclosure of the gang's activities?"

"Joe has been extremely helpful," remarked Peter. "We have a good deal of information that should put an end to many of the break-ins and assaults that have been plaguing the city lately."

Joe had started walking around the room again, muttering to himself. He looked at Laura and said, "It's my job to find the next safe house. I was wonderin' if ya know a place we can use."

"You're under protective custody," Laura said, shaking her head. "I'm not letting you go anywhere. Besides, it's too dangerous for you to go back with that bunch. You could get seriously hurt if they found out you've been here."

"I gotta make things right," Joe said grimly. "I ain't goin' to be a coward no more. I've been afraid ever since me Mum and Dad was killed. I never stood up for meself once. I always let Andy or Terry fight me battles. That ain't right."

"What did you have in mind, Joe?"

"You know how on video tubes they have them houses that have cameras in every room so you can see and hear what's bein' said? Well, if you had somethin' like that, you could watch the whole time and if there was any trouble you could come runnin'."

"When are they expecting you back?" she queried.

"We had ta lay low and meet in two days. So the day after tomorrow we all meet at the old sawmill at ten in the mornin'."

"Let me run it by my captain." She needed confirmation for something like this.

Laura left the room heading for the captain's office. She met him coming out of the rear of the interrogation room.

"I heard. It would take a bit of organising but it could be done."

Laura looked at him squarely. "What about Joe? Are you

prepared for the consequences if things go wrong? It's a big risk, Cap!"

"Look, if he wants to deliver these bastards, I'm all for it," was the captain's retort. "I'll talk to him. Let's go."

Peter and Joe were huddled together deep in conversation when the door opened, and the captain and Laura entered the interrogation room.

"Joe, this is my captain. I ran your idea past him and he's all for it."

The captain walked up to Joe and shook his hand. "Hello, Joe, I'm Captain Welsh. Do you understand what you are suggesting?"

Joe eyed the captain carefully, sizing him up. He then looked at Laura, who nodded.

"Yeah, I want you ta bug a house so you can see and hear what's said."

"All right, Joe. Are you doing this of your own free will?"

"Yeah. It was my suggestion, what's the problem?"

"In cases like this we have to make sure that you haven't been coerced by any member of my staff. The Department is covering its arse in case something goes wrong."

"I got ya. Nobody's done nothin' to force me into doin' this. It's all me own idea, Captain; no one put me up to it."

"I'll have Laura organise the details," the captain spoke with finality. "Until then you are a guest of the Department. Peter, you escort Joe to a safe house and remain with him. If he needs anything, have one of the other boys get it for him. Do you have any questions, Joe?"

"Yeah, the house ya have ain't too good, is it? 'Cause we ain't been livin' in the lap of luxury like. Oh, it will need an animal on the roof, or I ain't goin' in it."

"An animal!" exclaimed the captain. "Don't tell me you believe in animal totems?"

"Yeah," replied Joe firmly.

"I think I can accommodate you." Captain Welsh moved to the door. "All right, people, you know the routine, let's get started."

CHAPTER THREE

Nathanial awoke refreshed after his previous night's experience and readied himself for a visit with Barbette. The encounter he had with Kalareena the previous evening had awakened a strange feeling in him and he was looking for some answers. He wanted to know the extent of Barbette's involvement in all of this. While he was going over in his mind what he wished to discuss, the phone rang.

"Professor Belmont speaking."

"Hello, Professor. It's Sophie here, Mrs Phillips' secretary. Mrs Phillips is expecting you at ten o'clock this morning. Is that convenient?"

Nathanial stood dumbfounded with the phone to his ear. "Yes, of course," he suddenly replied, realising he hadn't responded to her question. "Thank you, Sophie."

"You're welcome, Professor," Sophie answered knowingly. "Until then, bye."

He stared at the phone, wondering how Barbette knew he was planning to visit her this morning. Shaking his head he replaced the handset. Barbette was not as she appeared to be. He had his suspicions about her origin of birth after reading the Phillips and Conway journals.

Arriving at her residence at the appointed hour he was

met at the door by a young woman in her mid-thirties. She stood her six feet with dignity and wore a bright-red knitted top over a dark woollen skirt that complemented her long auburn hair, curvy figure and fair complexion. She had a ready smile and introduced herself as Sophie. Having shown him into Barbette's study she announced his presence.

"Professor Belmont, Madam."

"Thank you, Sophie. Good morning, Nathanial. I trust you had a good night's sleep?"

"Yes, thank you," he replied, trying to hide the amazement in his voice at the splendour of her home. Her study was a large semi-circular room with redwood beams, Oregon panelling and hardwood flooring. Her desk was located on the left side of the room next to a pair of French doors that opened onto a garden. Opposite her desk were armchairs positioned around a small ornamental coffee table which caught his attention.

The coffee table looked like a small tree with its foliage forming the tabletop. Then he noticed her desk: each of the four legs was in the same design as the coffee table and the foliage formed the desktop. He had never seen its like. On further inspection he noticed the armchairs opposite were of a similar design. His attention refocused on Barbette as she spoke.

"Do you want to sit or walk around the room?" she asked as she rose from behind her desk. "I've been sitting long enough and would like to walk," she finished warmly.

Barbette always seemed to wear interesting clothes and

today was no exception. As she walked out from behind her desk, the sunlight streaming through the French doors heightened the colour of her dark-blue satin suit, under which she wore a very pale, blue silk blouse with pearl buttons. The ruffled collar of her blouse wafted gracefully about her neck complementing the style of the jacket. Frilled sleeves extended beyond the arms of the jacket to partly cover her hands. The gold buttons of the coat were purely ornamental. The jacket was cut so it flowed over the curvature of her breasts, fitted in to her waist and then fell to just below the crease of the knees in a gentle curve.

"Your study opens up into a garden, I see," Nathanial commented indicating the French doors. "Would you care for a stroll around it?" he suggested.

"That would be lovely. My husband and I used to wander its paths for hours admiring Nature," she replied.

"If you would find it disturbing we could stay indoors," he answered, feeling it could be difficult for her with her husband gone.

"Not at all. I couldn't wish for a better companion," Barbette said, smiling warmly while extending her arm.

He took Barbette's arm in his and they walked through the French doors into the garden. He stood transfixed at the sight before him. He expected to see a few acres of landscaped gardens; instead, it was an entrance to a forest of incredible size. Barbette stood quietly, allowing him time to absorb the grandeur. There was a seat at the beginning of a path that led into the forest. She sat him down and waited.

"When you mentioned how you and your husband could walk for hours, I thought you were exaggerating. But this! This can't be. It's not possible, Barbette."

"Are you all right, Nathanial?"

"Yes, no, yes, no, no, I'm not!"

"What's the problem, dear?"

"It is well documented Barbette that your property covers an area of four acres. The problem is this forest," he said. "It extends as far as the eye can see. It shouldn't be here."

"Nathanial, you're an intelligent man. Why don't you use that intellect of yours to figure it out? It's really not difficult."

He was looking about intently, something seemed familiar and then it struck him. This place was similar to where he'd met Kalareena in the Woodlands. "We're in the Woodlands," he remarked, surprised. "But the Woodlands are supposed to be behind the wall!"

"If you say so, dear. Come on, let's walk. There is a glade further along where my husband and I would sit and talk. Tell me what happened after I left you standing in the street the other day."

Nathanial explained that he had researched her family history and shared his findings with Renae. Then he mentioned the meditation Renae and he had done recently and how he'd entered the Woodlands. Next, he spoke of the surprise visit from Kalareena in the bookshop and the discussion they'd had.

When he had finished, Barbette said, smiling, "You and Renae have an incredibly strong bond of friendship and the

91

good sense not to spoil it with sex. Too many people confuse love and sex. They seek physical gratification as opposed to the mental and spiritual rewards that can be obtained through the respect of oneself.

"I look at this generation with sadness. They think that loving someone means you have the right to own or control them. The secret to loving someone is in allowing the person to be who he or she is without trying to change them. As for marriage, this younger generation wouldn't have a clue. Most think a marriage certificate is a bill of sale, or a right of ownership."

"I take it your marriage to your late husband was one of equality then?"

"Oh yes," Barbette replied, her eyes becoming distant with memories. Nathanial waited quietly and after a moment she continued. "There are many forms of love, Nathanial, and only one of them includes the physical joining of bodies." Barbette started to become quite emotional. "However, that's the first thing this society does! I think it's the try-before-you-buy generation.

"No morals whatsoever! In fact, I don't think they even know what morals are. They treat love as if they bought it on special at the supermarket – use it, discard it and replace it," she said, waving her arms to punctuate her statement.

She was quiet for a while, as if she had forgotten Nathanial was there. "Sorry Nathanial, I didn't mean to go on like that."

"That's all right, Barbette. I believe you first have to love yourself before you can truly receive love from others. Most people like to blame everyone else for their situation in life, rather than themselves. It has been my observation that the majority of people love someone because that person makes them feel good about themselves, rather than sharing the love that's within."

"That's a wise statement, dear. I wonder how many would understand it," Barbette said, smiling.

"Very few, I feel," he answered. "The love that Renae and I share is a deep and lasting affection based on trust and respect. What we have is far more valuable than a roll between the sheets; not that many people would understand that."

"I know what you mean," she agreed. "My late husband and I had our special friends that we loved dearly. It all comes down to respect of oneself and honouring that same quality in your partner. If every decision was made with love and kindness, there would be no disharmony in the world. Do you know why, Nathanial?"

Nathanial chuckled. He used to ask questions like that of his students to help them understand they were responsible for their lives. "Because the love and respect you have for yourself would flow on to your fellow human beings."

"Precisely. If you don't have love and kindness towards yourself, how can you communicate it to others? That's the problem with the world today: very few people truly love and respect themselves."

Barbette and Nathanial were walking along a path that wound through a beautiful forest. The sun's radiance shining through the trees was warm and comforting. On arriving at the glade, they sat on a unique set of chairs that were positioned around a table that grew around the large tree.

"Barbette, this is incredible," Nathanial said with astonishment. "The table and chairs are made out of living trees."

"Yes, dear. The Woodlands is like no other place in creation. Things transpire here differently. I suggested to my late husband that a table and chairs would be useful. Then a strange little man appeared and said he would arrange it for me. The result is what you see before you."

Nathanial looked at Barbette disbelievingly. Seeing the expression on his face she smiled warmly and simply nodded in the affirmative. "Amazing," he replied, looking at the depth of beauty all about him, feeling as if he'd stepped into the wonderland of myths and legends of his lectures.

"You have some questions for me, dear?"

"Yes. You're not a native of Telluric, are you?"

"Well, that's straight to the point," Barbette said, startled. "No, dear, I'm not."

"Then where are you from?"

"I come from a world called Terraqueous."

"Is there much difference between our two worlds?" he asked, his curiosity awakened.

"Not so much in appearance. We're a highly spiritually evolved race and everyone integrates their spirituality within their day-to-day life."

He became aware that he was seeing Barbette for the first time. The way she walked, her hand gestures, the manner of her speech. All that she did was a balance of spiritual harmony. She had stopped talking and was gazing at him.

"So," he said, regaining his composure. "Why are you on Telluric?"

"The Astral Plane is intruding into all the realms of Chimera, not just on Telluric. I was sent by the spiritual elders of my world to help bring about the investiture of the new Keeper of the Astral Plane."

"I see," he said, puzzled. "What do you mean by realms of Chimera?"

"Chimera is the material and spiritual realms of awareness Oletha birthed into being."

"Is the Astral Plane considered part of Chimera?"

"In a fashion. The Astral Plane is a realm of neutrality, a place where each soul wanting to send its eternal spirit to the material realm would decide the lessons it wishes to learn and the karmic debt to be repaid. It's also a place of rest between incarnations."

"Hang on a minute," he said, confused. "You said soul?"

"I keep forgetting you live by religious dogma on Telluric."

"I put no faith in religion, Barbette. To me, it's just a way for power-hungry people to control the masses."

"I couldn't agree more, dear. However, many people are so entrenched in religion they can't live without it."

"So what is the soul?" he reiterated.

"To explain the soul I will need to explain creation, so bear with me. Oletha is creation: she birthed herself from the cosmic void of spiritual essence to a wakefulness of life. Then from the compassionate radiance of love, she conceived the spiritual and material realms of Chimera. Drawing from her spiritual heart, she produced a life force and called it Gaia, bidding her make fertile in a diverse culture of life all the material worlds of Chimera."

"That's an interesting interpretation of creation," Nathanial mused. "What did Oletha mean by her spiritual heart?"

"She was referring to herself, the heart of creation. The spiritual heart in us knows without a hesitation of doubt, that it is the personification of the True Light, Oletha."

"Fascinating, and who is Gaia?" he asked, pondering over her remarks.

"Gaia is the one you refer to as the Earth Mother," Barbette explained. "Oletha birthed into being countless essences of angelic awarenesses of herself calling them a soul – her children. Are you following me so far?"

Nathanial felt a little annoyed at her question. "I'm not a child, Barbette, nor am I unintelligent."

"Sorry, Nathanial," Barbette said, while moving uncomfortably on her seat. "I didn't mean to belittle you."

"So if we are the soul of Oletha, her children, where does our eternal spirit come from?"

"Oletha bid that each of her children create an eternal spirit and infuse it with their essence. The eternal spirit is what each soul creates; it is the twin of the soul."

Nathanial looked at Barbette for a moment, digesting what she had been explaining. Something didn't seem right to him. "Why would we," he said, pointing to Barbette and himself, "if we're the children of Oletha, need an eternal spirit?"

"So the soul can be protected from any spiritual harm that may befall the spirit while within the realms of Chimera."

"All right," he said, thinking he'd found a flaw in her explanation. "Then where is the soul all this time?"

"The soul remains protected within a sphere of living energy in a place of Oletha's choosing," Barbette answered, looking intently at him. She could see he was having trouble accepting the concept of a soul and an eternal spirit.

"I think I understand," he replied thoughtfully.

"The eternal spirit is the twin to the soul," Barbette continued. "This means that anything it senses, feels or does is relayed to the soul. However, although the spiritual essences of those things are shared, any physical damage that may befall the spirit within a lifetime won't be manifested within the soul."

"So what you're saying is, if the spirit is spiritually harmed, the soul will have the awareness of the event, but won't have the disfigurement."

"Yes. That's why the Astral Plane is important: it's the place where the spirit can rest and repair before it's next incarnation."

Nathanial was allowing time to absorb all this ideology before continuing. "So you're saying that we are an eternal spirit with the soul of Oletha?"

"That's correct."

He was feeling a little overwhelmed. Barbette sat quietly, allowing him to digest all that she been describing. He couldn't help himself as he pushed onward with more questions.

"So where does Slegna fit into all this?" he asked, smiling.

"You certainly are a true Professor, Nathanial, always searching for the answers," Barbette commented warmly.

"So?" he replied questioningly.

"To bring about free will, there has to be a choice. To establish that choice, Oletha brought into being a spiritual essence of life devoid of compassion with a thirst for unwholesome awareness. This alternate choice she called Slegna."

"Charming," Nathanial replied sarcastically. "So Slegna stands for wrong choices and Oletha represents the right ones."

"Understand, Nathanial, there is no such thing as right or wrong, only Balanced and Unbalanced choices in life. Each realm has a mixture of Balanced and Unbalanced spirits co-existing together."

"How many realms are there?" he queried.

"Let me ask you a question first," Barbette replied. "How many forms of love are there?"

Nathanial looked at Barbette enquiringly and shook his head. "That's like asking how long is a piece of string, or how many drops of water does it take to fill an ocean?"

"Precisely," Barbette stated. "It all depends on one's level of understanding of love and kindness."

"I get the picture," he said, realising he wasn't going to receive a satisfactory answer. "What has any of this to do with me?"

"You and Kalareena are to reunite and become the new Keeper of the Astral Plane, thereby restoring balance throughout Chimera."

"Hang on, Kalareena told me she was a Keeper and guide. She's the next Keeper of the Astral Plane," he said, feeling the falseness of his statement.

"Yes and no. She is only one part of the whole," remarked Barbette. "Remember the vision Renae had of the child of Light that was born and then divided?"

"How could I forget?" Once more he felt the tender warmth wrap around him. Turning, he saw Kalareena walking toward them. She was still wearing the same clothing as when he'd first met her.

"Hello, Barbette, Nathanial." She looked at Barbette with a worried expression. "It was unwise to bring Nathanial into the Woodlands. Slegna is already aware of his presence."

"I'm sorry, Kalareena. I should have realised. We will leave immediately."

"I don't think Slegna will send his fiends to attack us while we are together," Kalareena commented. "However, I'd rather not take the chance."

While they headed back to Barbette's, Nathanial asked Kalareena some questions to which he needed answers. "I don't wish to appear rude, Kalareena, but how do you know where to find me all the time?"

Kalareena looked at him, startled. "Have you forgotten I'm from the enlightened realms? I can identify your spiritual energy anywhere. Besides we're connected through our golden thread of awareness."

"Of course, I hadn't thought of that," he replied, feeling a little foolish.

"That's all right," Kalareena responded compassionately. "You've had a lot to take in lately."

Assuming his professorial manner Nathanial continued with his questions. "From what I understand, Kalareena, we are the same spirit, but divided, yes?"

"Yes," she replied, smiling at him.

"Then how do we become one again and what happens to us as individuals?"

"The process of becoming one will be revealed when the full extent of your knowledge has been reawakened within you," she answered. "As for our individualities, I don't know."

Nathanial was feeling rather perturbed about the whole thing. "I don't want to lose my identity," he stated.

"By reuniting our spiritual halves into a single spirit, our soul can mature into our next stage of enlightenment," Kalareena continued. "What I do know, Nathanial, is that the masculine side of you is in me, as the feminine side of me is in you. We are one and the same."

"If you're referring to the depth of compassion and warmth I feel whenever you're around, then I know what you mean about being one and the same."

Barbette, who had been listening to the conversation, interjected.

"Nathanial, when you and Kalareena are together, what do you feel?"

Nathanial was quiet for a moment, thinking on Barbette's question, "An overpowering compassion," he answered; then he hesitated, trying to find the words to explain the changes that overshadowed him. "It's as if I'm complete, somehow."

"Complete, how?"

"Oh Barbette, that's brilliant," remarked Kalareena.

Nathanial was at a loss for a moment, until he realised what was being asked. "We're not two bodies, but one, a mutual blending of thoughts and spiritual awareness."

"What else, Nathanial?" Kalareena prompted.

He suddenly understood what was becoming obvious. He felt the look of astonishment cross his face. "We don't share love – we are love!"

"Nathanial, don't you see?" Kalareena said, smiling. "When we reunite we'll become the embodiment of love and we won't want to remain individuals because we will be complete within ourselves."

His mind was whirling. Could Kalareena be correct? Pulling his thoughts together as best he could, he replied, "Everything you're saying is registering, Kalareena, but I'm in two minds. I think I'll reserve judgement until all my knowledge has been returned to me."

"I understand, Nathanial. I will see you tomorrow evening in the bookshop. Be safe, my love, bye."

Barbette and Nathanial said their goodbyes and watched Kalareena disappear into the Woodlands. They were now standing at the beginning of the path Barbette and he had originally walked down. Nathanial's mind was numb and he hadn't registered where they were.

"Come on, young man, time to return," Barbette kindly announced.

"Young man? Of course, lovely lady," he laughingly responded.

"The passage of time is different in the Woodlands," she told him. "How long would you like to have passed while we've been here?"

"My pocket watch has chimed four times. I'm happy to keep it that way," he answered her.

"Very well, take my hand and think of the time as we walk through the doors."

They walked together through the double doors back into Barbette's study.

"Would you like a cup of tea, dear?"

"Yes, thank you, Barbette; that would be lovely." He was beginning to feel that his life was out of his control. Maybe awakening his spiritual abilities wasn't such a good idea. His emotions were being pulled in two different directions and it disturbed him.

Barbette went to her desk. Pushing a button on the intercom, she requested herbal tea for two as well as scones and jam, to be served in the parlour. She took him by the arm and they walked to the parlour where they made themselves comfortable. A short time later there was a knock on the door and a staff member entered carrying a tray with tea and scones. Placing it on a small table before Barbette, she nodded politely and left.

"Well, Nathanial, I know you have more questions. What would you like to know?"

* * *

Terry and Mick dumped the car over a gorge at an old abandoned quarry on the outskirts of town. Mick complained that it was a bit extreme as now they had a two-hour walk back to civilisation. Terry had been acting strangely all morning. Every now and then he would laugh hysterically. It was unnerving and Mick became afraid. Slegna was watching Terry closely as his spirit sank deeper into the realm of the Unbalanced. Very soon his mind would alter into that of the fiend he truly was. Suddenly Terry turned to Mick.

"Why don't ya bugger off? I'm sick of ya followin' me."

Mick didn't hesitate; he was off and running.

Slegna directed Terry to a secluded spot where they wouldn't be disturbed and waited calmly for Oletha to arrive. Slegna had no feelings one way or another about Oletha as she materialised beside him. Awareness passed between them.

"You're correct, Slegna. He seems more in tune with disharmony and confusion than the love of creation. Let's examine his life and see if he will accept responsibility for what he has done."

Slegna waited and watched while Oletha created a new reality for Terry where his life was rewarding and happy. Terry awoke from a good night's sleep to a new day filled with peace and contentment. He decided that a day at the movies would be fun. The movie was about a young man living in the slums. Terry's life unfolded before his eyes.

Every time an act of violence was committed, Terry would hoot and shout with delight. When it was pointed out that the violence was unnecessary, Terry would disagree. Entering Terry's reality, Oletha took the appearance of an usherette and Slegna a bouncer.

"Excuse me sir, would it be possible to keep your voice down?" asked the usherette.

"I have a right ta be here," Terry said angrily, glaring at her.

"Yes, sir, you do. However, your vocalising is disturbing the other patrons."

"Fine, then," Terry growled.

Within moments he was yelling once more. The man on Terry's right became angry at his foul mouth. "Hey mate! My lady doesn't need to hear that sort of language."

"How'd ya like me ta shove me bloody fist down ya fuckin' throat?" The man shook his head and said nothing.

The man in front of Terry was being booted with Terry's feet on the back of his seat; finally he'd had enough. He jumped up pushing Terry's feet off the seat. "Keep your damn feet off the back of my seat!"

Terry leaped up and over the seat swinging punches. The bouncer was there in moments. "I'll have to ask you to leave the theatre with behaviour like this."

"Fuck off!" Terry yelled.

The bouncer physically escorted Terry from the theatre.

"Young man," the usherette said, "don't you see that you're responsible for what has happened?"

"It's not my fault," grumbled Terry. "It's the other people's for complainin' and the man in front's for pushin' me legs. Then he grabbed me!" Terry said, pointing at the bouncer.

"Had you remained quiet, sir, and not become physical, I wouldn't have been forced to remove you from the theatre," replied the bouncer.

The usherette tried one more time for reason. "There is a code of conduct that everyone adheres to. That includes you. Don't you think that's fair?"

"Just because they want ta be a bunch of followers doesn't mean I have ta. I was only expressing meself."

"I see. Even though you were causing pain and upset to others," she continued. "Would you like it if someone insulted your partner, or kept putting their feet on the back of your seat?"

"How would ya like me ta close that smart mouth of yours, bitch?" was Terry's retort. Terry's mind suddenly went blank as he sank into an abyss; violence was his creed. He would be an exceptional fiend of the Unbalanced for he had locked his soul off completely from Oletha's influence and devoted himself totally to Slegna.

"The time has come, Slegna." Oletha pointed to one of the realms of the Unbalanced. "Terry can watch the fate that awaits him if he continues upon the path he has chosen. Within this realm all radiance of truth has been extinguished; there is neither light nor dark. They have brought about nothingness by destroying the essence of their souls."

Oletha, with power beyond imagining, delivered forth the means by which the entire realm of the Unbalanced started to implode. Then an explosion ripped the fabric of space and time causing a large gaping black hole to appear that engulfed everything within its vicinity.

When the last galaxy had been consumed and the solar system cleansed, Oletha reduced the swirling void of emptiness to the size of a small moon, leaving it as a reminder, that nothingness begets nonexistence. Slegna acknowledged the passing of nothing and the preparation for a new life.

Terry's life commenced once more. He wondered where Mick was. A sickening laugh of loathing escaped his lips as he headed towards the city. Remembering only a strange dream about exploding worlds, he started walking.

* * *

Mick was glad to be free of Terry; he was scary. Joe was different too. He couldn't wait for everyone to leave and Andy seemed preoccupied. Mick tried to talk to him, but

Andy wouldn't listen. Something wasn't right and Mick could almost taste the deception in Joe.

Terry needed time to wrestle with his demons, but he felt Joe was being devious. The walk back to the city gave him time to think. If he could find out how Joe chose the safe houses, he might discover what he was up to.

He decided to go to the library and use their crystal connectors for the information he required. Arriving, he sat himself down in front of the information centre, placing the headpiece over his eyes and ears and adjusting the mouth communicator.

Talking into the communicator, Mick requested an overview of the houses at the addresses he provided. The headpiece created a three-dimensional vision he could arrange as he wished. Studying all the houses they'd ever stayed in, he noticed that each house had a moulded animal on the roofline. Mick asked for the location of all houses with animal figureheads to be brought up. The list was large, so he requested a portable copy. Removing the headpiece he went to the copydesk.

The woman at the counter asked for his identification card; Mick slid it through the machine and waited. The woman smiled and handed Mick the crystal view tube with the information he wanted. Taking himself to the park opposite the library he sat under a tree and pulled the view tube out of his pocket. This was one of the newer ones. Wow! Looking through this tube certainly put you in the picture!

Mick let his mind wander around all the houses. Firstly,

he looked at the distances between the homes and then he looked at the suburbs, followed by the street names. There had to be some connection as to why Joe chose one house over another. Was it colour, shape, size, figureheads, what?

Slegna was impressed. Mick had never shown intellect before. Strengthening his loyalty to Andy had unlocked his dormant intellectual capacity for analysis. He would enjoy watching Mick's reasoning ability. The day had worn on and Mick still hadn't figured out Joe's method, but he would. It was time to find a place to stay for the night.

CHAPTER FOUR

The day started out like any other with Renae going over paperwork from the previous day's sales. Janelle, her second-in-charge, kept walking in and out of her office carrying a package. After the third time, Renae asked if she was all right, as the girl had a very perplexed look on her face.

"I have this package for Professor Belmont."

"He hasn't arrived yet so just put it on the table outside his room," Renae told her.

"For some reason I'm unable to," Janelle said, with a slight tremor in her voice.

"What do you mean?" Renae stared at her. "You simply walk out of my office and place it on the table in front of his office. It's really not that hard."

"I tried that, but it won't work. Watch," Janelle said, as she turned and walked out of Renae's office heading towards the table. Suddenly, to Renae's surprise, she vanished from sight only to reappear back where she'd started.

"Let me see the package," Renae requested, as she walked out from behind her desk. Removing the package from Janelle's hands she examined it carefully and then attempted to place it on the table only to find she was walking back into her office. "It's as if we're walking in a circle. It's almost like a time loop," Renae told Janelle. "We physically vanish but then reappear back were we started from," she said, amazed. "While I'm holding the parcel, see if you are able to leave." Janelle walked out of the office towards the stairs, only to reappear back in Renae's office.

"Who was the supplier that delivered the package; can you remember?" Renae asked Janelle.

"I don't know. I found it at the base of the stairs with the Professor's name on it. I tried to put it on the table as you did only to find myself in here. Renae this is spooky." Just then another staff member started walking into the office. She stopped dead in her tracks when both Renae and Janelle yelled to warn her to stay out.

"Sorry to yell like that, Gela, but we have a dilemma," Renae told her. "Please let everyone know that they're not to enter my office. If they need me, have them ring or stand outside."

"Very well. Mrs Phillips is downstairs. What will I tell her?" asked Gela, looking mystified.

"Do you know what she wants?"

"She asked me if you were all right. I said I'd check," Gela replied.

"Who's at the front counter?" Renae asked.

"I left Lon to look after things."

Renae went to the intercom and buzzed the front counter.

"Hello, Lon. Could you put Mrs Phillips on the intercom, please?"

"Of course," he replied.

"Mrs Phillips speaking."

"Sorry to talk to you this way, Mrs Phillips. I have a slight problem at the moment and I am wondering if you are aware of it?"

"Not exactly, dear, I only know you have one," said Mrs Phillips. "Can you say what the nature of the difficulty is?"

"Let's just say that another staff member and I keep returning to my office as soon as we walk out of the door."

"I will be right up, dear."

Mrs Phillips and Gela passed each other on the stairs. Arriving a few moments later, Mrs Phillips stood outside Renae's office while Renae explained what had transpired.

"Is the young lass with you courageous or skittish?" she asked.

"My name is Janelle and not much unnerves me, but this did give me a bit of a start."

"Yes, dear, I can see how it would. Renae, have you heard from Nathanial at all?"

"Only by answering machine. Something came up; he said he would see me later today."

Mrs Phillips looked disturbed. "I don't like the sound of that. What's written on the package?"

"It reads, Professor Belmont, Portal delivery, Telluric, and bracketed in very small print is 'his hands only'," answered Renae. "That's a strange way of addressing a parcel. There is nothing else written on it that I can see."

"Oh dear. What you have is a secured parcel delivery from another realm of reality. I'm sorry to say that neither you nor

Janelle will be able to remove yourselves from its presence until Nathanial retrieves it. What I don't understand is why you both kept walking into your office and not Nathanial's. Are you absolutely positive there's nothing else written on the package?"

Janelle and Renae re-examined the package. Janelle noticed, as Renae was turning the package over, that the bindings looked as if they had writing on them.

"Maybe I should untie ..."

"No!" Mrs Phillips screamed as Janelle reached over and pulled the tie undone. The ribbons undid smoothly and immediately wound around Janelle's hands binding them tightly together. "I'm sorry, dear, whatever you do, don't move your hands, otherwise it will tighten." The shocked look on Janelle's face said it all.

"What would happen if I unwrapped it?" Renae queried.

"I'm not sure, so don't try it." Just then there was a commotion from the ground floor.

"Renae! Get down here quickly, I think we have a ghost in the store," Lon yelled.

Mrs Phillips went to investigate and met Kalareena coming up the stairs looking agitated. "What are you doing here?" she asked, surprised that Kalareena had revealed herself.

"Nathanial is in terrible danger," Kalareena announced. "You and Renae must help me find him. I can hear his terrified screams! But I'm having trouble locating him."

I'm afraid we can't, dear. We have a problem of our own."

Kalareena looked at Barbette and then followed her to Renae's office. Noticing the package Renae was holding and Janelle's hands bound with a ribbon, she asked, "How many have touched that?"

"Janelle and I are the only ones who have handled it," Renae answered.

"Janelle, I am Kalareena. I'm not a ghost but a being from the enlightened realms. You tried to unwrap the package, why?"

"The ribbon looked as if it had writing on it," answered Janelle. "So I thought I would look at it more closely – and I know the difference between a ghost and an enlightened being, Kalareena. Can you get me out of this by any chance?" she asked, concern written on her face.

"I'm not sure. Renae, come to the doorway so I may have a closer look at the parcel, please."

Renae did as she was asked. Kalareena had her turn the package every possible way and then asked for it to be placed on the floor. She warned everybody to step back.

"As long as nobody else touches it, it's safe to move in and out of your office, Renae. Janelle, come closer and extend your hands towards me."

Janelle walked up to Kalareena with her arms extended. Kalareena placed her hand on the ribbon, which unwrapped itself and fell to the floor.

"How did you do that?" Janelle asked in surprise, relieved that her hands were free.

"Nathanial and I are 'one'," Kalareena answered. "Now, tell me what happened."

"I found this package sitting at the bottom of the stairs," Janelle began. "Noticing it was addressed to the professor, I tried to deliver it to his office for safekeeping. Instead, each time I ended up in Renae's office with the package. Renae also tried to deliver it and the same thing happened to her," Janelle finished.

"Why would it go to Renae's office if it's addressed to Nathanial?" Kalareena queried.

"We don't know, dear. I was trying to figure that out as you arrived," Barbette replied.

"Janelle, could you please kick the package out the door?" Kalareena asked.

Janelle gently put her foot behind the offending item and pushed it past the door's threshold and then gave it another push in the direction of Nathanial's office. It had only gone a couple of feet when it vanished, to reappear back in Renae's office.

"Renae," questioned Kalareena, "do you have anything with which to unwrap the package without touching it?"

Janelle grabbed a ruler from the desk and handed it to her. Renae nodded and then gently unfolded the wrapping from the package. This revealed a box that pulsated with a dark light. Kalareena looked stricken as Barbette cried out, "Oh no!"

"What is it?" asked Renae.

"That is an emotional trap box," Barbette replied. "A person is caught by his or her own denials within a dimension of time of their own making until they can face their true self. I thought they had all been destroyed."

"Oh Barbette, no!" cried Kalareena. "Look at the discolouration on the side. He's not in there alone; there are at least two hounds of despair with him. Not only will he have to confront his destiny; he will be fighting the hounds as well. That is too much for anyone to face. We have to get him out."

"I know, dear, but I'm not sure how," Barbette said, her face showing concern.

Seeing the stricken faces of Barbette and Kalareena was too much for Renae.

"I need to know what is going on, now!" Renae demanded.

Barbette turned to Renae. "Many centuries ago on another planet the fiends of the Unbalanced cruelly killed the wife of a scientist. Her husband vowed that they would face their worst enemy, themselves. So he designed and built an emotional trap box. He then sent one to all the Unbalanced who had been involved in the murder of his wife. Most died screaming in agony. Those who made it out were cleansed of their transgressions thereby returning to the True Light. Nathanial is in that box in front of you. I believe he is capable of removing himself. However, there are at least two hounds of despair in there with him."

"What are the Unbalanced?" Janelle asked, puzzled.

That's what you call the Mystery of the One Truth, dear," Barbette explained.

"How do you know Nathanial is in there?" Renae questioned. "And what are hounds of despair?" she asked, troubled.

"If you look at the box carefully you will see a very small portrait of Nathanial etched on the side, along with the hounds," Barbette said, directing Renae's attention to the portrait.

Renae looked to where Barbette was pointing and there on the side of the box was a likeness of Nathanial along with two horrible-looking beasts. "Are they the hounds you're talking about?" Renae asked, shocked.

"Yes," Barbette said matter-of-factly. "The hounds do the bidding of the one true ruler of all the realms of the Unbalanced. We call him Slegna. As I explained to Janelle you know him as the Mystery of the One Truth.

"I know who Slegna is; Nathanial told me," Renae advised her. "What exactly are you trying to say about the hounds?"

"I'm saying that the hounds are the worst nightmare in all of us. They create untruths that seem real and the mind is hard-pressed to tell the difference."

"Then how do we get him out?" Renae asked anxiously.

"If I may interrupt," Janelle said, "we still haven't worked out why the package went to Renae's office. Maybe it's broken?" Everyone turned to look at her. A voice echoing up the stairs interrupted their discussion.

"Is everything all right up here?" Lon asked as he stepped from the stairs to face Barbette and Kalareena. "So, you're not a ghost after all," Lon said, looking at Kalareena. "You do realise you scared half our customers out of their wits by appearing out of nowhere, don't you?" Lon asked Kalareena.

"I apologise for that," Kalareena said, looking radiant. "However, I have an emergency."

"Are you aware of how ethereal you look?" Lon remarked, his eyes glued on Kalareena's appearance.

Renae poked her head around the corner of her office. "Lon!" she called.

"Sorry, Renae," he said, feeling a little embarrassed. "Ah, it's rather hectic downstairs. What do you want me to do?"

"Politely escort everyone from the shop and lock up and then have all the staff come to the mezzanine floor, please," Renae advised him.

After Lon had ushered all the remaining patrons from the store and locked the shop, he assembled all the staff members on the mezzanine outside Renae's office. Once everyone was present, Barbette stepped forward and addressed Renae's staff.

"You all know me as Mrs Phillips; when we are in company that is how I wish to be addressed. However, while we are alone, I would like to be called Barbette; is that understood?" Everyone acknowledged Barbette's request.

"Now for some explanations," Barbette began. "The woman standing next to me shimmering radiantly is called Kalareena. She comes from the enlightened realms and is, in fact, not a ghost." Everyone chuckled. "She is, however, Nathanial's soul mate."

Kalareena acknowledged the people gathered about her as Barbette continued. "Kalareena has come with some disturbing news which I have just verified. Nathanial has been captured and imprisoned and we need to find some way to rescue him."

The staff Renae hired for the bookshop all had psychic abilities of differing degrees, so they were more than interested in Kalareena and what Barbette was saying. However, they also knew more was happening than Barbette was revealing.

"You seem rather calm about the whole affair, Barbette," Lon remarked, perturbed.

"Not really," Barbette responded. "I've simply been trained to stay calm in a crisis."

"Is Nathanial in any immediate danger, do you know?" Lon enquired worriedly.

"I see him moving through a forest," Fala announced suddenly, looking puzzled. "He seems to be lost, or running from something."

"I thought you said he was in prison?" Lon said to Barbette.

"He is," she affirmed. "It's the nature of the prison that's the dilemma."

"She's telling the truth, Lon," Gela remarked, looking at Barbette intently.

Barbette explained what had been transpiring and the predicament they were facing. Everyone immediately wanted to know how to help.

"Before you undertake such a perilous endeavour you need to know what you're up against," she warned them. "You will be fighting the most dangerous fiends from the realms of the Unbalanced. The ruler of those realms is called Slegna; you know him as the Mystery of the One Truth. The Mystery of the True Light is called Oletha. Believe me when

I tell you, this fight will take lifetimes. Also, for those of you who haven't worked it out, Telluric is not my planet of birth."

Barbette waited for that piece of information to be digested before she continued.

"I'm a teacher of spiritual consciousness from a planet called Terraqueous. If you are to join this fight, I will need to train you, in which case you will do everything I say without question. I have been teaching Renae for twelve months now without her being aware of my identity."

"You're the teacher from my dreams?" a surprised Renae asked.

"Yes, dear, sorry for the deception. However, it was necessary because of the nature of the foe we are facing. If you all make a decision to enter this battle, you cannot later decide to withdraw. Slegna will know who you are and will target you every chance he gets. So decide very carefully. Those of you who wish to join Kalareena, Nathanial and myself, say so now."

"I'm sorry, Barbette, but I would like proof of who you are. Do you have something I can hold?" Gabbryel said, stepping forward.

Barbette reached into her pocket, withdrew an object and handed it her. Gabbryel's face registered several different expressions as she slowly turned the object over in her hands. Returning it to Barbette she nodded, accepting the truth of her words.

Lon gently placed his hand on Barbette's forehead and after a moment stepped back. "Your spiritual essence is different enough to substantiate your claim," he said, obviously curious and interested.

"That's most generous of you, Lon," intervened a new voice. Everyone looked in Janelle's direction as her guide Maaten continued. "Time for the new order has arrived, the moment of prophecy has come to pass." Then he left leaving Janelle standing bewildered.

Lon directed his attention to Barbette. "We have never had a teacher," he stated, deep in thought. "It would be wonderful to have someone who truly knows what they're talking about and can validate what they teach." Lon's expression changed becoming serious. "However, we won't be ordered about like children. Nor will we do what you say just because you say it. We here," indicating to the rest of the staff, "are more than work colleagues; we're family. This shop is the one place where we all feel at home."

"I understand that, Lon," Barbette said earnestly.

Lon continued. "The head of our little family is Renae. Her guidance and counsel are always respected, even if not always taken. If you can respect our rights, then I anticipate that you'll have some new students."

"Well spoken, Lon. You know your family quite well," Barbette replied. "I think we've found our pathfinder, Kalareena."

"It would appear so," Kalareena responded thoughtfully.

Gabbryel had been watching Barbette carefully. She had received quite a lot of information from the item Barbette had given her and she was waiting for Barbette to explain.

Sensing that wasn't going to happen, she decided to ask, "That item you gave me before, Barbette, told me a lot. I know you're the one who brought us together, but we're more than work colleagues. Like Lon said we're a family. If you attack one of us, you attack all of us."

"My, my Gabbryel, you can be fiery, dear! Do you all feel the same about this?"

Everyone looked at Renae and nodded. "I believe they do," Renae replied.

"There is an animal on my world that you don't have on yours, called a wolf," continued Barbette. "They are fierce creatures when threatened. They are independent of each other while working for the common good. Family is extremely important to them and they are fiercely loyal to their mate and the pack. They're considered one of the greatest teachers of wisdom on my world. You all exhibit the same traits as a wolf pack.

"Renae is the leader of your clan and Lon, the pathfinder. Each of you has abilities that can support and strengthen the others. This makes you a formidable force to be reckoned with. However, your abilities are no match for the fiends of the Unbalanced. I can train you, as the masters of my world do, but it will take discipline and dedication."

"What do you mean when you call Lon a pathfinder?" Gabbryel asked Barbette.

Barbette looked at Gabbryel with understanding as she replied. "Lon is a maverick and explorer, dear," Barbette explained. "Being a free spirit means everything to him.

He also recognises the importance of belonging to a select group of people," she said as she gestured towards Renae and her staff. "This makes him the perfect pathfinder and protector of his family."

Gabbryel looked at Lon. "Is Barbette correct?" she asked, looking at Lon strangely. "Are you our protector?"

"I hadn't thought of it quite that way, Gabbryel," Lon replied. "But since Barbette has mentioned it, yes, she is correct."

"Now," Barbette began. "Do I have some new students, or not?"

"What you are offering is sweet to our ears," Janelle answered. "However, we have all learned on the road of hard knocks so we won't blindly follow."

"Are you not blindly following Lon now, Janelle?" Barbette questioned.

"You are an unproven item, Barbette. My guide and I know Lon; his healing ability and his intuition are impeccable. You said yourself, he is a pathfinder."

"Very good, Janelle."

"There is something you're not saying, Barbette, why?" Gela prompted.

"I was wondering how long you were going to keep quiet," Barbette said, smiling warmly at Gela. "Each one of you has grown up in a world below your level of spirituality. Your potential is phenomenal, but your training has been appalling. You have no masters upon this world, for you are to become the future masters."

Renae spoke up. "I have been training with Barbette for twelve months now and I can tell you that she is the toughest teacher I've ever known. The simple reason is that she is the only true master I've ever encountered. Barbette teaches in a similar vein to the way I run this store. If you want to develop beyond your present level of spirituality and you don't mind hard work and dedication, then walk your talk."

"It is my belief," Lon interjected, "that a tutor is only as good as the student and a student is only as proficient as the tutor allows. If the student has potential, then it's the educator's responsibility to encourage that student to move beyond their limitations. That is the way Renae manages this bookshop. Is that how you teach?"

"Well, Lon, you really are a pathfinder and protector of your clan!" replied Barbette, sounding pleased. "Yes, that's how I teach."

Lon gestured towards Gela. "Is there a hidden truth behind her words?"

"There is caution in her comment, Lon, although she believes she speaks the truth."

"Janelle," continued Lon, "a question for your guide Maaten: is our family's destiny joined with Barbette's?"

Janelle relaxed, allowing her guide to speak. "All your lives are interwoven, Lon."

"Thank you, Maaten. Fala, would you like to comment?"

"She is one of the instructors we have sought, Lon."

Lon walked towards Barbette with purpose. Standing her ground she held his gaze, admiring his manner and forthrightness. "People feel uncomfortable having their word questioned, Barbette. We don't like it and I suspect neither do you," Lon said respectfully. "I would like to be your student, as would the others, I'm sure. I'll confess now that I am inquisitive and will ask many questions. If you can deal with that, then, gracious lady, we are yours," Lon finished with a bow, trying to lighten any misunderstandings.

"Is he always like that?" Barbette asked Renae.

"I'm afraid so."

"That's all I need – now I will have two of you to contend with!" Barbette said, shaking her head. "I take it that I now have some new students?" Everyone answered in the affirmative and refocused their attention on the box.

"If I understand you correctly, Barbette, you believe that the professor is in that small box," asked Janelle.

"He is," Lomasi said, staring intently at the trap box. "I can just make him out."

"You have quite an interesting group of people working for you, Renae," Kalareena said, turning to face her.

"They are unique," she replied smiling.

Kalareena turned her attention towards Janelle. "Janelle, that box is an Epoch Dimensional Distorter, meaning that the time and space within its boundaries are different to its exterior proportions. Its inventor simply called it a trap box," Kalareena explained.

"Hang on a minute. How would the professor become trapped in there? He's no fool!" Gabbryel exclaimed.

"Gabbryel, that's not its original size," Kalareena explained.

"It reduces after someone is within its borders. It's irrelevant at this point how he got in there. He's in there and we have to find a way to get him out."

"All right," Renae began. "We need to put our collective abilities together and come up with a way to either help, or remove, Nathanial from that thing. Kalareena, do you have any ideas?"

"Yes, I believe so. Renae, you and Janelle pick the box up and see if you can carry it to a position four feet from the head of the stairs. That way it will be directly over the portal on the ground floor."

Everyone moved away from the door and watched as Renae and Janelle picked up the trap box and slowly walked out of the office, heading towards the location Kalareena had suggested.

"Kalareena, this thing is trying to return to my office," Renae announced, sounding anxious.

"I want you both to concentrate all your energy on translocating it to where I said."

"Translocating?" Janelle said, uncertain.

"Yes. You need to see yourselves and the box already where you want to be while carrying it."

The staff were astonished when Renae and Janelle vanished from sight, only to reappear back in Renae's office.

"Remember your lessons on energy transference, girl," Barbette said, with frustration in her voice.

"All right, Janelle, let's do it again. But this time don't think about where we want to go, only that we have arrived, agreed?" Janelle nodded and they walked out of the office once more. When they reached the place they'd disappeared from previously, it happened again, only this time they reappeared where Kalareena had requested.

"That was awesome," Janelle commented with amazement. "It was like walking through time."

Renae laughed. "I suppose that's one way to look at it." She explained, "Everything is made up from living energy, Janelle. All we did was place our essence where we wished to be and then flowed into it."

Kalareena cut short any further explanations. "Now I want you to relocate it to the ground floor into the centre of the portal."

Everyone stood and watched as Renae and Janelle suddenly disappeared. Kalareena and the others walked downstairs to see them both standing at the base of the stairs. Kalareena asked Renae and Janelle to join with everyone else to form a circle eight feet in diameter around the box, leaving the box in the middle of the portal with her.

Having joined the others forming the circle, Renae attracted Kalareena's attention. "Kalareena, what is it you wish us to do?"

"Sorry, Renae, I should have explained. "I want all of you to concentrate on the box. First, I need Lomasi to use her spiritual sight again to look closely at the discolouration and tell me what she sees."

Lomasi concentrated. "There is a small tear in the fabric

of its makeup. I can see light escaping from it. Does that help?"

"Yes, but I need you to look closer. I have to know why it kept returning to Renae's office and not Nathanial's."

"I'm sorry, Kalareena, but I'm not seeing anything. Gabbryel," Lomasi said suddenly, "could you gently glide your hand across the section of the box that looks tinted?" she asked.

Gabbryel kneeled before the box, looking at where Lomasi was indicating. "Just here?" she asked, aware of a slight discolouration.

"Yes. What do you sense?"

"Oh my, it tingles to the touch. I have never felt its like before." Gabbryel's hand stopped moving as a look of horror clouded her face. "Nathanial entered this thing thinking that by doing so it would save Renae's life."

"So that's why the box returned to Renae's office and not his," whispered Kalareena. "His concern for her was imprinted on the box." Kalareena then addressed all present. "I believe Nathanial can be rescued. However, I'm not sure how long it will take; I will have to wait to the last possible moment to remove him. It will require a mantra meditation from all of you until he is free. Can you do that?"

"We can, but we will need to take care of some personal comforts before we start. I want chairs or cushions for everyone, along with a glass of water in case the throat becomes dry during the mantra," Renae announced firmly.

Everyone moved in harmony to complete the task Renae

had requested. Lon had gone to the trouble of removing an armchair from the mezzanine for Barbette. When he offered it to her, she smiled, patting him on the cheek. Except for Barbette, everyone else sat on cushions. Lon delivered a glass of water to all and made sure they were peaceful.

"Is he always like this?" Barbette asked Renae, looking at Lon.

"Yes. He believes it's his position as healer to see to our comfort whenever we meditate. If one of us is feeling out of balance he uses his ability to realign our chakras. Lon was the second person I employed, and since that time no one has had a sick day.

"The girls go to him for everything, physical and emotional. He's extremely professional and takes his abilities very seriously. They all defer to him in matters of wellbeing." After Lon had spoken to each of them, he asked Kalareena if there was anything he could do for her.

"Thank you for your kindness to everyone, Lon. I do have a request. Nathanial's mental state may have altered; he will require immediate attention. Do you feel competent enough to deal with whatever transpires?"

"I will place myself in a position I feel is the most appropriate to receive him. I will not let you down, Kalareena," Lon asserted.

Kalareena smiled and then nodded to Renae to begin.

"Our task is a simple one," Renae stated. "We must keep a mantra running no matter what happens. The energy must be built to a high level and maintained. There is a flaw within the structure of the box that Lomasi will keep an eye on. She will let Kalareena know the exact moment the weak spot can no longer resist the energies directed at it," Renae said, looking at all present before continuing.

"Kalareena will then enter. Our efforts will have to be intensified at that point, for, if we falter, we lose Kalareena and Nathanial." Renae directed her next comment to Lon. "You will need to remain mobile, but available for Nathanial." Lon nodded.

"I will start the mantra now. When I have completed two cycles, one after another you will each join in. It will continue until I say otherwise; is that clear to all?"

Everyone nodded, and Renae began her mantra.

Ohm Ma Rom Ma Roo
Ohm Ma Rom Ma Roo

After the first two cycles were completed, one after the other they began to chant. The energy built up quickly while Kalareena manipulated the power and directed it to the flaw in the box. The light in the room was intense as the portal awakened to add to the power that was being generated. The box began to pulsate with the intensity of the energy being directed towards it.

Suddenly Lomasi screamed and started to cry uncontrollably. Lon was by her side in an instant, giving her healing. She clung to his arms while describing what she was seeing. "Nathanial is running for his life, his clothes are torn and bloody and he's being chased by some huge beasts."

Healing poured from Lon like water from a tap, restoring Lomasi's balance, giving her courage to continue. Renae intensified the mantra; this strengthened the moral fibre of the group and reinforced their concentration. Lomasi was trying not to break down again. Lon was by her side, once more speaking softly to her.

"Allow all emotion to pass you by, focusing your attention on what you're seeing only," Lon repeated while loving energy enveloped her.

Lomasi's eyes were glued to the box as she spoke clearly to the circle.

"Mystery of the True Light!" Lomasi suddenly exclaimed. "Nathanial's drenched in blood; he's fighting to get a hound off his back while kicking his legs to stop the other one from gnawing on them. We have to help him, Lon. We have to!"

CHAPTER FIVE

Nathanial left Barbette's place at one in the afternoon, deciding to walk, giving himself time to digest all that she had said. He had been wandering for around two hours when he realised he had unconsciously walked to the gaslight. Crossing the road he entered one of the gardens; this would be a good place to reflect on Barbette's words.

"Nathanial," a voice called.

He turned to see who it was. "Hello, Darshan. How have things been with you?"

"Weird. Remember Troy's call for help the other night?"

"I was going to ask you what happened there," he said, as his mind reflected back to his meeting with Kalareena.

"Well, by the time I got to him he was on the ground with these blokes kicking into him. I king-hit one of little shits and laid into the other two with my truncheon and they ran off.

"Now this is the strange part. A fourth bloke just stood there with tears in his eyes. He said his name was Joe and he was sorry for what his mates had done. He helped Troy to his feet and left." Darshan's face showed bewilderment as he continued, "He was the gentlest person I've ever met; there was no violence in him."

"That is strange," Nathanial said, intrigued.

"There's one more thing." Darshan looked concerned. "I've discovered a way into the Woodlands."

"What!" Nathanial was surprised. Firstly he had discovered that the Woodlands could be entered via Barbette's; now Darshan had found an entrance!

"We had to barricade off parts of the garden. We've used the excuse of vandalism, but that's not the real reason," Darshan said nervously. "Nathanial, people are disappearing." He indicated for him to follow. Darshan and Nathanial moved through several small gardens until they arrived at the barricade.

"This should be right up your alley," he said ruefully. "You're not the sort of person who panics at the unexpected, are you?"

"No, I don't panic," Nathanial answered, relieving Darshan's concern, but curious about his question.

"Good."

Crossing the barrier they walked deeper into the garden. A slight mist was forming around their feet the further they continued towards the wall. The mist had become so thick Nathanial could scarcely see his hand in front of his face. Finally, he called a halt.

"Darshan, we have walked much further than the garden goes."

"Look behind you," he directed.

Turning around, he could just make out the inside wall that surrounded the outskirts of the Woodlands. The mist had somehow allowed them to move through the wall and enter the Woodlands.

"We're inside the Woodlands," Darshan commented. "There's something else I need to show you." They finally stopped walking near a circular disc eight feet in diameter. Nathanial recognised it immediately as a transport portal.

"Do you know what this is?" he asked.

"Yes. It's a transport portal between different realms of reality," he answered. "That's part of the secret of the Woodlands. The reason the wall was built was to protect the public from inadvertently becoming lost or disorientated within its boundaries. Is your side of the wall the only place the mist is occurring?"

"To my knowledge, yes," Darshan replied with caution. "The funny thing is, sometimes the garden is normal; then, without warning it's like now. We'd better get back. This may sound strange but ..."

"Time is different in the Woodlands," Nathanial said, finishing his sentence.

"How did you know?"

"It's a long story," Nathanial sighed, not wanting to explain.

An evening mist was rolling in by the time the two men found their way out of the Woodlands and back into the garden.

"It's really weird. Every so often, time stands still when you're in there," Darshan said, pointing over his shoulder towards the Woodlands. "At other times, time flies, like now," he remarked looking at his watch. "Three hours have gone by and it's time for me to finish my shift."

"You had better let your colleagues know that if they get caught behind the wall, the simplest way out is to walk into the mist towards the wall, think of where and when they want to be and that's what will happen."

"That's good to know," Darshan commented thoughtfully. "I take it your investigation into the Woodlands has been beneficial?" he continued questioningly.

Nathanial smiled at Darshan's attempt to acquire information. "You could say that," he replied.

"All right, no more questions about the Woodlands. I will, however, pass on your information to my workmates. Where are you off to now, Nathanial?"

"Somewhere for dinner," Nathanial replied, unsure.

"Then you're coming home with me," Darshan responded with finality.

"I don't wish to put your good lady to any difficulty," Nathanial said hesitantly.

"Then why don't I give her a call and leave it up to her?" he suggested.

"Done."

They walked to the local communication booth at the end of the street where Darshan placed a call to his wife.

"Darshan and Oonah's residence, may I help you?"

"It's me here, love. I was wondering if you have prepared the evening meal yet."

"No, darling, not yet, why?" she enquired.

"I'm with Nathanial and would like to invite him home for dinner. However, neither of us wants to be a nuisance and, as you're the chef, the decision is up to you."

"Of course he's welcome," she replied. "What time shall I expect you both?"

"About an hour or so I'd say," he estimated.

"You let Nathanial know he is more than welcome and I will see you both when you arrive. Bye dear."

"That's settled Nathanial. She's delighted. Now I need to report back to the office and sign out. Then we're off."

They walked to the office complex in the Phillcon Enterprises building across the way. Darshan introduced Nathanial to his supervisor and he advised him of how his security guards could remove themselves from the Woodlands if ever the need arose.

Darshan and Nathanial then headed to Darshan's residence for a home-cooked meal. Oonah greeted them as they entered the premises.

"Hello, Nathanial. I'm delighted you accepted Darshan's invitation. You are welcome."

Walking into the dining room, Darshan indicated the seating positions and poured the wine. It was a round table with a candelabrum as the centrepiece with a spice and sauce set next to it. There were silver platters of food set about the table for easy access. Darshan uncovered the food and began serving the evening meal. Nathanial made a circle with his hand and pointed to the table.

"Equality. Correct, Oonah?" he enquired.

"I believe everyone is equal and a round table exemplifies that perfectly."

The evening progressed well, with good wine, good food and good conversation.

* * *

Terry awoke the next day with his head full of questions. He had been going over his life and recent events. That strange dream about the worlds imploding into nothingness really affected him. Something deep inside him knew it was more than just a dream; it was a vision.

Then there was the new awareness about the Mystery of the One Truth and the Mystery of the True Light. He had grown up hearing about the different Mysteries, but this was the first time they seemed real to him. He would have to think on it more. He decided to mull it all over while he had something to eat as he knew it was important.

After he had eaten, he went to the park that surrounded the Woodlands. No one would bother him there. He reasoned that the Mystery of the True Light wasn't as strong as the Mystery of the One Truth because fear ruled the world.

Besides, if it were otherwise, his life wouldn't have been as it was. After all, he had no control over his life, or the way people treated him.

Terry concluded that the Mysteries were real and that he preferred the Mystery of the One Truth. At least he could have a better life if people were afraid of him, instead of the other way around. A sinister laugh erupted from deep inside of him; yes, he was right.

Then the vision came to mind. If he were to follow the Mystery of the One Truth, he would need to be careful. Otherwise he could perish as those in the vision had done when all light to their souls had been cut off and ultimately they had become 'uncreated'.

Terry grew up hearing about how each person had a soul and eternal spirit. He wondered what his soul would look like but then realised it didn't matter. He could see it any way he wished. He imagined himself as a fern with his roots deep in the ground and the fronds reaching upward into the light of day.

The nourishment he received from the earth would be the One Truth and the True Light would be the daylight. His body would be the outer aspect of the fern with his spirit beneath, and his soul the core. In this way he would always be connected to the Light and not be uncreated like he'd seen in his vision.

He laughed ruefully with the recognition that he was right. For the first time in his life he belonged to something special. He understood aggression and violence; there was a perverse stability to it, a constant. Real power was not money or possessions. It was the control over people's lives and from that you could obtain all the material things you wanted. Fear, real fear about the fact that you might torture or kill a person's family or friends if they didn't do as you said – that was true power.

Terry was aware of something else; his inner sense seemed heightened. A couple of people had walked past him in the garden and he knew their fears. He even knew how to manipulate them to get what he wanted.

He liked these strange new feelings and couldn't wait to use them. Nothing would stand in his way now, not even Andy, and if that poonce Joe started in on him about his aggression, he'd kill him. That went for everyone else too. No one would ever push him around again.

Slegna was highly skilled in the art of deception, distorting people's emotions to his will. So it was with Terry, playing on his fears of insecurity and rejection. Terry had moved beyond being a simple fiend of the Unbalanced and was now demonic in his actions, something that normally took many lifetimes to accomplish. This Terry would suit his purposes nicely.

Oletha had also been listening to Terry's reasoning and appeared by Slegna's side in the ether. They both appeared as auras of light, Slegna choosing the heavier waif-like shadows while Oletha adorned herself in the glow of ethereal beauty.

"He truly belongs to your realms of the Unbalanced, Slegna. His mind is bright and quick. He remembered the vision I gave him and has opened a direct connection to the realms of the Balanced. Thus he has ensured that his soul will always receive the Light. He is now a demonic fiend with powers far greater than this realm of learning is accustomed to.

"You cannot deceive me," Oletha said, looking intently at

Slegna. "You have chosen Terry as your agent of the realms of the Unbalanced to contend for the world of Telluric. You believe they have fallen so far?"

"They wallow in the filth of corruption, Oletha," declared Slegna. "Their spirits are tainted with perversion; this world is mine."

"So you have chosen your arena," Oletha quietly announced. "As you wish. We contest to see if Telluric will belong to the Balanced or Unbalanced." Then Oletha's presence faded from Slegna's side.

Terry felt compelled to find a secluded part of the garden. He lay down on the grass and, closing his eyes, drifted into a strange sleep. In his sleep he felt a familiar presence. His memories returned from the previous night's terrors of the hound, the voice, everything. This time though, there was something else, a malevolence so profound that he knew he was in the presence of the Mystery of the One Truth. Terry didn't hesitate and surrendered himself completely.

"What may I call ya, master?" Terry cried out with reverence, in his sleep state.

"I am named Slegna."

"I dedicate meself to ya, Slegna."

"You are now my disciple. Your name is Enoch. All are to call you by your true name." Terry was thunderstruck as information on how to manipulate matter and transport himself to wherever he wished filled his mind.

He became aware of the dimensional makeup of Chimera as Slegna continued. "Many people will be drawn to you and

I invest in you powers to aid my cause. You are already aware of some of these. Trust your intuitions, they will not let you down.

"There is a task to be done and I will send with you the hounds of despair. They will do your bidding. Whenever you need more they will come to you; use them freely." Slegna's presence became stronger and his voice menacing.

"I seek a man called Nathanial. He will be walking home late this night; I will show you where. You will find a trap box when you awake and will know how it works and what is to be done. Now awaken and be reborn, disciple Enoch."

Enoch awoke from his daydream with renewed energy and a strong sense of power. Slegna was his master now; no longer would he fear anybody or anything. All his fears had been removed and he was reborn. He strode with a sense of invincibility and purpose, afraid of nobody and nothing.

Enoch moved to the location he was given in the Woodlands. Before him was a circular disc eight feet across with a box in its centre. Enoch's laugh was deep and low. With his increased spiritual awareness from Slegna, he knew this was an Epoch Dimensional Distorter and that was where this Nathanial would spend the rest of his life, in agony.

Hearing a noise, he turned to see two hounds of despair moving through the bushes towards him. However, they weren't as they had been the first time he saw them. Nevertheless the sight of two oversized, grotesquely deformed bodies, larger than a dog that rippled with foulness, would instil fear into anyone. This time though, they were his companions and friends.

There was much to be done if he was to have everything prepared by the time this Nathanial arrived. Following Slegna's command, Enoch arrived at Enigma Books at the appointed hour and programmed the trap box to the exact proportions of the front door. Then he went to the local eating-house across the way and settled in to wait. Enoch's heightened spiritual awareness told him when Nathanial was arriving. Leaving the restaurant he called the hounds to him as he walked towards the bookshop; then at the right moment he sent them in Nathanial's direction.

* * *

The evening had been progressing wonderfully, but it was time to call it a night. Nathanial thanked Oonah once again for the lovely meal and Darshan for the invitation.

"Nathanial, real friends are rare. This door is always open to you and you don't need to ring first," Oonah announced.

"I have been a recluse for many years, Oonah," he declared frankly. "Darshan's friendship over the last eight years has been the one constant in my life, keeping me connected to the real world."

"It isn't difficult to be your friend, Nathanial. You never ask anything of me that you wouldn't do," Darshan warmly emphasised. "Besides, I think that having one's head stuck in books all the time tends to give a false sense of security. You need to put into practice what you've been learning."

"That's one of the things I like about you, Darshan, your frankness. Now you remember what I said, young lady. I would be delighted to continue your education as your private tutor."

"Only if I can pay you for your services," she bargained.

"All right, Oonah, if you insist. It will cost you a home-cooked meal."

Darshan laughed. "You're not going to win, my love. I know Nathanial when he makes his mind up."

"Okay, Nathanial, a home-cooked meal it is," Oonah confirmed.

"Oonah, until a couple of days ago I only ever ate at the university café, but now I eat at eating-houses. So a home-cooked meal with genuine friends is a rich payment to me," he said. Suddenly he remembered he was supposed to contact Renae. "I need to leave a message for Renae; may I use your phone?"

"Of course, it's just beside the hallstand," answered Darshan.

Nathanial rang the shop and left a message for Renae, telling her something had come up and he would call her later. "Well, I had better keep moving, goodnight."

"Goodnight, Nathanial," the couple replied.

They watched Nathanial walk briskly towards the transportation terminal as they closed the door. The glider was a marvellous piece of crystal technology. It sat on a single rail suspended twenty feet above the ground by pylons. The lower wall of the glider wrapped around the sides of the rail and a cushion of energy between the rail and the glider provided the movement and stability. The glider had window seating for six people in armchair comfort with a destination panel by each seat and a clear domed roof gave everyone an uninterrupted view of their surroundings. Nathanial climbed the steps leading to the terminal lounge where he waited for the crystal glider to arrive. He entered the next glider that stopped. Deciding to return to the bookshop first, he recorded his destination on the control panel and waited for the glider to move.

Arriving at his destination he alighted from the glider and slowly walked down the steps from the terminal. Something didn't seem right but he couldn't put his finger on it. He froze when he heard howling coming towards him and feelings of dread ran down his spine.

What was causing that dreadful sound and from which direction was it coming? The howls became louder as they reverberated off the surrounding buildings. He started walking nervously towards his destination, looking for the origin of that gruesome noise.

Suddenly he remembered where he had heard that sound before. It was the night he first met Kalareena. She had called them hounds of despair. On entering the street of the bookshop, two hideous-looking creatures larger than a dog with skins that rippled with a thriving mass of filth loomed before him. He froze with dread as the drooling beasts with burning orange eyes stared him down.

Before he could regain his composure they attacked, knocking him to the ground. One of the hounds sank its teeth into his arm as he tried to fend it off, while the other grabbed his leg, tearing at his flesh. He screamed with the pain as he fought furiously, kicking and punching with all his might.

Enoch watched in delight as he put the next part of his plan into action, calling one of the hounds to him. That slight reprieve, plus the adrenalin running through Nathanial's body, provided him with the strength he needed to finally grab hold of the beast and slam it into the side of a building. It was almost his undoing as the weight of the hound was formidable. Bloodied, torn and shaking, he looked for the other hound.

What he saw, however, was Renae walking out from the bookshop unaware that a thug was heading towards her. Nathanial screamed for her to stop as he raced towards the shop with a hound of despair right behind him. He hit the thug at a full run, catapulting the thug and him through the shop door with the hound of despair right behind them.

Nathanial was bewildered when he realised that it was a hound he was wrestling and not some thug. He fought frantically to escape the gnawing teeth and razor sharp claws. When the other hound joined the fight, he was being systematically cut to pieces.

His mind felt as if it was being torn apart with every

bite and gouge, and he cried out with the unbearable pain. Then, without warning, the hounds ceased their attack and withdrew from sight.

Enoch laughed till his sides hurt. The mind control he'd used on Nathanial to make him think he was saving Renae from an attacker was perfect. That thug was the other hound! Nathanial was in there with two hounds of despair. How sweet!

The trap box automatically reduced to the size of a shoebox once it had been activated. Enoch picked up the box and took it to the portal in the Woodlands where he wrapped and addressed it to Professor Nathanial Belmont, Security Portal Post, for his hands only. Whoever handled this package would be caught as well. Then he left and went about other business.

Nathanial was in tatters emotionally and physically. His body was bloodied and bruised and his clothes hung in rags. Rolling onto his knees brought a wave of pain that almost had him unconscious; blood was streaming from open slashes on his arms and legs.

He slowly stood up, on guard for the next attack. As none was forthcoming he removed his jacket and used his shirt to make bandages for the wounds. The realisation that he wasn't in the bookshop gradually sank in.

He was mystified; this wasn't making sense. He had gone through the door of the bookshop, hadn't he? Except … this was a forest. Well, at least it was still night – he had that part right. He was totally confused. Wherever he was, he needed to find a way of defending himself from those hideous beasts.

Limping along a path that wound its way through the trees he picked up sticks and hit them against a tree to see how sturdy they were. Unfortunately they all broke. He wondered why the hounds had stopped attacking him.

He needed to find some water to drink and clean his wounds. His instincts told him that the safest route to travel would be deeper into the forest. He had been hobbling along that path for what seemed like hours and needed rest.

Hearing a sound he turned quickly, ready for another attack, but it was only a night bird winging its way from tree to tree. He needed a safe place to rest. Noticing the bird's tree, he saw its branches were thick and strong. However, they seemed out of reach. Still if he could just manage to reach them he could rest safely for the night.

Hobbling in the direction of the tree he realised it was gigantic with limbs that grew out from the trunk in every possible way. Falling against the trunk, he spoke to it. "My beautiful friend, I need your protection. Please lend me your strength to climb your branches to safety."

This was said out of the need to hear a familiar voice rather than the need to address the tree. Looking at the branch overhead it looked much lower than before; he looked at it puzzled as a breeze rustled the tree's branches.

That must have been it – the branch was moving in the wind. He dragged his aching body over to the branch and struggled to climb it. Once on it, he carefully moved higher until he could go no further. Making himself as comfortable as possible, he slept.

* * *

The sun's rays filtering through the leaves shimmered on his face, awakening him to a new dawn. He awoke stiff and sore and tried to get his bearings. Lying on his back on a tree branch, he rolled to his side, coming to a startled stop when he noticed the ground was twenty feet below him.

"How in the blue blazes did I get up here?" he said, surprised.

He carefully started to climb down; however, this proved to be a painful exercise. Once on the ground he turned to look at the tree and then gave it a hug. "Thank you for your protection and the use of your branch as a bed."

He hobbled towards a river he'd seen from his perch in its branches. It was much further away than it appeared and by the time he reached it, he was exhausted. Sinking to his knees beside the water, he quenched his thirst and then washed and dressed his cuts as best he could with pieces of torn clothing. He found some fruits and berries growing near the water's edge to satisfy his hunger.

"I wonder where I am," he said aloud.

Nathanial tried piecing together the events from the previous night, but there seemed to be gaps in his memory. He couldn't remember where he was or how he'd arrived here. "By the True Light, I vow I will find my way home," he said out loud. At the mention of the True Light, the hounds of despair let out a cry that chilled him to the bone. He didn't know where they were but it sounded close and he decided to cross the river, hoping it would put them off his trail.

The sun was warm and he was pushing himself hard. He couldn't keep this pace going for long, as he wouldn't have the strength to defend himself if the need arose. He felt the hounds closing the distance between them so he moved out of the forest and was limping his way across a rocky wasteland when he rounded an outcrop of rock and moved into an alcove that looked like a dead-end.

He was about to turn around when he saw a fissure between the rock walls just large enough to squeeze through. His intuition was warning him that this could be a trap. He hesitated for a moment and then decided to retrace his steps.

That's when the hounds attacked. Leaping from a rock ledge, a hound landed on his back while the other came from behind. He screamed with shock and pain. He swung around, trying to loosen the grip of the hound on his back, while attempting to keep the other one from sinking its teeth into his legs.

He fell to the ground kicking and managed to grab a rock and started bashing at the hound on his back. Regaining his feet, he ran backward into the rock face, slamming the hound against the wall.

Feeling the hound weaken he redoubled his efforts, continually backing into the rock wall. The hound finally dropped to the ground. Nathanial didn't hesitate and ran to the slit in the rocks, squeezing through while the hounds tore at his legs.

Once through the crevice he collapsed, gasping for breath. His mind was numb with pain; he had scraped off a great deal of skin in forcing himself through the fissure. Struggling to his feet, he moved onward with blood running down his back and legs. "By the True Light, I will not give in! You stinking beasts!" he yelled. The hounds howled their response.

* * *

Lon was helping Lomasi regained her composure. "Nathanial's drenched in blood," Lomasi described tearfully. "He's fighting to get a beast off his back while kicking his legs to stop the other one from gnawing on them." Lon enveloped her in soothing energy while speaking softly to her. "Remove yourself from the emotion and see only what's before you," he repeated constantly while giving her healing. "Nathanial's managed to dislodge the beast from his back and has squeezed through a crevice in the rock. He's safe for the moment," she finished, relief sounding in her voice.

Oletha was communicating with Barbette. It was time for the chosen ones to know who they were. Now that Lomasi was composed, Barbette asked Renae to stop chanting and Lomasi to check if Nathanial was all right.

"Yes, Barbette, he escaped those things. Do you know what they are?"

"They're hounds of despair, Slegna's personal tormenters," Barbette replied. "They not only tear the flesh, but poison the mind and spirit as well, leaving one feeling disorientated and alone. However, Nathanial is safe for the moment and it is time for you to know whom you really are," Barbette informed them. "You were all born on different material realms and brought here for safekeeping. Each of you has skills far beyond your understanding and it's time to meet the one who bestowed them upon you."

As Oletha's presence filled the room, everyone felt a warmth of love so profound they were speechless. Kalareena, smiling, was levitating within a radiance of white light. Lon was the first to make a comment.

"We're in the presence of the Mystery of the True Light, are we not?"

"We are. Where I come from we call her Oletha, Creator of Life. I am her disciple. Each of you has been chosen by Oletha and given the gift of knowledge you call spiritual awareness. You would not have received these abilities if you weren't capable of learning how to use them proficiently. Oletha calls you her chosen ones and from this moment she has empowered each of you with the True Light."

"I knew we were all different," Lon announced. "But different worlds? Were our parents so horrible that we were taken from them?" he questioned.

"No, dear, not at all," Barbette said compassionately, resting her hand on his arm. "Each of you was orphaned at birth. You may not realise it, but you chose the lifestyle you're living," Barbette explained. "You were born to be Oletha's disciples and she asked me to bring you to Telluric and protect you from Slegna. That awareness is in each of you.

Everyone looked at each other for a moment and nodded as they realised the truth of Barbette's words; then Lon continued. "This may seem like a stupid question, Barbette, but what exactly does it mean to be empowered with the True Light?"

"Lon dear, you're a gem."

"I do my best to please," he said, smiling.

"To be empowered by the True Light is a realisation that there is no right or wrong, good or bad and that there are only different forms of love and kindness."

"Oh my." Everyone turned to look at Janelle. "I understand now the differences between the Balanced and Unbalanced, the reason for life and why the Unbalanced is important." Janelle's physical appearance seemed to alter slightly as if she was bathed in a soft light.

"It's a wonderful feeling, isn't it, dear?" Barbette quietly affirmed.

One by one they all became empowered with the profound spiritual consciousness that is Oletha. They understood the reason for the creative realms of Chimera, that Gaia was the spiritual heart of Oletha and that Slegna was simply a choice. They knew they were the soul of Oletha, her children. As they totally accepted Oletha's overwhelming love of being, they become at one with the True Light.

"Oletha isn't a he or a she any more than Slegna is," Lon said in awe. "However, I understand why you refer to her as a she. Being the embodiment of love and kindness is the quintessence of creation that is Oletha, meaning she is constantly pregnant with everlasting life."

"You have a lovely way with words, Lon. Yes, that is the reason we refer to Oletha as a she and Slegna as a he. I know you would like to discuss what each of you is experiencing, but unfortunately, Nathanial is still trapped in that box. Renae, could you recommence the mantra, please?"

Renae started the mantra again:

Om Ma Rom Ma Roo
Om Ma Rom Ma Roo

The light of Oletha had more brilliance and greater intensity than a sun. Her disciples, being endowed with the True Light, now had a never-ending wellspring of power within them to draw upon. So when they resumed the mantra the energy within the portal became immense.

CHAPTER SIX

Nathanial was battered, bruised, cut, exhausted and angry. The little clothing he had still remaining was tattered and soaked in blood. He had torn the legs of his trousers off to make bandages. Wearing nothing but ripped-off trousers as shorts and a tattered jacket, he hobbled through the barren wastelands under the blazing sun looking for a safe place to rest.

He could see forests in the distance to the South. However, his instincts were telling him to keep moving West. The rocky outcrops had given way to desert sands that the prevailing winds were whipping into a frenzy. This then blasted his exposed body, adding insult to injuries. A howl in the distance told him that he hadn't lost those demonic hounds.

He didn't really know what kept him moving. His head began spinning and his legs gave way as he fell to his knees. What he really needed was an oasis like he'd seen on travel brochures. He was exhausted and very light-headed due to loss of blood. Closing his eyes, he collapsed. Lying on the ground, his thought processes were numb so he couldn't organise his thinking properly. He could go no further; he had to have water.

Suddenly the sound of running water caused him to open his eyes. There before him was a small waterfall emerging from a rock face that ran into an oasis surrounded by shrubbery and several palm trees. He could have sworn it hadn't been there before. Crawling to the water's edge he satisfied his thirst. Looking about, there were sand dunes on three sides and a path leading from the oasis heading to an outcrop of rocks.

Having quenched his thirst and washed as much of the sand out of his wounds as possible, he sat down to think. He knew the sun could play tricks on the mind. However, the way his surroundings would change so dramatically wasn't natural. This whole place didn't seem real; it was like a bad dream.

"No!" he cried out loud. *"That oasis appeared because I needed water. Think, Nathanial think! If my thoughts controlled my environment, then it's reasonable to assume that I can think my way out of here. Every time I have needed a way to escape from those hounds, or a safe place to rest, it has appeared. Why? Also why is it I believe that travelling West is the way to escape?"*

Shakily standing and then while stumbling around the oasis he muttered to himself. *"Come on man, keep talking to yourself and reason it through. What did Barbette say? You're an intelligent man, Nathanial, so use that intellect to work it out. So work it out, come on. This place seems unnatural: the sky to the West has a discolouration to it and there is no way I could have travelled those distances with the injuries I've sustained. So what am I saying? That my surroundings aren't natural? Then what* are they, memories from my subconscious, brought to reality by an overactive imagination, coming to life in a dream? More like a bloody nightmare!"

Nathanial's mind didn't seem to want to work. He felt so frustrated and he sat back down to think. Hearing the beasts in the distance he got to his feet and yelled, *"No! Don't stop talking out loud. It keeps the brain clear, and why does Barbette keep coming into my mind? What is it, Barbette? Talk to me. We spoke on so many things in your parlour; let me hear your voice."*

Visualising Barbette in front of him, he went over the conversations they had after returning from the Woodlands. He could hear her voice clearly. She was talking about the Unbalanced and the punishment they faced for the deeds they perpetrated against themselves and society.

He had asked, *"Do they ever really suffer as much as their victims with their wanton acts of cruelty?"*

"They suffer greatly," Barbette had replied. *"We don't always know about it, so we think they are unpunished. If you propagate the seeds of disharmony then you will have to partake of its fruit when ripened – you have no choice."*

"I understand choice and consequence," he observed. *"Consider others as you would have them consider you, or what you dispense you harvest. I sometimes feel that incarceration without consequence is pointless. It's a pity they can't be made to face their deeds in some way so they can understand that their actions are not productive to a happy life."*

"There was a scientist on another world, Nathanial, who

made a device that trapped people by their own emotions. To be incarcerated within a prison of emotional trauma is terrifying."

"That seems a cruel prison." Nathanial shuddered as he thought of it.

"Yes, dear, it is a very cruel prison for anyone, let alone the fiends of the Unbalanced. It was called an Epoch Dimensional Distorter, or trap box for short. It ensnared its victims with their own emotions. A person is forced to take responsibility for his or her actions. A whole world is recreated within the Dimensional Distorter in the fashion of their deeds. Then situations arise that make them confront what they have perpetrated against themselves and others. Once they can truthfully accept responsibility for their actions the device disintegrates."

Nathanial pondered over Barbette's comment as the realisation hit him.

"That's where I am," he screamed to the air. "Somehow I've been trapped in an Epoch Dimensional Distorter, but how? That doesn't matter now. What does matter is that I can now remove myself from this abomination." Then a thought hit him. "Hang on a moment; something has to be keeping me imprisoned in this thing. What is it I can't or won't face in my life?"

Nathanial lurched around the oasis several times while going over his memories. It was a difficult process forcing the mind to work as there seemed to be gaps in it. "Love!" he suddenly yelled. "It's love." Feelings of remorse moved throughout his body as he remembered his broken relationships and the failure he felt at the time. He suddenly stopped walking and called out to the sky,

"I take full and complete responsibility for all my actions in life. I realise that I could only respond with the knowledge and understanding of life I had at the time and have no reason to find myself wanting."

A surge of energy shot through his consciousness. He had broken free of his prison and his surroundings disappeared. His mind started to clear as memories flooded back. Renae, where was Renae? He realised she had never been there and it had been all some form of illusion. The trap box had been placed in front of the bookshop and he had inadvertently entered it when trying to save her. What a relief it was to know she was safe. Now where was he?

He landed with a thud as he was transported to another place. To his surprise, he found himself surrounded by all the sounds and smells of a living forest. This wasn't where he thought he would end up. He should be back at the bookshop.

* * *

The power within the circle had been growing steadily, with Kalareena focusing on the weakness within the trap box.

"Barbette," Kalareena called. "With the amount of energy we're directing into the trap box, Nathanial is using it to move from the box to a realm within the Woodlands and back again. I don't think he knows he's even doing it. If I could reach him when he next enters the Woodlands, I can remove him."

All of a sudden Lomasi called out as an explosion of light

filled the room and the box disappeared in a flash. Everyone looked on in astonishment.

"Lomasi, what happened?"

"I don't know Kalareena. I saw Nathanial stand and call something to the sky; then this light appeared and 'poof' the box was gone."

"He must have figured out where he was. Barbette, did you ever talk to Nathanial about the trap box?"

"Yes, dear, I did. Kalareena, with the amount of power we were adding, he could have been transported to almost anywhere."

A male voice entered the conversation as Janelle's guide Maaten spoke. "He is safe for the moment within the realm of nature. However, the hounds of despair are still with him." Janelle shook her head but then also spoke. "Sorry. I didn't know he was going to speak," she apologised.

"That's all right, dear. Fala, are you receiving anything at all?"

"Yes, Barbette, but it doesn't make any sense; I am seeing a world similar to Telluric, in that it has oceans, lakes, mountain ranges, flatlands and deserts. The forests are magnificent. I've never seen their like; the average tree is well over nine hundred feet high and sixty feet wide at the base.

It looks like Nathanial is sleeping at the base of a tree. There must be a wind as leaves are falling on him. I'm also aware of speaking. I have been given the impression that the entire planet is devoid of human life. So, who's doing the talking?"

"Oh dear, if Nathanial doesn't realise where he is, he's in danger."

"What are you talking about, Kalareena?" Gela asked.

"You've heard about Mother Nature, haven't you, Gela?"

"Yes, but she's not real."

"She's very real and Nathanial has transported himself to a realm that belongs exclusively to her domain. Those voices that Fala heard were the land itself, and all that live there, communicating with each other."

"Are you saying that all the flora and land can talk?"

"Yes, Lon, that is exactly what I'm saying," Kalareena explained. "Trees are called Standing People; they're considered the wise ones. The Rock People are the Record Keepers; they have the complete accounts of all the lives you've ever had since you reincarnated into the material realms. There is an immeasurable amount of knowledge within the realms of nature, providing you know the correct protocol to access it."

"Well, if it's such a knowledgeable place, the professor should be right at home."

"Gabbryel, finding yourself in the middle of a forest that is sentient aware isn't where you want to be, if you are unaware of it."

"What possible harm could befall him?"

"Gela, if you were cold or wet what would you do to keep warm and dry?"

"Light a fire, of course," Gela replied quickly.

"Very good, except on this world everything has a living

spirit," Kalareena told her. "So if you were to break some branches, it would be like me breaking your arms and legs and setting fire to them. The same goes for drinking water. You have to ask permission from the water spirits. However, if you don't know they exist and take a drink, it would be like me drinking your blood. The same with any food that Nathanial may find; to eat without permission is to commit murder."

"Come on, Kalareena," Gabbryel said mockingly. "What are they going to do, yell at him?"

"For a bright girl, Gabbryel, you're exhibiting a great deal of ignorance," Kalareena commented, concern written on her face. "The trees can hit with their branches, the rocks can throw themselves, the fruits can turn poisonous and the water spirits can drown him. Shall I continue?"

"Then what do we do?" Renae asked with concern.

"The only thing we can do, Renae," Barbette responded, "is focus our energies so that Kalareena can extend her spiritual sight to search the realms of Nature until she can locate the world he's upon."

"There may be another way, Barbette," Kalareena said thoughtfully. "I'll travel to the Woodlands and see if I can locate him through our golden thread of awareness."

"Then what?" Janelle asked hesitantly.

"Once I've located him, I can travel to the world he's on through a transport portal. Once we are together our spiritual energies will exceed that of the realm we are in. It will just be a matter of bringing him back here so Lon can heal him."

"Kalareena, if Nathanial is badly hurt, wouldn't it be better if I were to go with you?"

"Thank you, Lon, but it's not that easy. You haven't been shown how to travel inter-dimensionally through the portals into the different realms. You could become disorientated or lost in another dimension of time."

"Kalareena, I'm worried for Nathanial. He's like a father figure to all of us. Lomasi doesn't exaggerate. If Nathanial is badly hurt, the quicker I can reach him the better." Lon spoke quietly but firmly.

Kalareena looked at Barbette. "Will he do exactly as he is told, no matter what his eyes show him?" she asked intently.

"I can answer that, Kalareena," Renae said. "Lon is very well respected among the staff; he follows instructions to the letter."

"Very well, Lon, you have your wish. Barbette, please instruct Lon in the basics of mental disorientation and energy pressures between the different realms. I shall return shortly. Everyone sat listening intently to Barbette's explanation of inter-dimensional portal travelling.

"When you move through a portal, there is a period of disorientation that isn't real. It's a trick of the eyes and mind. It is similar to having a bucket of water and putting a stick into it. The stick appears to bend, when in fact it is still straight. A similar thing happens as you move within a portal; you think you are bending or falling when you're not.

"There is a lot of theory about this phenomenon which I haven't got time to go through. So I will simply lead you through. Would everyone remove themselves and their belongings from the disc of light, please?"

Barbette waited until the area was cleared of belongings and people and then took Lon's hand and disappeared from sight. A moment later they were back where they had started. Lon looked a little worse for wear.

"Okay, Lon, tell me exactly what you experienced," instructed Barbette.

"It is similar to motion sickness, my head is spinning and I feel like I want to throw up. Renae, there are some herbs in a brown bag tied with an orange string in the counter drawer. Could you crush some up in water for me, please?"

As Renae went for the herbs, Janelle fetched a glass of water. Renae then crushed some of the herbs into the water. They dissolved and turned the water green. Lon gulped the liquid down. Looking pale, he sat down with his head in his hands.

"Does everyone go through this, Barbette?" Janelle asked.

"No, dear, the effects alter depending on which realm you come from. Each one of you is from a different realm of learning, so you will all experience a different effect. It has to do with the differing rhythmic resonances between the body and the realm you're coming from and going to."

Lon spoke up. "I'm all right now." Everyone looked in his direction; he appeared as if he had just woken up from a good night's sleep.

"That must be some amazing stuff, Lon?" Barbette asked.

"It's my own concoction of herbs and pick-me-ups, I give it

to the girls when they're feeling seedy. Could you explain to me how you travel? I feel that could be part of the problem."

"Each portal has a rhythmic energy that produces a colour," Barbette began. "Each colour is a destination; you simply envisage your destination and arrive."

"If I don't know the colour of the portal, but I know my destination, would I still arrive?"

"Yes, you would. Why Lon, where were you planning on going?"

"To the forest we went to before. If you would be so kind as to take my hand, that way if I mess up you can save us."

"Only if you're a good boy," she said humorously. They walked into the circle of light and disappeared, a moment later they reappeared.

"That was very well done, Lon, how are you feeling, dear?"

"No ill effects at all. Concentrating on the destination is the key. I would like to try something else, if you would take my hand again."

Barbette did so and they were gone. They appeared on a large flat rock on top of a mountain and then vanished, reappearing above an ocean. They vanished again and reappeared in the clouds. Barbette looked at Lon enquiringly.

"It's just like healing, Barbette; you follow the energy flow," Lon explained excitedly. "This is wonderful," Lon said, smiling happily.

"Very good young man, now return us home, please."

"Your wish is my command," he replied.

They suddenly reappeared in the bookshop. Barbette

went over to the armchair Lon had brought down from the mezzanine and sat. Everyone wanted to know where they had been. Hearing of their destination they looked to Lon for an explanation.

"Do you realise how dangerous it was to materialise above the ocean and in the clouds without advanced training in levitation techniques, young man?" Barbette chastised.

"There was absolutely no danger at all, Barbette. I could see the healing energies within the realms we visited. Did you know that everything is made up of sound?"

"Yes, dear, I did. You have come a long way in a short space of time. It'll be safe for you to travel with Kalareena."

Lon had been standing within the circle of light when suddenly the portal lit up in a brilliant white flash that filled the entire room. When the light diminished, Lon was nowhere to be seen. Everyone was in shock; Barbette was moving towards the portal when Oletha's presence filled the bookshop. Her awareness filled them all with profound feelings of love as she advised them that Lon was on the planet Terraqueous for training. He would be returned later if his training were successful. Then her presence left.

* * *

Mick awoke the next morning feeling refreshed and ready for the day's challenges. He wasn't going to let Joe outsmart him; he must have a method of choosing the safe houses. During a morning meal at a local eating-house,

Mick reviewed all his notes on his crystal note screen and securitised the houses on his view tub once more.

So far, all he had determined was that all the safe houses had figureheads on the roofline; other than that he was stumped. He couldn't seem to find the common denominator. He was so engrossed in his endeavours that he hadn't noticed the time or Terry standing across the table watching him until he spoke.

"What's ya up ta, Mick?"

Mick nearly left his seat and started shaking. "Shit, Terry, ya scared the life outta me."

"Yeah, I noticed that. By the way, I've changed me name ta Enoch.

"Yeah Terr ... Sorry, Enoch, whatever."

"Not whatever, Mick. I wouldn't want ta have ta remind ya. Got it?"

Mick took one look at Terry's face and knew never to slip up. Fear travelled through him and he thought he was going to soil his pants. Who was he to argue? If Terry wanted to be called Enoch that was fine by him.

"So what are ya doin' here?" Enoch enquired.

"I'm tryin' ta work out how Joe chooses the safe houses. What have you been up to?"

"I've just been wandering around and saw ya in here."

"So what are ya goin' ta do the rest of the mornin', Enoch?"

"Mornin?' Are ya simple in the head? It's two in the afternoon. I'm off, see ya tomorrow."

Mick looked at the clock on the wall in amazement. He

stared at it for a long time until he realised what had caught his attention. The face of the clock was covered with animal figureheads.

A couple of centuries ago animal totems were all the rage. Many people formed clans and lived in communes, taking on the attributes of the animals they followed. The practice still went on today; however, it wasn't as widespread and that's what had caught Mick's attention. The clock signified it had once belonged to the Cat Clan; every minute was a cathead indicating the passage of time around its face. All the safe houses Joe chose had a figurehead from the cat family on them! Mick was feeling pleased with himself and decided a celebration was in order.

* * *

A white light of intense love emanated from every part of Lon's being. As the sensation slowly diminished he found himself lying on a bed in unfamiliar surroundings. His vision seemed unnatural, as if he was seeing through a silken veil. A woman appeared before him who looked translucent; her soft gentle features were warm and inviting.

"I am Harpreet, a devotee of Oletha. I will be your instructor in the spiritual arts."

"Hi, I'm Lon, where am I?" he asking rising from the bed.

"You're on Terraqueous," she answered.

"That's Barbette's home world," Lon observed.

"Correct."

"How did I come to be here and when will I be returning home? My family needs me," Lon was concerned.

"Oletha brought you here to learn," Harpreet explained. "You will be able to help your friends more easily once your spiritual skills have been developed.

"Harpreet, all I can see are different shades of white. It's a little unnerving," he explained looking around the room uncomfortably.

"As your understanding grows in the spiritual arts, your sight will become clearer. Let us begin." Harpreet indicated for Lon to be seated. "Do you know who Oletha and Slegna are?"

"Yes. Oletha has empowered me with the True Light."

"Then you know I Am That I Am, Oletha, is the spiritual heart of life from which our soul was born and that each soul created the eternal spirit to wander the realms of Chimera. You also know that Slegna is nothing more than a choice between a Balanced and Unbalanced life."

"Yes, I know that."

"Good. Then you will appreciate it's the spiritual ambiances of life that are the building blocks of creation."

"If by spiritual ambiance of life you're referring to the creative power that brought life into reality throughout the realms of Chimera and that our environment is nothing more than a collection of harmonic vibrations, then yes."

"Interesting interpretation, Lon," Harpreet said, moving closer to him.

"I became aware of the aspects of what we call life, after Oletha empowered me with the True Light," Lon explained.

"Then you also know that everything you sense, see and come into contact with is made up of sound," Harpreet continued. "What blends sound into music is love and the greatest form of love is compassion. If your entire decision making was in harmony with the resonance of love and kindness, then the Unbalanced would be unable to influence your life," she finished, sitting beside him.

"You can't possibly believe that by 'thinking' love and kindness, nothing untoward will happen to you," Lon scoffed. "Come on, Harpreet, you're living in a dream world," Lon continued disbelievingly.

"Your environment is everything that you sense, see, smell and touch within the physical and spiritual realms of Chimera, Lon. By allowing every decision to resonate in love and kindness, you wouldn't be able to misrepresent the integrity within yourself, or others."

"So you say, but you've never lived on Telluric; many people are cruel," he pointed out.

Harpreet's face showed gentleness and wisdom as she continued. "Lon, compassion is the empathy that recognises that all beings are created free and equal."

"Which means every person is free to be cruel or kind. Harpreet, thinking loving thoughts won't have people being sympathetic towards you."

"You're using the emotions of your mind to reason with, Lon, instead of the feelings of your spiritual heart. Love is the essence that folds and binds all the realms of Chimera together. You are love, a pure, unadulterated essence of creation."

"I must admit," Lon responded, his mind and spirit working to coalesce his newfound knowledge, "since Oletha empowered me with the True Light, I view life differently."

"That's because Oletha isn't outside of you, but a part of you. Love isn't something you have to find, for you are love."

"When it's put that way, I have all the love I will ever need," observed Lon.

"Yes," Harpreet answered, smiling. "By truly loving yourself you won't need the affections of others to make you feel a person of consequence, because you are love. Do you know why?"

Returning Harpreet's smile, Lon answered, "Because I'm already the embodiment of love that is Oletha."

"Now you have that understanding, Lon, do you know what chakra points are and where in the body they're located?"

Lon made himself more comfortable before answering. "Yes, there are seven points within the body that the spirit uses to harmonise the material and spiritual essence of creation. They're located at the crown, forehead or third eye, throat, heart, solar plexus, pubic bone or sacrum and coccyx," remarked Lon dutifully.

"Good." I want you to meditate on your heart chakra, creating a state of peace throughout the mind and body," Harpreet explained. Lon gently closed his eyes as she continued to explain what she wished him to do. "Once that has been achieved, visualise a silver disc emanating from your heart chakra outward from your body to the distance of your fingertips if your arms were outstretched. It must be of the purest silver, without any imperfection."

Lon had been meditating most of his life so he was in a state of peace within moments. Opening his awareness, he visualised a silver disc emanating from his heart chakra as Harpreet had described. The energy was undulating outward from the heart like waves on an ocean; no matter how much he concentrated he was unable to maintain the type of silver he wanted.

Harpreet, aware of Lon's difficulty, entered his mind. "You are of the True Light, not the mere thought of mind. Start over."

Lon recommenced his meditation. This time he controlled the wrinkle effect the disc of light had previously made, but now the silver looked wrong. Harpreet's awareness entered his mind once more.

"You are of the True Light, not the mere thought of mind. Start over."

Lon decided he must be missing something in her comment and decided to ask.

"What is it I'm not hearing you say?"

"Your mind is hearing my words and doing as it's asked. However, you are of the True Light, not the mere thought of mind. Start over."

Lon started over as requested, only to have Harpreet's awareness enter his head yet again, repeating her phrase. He was becoming frustrated with her continued response. While wondering what he was doing wrong, he became aware of another part of himself that he hadn't been conscious of before.

"Harpreet, there's a part of me I haven't consciously been aware of before."

"Yes, Lon. It is your true self."

"Of course," Lon replied in amazement. "My eternal spirit."

"The spirit is the soul's representation of the True Light within the realms of Chimera; the power at its disposal is awesome. To protect the mind's free will, the spirit becomes a muse for the mind."

Lon looked puzzled. "What's a muse?" he questioned.

"A muse is one of nine sister goddesses who preside over all themes of learning, together with the arts, in the mythology on my world," Harpreet answered. "Like any good educator they never impose their own ideas upon their students, but encourage them to think for themselves, guiding a person beyond their present level of education to where they can discover the answers in their own way."

"So you're saying that the spirit created the muse as a teacher?"

"Yes. The muse then created the subconscious mind in such a way that the mind thinks it created it. Your muse knows the edification you chose, and the manner in which you decided to learn, because in reality it is your eternal spirit, which was created by the soul."

"I don't think I would have chosen some of the experiences that have happened to me," Lon said drily.

"Nothing is an accident, Lon, and everything happens for

a reason. The muse is the ambiance of compassion, love and beauty; nothing that isn't constructed from love can come from the muse," Harpreet explained while moving to face him.

"You're saying that the inner voice that won't let me give up and keeps me searching for my spiritual truth is the muse."

"Yes."

"So the muse is my spirit and the embodiment of my soul, which is Oletha."

"Correct," continued Harpreet. "The muse is the strength of mind that responds to a sensation or belief that won't quit, even in the face of overwhelming odds, because in reality it's Oletha."

"Then I should be meditating with the love of spirit; not with the strength of mind."

"Shall we start again?" Harpreet suggested, smiling at Lon's understanding.

Focusing on his spiritual heart, Lon drew forth the creative energies of love and kindness. He then allowed those feelings to embrace his heart chakra and was pleasantly surprised at how easily he created the silver disc Harpreet had requested.

Her words echoed in his mind. "Love is always the answer, Lon."

She then filled his mind with a vision. Silver energy travelled through the chakra points of the body and along lines of energy called meridians, in both directions simultaneously. As it reached each chakra, a silver disc of energy formed, identical to the heart chakra; this continued until it reached the crown and base chakras. Once the discs had formed, a shaft of silver shot from the base chakra, connecting to Gaia, while an equal shaft of silver shot skyward, connecting to the universe.

Lon knew what was required of him and set about duplicating the vision he had been shown. He had accomplished the task several times, only to realise the silver was inconsistent and he would have to start again. After many unsuccessful attempts, he finally succeeded in duplicating the vision. As the light simultaneously connected to Gaia and the universe, Lon's awareness reawakened to the oneness of soul, spirit, mind and body as they became a complete entity.

It seemed so easy now he knew how it was done. The chakra points reminded him of a set of scales with the heart chakra as the fulcrum. He simply allowed the heart chakra to overflow with love, thus transferring equally throughout the other chakras, above and below.

Harpreet's awareness once more filled Lon's mind. "Return now from your meditation, please."

It took a little while for Lon to completely return to mental awareness. His mind seemed more in harmony with his body, as if he had been reborn. There was something else, something he hadn't really thought of before, something that now seemed so natural he laughed quietly to himself. He was the complete embodiment of love. Finding his voice, he addressed Harpreet.

"That was awesome Harpreet, I feel wonderful..." Lon stopped in mid-sentence as he realised he could now see his surroundings. A ceiling-to-floor window filled the entire wall opposite providing an uninterrupted view of nature. The room itself was rather plain with minimum seating for three people, the bed he occupied and a small worktable. The remaining three walls were an off-white colour and the door was palest yellow. Standing beside the bed was his teacher who indicated that he should remove himself from the bed and sit on one of the seats.

"Hello Lon. Yes, I am Harpreet. You see me differently now. Welcome again to Terraqueous."

Lon stared open-mouthed at a woman of extraordinary loveliness. Standing six foot with straight auburn hair that rested gracefully upon her shoulders, her every movement was precise and delicate as she seated herself on the chair seat next to his. Intelligence born of time emanated from intense green eyes and her presence was almost ethereal. Her soft mouth creased in a welcoming smile that radiated warmth and understanding as she regarded him.

"What you see around you will undoubtedly seem strange," she said, with a serene voice of authority.

Realising his mouth was still open, Lon shut it quickly and cleared his throat before speaking. "You and everything I see feels unearthly," he said, looking around intently. "As if you're lacking substance," he finished uncertainly.

Smiling knowingly, Harpreet explained. "Our illusions of life aren't as cemented in delusions as on your world, Lon."

Lon reached out tentatively to touch Harpreet's arm and a peal of laughter escaped her lips at the surprised expression on his face. "We still have substance, Lon," she clarified. "However, because our species is harmonising at a different spiritual vibration than you are, we seem less opaque. Of course that's all just an illusion anyway," she finished.

"What do you mean an illusion?" Lon asked, suddenly feeling very tired.

"Nothing is real, Lon. Everything you think of as real is a fabrication of the spirit, an illusion. Even my world is an illusion; it's just a more refined one."

Lon put his hands to his head. He needed to think but his mind didn't want to work; he was tired and hungry. Harpreet recognised his dilemma.

"You may feel a little disoriented at the moment, Lon," she said, resting her hand on his. "There is food and drink provided for you at the guesthouse. Please refresh yourself and we will talk on the morrow."

Lon looked at her. "How long have I been here?" he asked, feeling drained.

"Oletha brought you here twelve months ago," she informed him.

Startled, Lon asked. "Did you just say I've been here for a year?"

"Yes," Harpreet replied gently.

"I don't recall eating or drinking. How have I survived?" he asked, confused.

"On spiritual energy." Harpreet raised her hand to forestall any more questions. "I know you have questions Lon," she replied sympathetically. "But allow yourself to follow my advice and rest. I'll return to answer all your queries tomorrow." Harpreet gestured towards a woman who had just entered the room. She advised, "This is Winna. She will escort you to your quarters at the guesthouse." Lon nodded his head and went with her.

CHAPTER SEVEN

She had come into being the moment Oletha had given her of her spiritual heart. She has been in existence since the universes were created. She is the fundamental nature of being that nurtures and mothers all things; she is the life that formed all the material realms of Chimera. The name she goes by is Gaia.

She had known from the beginning that he was coming. His Staff of power started growing from the One Tree of Consciousness the moment the realm of nature came into existence. The Tree of Consciousness contains within its essence all the knowledge of the realms of Chimera.

It will be Lon's task to combat the forces of the Unbalanced and infuse his essence with the Staff of Life, completing his transformation into Umi 'New Life', becoming Malachy, Oletha's Supreme Being and Kyros, Consummate Healer of all the realms of Chimera.

* * *

Harpreet entered Lon's bedchamber to see if he was awake; noticing his slight movements she retired to the lounge area. The clever use of nature's warming colours created a gentle atmosphere, and an uncluttered appearance gave the impression of spaciousness, in what was really a small chamber where Lon was rousing himself from sleep.

A ceiling-to-floor window at the other end of the bedchamber had awakened Lon to a blue sky and bright sunshine. Having dressed, he went from his sleeping quarters to a compact kitchenette and lounge area, where he found Harpreet sitting comfortably in one of the large lounge chairs.

"You have rested well, I see."

"Yes, thank you, Harpreet," Lon replied absentmindedly, while coming to terms with a new balanced awareness.

"To answer your earlier questions, Lon," Harpreet said, while indicating the food that had been provided on the table, "you have spent the last year learning to be in command of your spiritual energies. Each chakra point has a cadence, which, while resonating, creates a specific colour. You not only connected and purified your chakra points, you also had to balance your aura while maintaining the integrity of the silver discs."

"Didn't you say that everything was an illusion?" Lon asked, making himself comfortable on a lounge chair opposite while helping himself to the cuisine.

"No. I said that all the realms of Chimera are illusions."

"So what I am seeing isn't real?" he asked around a mouthful of food.

"It's as real as your reality can create, Lon."

"Now I'm lost, please explain," he asked.

"Philosophy is the divine truth of being and this knowledge is imparted through different levels of plausible illusions. Each one of us has many differing degrees of illusions that are constantly being reinforced by our environment.

If we allow only the mind to do our thinking, then before long we become entrenched in the illusions of a material life. We deceive ourselves that this life is all there is. When that happens, our illusions become multifaceted and mature into delusions becoming figments of the imagination and figments of the imagination are far more complex to negate," Harpreet clarified, while picking up something to eat.

"So why do we have illusions?" he queried.

"They are the clothing within the realm of existence we have incarnated into. In essence, illusions are the building paraphernalia that the creative imagination, or subconscious mind, utilises to demonstrate the joy of being."

"Didn't you say that the subconscious mind was the muse and that the muse is the spirit, which was created by the soul?"

"That's very good, Lon," Harpreet said, wiping her hands on a napkin.

Lon leaned forward with his elbows on his knees and his chin on his clasped hands, deep in thought but then sat upright. "So you're saying that the spirit is responsible for what surrounds me?" Lon enquired.

"Yes. Illusions are neither good nor bad; they simply are," Harpreet replied, making herself more comfortable. "It is the varying ambiances of love which bestow upon you the differing moods of illusions that can produce feelings of compassion."

"So illusions have to be, so we can learn and grow?"

"Yes, if you look in the bowl behind you, Lon, you will see brown and white earth fruits. If you were to peel one, you would find that there is nothing inside, because they are made up from many layers of skin."

"We call those onions on my world," Lon commented.

"Then think of your life as an onion and the skin as your illusion," continued Harpreet. "Your task is to remove all the layers to reveal the truth of who you are. Sometimes accepting the things you have done is too much to bear, so you create another illusion to cover the first. Consequently, you establish a foundation of delusions to protect your denial."

"So if I'm feeling guilty about something but then convince myself that I was justified in my action, I have created a delusion on top of an illusion, correct?"

"You catch on quickly, Lon."

"Not really," Lon answered, disappointed in himself. "I simply recognise what I've been doing in the past," he said, picking up an apple.

"Life is too precious to waste on self-doubt and self-abuse, Lon," Harpreet responded compassionately. "A foundation of love and kindness inspires a gentleness of purpose, not a need for control."

"I understand," Lon answered thoughtfully. "It's the

need for control that most people need to make them feel empowered in life, instead of self-love."

Harpreet leaned forward in her chair. "Lon, where does healing come from?"

Lon finished his mouthful of apple. "All healing comes from Oletha. A healer is someone who can control the energy flow to repair the spirit and body. However, unless the body has been seriously damaged, by healing the spirit the body will automatically repair itself."

"Oletha brought you here to learn that One Truth and this you have done," Harpreet said. "Are you happy with what you have learned?"

Since being empowered with the True Light of Oletha and having balanced his soul, spirit, mind and body through the chakra meditation, Lon knew something more was going on other than what Harpreet had so far explained. "Harpreet, I could have learned this on Telluric. What am I really doing here?"

"What do you want from life, Lon?"

"I'm Oletha's disciple, Harpreet. All that I am, or will become, is done with her blessing or not at all. Does that answer your question?" Lon explained while reaching for the water jug.

"Perfectly. Let me share an anecdote with you. Before there was life, there was something else; no one knows what it was but Oletha created herself from it. She then created the Realms of Chimera and at the same moment they were formed, she brought into existence an essence of being to mother all things. This she called Gaia. The instant Gaia's awareness became she created the One Tree of Consciousness, the only one of its kind.

It's the Record Keeper of all knowledge and Gaia planted it on the first world Oletha created. Its root system encompasses the entire planet. The tree began growing eight healing Staffs of Knowledge at the beginning of its life. When the deeds of the Unbalanced become too much to bear, a healer is called upon to claim a Staff and heal the rift of knowledge. Each Staff comes to fruition at the appointed time.

The eighth Staff, however, is unique in that it is sentient aware and has all the knowledge of the parent. The healer who would claim this Staff has to undergo a physiological change."

Lon got to his feet and started pacing around the room while Harpreet continued her explanation.

"The second world Oletha created was of crystal. Gaia infused the crystal with the ability to extend life almost indefinitely. For the true healer to become Kyros, he or she must infuse their essence within a liquid crystal. That, Lon, is the position of ultimate healer, the true master: Kyros."

Lon returned to his seat and sat silently for a moment. "That is a fascinating story, Harpreet, although I don't think you told it to me for its amusement value."

Harpreet's manner became serious. "Oletha brought you here to train so you may become Kyros. Do you accept?" she asked with finality.

Something deep inside Lon recognised the truth of Harpreet's words. All his life he had been healing people; he was fascinated with the workings of the mind and body, but was frustrated with orthodox medicine.

Rising from his chair once more he walked from the lounge area onto a veranda that overlooked a lake and gardens. He already knew his answer, but there was something else bothering him. He turned to face Harpreet, who had followed.

"Harpreet," he asked, concerned, "if you and Barbette are from the same world, how is it her appearance is different to yours?"

Smiling, she clarified. "Because we are the embodiment of our spirituality Lon, we're able to manipulate the outward appearance of our physical density. Barbette is as opaque as I am on her home world. However, she couldn't walk around Telluric looking that way as she would draw too much attention to herself."

Chuckling, Lon nodded his head. "I see your point. What do I do now, lovely lady?"

"First, you visit the world of liquid crystal and blend your essence with theirs."

"How do I do that?"

"I don't know, Lon. Oletha believes you already have that information or she wouldn't have chosen you. After you and the crystal are one, you will travel to the world of the Tree of Consciousness and claim the Staff. You cannot obtain the Staff without first joining with the crystal. Do you understand?"

"Yes," he said.

"The essence of the True Light is within you, Lon. You must use what you know. I can show you the portal that will take you to your destination, but you must go alone."

* * *

Lon stepped onto the portal and disappeared. He emerged into brilliant light that dazzled the senses. Shutting his eyes quickly he pulled a handkerchief from his pocket and tied it around his head, protecting his eyes. Harpreet had said this world was liquid crystal so he wasn't going anywhere just yet. He carefully located an outcrop of flat crystal to sit on and made himself comfortable.

While waiting for the light to dim he thought over his life. He had lived with his foster parents in a middle-class neighborhood. His family wasn't rich, nor were they on the breadline and when he showed an interest in becoming a doctor they happily supported him. Having finished his medical training and become a qualified medical practitioner, he found that he couldn't refer to himself as a doctor, nor practise in the style of his education.

Lon believed in a holistic approach to his patients' health. He reasoned that the spirit had feelings that influenced the mind. The mind then transferred those feelings into emotions throughout the body and created a person's responses. If those emotions were ignored then the body suffered discomfort and eventually illness. However, everything Lon was taught denied the existence of the spirit and concentrated solely on the science of the body. He couldn't come to terms with the lack of compassion and spirituality in his studies, believing that to treat just the body was to only address the symptoms. He had almost been expelled twice for arguing with his tutors about holistic healing. Despite his constant questioning he passed all his studies with the highest honours becoming a qualified medical practitioner.

However, he was disheartened with his profession and was wandering around the streets wondering what he was going to do with his life when he came across an advertisement for a librarian in a bookshop window. On impulse he entered Enigma Books and located the manager, Renae, and introduced himself. There was something about the store that drew him in and Renae made him feel at home. After a satisfactory interview he now had employment as a librarian.

He moved from his family residence and rented a small apartment close to Enigma Books. Lon knew his foster parents were disappointed with his decision. His experience with Oletha had verified his beliefs about healing and now he was being given the chance to become a true healer. He felt both terrified and elated at the same time.

He didn't know how long he waited for the light to dim. When he finally removed his handkerchief and opened his eyes he could see mountains, rivers and a type of flora, all constructed from crystals of various shapes and sizes. It was a breathtaking but dangerous terrain. The sun had completely set and another was rising by the time he decided to have a look around. It must have been an old sun as it wasn't as bright, though it illuminated the surrounding area sufficiently for him to see without any problems.

Lon decided to meditate on how he should best proceed. After a while he heard voices and opened his eyes to see who was there, but could see no one. Wondering, he resumed his meditation. The voices returned. He deepened his meditation and sent his thoughts out to the voices hoping he could communicate with whoever it was telepathically.

"My name is Lon," he sent outward from his mind. "I have come here from another realm of learning to blend with a crystal of life. The Mystery of the True Light, Oletha, has asked this of me. I am her disciple." To his surprise a female voice answered.

"I am Me-i, the voice of the crystal and I hear your request. You must find the crystal with which you harmonise with the most and share your essence with it."

"How do I blend my essence and the crystal's essence as one, Me-i?"

"If you are as you say, you will know." Then the voice was gone.

He didn't try to mentally work out what had to be done; he had faith his inner knowing would guide him. He opened his eyes and started walking and had gone some distance from the portal when he heard running water.

On closer inspection he saw a crystal river of sapphire and his heart leaped with joy at the sight. His whole being started to resonate with anticipation as the crystal communicated with him. This was the crystal he wished to share his essence with. Walking to the river's edge, he crossed to a crystal sandbank where he sat down and meditated, sending his thoughts to Me-i.

"Me-I, if you can hear me, I wish to be as one with the sapphire crystal."

Suddenly the crystal sand dissolved beneath him and he found himself immersed within the swiftly flowing crystal river of sapphire. Strong currents buffeted him over crystal shards that protruded from the river and bounced him from one outcrop of crystal to another. Each encounter brought agony as the ends of the crystal cut deeply into his body. With great effort he finally managed to heave himself upon an island in the middle of the river, while the river sped past threatening to drag him to its liquid depths.

Gasping for breath, he spat the liquid crystal from his mouth. Intense pain assailed his mind and body; blood was running from the gashes he had sustained. Ripping the tail of his shirt into bandages he tied them around his wounds as best he could. His mind was screaming for a reprieve as the liquid crystal moved through his veins like burning sludge. If he didn't regain some form of control over his mind and body he felt his life would be at an end.

Forcing his mind to follow his demands, he immersed himself completely within the love of Oletha, finally achieving a state of spiritual peace, ignoring the agonising pain of his body. Then he performed the disc chakra meditation technique Harpreet had taught him. However, the disc of silver was changing to a rich sapphire blue. If there was to be a sharing of essences, it would have to be a silvery blue. The distribution of essences must be equal or he couldn't survive. His mind was disorientated from the depth of anguish he was experiencing.

It took all of his mental and spiritual power not to give in to the intoxication of the sapphire. Like a drug of sweetest delight the embryonic crystal sapphire essence used every ounce of its subtle persuasion to seduce Lon into relinquishing control of his mind and spirit. When that failed it attacked him with such force as to almost render him unconscious.

The spirit of the sapphire was trying to change the silver around Lon's chakra points. Each time the blue would gain the advantage; Lon would swamp the crystal with the love of Oletha, thereby dispersing the rich blue into a more harmonious blending of silvery blue. The battle raged back and forth as each fought for control.

Lon recognised that neither could win this battle; there had to be a mutual blending or both would forfeit their lives. The battle was titanic as Lon communicated with the crystal spirit sapphire advising him that if it didn't cooperate they would both perish. The crystal recognised Lon's words as truth and finally agreed to blend their spirituality as one.

So it was that Lon eventually successfully transcended the blending of the crystal into the silver disc around the heart chakra and it became a beautiful rich silvery-blue that dazzled the senses. The conversion of the remaining discs was a steady progression of energy that emanated from the heart chakra. When the base and crown chakras were complete a shaft of blue light shot from the base chakra downward while a shaft of silver flared upward. The blending of essences was complete. Lon felt peace melting into his spirit, mind and body.

"Open your eyes, Lon, and see what you have become," echoed Me-i's voice in his ears.

Opening his eyes, Lon was greeted with the incredible splendour of Me-i's home world. The island that had been his refuge was no longer a sandbank with crystal shards protruding from the ground, but a beautiful landmass of flowers and shrubs. A river of deepest sapphire-blue flowed gently around it and standing next to him were Me-i and her helpers.

There was no mistaking their gender as they were completely devoid of clothing and created entirely from liquid crystal that constantly moved rhythmically throughout their bodies, the consistency of which resembled mercury. However, their skin altered in colour depending on the crystal essence to which they belonged. Me-i's appearance was breathtaking as her body pulsated with a beautiful lilac that changed to tranquil shades of pink, white and yellow as she moved. Lon couldn't help but stare.

"Do you need help to stand, Lon?"

"I think I'll be all right, Me-i." Lon gently rose to his feet as Me-i's helpers smiled kindly towards him and continued to pack their equipment.

"Please excuse me if I'm staring, Me-i, as I don't mean to be rude."

"That's all right, Lon, I've been looking intently at you too. You're certainly an interesting species. Do your kind always cover their bodies with..."

"They're called clothes, and yes, depending on the nature of the weather and where we are at the time."

"Your bodies are very frail, aren't they?"

"Compared to yours, yes. Me-i, I don't wish to sound discourteous, but which crystal are you?"

Me-i's laugh was rich and full of life. "That's not an impolite question, Lon. I'm of the Crystal Clan Danburite."

"Does your race always change colour?"

"It's strange, but I didn't realise we did until you mentioned it. It's amazing how one takes things like that for granted. Our complexion alters as our emotions fluctuate."

"The lilac you're displaying seems more dominant than the pink, yellow and white that are moving through your body Lon commented, indicating her form, "whereas your nursing staff are changing colours more rapidly."

"I'm a very old spirit, Lon, and have more control over my emotions than my nursing staff. If I'm correct, your species has a relatively short life span and would reincarnate quite frequently."

Lon nodded. "Compared to your species, our average life span is around ninety years."

"To you we would seem to have eternal life, which of course isn't true," Me-i explained. "Our essence is simply on a different time line from yours. Now you've joined your essence with ours, when you return to your world you will be immortal in the eyes of your kind."

Lon looked down at his body, surprised that he was as naked as Me-i. His appearance was of ever-changing colours of blue, yellow, green, black and purple, also the consistency of mercury. It struck him as interesting that in the genital area, the crystal would darken form, virtually rendering one's gender invisible.

"Me-i, would you mind if I asked an anatomical question?"

"This could prove interesting, please continue," she said, smiling.

"It's obvious from your figure that you are a female and it's obvious I'm a male. Yet I'm unable to identify any genitals to support my observations, either on you or myself."

"From what Oletha has said of you, you are a healer and your knowledge of anatomy is quite extensive. Am I correct?" asked Me-i.

"That's correct. I'm a qualified medical practitioner or doctor on my world."

"Then watch." Me-i stood facing Lon with her back towards her staff. The uniformity of her body changed revealing her gender and then returned to its original form. "You use clothing to cover your masculinity, Lon. However, at the moment your mind is interacting with your crystal form and covering your genital area for you."

"Really," Lon said, amazed. "So if I want to expose myself I just think about it and it will happen?"

"Yes," Me-i replied with a laugh.

Lon concentrated his thoughts on his masculinity, revealing his naked form. "Well, will you look at that, I did it!"

Everyone present turned to see what was transpiring and laughed at the sight of Lon continually looking at himself while dressing and undressing.

"Sorry, I didn't mean to cause embarrassment to anyone," Lon said, suddenly realising what he was doing.

"I'm a doctor and my staff are all qualified nurses; you don't have anything we haven't seen before," Me-i reassured him, smiling. Lon laughed while he admired the depth of colour and movement of energy within his being.

"You're highly spiritually evolved Lon, for you are running the full spectrum of colours of the Clan Sapphire. You are most handsome indeed in your crystal form," she observed.

"If I'm handsome, Me-i," Lon said, flirting outrageously, "it's only because I'm basking in the radiance of your beauty."

Me-i smiling bowed to him. "Why thank you, kind sir. It is most gracious of you to say so."

Something was still nagging at Lon but he couldn't put his finger on it. Finally it hit him. "Me-i, I can see you!"

"Of course," she replied. "Once you blended with the crystal you gained crystal sight."

"Are the others in your team, specialists?" he asked.

"We're a special medical team specifically trained in the rejuvenation of the physical and crystal embryos as a single life form, assisting the two bodies to metamorphose into a single material form," Me-i answered.

Where once Lon had only seen magnificent crystal outcrops, high mountains now surrounded the island he had finally crawled onto. Life was in abundance all about him. He could see forest-covered mountains everywhere. Me-i must have constructed a small bridge as one now stretched from the island to the far bank. Moving across the bridge they walked along a path that wound out from the gorge to a vast plain that ran between two mountain ranges.

Although Lon could distinguish the plant and animal life, it seemed strange, as everything was created from living crystal. The forests were similar to Telluric, with one exception. Each colour was a different crystal essence and they all flowed together effortlessly. Me-i interrupted his thoughts.

"Many only see us as a form of rock, something to cut and polish and hang around their necks or put on their fingers, but we are as real as you are, Lon."

"I confess, Me-i, I'm as guilty as the rest. For all I saw when I arrived were differing shapes and sizes of beautiful crystals."

On inspecting his body, Lon realised his wounds were completely healed.

In fact, he could scarcely see where the cuts had been.

"Me-i, how long have I been here?"

"In our time, you have only just arrived. In your time, around four years have passed."

"Four years!" Lon replied, shocked. "It took that long to blend my essence with the crystal?"

"Time is but a measurement of a journey you think you are on and nothing more. We expected it to take centuries. You truly are Oletha's disciple. A great many changes have taken place with your transformation, Lon," Me-i said, looking at him intently. "You're now of the Clan Sapphire. The earth is the Record Keeper of all life and you will be able to access that knowledge. Many things will be known to you; use this insight wisely."

"Me-i," Lon suddenly asked, looking about anxiously, "where are my clothes?" He felt concerned as he didn't want to continue his quest naked.

"The same place they were when you arrived. All you need do is concentrate on your human form and you will revert to that outward appearance."

Me-i and Lon talked continually while walking back to the portal. What had once been large outcrops of crystal were now strangely designed buildings, shops and residential areas. Arriving at the portal Lon reverted to his human incarnation. He thought it would feel strange, even unnatural, but there was no difference in sensation at all. He saw his torn shirt and shrugged; Me-i simply smiled. Joining with the crystal had given him crystal sight, so being in his human form made no difference to what he now perceived.

"It's time for me to continue my journey, Me-i. Before I go, would you answer a question for me?"

"If I can," Me-i replied gently. "What is it?"

"I had no idea how to become at one with the crystal. If I

hadn't sat on the quicksand or, in this case, quickcrystal, and accidently fallen into the river, would you have helped me?"

Me-i looked surprised as she turned to face Lon. "What makes you think you were accidentally immersed within the crystal river? Didn't your heart genuinely wish to become at one with us and share your essence with its beauty? We heard your request and knew your life story. We chose you, Lon; you didn't choose us. Those who drink of the crystal waters without our consent die horribly."

Lon gave Me-i a hug. "Do you often embrace crystals?" Me-i said laughingly. "No, this is a first for me, thank you, Me-i." Lon stepped onto the portal and vanished.

CHAPTER EIGHT

What confronted him when he appeared upon the world of the One Tree of Consciousness had his senses reeling. The trunk of the One Tree filled the entire landscape before him in a pulsating soft brown glow. Ever-changing luminescent green leaves of the One Tree covered the sky in every direction. Alien life forms moved among curious luminescent plants of varying colours.

An orange plant propelled itself to a different location in front of his eyes, turning yellow when it landed. Others shot colourful spores that danced in the air before drifting on the breeze, while continually changing coloured vines of blue and white laced the branches overhead. Regaining his composure, Lon walked to the trunk of the One Tree of Consciousness and introduced himself.

"Hello to you, my friend. My name is Lon. I am a disciple of Oletha and have just come from the World of Crystal where I had the honour of joining with the Clan Crystal Sapphire. I am on a quest to acquire the Staff of Knowledge and ask your permission to do so."

"So you have come, disciple of Oletha. I call myself Zaki. The Staff you seek is in the Baleful Forest of the Damned. The Unbalanced protect it jealously and wish it not to be removed from its place of birth. It only awaits your touch to complete its transformation into life," Zaki's rich baritone voice intoned.

Travel the Path of Neutrality and you will reach the Baleful Forest. There you must use your own skill to retrieve the sentient Staff of Life. I warn you, the hounds of despair are born within that forest from the woeful deeds of humanity."

"Thank you for your wise counsel, Zaki, and the trust of your name," Lon answered respectfully, privileged to be entrusted with Zaki's name.

"No matter where you are upon my world, I can hear you. To reach the Path of Neutrality, follow the branch you are now under to its end. There you will see the division of the Balanced and Unbalanced and the path between. Eat not of the fruits that grow within the borders of the Unbalanced and only the red fruits from the Balanced. Accept nothing that is offered to you and drink no liquids."

Lon walked up to the trunk of the tree and embraced it. The branch he was to walk under was larger than the mighty redwood trees of Telluric; he had never seen anything this large. The enormity of what he was seeing staggered the mind. Nodding to Zaki, he headed in the direction indicated.

As he walked, leaf creatures the colours of autumn leaves flitted about his feet and then flew into the overhead branches. Flocks of birds sang their eerie cry as they flew overhead. Their brightly coloured plumage of red, orange, yellow and blue looked like splashes of paint as they dipped and turned overhead. Lon didn't know how long he had been walking but decided that he needed to rest.

"Zaki, would you mind if I were to climb your branch to rest awhile?"

Zaki didn't say a word as vines snaked down from overhead and encircled him, drawing him up into his branches for safekeeping. Seven times Lon was lifted into Zaki's branches. He wondered if he would ever get to the end of this branch. At last the sun started to filter through the leaves and a slight breeze was a relief from the humidity. Finally he could see the end of the branch in the distance.

"Zaki, I'm unable to estimate how long I've been walking because of the lack of sunlight. How many days have gone by?"

"Seven days have passed since you started walking, Lon."

"Thank you. Oh, are they a twenty-four hour day like on Telluric?"

"Yes."

"Thought I'd better ask."

Lon's legs were telling him it was time to rest again. He thought it would be still another full day's walk until he was out from beneath Zaki's protection. Once more the vines delivered Lon into Zaki's branches to rest. He awoke refreshed and ready to continue walking as the vines lowered him to the ground. By this day's end, it would have taken him eight full days to walk from under this one branch. Lon emerged from under the last of the branch's leaves into a darkening sky. He had better find a place to stay for the night.

"Zaki, I haven't seen any wild animals but that doesn't mean there aren't any. Is it safe to sleep in the open?" Lon asked warily.

"You are safe in the neutral area only, Lon."

"Thank you for all your kindness and the spiritual nourishment you have been giving me to forestall my hunger, Zaki."

Lon found a cosy spot to sleep in a small glade covered with thick moss. The sun's rays shining in his eyes woke him the following day. Stretching, he stood ready for another day's walk. He was becoming a little hungry now he wasn't receiving spiritual nourishment from Zaki and hoped he could find some red fruits. Walking in the full sunlight was enjoyable after days of nothing but a luminescent glow to light his way. He would have liked to have seen rolling hills and snow-peaked mountains but this wasn't to be. Heading into the distance, as far as the eye could see, was a single path flanked either side by forests.

Lon started walking; this had to be the Path of Neutrality. He had been walking for around six hours when he became aware of Balanced and Unbalanced Emanations coming from the forests either side of the path. They were intoxicating and frightening. Lon felt as if he was in the middle of a tug of war as memories of all the lives he ever had and the decisions he had made flooded his mind. The torrent of information that assailed his senses was astounding.

Since becoming at one with the record keepers of the liquid crystal, all his previous incarnations were at his disposal. Lives he couldn't consciously recall were returning with crystal clarity. He was being assaulted by the Balanced and Unbalanced alike, as each one encouraged him to walk off the path into their protection. His legs were becoming too heavy to lift and he felt like the weight of the world was on his shoulders. His mind was spinning with confusion. Putting his hands over his ears he fell to his knees screaming for the onslaught to stop.

However, it didn't stop and his mind reeled from deeds long forgotten. So many memories, so many lives lived, his mind was being tormented with the guilt of past indiscretions. He had to regain control of his mind. Taking a deep breath, then another and another, he focused his attention on breathing. This gave him strength of mind to start a mantra meditation and regain full command of his faculties. Filling his chakra points with the power of love and kindness and allowing it to flow throughout the mind and body, he purged the unwholesome thoughts from his mind.

Now he was thinking clearly. Deeds of the past, whether Balanced or Unbalanced, had already been accounted for through the cosmic law of cause and effect: karma. He was also a Record Keeper now and the first record he would check was his own. He delved deep within the memories of his lives like an accountant examining the account books. There were no outstanding karmic obligations. His accounts for the lives lived had been paid in full, the only one left was the current one and up to now he was in credit. He was free from all the torment of past doings and his way ahead was clear.

Lon began walking once more – this time the emotions that assailed him were like water off a duck's back. He could see fruits of varying types on either side of the path and his mouth watered with the thought of biting into a succulent piece of fruit. The urge to eat had become so strong that only at the last moment did he withdraw his hand from penetrating the veil into the forest of the Balanced.

A beautiful woman suddenly appeared and offered Lon the fruit he almost reached for.

"Please, kind sir, take this gift of life to quench your thirst and appease your hunger."

"Thank you, but I must decline," answered Lon.

"But sir, the bush is laden and many of the fruits are rotting on the ground. Just one cannot hurt. Did not the One Tree of Consciousness say you could eat of the red fruit?"

"It is true I was told I could eat of the red fruit, but no, thank you."

"Sir, I did not offer you any of the other fruits that are also abundant, for I know it's only the red fruit you are allowed to eat. What possible harm could there be? Look I will eat first."

With that, the woman started eating the fruit with obvious delight. Lon watched as the juices ran from her mouth across her chin and slowly trickled down her neck to gently run between her breasts. He was salivating with the thought of eating such a delicious piece of fruit. When she had finished, she picked another ripe red fruit and started eating and while it was in her mouth, she pulled another from the bush and handed it to him; the temptation was incredible. Lon felt his will weakening, as his hand seemed to reach involuntarily toward the offered fruit.

"Please, kind sir, Tree won't mind."

Something inside Lon was warning him against accepting the fruit. He wrestled with his mind for a while and then remembered what Zaki had said: 'Accept nothing that is offered to you'.

"No, thank you, I will not partake of your fruit."

The woman disappeared from sight; all the desires wants and needs vanished with her. Lon continued walking. Further down the path, leaning outward from the forest of the Balanced was a branch laden with ripened red fruits. Lon picked one and ate eagerly; his hunger and thirst were totally satisfied. He thought about picking some fruit for later on but then decided against it.

The sun was waning in the evening sky as Lon searched for a place to bed down. He found a relatively secure spot in the middle of the path behind a boulder. He was thankful the path was wide enough that he couldn't inadvertently roll into the forest on either side. He awoke the next morning feeling rejuvenated; those fruits certainly had done the trick. He was off and walking once more. Halfway through the day his body reminded him it needed to perform certain functions.

"Zaki, I have a slight problem, I need to relieve my body of waste products. Could you suggest where this could be done without causing embarrassment to anyone?"

"There is a bush that grows only on the path that has large purple leaves. The ground around it is very soft. The waste products will be good for it."

"Thank you, Zaki."

Lon kept walking until he arrived at the purple bush. On close examination he saw that the ground was soft enough to scoop out a hole with his hands. Having taken care of his needs and using the leaves on the bush to full advantage, he moved on. Another day came to a close as he bedded down for the night. He awoke to an overcast day and a cool breeze.

Lon had noticed that the weather wasn't affecting him. He knew there was a cool breeze blowing, but he seemed impervious to it and his body suffered no discomfort from all the walking. He was also aware of other changes in his mental abilities. When he meditated there were areas inside his mind that weren't available before. A whole library existed; he could mentally walk into a building and speak to the librarian. A bird cry caused him to scan the sky overhead and he saw it clearly several miles in the distance winging its way over a mountain range. He was coming to terms with his new abilities and a greater awareness of a new self as another day drew to a close.

He awoke to a new day, trekked through it – and then many more. Food appeared whenever he needed it and the emotions emanating from the forests no longer affected him.

Sharing awareness with liquid crystal certainly broadened his perception. One day seemed to run into another as he walked the seemingly never-ending Path of Neutrality.

He reasoned that he had been walking for about a month and there didn't seem to be an end to the path underfoot. A branch of red fruits was hanging out from the forest of the Balanced and he helped himself to one. After he had eaten he started walking once more. The path took a sudden turn to the left, then to the right and stopped.

There before him was the Baleful Forest. Lon stopped, staring hard at the densely oppressive forest of the Unbalanced. It was aptly named, its thick vines interlacing twisted deformed trees with coarse shrubbery underfoot. An oppressive heat accompanied the depraved ghostlike emanations coming from it as large shadowy beasts moved within its borders. Once he entered its boundaries he would be on his own.

"Zaki, I'm about to enter the Baleful Forest; do you know how far I need to travel to reach the Staff I seek?"

"What you want is in a clearing not eighty paces directly in front of you. The distance is not the problem Lon – it's the hounds of despair."

Lon's mind was awash with apprehension now that he had arrived. "Is there a time limit as to when I must enter the forest?"

"There is none."

"Then I'll meditate and take myself to the library before entering, thank you."

Lon sat down and placed himself into a deep meditative state. His reality changed, as he actually seemed to physically walk into the library and speak to the librarian.

"Hello. I wish all the information you have on the hounds of despair, please."

The librarian responded in a loud clear voice. "The hounds of despair survive on the unwholesome emotions within the mind. They feed the mind with doubts and falsehoods, undermining its strengths. The bite and claws of a hound not only cause physical damage, but cripple the mind's ability to think clearly while shredding one's faith of the spirit."

"What is the best defence against them?" Lon asked, hoping for some form of miracle.

"The Mystery of the True Light," was the crystal-clear response.

Lon returned from his meditation knowing what he had to do. He created the silvery blue discs around all his chakra points, connected his base chakra to the earth, his crown chakra to the heavens and Oletha, and then stepped into the forest.

The hounds attacked him immediately but with little success as the love of Oletha was the epitome of his defence. He kept a steady pace as he worked his way through the dense underbrush. The hounds were going crazy trying to get to him but they disappeared as he broke through the last of the foliage.

There in the clearing was a large tree with one of its braches lowered to the ground and growing from that branch was the Staff. It didn't look all that remarkable from where Lon was standing and beside the Staff was a hound of immense size.

Its large deformed body rippled with disdain; filth hung from its form in the manner of wet knotted hair. Its strong twisted legs supported its weight and claws protruded from oversize feet. An equally oversized head held penetrating orange glowing eyes and fangs showed through the snarling mouth. Lon walked steadily closer to the Staff and when he was six feet away from it the hound spoke.

"You puny little human, do you think you can get by me?" Its deep guttural voice oozed with malevolence.

Lon didn't even acknowledge that it had spoken as he started towards the Staff once more. The hound let out a cry of malice and then sprang. Lon was ready for the attack and leaped at the hound with all his strength. They met in midair, locked in an embrace of death as fangs snapped and claws endeavoured to rip Lon apart. He locked eyes with the hound and screamed, "You have no control over me, beast! Be gone!" as he poured forth Oletha's love.

They landed in a tangled mess, each one trying to gain a footing first. The hound shook and whined as if it had been hurt but then lunged again. Lon knew the only way to defeat the hound was to embrace it with Oletha's love. So it was, he continually met each charge with one of his own, wrapping his arms about the hound's body while trying to keep it from tearing him apart. The lunge was sudden but to no avail as Lon met the charge head on, and again they went down. Lon had sustained several nasty gashes each time they met. He couldn't allow himself to register the anguish his mind and body felt with each attack.

The hound moved off and started circling his prey. Lon smiled, intensified his love for all things and charged the hound with open arms. The hound responded. Jaws gaping wide, it lunged for Lon's throat but it wasn't quick enough as Lon wrapped his arms around the hound's neck in an embrace of love. Pouring the light of Oletha into the hound, Lon's embrace held firm. The hound twisted, squirmed and howled as the Light of Love took hold. Then all movement ceased and Lon let the hound's limp form fall to the ground.

He watched as it dissolved into the earth at his feet. The attack had left him mentally and spiritually fatigued; his torn flesh was a constant trickle of blood and he still had to retrieve the Staff and return to the Path of Neutrality past the other hounds. Falling to his knees, he felt spiritually, mentally and physically exhausted after his ordeal. He rested awhile before risng to his feet. He walked over to the Staff and spoke to it.

"Well, my friend, you certainly ask a lot of a person. I trust you're worth it?"

Placing his right hand around the Staff, he wasn't expecting what happened next. His hand was frozen to the shaft of the Staff as fine needles penetrated the palm of his hand. He felt his blood mingle with the Staff and the sap of the Staff enter his bloodstream. The pain drove him to his knees. Again he was forced to balance his energies through his chakra points until all was in harmony. He watched as the Staff separated from its place of birth. It pulled itself free and integrated its root system back into itself.

With the Staff in his hands Lon struggled back the way he had come. His mind was numb; he had no real feelings one way or the other for the Staff he had fought so hard for and now carried. Once he was safe outside the forest, he collapsed to the ground in an exhausted sleep. He awoke many hours later feeling hungry and thirsty. It took a great effort to scramble to his feet and stagger back to the tree of red fruits where he ate his fill. He then curled up and slept again. Later he had some more fruit and decided to have a good look at the Staff. It was truly a work of art. The designs were incredible; there were trees, mountains and scenery all engraved upon it.

"You, my friend, are truly exquisite," he said to it.

"Thank you," the Staff responded, its voice sounding exactly like Lon's.

"You can talk? Of course you can, you're sentient."

"I believe you'll find that I am worth the effort, Kyros."

"Kyros?" Lon said, confused.

"That is who you are: Master Healer of all the realms of Chimera."

Lon suddenly remembered his wounds and investigated the extent of damage he had received from the hound of despair. To his surprise there were none. He heard a chuckle and looked at the Staff.

"Your injuries healed while you were sleeping."

"How long was I asleep?" Lon asked, amazed.

"Three years," the Staff replied. "Your body needed to undergo similar changes as when you blended with the crystal."

"Time flies when you're having fun," said Lon, taking refuge in humour. "What do I call you?"

"We are Malachy, but all will call you Kyros. Call me by our true name, Malachy."

"What is the meaning of Malachy?"

"Angel of the True Light, messenger of Oletha," the Staff replied.

"Well, Malachy, it's time we were off."

The walk back to the portal gave Malachy and Kyros time to understand their unification. As Lon and the crystal had blended so had Malachy and Lon become as one. An interesting awareness settled within the consciousness that was Malachy. If he so desired he could separate into three separate entities, Human, Nature and Crystal. When separated, each entity was a perfect effigy of Lon, unless the Crystal or Nature entities chose a female form.

For the most part, Malachy and Kyros would remain a unification of one. While Kyros could materialise Malachy whenever he chose, Malachy's ability to change form would prove beneficial as he could appear as a Staff, walking stick or a person.

When they were divided, they still remained unified spiritually and mentally. By the time Malachy reached the branches of the One Tree of Consciousness, the person who was Lon no longer existed for Kyros and the Staff was Malachy and inseparable, their minds and spirits being in complete harmony with each other. Lon knew all would call him Kyros, his Staff Malachy, and his friends and family Lon. With obvious pride and a sense of fulfillment, Lon with Malachy in hand, continued walking.

Arriving at the base of Zaki's mighty trunk, Kyros thanked him for all he had done and for Malachy's birthing. A sense of pride ran through Zaki's branches as they quivered with pleasure for his offspring and Kyros. Lon moved toward the portal, turned once and waved and then stepped onto the portal and vanished.

He reappeared on Harpreet's home world. Stepping from the portal he headed for the place he had stayed the last time he was there. Harpreet met him at the door.

"Harpreet, I believe you have some clothing for me?"

"Yes, Kyros."

Lon smiled at the use of his title. Showing him to the wardrobe, she watched as he selected the appropriate attire. He chose supportive undergarments, a deep blue homespun pair of comfortable trousers with a leather belt and a pouch. He also chose a three-quarter jacket of the same colour that wouldn't restrict his movements and a black roll neck fitted skivvy for underneath the jacket. His footwear was a soft and durable pair of moccasins, beaded with a wolf's head.

"Your body has matured," Harpreet said admiringly. "There is a reflecting tube in the other room if you'd care to see yourself?"

Kyros followed her into the other room and looked at his reflection. To his surprise, the reflecting tube was a three-dimensional viewer that showed what he looked like from any direction. He judged himself to be in his early thirties with a fit athletic body and rather handsome in his new attire.

"Thank you for all you've done, Harpreet. It's time for me to leave."

Harpreet accompanied Kyros to the transport portal. He gently embraced her, kissed her on the forehead, then stepped onto the disc of light and vanished. He reappeared at the base of the stairs in the bookshop. Everyone was milling around Barbette talking. The room went silent as all eyes turned to see who had arrived.

Dressed in his deep blue pants and three-quarter jacket with his black skivvy and beaded moccasins, standing his full height and holding Malachy in his right hand, Lon was an imposing figure.

CHAPTER NINE

Nathanial found himself in an unfamiliar environment; cautiously he surveyed his surroundings. This forest was truly magnificent; he had never seen flora like this before. A howl in the distance told him he hadn't lost his tormenters. He had to find a way out. However, he had no idea where he was so he decided to rely on his instincts and follow his feet. The going was quite difficult as he was moving through virgin bush. Trudging through the underbrush, at the back of his mind he could hear the sounds of someone in pain.

"Is anybody there?" he called. Receiving no response he kept moving. Something felt very wrong but he didn't know what it was. He had reached the limit of his endurance both mentally and physically and those blasted beasts were still after him.

He stumbled out of the forest and found himself standing on the edge of a cliff with the roar of water filling his ears. In the gorge below was a river that wound its way out of the mountain pass and through a length of flatlands before dropping out of sight. Behind him were snow-covered mountains. There was a steep drop to a ledge farther down the mountainside with a rocky outcrop all the way to the river. If he could reach that ledge below him he could climb down the rocks to the river.

Hearing a growl behind him he turned – without warning a beast lunged. They met in a tangle of claws, teeth, arms, legs and bodies as they tumbled over the side of the mountain. Saplings cracked, then snapped, and rocks dislodged as Nathanial frantically fought for his life, dodging the beast's gnashing teeth and razor sharp claws while rolling and bouncing down the mountainside.

Finally he managed to wrap his arms around the hound's mouth as they came crashing onto the ledge below. With tremendous effort Nathanial manoeuvred his legs under the beast and pushed hard. The hound sailed through the air over his head, plummeting to the rocks below. Nathanial's head was spinning as everything went dark.

* * *

Silence filled the room as Kyros walked from the portal. The shocked look on everyone's face was evident as they observed the changes in him.

"I trust I haven't been the subject of too much concern?" he asked gently.

Barbette walked forward and bowed slightly, saying, "Oletha explained that you were in training. I see much change in you. Would you do the honour of introducing me to your companion and advise me of how you wish to be addressed?"

"We are Malachy. I have earned the title of Kyros and my companion goes by the name that we are. My friends call me Lon in private; otherwise, I am addressed as Kyros."

Everyone huddled around Lon listening to his response to Barbette's question. Barbette raised her hands, forestalling any other questions. "The word Kyros means 'Master' and refers to his being the supreme ruler of knowledge and abilities in the healing arts. To earn this title Lon had to undergo several rigorous challenges that would have claimed his life had he failed.

"The Staff you see before you is not merely a piece of wood but a sentient being of incredible knowledge far beyond our understanding. For Lon to be in harmony with Malachy he had to join his essence with a crystal entity. He then had to fight his way past several of Slegna's hounds of despair to retrieve the Staff of Knowledge and join his essence with it.

"Malachy means Angel of the True Light, Messenger of Oletha. The Staff and Lon are one. They are totally devoted in soul, spirit, mind and body to Oletha. They are her spokesperson upon all the realms of learning. There has never before been their like and their coming has been foretold down through the ages. Behold Kyros."

The last was expressed with pride and admiration.

"We here are a family," Lon told them. "Each one of you in turn will have to face your fears and doubts to become what you may be. I have learned of a race of people who are pure in mind and body. They live their lives in a similar way to that of a wolf pack. After what Barbette said about our family," Lon explained to all the staff of Enigma Books, "that we mirror the ways of a wolf pack, I couldn't think of a more fitting way to represent our family. We are to be known as the Order of the Phelan.

"Phelan means wolf in a different language. I chose that spelling so no one on any other realm would connect the two." Lon then began intoning a mantra while gently moving his hand over his heart chakra. When he had finished, seven glistening rich blue sapphires in the form of a wolf's head sat in the palm of his hand. All gasped as they stared at the sapphires.

Renae was the first to receive Lon's gift, followed by Lomasi, Fala, Gabbryel, Janelle and Gela. They all looked with astonishment at the wolf's head in their hands.

"We are the family of the Phelan," Lon intoned.

Lon held the seventh sapphire towards the Staff. All watched as Malachy transformed into his male form, an exact replica of Lon. Taking the sapphire from Kyros in his left hand he placed it on the second finger from the right on his right hand. An intricate design of nature appeared around the sapphire making it seem as if the wolf was looking out from some bushes, thus forming a ring of enormous beauty.

"Lon," Gela said, breaking the silence. "It has been twenty minutes since your disappearance. Now you stand before us as a different person. Your eyes are no longer green but a beautiful deep blue. Your hair has changed from a mousey blond to a rich silky blue-black, although it's still soft to the touch," she said, gently running her fingers through his hair and over his skin.

"Your skin is a luxurious golden tan and soft as a baby's. You have an air of great knowledge and you reek of power. You also show signs of having gone through profound trauma to acquire your abilities and physically look the age of a thirty year old. Beside you stands your replica called Malachy. I can feel the truth of you and therefore will treasure your gift of the heart."

Lon leaned forward and encircled Gela in an embrace, allowing her to feel the truth of him. When he released her, she turned to Malachy and bowed. Malachy also embraced Gela and thanked her for the honour he felt she had given him. Everyone was stunned to hear Malachy speak.

Lon looked at them. "Please, I ask you all not to place Malachy and me on a pedestal. Each of you will be the best you can be and masters in your own fields of expertise. We all have much to learn from each other and many students to instruct. Always remember that we are, first and foremost, the Order of the Phelan, a family."

"How shall we address you?" Renae asked.

"By my name, of course. Remember Barbette's comment about addressing her in private as opposed to in public? Nathanial said the same when we all started working here. I have earned the title of Kyros and all but my friends shall call me that."

"Lon, your gift is beautiful beyond words; never has anyone ever given me such a special jewel. How may we mount it?" asked Gabbryel, her eyes shining.

"Anyway you like."

"I loved how Malachy incorporated his wolf's head in a ring of nature. The closest thing I could think of is to have a gold ring constructed around the sapphire in the same manner," Fala said, looking at Malachy's hand.

"Ladies," Barbette called, "if you would like your sapphires mounted as rings, I know just the person for the job."

Everyone talked amongst themselves for a moment and all agreed that rings would be the perfect way to display Lon's gift. Barbette asked them to wait, stepped onto the transport portal and disappeared. Movement at the portal caught everyone's attention as Barbette returned with a strange little man. She introduced him as Gair, a priest of metals, from another realm.

Standing a little over three foot high, rumpled as if he had just got out of bed, Gair had a thin body with a large head and delicate fingers. He was dressed in leather with a bag over one shoulder and a toolbox hanging from a strap over the other. They thought his age would in the nineties.

The scruffy-looking visitor walked over to the ladies and held out his hand for the sapphires, which he examined very closely. He then went over to Lon and bowed. Lon regarded the man before him. As Kyros, Supreme Healer of all the realms of Chimera, he recognised the affliction that was attacking the priest's body and knew the pain he was suffering. "Master priest, before you commence your work, please be seated," Lon requested, pointing to the closest seat.

Gair did so. Approaching the little man, Kyros held up his hand and intoned words unknown by anyone there. Gair was engulfed within an aura of white light of such intensity that all covered their eyes or turned away. When the light diminished Gair looked fifty years younger.

"Your affliction has been removed, good priest, be well," stated Lon.

Removing himself from the seat, Gair cleared his throat and bowed deeply. His eyes glistened with moisture and his mouth quivered slightly, but he didn't say a word. He cleared a desk and unpacked his kit and then set out an array of tools and other devices unknown on Telluric. Pointing at Renae, he indicated that she was to be seated next to him. He then pointed to her fingers, querying which one would hold the ring. Before he started work, Lon spoke.

"Choose carefully the finger you wish the ring to be on for it will become part of you. The gold that will be used isn't of Telluric, but living gold from Gair's home world. It is of the finest quality in all of Chimera. If any of you don't wish this, say so now, for it can't be undone."

"How do you know that?" Gabbryel questioned.

Smiling, Lon turned to her. "When I became Malachy I gained the knowledge of a great many things."

Everyone nodded. They watched in fascination as the little man pulled a rod of gold from his leather bag and placed it in a machine that resembled a lathe. He hummed a strange tune as he worked. When he had finished he pointed to Renae's finger. As she extended it, he placed a filament of gold upon it that snaked around her finger intertwining as it went, until the gold and the finger were melded into one. Placing the sapphire wolf's head on top of the ring, he added another thread of gold. Encircling the gem, the gold travelled completely around the ring forming an intricate design of nature so that the head of the wolf appeared to be looking out from the bushes. He then made a gesture with his hands and indicated he had finished.

Renae examined the ring carefully; she had never seen its like. In fact, she couldn't even feel the ring on her finger. Leaning forward, she put her hands on either side of Gair's head and drew him closer, kissing him soundly on the forehead. The little man was so surprised he almost fell off his seat.

"Kind sir, no words could ever convey the joy in my heart. You have complemented Kyros's gift to me with the same love and kindness he has shown in presenting the gift in the first place."

The astonishment on Gair's face said it all. He turned to face Kyros, who smiled kindly. Never before had he received such praise for his work. To him it was a simple matter. Kyros walked over to him and placing his hand on his shoulder said, "Your skill has long gone unrewarded, you have harmonised with my gift admirably."

The little man shook his head and then indicated for the next person to be seated. This continued until all the rings had been fashioned. Everyone was admiring each other's ring. Renae drew her staff to one side and spoke to them; they nodded in agreement and then formed a circle around Gair.

Joining hands they sang a song of thanksgiving that farmers sing each year for their harvest. When the song was finished, one after another stood in front of him and bowed their head in respect. The love in which all this was being done was too much for Gair as tears flowed down his face. Barbette approached him and embraced him warmly.

"Barbette, can he not speak our language?" Renae asked.

"No, although he does understand what you are saying."

"We didn't mean to cause him any embarrassment," Lomasi explained.

"He knows that, dear."

"I don't wish to be forward, or to create further awkwardness, but in what manner will he be paid for his work?" Renae enquired.

It was obvious that he had understood the question. He shook his head and waved his arms to indicate there would be no payment. Renae walked up to Gair and kneeled before him; looking him in the eye she spoke. "Thank you, Gair. Please know that if ever you are in need, we will be there for you. You can contact us through Barbette."

Gair reached out, lightly touched Renae's hand and nodded. Then he began to repack his tools. When he had finished, he walked up to Kyros and embraced him. He then bowed to everyone and joined Barbette on the portal. They promptly vanished. A moment later Barbette reappeared.

"Barbette."

She turned to look at Malachy.

"I have a gift for you."

Barbette walked over to where Malachy was standing next to Lon. Malachy held a deep golden ball that looked like sap that he placed in Barbette's left hand.

"In the palm of your hand is an Orb of Knowledge. If you accept this gift, know that whatever understanding you are searching for, circumstances will present themselves continually, so you may learn. As you know, knowledge cannot be given. It is in the manner of your learning that growth becomes wisdom. What I am offering is a gentler manner of gaining wisdom in that if you have not understood your lesson, an inner knowing will advise you of a different approach to achieve your goal."

"I most humbly accept your precious gift, Malachy," Barbette said gratefully.

The orb then dissolved into her hand. Lon moved forward to support her as her legs gave way while the essence of knowledge moved through her.

"Oh my, I have a presence inside me," she said with reverence. "The depths of love I'm feeling is extraordinary, like a wise and compassionate teacher who won't let you deceive yourself." Barbette gently embraced Malachy who promptly hugged her in return.

"Flirt," Lon remarked as everyone laughed.

"Remind you of anyone, Gela?" Janelle said pointedly.

"I couldn't have said it better," Gela agreed.

"I will have you know that I'm a changed man, ladies," Lon replied.

"The only thing changed about you, is that you now have

a greater collection of knowledge in how to have your way with the ladies."

"Why Lomasi, I'm shocked."

"As Barbette would say, of course, dear, we all believe you," Renae commented.

Everyone, including Barbette, burst out laughing. Then Malachy walked up to Lon and merged with him again, leaving only Kyros standing before them.

"May I see the rings, please, ladies?"

They all crowded around Lon presenting their hands so he could admire their rings.

"He really does fine work; they are exquisite and they enhance the wolf's head perfectly. You would swear the rest of the wolf was just behind the bushes," Lon said. Then his manner changed. "The reason for the wolf's heads is twofold. Firstly, they represent the Order of the Phelan and secondly, they're a communication device."

Lon watched in amusement as Janelle put the ring to her ear and then tapped it. "What do you mean, Lon, like a phone?"

"Exactly. The difference is you can only call each other."

"So how does it work?" Lomasi asked, holding the ring up, and watched as the light sparkled on the sapphire.

"You direct your thoughts towards the wolf's head and the person you want to contact. They will hear you and answer in the same way."

"I wish Barbette had one; she is part of the family too."

"Oh no, Janelle, my gift was perfect, believe me." Barbette

nodded at her. "All of you have much to do. Remember, as Oletha's disciples, you will be expected to do many things that will put your lives in constant danger. You are her chosen ones. That is why the Order of the Phelan was created. Lon chose wisely to call you that."

Gela was looking at Lon and everyone knew what she was wondering. He turned and caught the look in her eye and smiled. "As you all know, before I was whisked away by Oletha, Gela and I were becoming involved.

"As she is a bright intelligent young lady, I could never entice her into anything disrespectful, meaning that her virtue has stayed intact. Also, being the only male working here, I've had a lot of fun flirting with each of you, except for Fala and Gabbryel, who are too young.

"However, what you do not know is that I won't age. I will remain the way I am until I die which will be close to eternity. One of my tasks was to become one with the crystal. I won't explain the process but what flows through my veins is more liquid crystal than blood, hence the deep blue eyes and blue-black hair. I am, in essence, now made of crystal."

"Are you serious, Lon?" Gela asked.

"Very much so, watch."

Lon concentrated on his crystal form and transformed before their eyes into the most beautiful coloured sapphire effigy. Everyone stood in stunned amazement as he changed his colour tone as if he were changing articles of clothing. Colours started to swim throughout his body with the consistency of mercury. As rich blues and deep blacks swirled amidst exquisite golden yellows that twirled around warm greens and gentle mauves. The only thing that remained constant was a set of gorgeous blue eyes. Then he reverted to his human form.

"But that's not the end of it," he continued as if he had done nothing special. "On the first world, Oletha created is a tree so large that it would take years to walk around its base. I walked for eight days just to get out from one of its small branches. Malachy is the offspring of the One Tree of Consciousness and has all the wisdom of the parent." Lon was quiet for a moment while everyone absorbed what he had just explained.

"He is the only sentient-aware being of his kind. To be at one with him, a sharing of essences had to take place; I am as much Malachy as he is me. Our merger also changed my physical structure. After I had blended with the crystal my skin was a deep yellow. Merging with the Staff of Knowledge changed my complexion yet again to the golden colour it is now. So you see, my life is not my own to do with as I please. I would love to pick up where we left off, Gela."

"You mean when you tried to get me into bed and I said no?"

Everyone burst into laughter; Gela always knew how to lighten the mood.

"Yes, there was that," Lon laughed. "However, that's not what I meant though. I was hoping for a great deal more. I love the quickness of your mind and the depth of your spirit.

You know how to lighten my seriousness. You fill me with such tenderness. Life has been so beautiful with you as part of it and ..." Lon paused.

"Don't stop now, Lon. This is the most direct and honest you have ever been," Gela said, pretending surprise.

"I'm trying to be serious here, Gela."

"If I've understood correctly, Lon, you and your Staff or your wooden effigy are Malachy, right?" Gela asked.

"That's correct."

"Then if I ask you a question, I'm also asking Malachy the same question, correct?"

"What are you driving at?"

"Am I correct?" she persisted.

"Yes," Lon replied.

"Then I have a question that you both must answer and I will hear that answer from the both of you. Do you understand, Malachy?" Malachy materialised beside Lon taking on his masculine form and in unison Lon and he responded.

"We understand, Gela."

"Do you love me, or are you in love with me?" she asked intently.

"I am in love with you, but it cannot be, for I am no longer mortal," they both replied.

"Oh Lon, my darling, for all your knowledge there are some things of which as yet you are unaware. Fala has had a vision that she only now understands. You had better enlighten him, Fala." Gela smiled at Lon.

"I was given a vision about a group called the Order of the Phelan but until now didn't understand its meaning," explained Fala. "I was told we are to be taught something called the Chakra Disc Meditation Technique and shown a world completely made of crystals that we will have to go to. It was truly beautiful."

"Yes, and very deadly if you fail," Lon and Malachy responded.

"I also saw the two of you becoming one," Fala finished.

"Gela, you know the truth of my words and the depth of my love; you also know my fear. I hid nothing from you, so I ask you the same question you asked us."

"Then Lon, as Kyros, see the truth of my answer, for I know you would not invade my privacy or anyone else's," Gela stated. "Your sense of honour and professionalism would not permit it. My feelings for you are like a foundation of strength and I return your feelings of love in equal proportions."

Tears filled Lon's eyes and he smiled as Malachy merged with him and he took Gela in his arms.

"You do know, my love, that wolves mate for life?"

"What a marvellous idea, my love." Gela replied.

"Oh Fala, did your vision also tell you that to join with the liquid crystal is to become infertile?" Lon looked on in amusement as the ladies' faces went through a range of emotions. "You ladies will never have to worry about your cycles again," Lon casually informed them. Everyone looked at each other, wondering if Lon was joking.

"Barbette," Janelle said, changing the subject, "do you know when Kalareena will be back?"

"Sorry, Janelle, I can't answer that."

"In that case, let's eat. I'm starved," she said.

"That's a good idea. You don't happen to have any rocks handy, do you, Janelle? I could really do with something solid to chew on." Everybody stopped and looked at Lon.

"Didn't I tell you, once you become one with the crystal, all you can eat are rocks?" Lon said, keeping a straight face.

Gela covered her mouth with her hand to stop from laughing. Barbette just shook her head and headed towards the kitchen.

"It's nice to see you still have your sense of humour, Lon," Renae said, as she directed the others towards the kitchen."

"Come on, my little Phelan, let's go eat," Lon remarked to Gela as they followed the others.

* * *

Nathanial groaned with pain as he moved and then everything went dark. Twice he had awoken only to be rendered unconscious again. The warmth and light of the sun on his body caused him to gently open his eyes. He struggled into a sitting position. He found a new meaning for pain every time he moved. It was all he could do not to pass out.

On investigation he discovered there was an open gash across the left side of his body that travelled from under his arm to the navel. A rib was sticking out of his chest and another had punctured the left lung. The pain was excruciating as he tried not to double over as he coughed blood from his lungs while racked by a sudden bout of coughing. Travelling in this state was impossible, so gritting his teeth, he pushed his fingers into the open wound and removed the broken rib from his lung. He blacked out.

He regained consciousness some time later and found that although breathing was difficult, it was not impossible. A growl from above told him that staying put wasn't an option. However, he still had a rib sticking out of the side of his chest and the gash was open to the environment. Looking around the ledge, he saw some vines and large leaves that had been dislodged in the fall.

He carefully retrieved a number of large leaves and a length of vine. Placing the leaves over the open wound he tied the vine around his chest to hold the leaves in place, binding it as tightly as possible. His breathing became ragged and his body was trembling with the effort. When he had finished, he closed his eyes to rest and passed out again.

The sun was high in the sky by the time he regained consciousness. He couldn't stay where he was, so on shaky legs he started to climb down the mountainside. This took the better part of the day. The sun was waning as he reached the river. The beast he had thrown off the mountainside was nowhere to be seen. Crawling to the water's edge he took small sips of water. As the water travelled down his throat he started coughing violently, doubling up in pain as the spasm ran its course.

Then he heard that horrible guttural growl behind him. Without thinking, he plunged headlong into the water toward a small sandbank in the middle of the river. Dragging himself onto the island, he expected the beast to be right behind him. To his surprise, it was still on the far bank, pacing the water's edge and howling every time its foot touched the water. At last a reprieve, he thought, as he dragged his battered body further onto the island and propped it against a fallen tree.

Night was falling and the temperature was dropping. All around him were broken pieces of driftwood and bark. Crawling, he gathered as much of it as his strength would allow. Pulling a lighter out of his trouser pocket he prayed that it still worked. After several attempts it finally ignited; he had a fire for warmth. Nathanial drifted in and out of consciousness, mumbling and crying out throughout the night. When he was lucid he added more fuel to the fire.

The morning saw him feeling very sorry for himself. The beast was still on the far bank, joined by its partner. What did it take to kill these things? He thought that the fall off the mountain ledge would have been its demise. The water was starting to rise, so that put an end to his island haven. Moving to the water's edge, he once again heard the sounds of someone in pain. He couldn't worry about that now; the water was really becoming quite strong. If he was going to make it to the opposite bank to those beasts he had better get started.

The moment he entered the water it turned rough. He had to swim sidestroke as it was and that wasn't easy at the best of times. Swimming had never been his forte. He was halfway between the island and the riverbank when he felt something pulling on his legs. The harder he kicked the stronger the restriction became. The water was becoming violent as waves pounded him. He felt himself being dragged under. He grabbed half a lungful of air as he went under and saw iridescent people pulling at his legs.

Kicking his legs as best he could he finally managed to break free, his head spinning, and he almost lost consciousness with the pain. A fallen tree became his life raft and he clung to it as the water assailed him. Exhausted and battered, he had reached his limit; there was no more left in him. He didn't know why he even hung onto the tree. The bank was no more than ten feet away but he didn't have the strength to try for it. To make matters worse, the water was becoming increasingly colder and icy. He cried out, "Oletha, I am yours; do with me as you will."

* * *

Everyone was sitting around talking when Kalareena appeared. "I've found him. Lon, come quickly," she said urgently. Holding Malachy in his right hand, Lon walked briskly to where Kalareena was standing. She looked at him intently and then spoke. "Barbette, is Lon Kyros?"

"Yes, dear, I will explain later," Barbette answered.

Kalareena and Lon disappeared and reappeared in a forest of virgin bush. They found Nathanial half-lying over a tree branch, waist deep in water that was turning to ice. Two huge misshapen-looking creatures paced the riverbank, their skin crawling with filth and their low guttural growls menacing.

A tremendous shudder shook the ground as Kyros planted Malachy in the earth. The hounds of despair howled for the last time as they quivered and died. Healing energy travelled to Nathanial and the water spirits.

The ice started melting, warming the water around Nathanial. Kyros kneeled and spoke quietly to the water spirits. The river parted, allowing Kalareena and Kyros passage. They removed Nathanial from the branch and placed him upon dry land. Kyros kneeled next to Nathanial and laid Malachy along his body.

"I have placed him in a deep trance and slowed his heart; healing energies are being administered by Nature. Stay with him, I travel to Terraqueous; I will return shortly," he said gently.

Kalareena acknowledged Kyros; then he returned the way he had come and reappeared in the bookshop. Everyone looked to see if Nathanial had come back.

"Barbette, we have need of you," requested Lon.

Barbette didn't hesitate as she stepped next to Kyros on the portal and vanished. They reappeared on Barbette's home world of Terraqueous.

"We seek my teacher, Harpreet," Lon told Barbette.

Kyros walked off at a brisk pace with Barbette trailing behind. He entered the house of his teacher where she was working with some students.

"Forgive me, Harpreet," he told her. "I have no time for formalities. I believe you two know each other," he said, gesturing to Barbette. He then continued speaking. "I need two physically strong healers and a stretcher to carry a man my size. We will need surgeons skilled in lung regeneration, bone repair and deep tissue lacerations."

Harpreet went to a communication device on the wall and spoke.

"Kyros requests a full restoration-healing team to be assembled at the portal immediately." Switching off the device, she faced Kyros. "They will be there by the time you arrive, Kyros."

"Thank you, Harpreet. Before we leave, this is for you." Kyros put his hand over his heart manifesting a beautiful sapphire.

"This sapphire is also a communication device," he said, smiling at her. "By concentrating your thoughts on the gem, I will receive them. I can answer you by sending my thoughts in return."

"You honour me, Kyros. Do you require my services further?"

"Could you travel to Telluric with Barbette and return with the chosen ones?" he asked her. "They've never travelled through a portal before. Harpreet, I have chosen you to be one of their teachers, if you are agreeable."

"The chosen ones? Oletha's chosen ones? Oh Kyros, I don't know what to say." Harpreet looked overwhelmed.

"Yes, seems appropriate to me," he stated. "Let your class know I apologise for the disruption. I will return to Nathanial with the medical team now."

To Kalareena's surprise, Kyros appeared with a full medical team. They examined Nathanial carefully, transferred him to the stretcher and returned to Terraqueous Medical Centre. While Kyros healed the rifts in Nathanial's spirit caused by the hounds of despair, the surgeons used their advanced specialist abilities in matter manipulation to repair the physical body.

CHAPTER TEN

Kyros walked out of the door leaving a class full of students in awe and a stunned Harpreet standing with Barbette. Harpreet turned to her class. "Class is dismissed for the rest of the day; however, I expect you to work harder tomorrow. To the question on all your minds, yes that was Kyros."

"Children are so easily impressed. I haven't seen you for some time, Harpreet, how have you been?" asked Barbette.

"Until Kyros entered my life, I've been plodding along nicely, thank you," she said, smiling.

"I know the feeling; we'd better do as his master's voice requested."

"His master's voice?" asked Harpreet.

"Yes, dear, Kyros," confirmed Barbette. "You're about to meet your new students for the first time. They've never had a tutor before. All their development has been self-taught."

"What sort of world do you come from that there are no teachers of spiritual truth?" Harpreet questioned.

"A primitive one," Barbette replied mildly. "At Oletha's request each one was transported to Telluric for safekeeping from Slegna, including Nathanial. I have been supervising their lives without their knowledge ever since. They're a rag-tag set of individualists whom I love a great deal."

"Did you see what he gave me?"

Barbette looked at the sapphire in Harpreet's hand, not surprised to find it was in the design of a wolf's head. "This is larger than those he gave your new students. I think, my dear, that Kyros has chosen you to belong to a select group of individuals."

They walked out of the classroom to the transport portal, disappearing and then reappearing in the bookshop. Harpreet surveyed her surroundings carefully.

"Barbette, what has happened to Nathanial and who is your friend?" Renae asked.

"If you would all gather round I will do the introductions," Barbette began.

"That won't be necessary, Barbette, if you don't mind I will conduct the introductions."

"As you wish, Harpreet." Hiding her smile, Barbette nodded and stepped to one side.

"My name is Harpreet; I am a spiritual teacher of awareness and truth. I'm to be one of your tutors. I come from a world called Terraqueous."

"That's the same planet as Barbette," Renae commented.

Harpreet looked at who had spoken. She saw a woman with short mousey-blonde hair, a firm disciplined body and a rugged beauty, blue eyes and a no-nonsense look to her face.

"You are Renae and you were born on the 2/4/1964," Harpreet stated.

"Yes," confirmed Renae, wondering how she knew.

"You are presently learning energy control with Barbette. You are also the leader of your group."

"That's correct."

The next person Harpreet regarded was a young woman of twenty-six years. She stood her seven feet with pride and had luxurious dark skin and long delicate fingers. Black wavy hair cascaded over her shoulders, complementing her brown eyes and a slim body.

"You are Lomasi, born on the 5/1/1982?"

"Yes, Harpreet."

"You see the spiritual content in material things. This gives the impression that you can see through solid objects, including clothing."

"Yes," Lomasi responded, blushing.

Harpreet turned to an attractive thirty-five-year-old woman, with long light brown hair, piercing blue eyes and full lips. She was barefooted and stood about five foot six inches.

"You are Janelle, born 4/2/1973 and you're a trance-medium."

"Correct."

The next individual Harpreet moved to had bright green eyes and a round face with fiery red hair. She stood five feet tall and was covered in beads, rings and brooches in gypsy fashion. She looked no older than seventeen.

Harpreet nodded. "You would be Gabbryel, the second youngest of the group, born 13/2/1991."

"Yeah, that's me," Gabbryel said cheekily.

"You work with rhythmic vibrations and their interpretations," Harpreet said confidently.

"What!" exclaimed Gabbryel.

"You can read something about a person from whatever they have handled."

"Oh yeah," Gabbryel murmured.

Moving from Gabbryel, Harpreet locked eyes with a young woman so petite she didn't look real. Her bone structure was perfect for her five feet two inches in height; her skin was as white as snow and looked soft as fleece. Her blue sparkling eyes shone with mirth, merriment and wisdom. She wore flattering but plain clothing and her long golden hair cascaded down the full length of her back. She presented well for her twenty-six years.

"You are Gela, mate to Kyros, born 18/6/1982, and you know untruths when spoken."

"You speak the truth, Harpreet."

Lastly, she turned to face another young lady of seventeen. She had brown curly hair, a lively disposition and an olive complexion. Her eyes were a deep brown and her arms hung gracefully by her side. Standing five-feet eight inches tall with a well-formed body she looked most striking.

"You are Fala, the youngest, born 10/5/1991 – a seer."

"Sometimes, Harpreet."

"It is a pleasure to meet you all. Looking around, I see you are all recently acquired disciples of Oletha. The importance of this has not yet sunk in; let me point out some obvious similarities between you all.

"Each one of you was born on a different world and brought here by Barbette for protection. You all have a spiritual talent. Numerologically, each of your birthdates adds up to an eight and your ages add up to an eight, as does Lon's, who was born on the 17/7/1982.

"Also, your workplace address is an eight and there are seven staff members plus your employer who work here – eight people. Your calendar shows that you are in your ninth day of your ninth month of your eighth millennium. This adds up to an eight yet again. The number eight is significant in that it has no beginning and no end; many regard it as the sign of infinity.

"Your rings, plus Malachy and Kyros's gift to me, make eight sapphire wolf heads. We are all united in an alliance of the Mystery of the True Light, Oletha. She requires you to walk your talk and be the best you can be." Harpreet enquired, while walking quietly among them, "Are there any questions?"

"How did you know all that stuff, Teach?" asked a cheeky Gabbryel.

Harpreet looked at Gabbryel, as one would view a young child. "Would you like to rethink that question and your end response, Gabbryel?"

"It was a silly question and I was stupid for asking the obvious," Gabbryel said, her voice wavering slightly. "I'm sorry, Harpreet."

"There is no such thing as a stupid or silly question," Harpreet said kindly. "However, I will require you to think before you speak. Otherwise you could make yourself look ridiculous."

Harpreet looked at Barbette and nodded.

"Harpreet and I are here to teach you how to travel through the transport portal. Nathanial is badly hurt and needs his family around him for support. The world you will be travelling to looks similar to Telluric, but is very different in spiritual understanding."

Barbette stepped forward. "So, you appreciate the level of respect Harpreet's expertise deserves. She would be classed as the top-ranking professor in her field on this world," Barbette confirmed.

"Lon said that travelling through the portal was similar to travel sickness. I could mix up some of his herbs if you think that would help?" Renae asked.

"That's thoughtful of you, Renae," Barbette answered. "As I have already explained, the sensation is different depending on the realm you were born on. Is there any among you who suffer from travel sickness?"

"Lon was the only one, he used to get it quite badly at times," Lomasi answered.

"Thank you, Lomasi. Very well then, you all know the technique. I will describe the destination and I want you to form the vision in your head. Once we're on the portal, imagine we have already arrived. Renae, I will start with you."

Everyone listened closely as Barbette described their destination. Then she and Renae stepped onto the portal, Barbette nodded and they vanished. They reappeared precisely where they intended. Barbette asked Renae to move off the portal and wait. A moment later she appeared with Janelle, who moved to stand beside Renae; then Barbette disappeared again. Harpreet was the next to arrive with Gela and so the procession continued until everyone was present.

"I will escort you to the guesthouse for safekeeping and I will then check on Nathanial and advise you of his condition," Harpreet told the assembled group.

She escorted the chosen ones to their lodgings. The walk gave them time to observe their surroundings. It didn't look much different from Telluric. The houses were slightly different in design as they incorporated landscaped gardens within their structures. Harpreet settled them into their quarters and advised them to make themselves at home.

"Please remain in the home, no matter how tempting it might be to look around. You will be given a tour of my world a little later. "

Renae assured Harpreet they would do as they were told and Harpreet left.

* * *

Laura called around to where Joe was staying to advise him that the safe house was prepared. "Hello, Joe, everyone been looking after you all right?"

"Yeah, thanks."

"I thought we could take a ride to the safe house and show you what we've done," Laura told him.

"That'd be great."

Laura and Joe headed off in the detective's vehicle. They had almost arrived when Joe asked her to pull the car over.

"What's the problem, Joe?"

"I know this section of town and it ain't too healthy for coppers around here. I can't be seen with ya, nothin' personal like. It just ain't safe, that's all."

"I understand, Joe," Laura said, nodding. "The house is in the second street to the left, number eight. Have a good look around and let me know if you can see any of the cameras. If you can, then the job hasn't been done correctly. I'll wait here."

Joe got out of the car and walked to the safe house. He carefully inspected every room looking for the hidden cameras but without success. He then walked around the exterior of the house. Something wasn't right, but he couldn't put his finger on it. He stood looking at the house from the street. That was it! The animal figurehead on the roof wasn't his totem protector. A cold shiver ran down his spine; it was too late now. Joe headed back to the car.

"What's the matter?" Laura asked when he hopped into the car.

"When I asked for an animal on the roof, I forgot ta tell you it had ta be from the cat family. Without my totem I'm not protected." A deep expression of foreboding crossed Joe's face.

"Joe, we will protect you – nothing can happen that we won't notice. The moment you give us the sign we'll be there, agreed?"

"Yeah, can we go back now?" Joe wasn't happy and felt helpless.

Joe wasn't convinced of his safety and Laura knew it. He was one of those people who believed that animals had special powers. She would have to do something about it so she decided to detour to a large shopping complex where she knew there was a new age shop that sold totem animals.

"Joe, I have to drop into the shopping centre before we return. It won't take long. Do you mind?"

"Nar, that's all right," he replied.

Joe didn't say a word throughout the journey. When they arrived, he insisted on remaining in the car. Laura knew where she needed to go, having recently purchased something similar for her niece. The shop had changed so much since she had been here last that she hardly recognised it; in fact, she had to take a double look to see if she was in the right place. The windows at either side of the door now contained a lifelike replica of an animal. The shop itself was full of animal facsimiles of all shapes and sizes along with many of their habitats. She could be forgiven for thinking she had entered a zoo. As she tentatively walked through the door a slim woman approached her. She was around five feet six with short red hair and wore a tightly fitted dress that flowed out from the waist.

"You appear in need of assistance?" she remarked with an odd accent.

Laura looked at her intently. "Yes, I have a friend who believes that the cat family is his totem and he is going away on a trip. Which animal would you advise?"

"That depends on the person. Is he courageous or timid?"

"He believes he is are timid, but I think otherwise, and what he is about to undertake is very courageous," Laura replied.

"I sense that the medicine needed is from the darkest cat of all."

The woman went to a side stand and removed a cat as black as night and then found its box. "This is Midnight Black of the Panther Clan. There is a poem that goes with it. It reads:

> *Midnight black of the Panther Clan*
> *Strengthen my heart with your love*
> *So I may know that dark unknown*
> *As I bravely leap all alone*
> *Fortified by your courageous spirit."*

"That's perfect. I'll take it," Laura acknowledged gratefully. Returning to the car she found Joe quietly brooding.

"I have a gift for you, Joe," she said, quietly slipping it into his hands. "I ask that you accept this in appreciation for all you are doing."

Joe took the gift and opened it carefully. Tears sprang to his eyes as he saw what it was. He couldn't believe she had done this for him. "This is a precious gift; I will treasure it always, thank ya," Joe managed to choke out.

Laura started the car and headed back to where she had picked him up. The panther was small enough to hang around his neck on a chain or attach to his keys. Joe kept handling the panther and reading the poem over and over. He didn't speak a word until they arrived.

"Laura," he said quietly. It was obvious he would like to show her some form of affection in gratitude for her gift. All he could do was to say her name.

"Joe, you are truly welcome. You had better go in now." Joe nodded, got out of the car and went into the house where Peter was waiting.

"What's up?" Peter asked, watching Joe walk back into the house.

"Joe forgot to tell us the totem animal had to be from the cat family. When he noticed the totem was from a different family he freaked, so I went to the shops and bought him a panther totem for luck," Laura explained.

"You have no idea what a plus you'll have achieved in giving him that panther. I'm surprised he didn't hug you," Peter stated.

"The look on his face and his body language said he wanted to," Laura remarked, wondering if she should have let him show her some form of gratitude. "I told him I understood and suggested it was time to go to the house."

"I don't know if I could have remained sane if I'd had his life. Every so often he would relate some of his story. I thought I was a hard-nosed cop until I heard what he'd gone through. The one thing that kept him from going over the edge was a woman who introduced him to totem animals."

"I only hope it helps," Laura answered. "We will see what

tomorrow brings when he meets his colleagues at the old sawmill. Until then, bye, Peter."

Laura drove off and Peter walked back into the house to keep a protective eye on Joe.

* * *

Night had fallen as Lon and Harpreet strolled back to the guest residence, deep in conversation. Gela spotted them. "Lon and Harpreet are coming," she called out to the others.

Everyone crowded around the pair as they came through the door. Harpreet indicated that they all talk together in the relaxation area of the house. Once they were all seated Lon addressed them.

"Nathanial will be okay. The healers here are the finest. You will be able to visit him tomorrow."

"Lon, this will probably sound disrespectful, but if you're Kyros, the supreme healer of all the realms of Chimera, why couldn't you have healed Nathanial?" Gabbryel queried.

"I could have. However, his injuries were so severe that I would have had to put him into a state of suspended animation while I repaired his spirit. We didn't have that much time. As it is, it has taken twelve hours for myself with the aid of several skilled surgeons, to restore Nathanial to health again. I don't need to prove how good I am, Gabbryel; this isn't a competition with me taking first prize. It's about what's best for the person under my care," Lon stated, still coming to terms with his new abilities.

The room they were in had large double doors that opened onto a verandah with steps leading down into a garden. The evening sun shone a copper glow that radiated gentle warmth, calming the mind and warming the body. A meal had been prepared and served out on the verandah where all were enjoying a relaxing twilight repast. Towards the end of the evening, Lon walked to the head of the stairs leading to the garden but then suddenly advised everybody to remain indoors.

"What is the problem?" Harpreet enquired with concern.

"Slegna's coming," he stated, coldly turning to look at them. "I want all of you to say nothing and do nothing, no matter what! Is that understood?"

Everyone watched a light start to appear in a large grassed area of the garden. Lon turned to them and reiterated his previous statement with such force that they sat frozen in their seats. He then walked across the verandah, went downstairs and out onto the lawn, where he lazily leaned on his Staff as if it was the most natural thing in the world to do, and waited.

The light intensified until the shape of a man appeared before him. Standing six feet tall with soft facial features, rich brown eyes and a full mouth, his skin was flawless and his hair well groomed. Dressed all in dark shades was a man of incredible stature.

Kyros spoke. "Whom do I have the pleasure of addressing?"

A voice as sweet as honey, with seduction flowing from every word, replied.

"I am called Slegna." An audible intake of breath could be heard from inside the house. Slegna smiled. "With whom do I speak?"

"Kyros is the name I am given."

"I have come to meet you, Kyros." Lon felt the true power behind Slegna's words as an intention to weaken Lon's faith in Oletha. Waves of dark spiritual energy assailed him as Slegna attempted to find a weakness in his defences.

"Are you unwell, Slegna, that you seek my services?" Lon asked smoothly, wondering how he would respond if Slegna's assault on him increased.

Slegna's laugh contained no humour. Those in the house could feel his seductive power as they were beginning to succumb to his honeyed voice and silver tongue. "I wish to meet the one who removed the sentient Staff of Knowledge, and learn its name."

"Wood," Lon replied calmly.

"Wood!" Slegna said, shocked. "You called the most enlightened sentient being of all the realms, Wood?"

"Well, yes. After all, that is what it is," Lon suggested. "A piece of wood."

Slegna took a menacing step closer. The onslaught of power was overwhelming and Lon knew that fighting against it would only weaken him. So he absorbed it into himself and redirected it to Gaia. The look on Slegna's face told him he hadn't expected Lon to be able to do that. Indifferently, Lon moved his Staff from one hand to the other and scratched a supposed itch on his neck. He looked around lazily and then moved the Staff back to the other hand.

"It seems I have interrupted a party in your honour, Kyros."

"No, these people were simply kind enough to invite me to share in their buffet," Lon told him dryly.

Slegna started to extend his energy into the house. The moment Lon felt the movement towards his family he tightened his grip on Malachy and healing energy met Slegna's power with a blinding flash lighting up the immediate area.

"Was it not I you wished to see Slegna?" Lon responded, feeling Oletha's love enveloping him.

"Are you challenging me, Kyros?" Slegna asked, amused.

"Only a fool would challenge you, Slegna. I feel no animosity towards you."

Lon was ready for the attack that followed. With the Staff firmly in front of him, he blended entirely with it, becoming Malachy. Reams of spiritual energy discharged from Slegna in frightening succession, to be met with Malachy's protective healing aura of love.

Malachy poured forth equal strength of energy, countering Slegna's every move. Night had turned into day as the surrounding area was lit with bolts of energy that exploded in an array of astounding colours and ear-splitting sounds. So intense was the combat that the world was engulfed in an aura of extreme glowing energy as the struggle intensified with every volley Slegna expended.

Malachy drew on the love and kindness of Creation,

countering with forgiveness and understanding. This only enraged Slegna to greater and grander outbursts. Harpreet and the others ran from the premises as the volley of fire increased.

Harpreet had just ushered the last person out when a councilman approached her and they re-entered the house for a moment. Suddenly the house and the surrounding gardens vanished in a volley of fire that staggered the mind and sent the spirit reeling. Kyros and Slegna were no longer visible, engulfed totally within the explosive energies.

Slegna knew this battle could continue for centuries this way. Kyros wasn't attacking; he was only defending, using his own power against him. He also knew he would eventually win, but at what cost? He would be considerably weakened and would have to spend aeons recovering. Slegna moved to physically grab Malachy. Sensing the move, Malachy leaped into Slegna's arms embracing him with the love of Oletha. The shock of Malachy suddenly being in his arms pouring forth love was too much for Slegna to endure.

He flung Malachy from his embrace and poured such loathing upon him that all went pitch black. The air became still and the silence was deafening. Then the faintest light began to glow within that horrid darkness, growing in power and splintering the darkness to the four winds. Slegna was at a loss to understand the emotions of love for it wasn't part of his makeup. In wild frustration, he poured forth all the power at his disposal. The torrent of energy that struck Malachy was horrific.

Beneath that appalling onslaught, Malachy held firm. Gaia could take no more outbursts without grievous damage. Already she was seriously wounded with the extent of power that surrounded her. So Kyros redirected Slegna's energy to the universe where it could be dispersed.

Harpreet advised the other gathering council members that Slegna had come to battle with Kyros and that the fate of their world depended on the outcome. Everyone was in awe of Kyros's abilities, for to fight the ruler of the Unbalanced realms was supposed to be something only Oletha could do and win.

"Renae!" Harpreet unexpectedly screamed. "Stop Gela from trying to help Lon!"

Renae made a grab for Gela and swung her around. "You heard what Lon said!" She yelled over the noise of battle, "Keep out of it!"

The surrounding countryside was slowly being engulfed with the prevailing spiritual energy outbursts. More and more residents were evacuated from their homes as the energy extended ever outward. They were now over a mile from the house from where the conflict had started. All that could be seen were intense flashes of light that exploded on impact. Many people had been knocked to the ground with the explosions. Great eruptions of energy would burst skyward illuminating the entire night sky. All wondered about the fate of Kyros and how long he could hold his own.

As an explosion blasted from the middle of the conflict, the intensity was so immense that no one within a radius of five miles was left standing, and everyone feared the worst. However, the hostilities began again. As the people of Terraqueous reeled under the onslaught, a firm compelling female voice, emanating from the heavens, called, "Be still."

Silence blanketed the night as people slowly rose to their feet, many trembling in fear. Harpreet and the chosen ones found transport and headed toward Harpreet's home and the battle zone.

Then a warm wraithlike glow descended from the heavens projecting a calming influence that encompassed the entire world of Terraqueous.

On arrival at Harpreet's home, they saw that Slegna and Malachy were suspended in mid-battle. Gela stared at Lon in stunned amazement for he was Malachy and extended out from him was his open hand of friendship into which Slegna was spewing his wealth of dark energy. This, Malachy then directed outward to the heavens. Even more surprising was the compassion on Malachy's face, compared to the dispassion on Slegna's. Nothing remained of the garden.

As the luminosity touched the earth it transformed into a woman of extraordinary beauty. She was stunning beyond belief, her ethereal appearance holding everyone speechless as she flowed gracefully toward Slegna and Malachy.

She wore a white silken gown that flowed over her head, across her shoulders and down her arms. It covered the full curvature of her body while sweeping the ground beneath her feet as she moved.

Around her waist she wore a golden cord that encircled

her twice before being tied in a knot, with the remaining length of cord dangling from her left hip to just above her knees.

Her outer garment was a sky-blue cape, which descended over her head, shoulders and across her arms to travel the full length of her body to the ground beneath. Her angelic face had a flawless complexion and her hands made exquisitely graceful movements as she spoke.

Stopping between Slegna and Malachy, she made a slight movement with her hand and the two combatants were returned to their former selves. Slegna appeared indifferent to Oletha's presence.

"Hello, Oletha, what are you doing here?" he said in a neutral tone, looking around to see what else was happening.

"This is not allowed, Slegna; you know that," Oletha informed him.

"I just wanted to see what Kyros was made of." Slegna's voice was perfectly calm.

"Now you know, you can leave."

Slegna looked at Kyros, who was now standing calmly with Staff in hand. He bowed politely towards him, nodded to Oletha and vanished. No one had ever seen Slegna before, or Oletha. Oletha's voice resonated with a divine empathy that filled the spirit and soothed the soul. Every tone uttered was like a choir of heavenly revelations.

"Thank you, Oletha, that could have gone on for a very long time before his energy eroded me to nothing. As it is, I feel a little worn," Lon commented wearily.

Gela ran up and flung her arms around Lon's waist, squeezing him tightly.

"Well, little one," Oletha said. "I see you are in love with my champion and the feelings are returned. For you to share a full life together you must first join with the liquid crystal. Are you prepared to do that?" Oletha enquired.

The smile that radiated from Gela spoke volumes. "Very well then, but know that in doing so you will seem eternal. You are at present my disciple of this one life, free from service upon the passing of your body. To join with the crystal essence, your fidelity to me must be without question. If it is not, then the joining will not take place and your body would eventually suffer a horrific death. Are you prepared to dedicate your existence to me as Lon has done?"

"Yes, Oletha," replied Gela. "For as much as I am deeply in love with Lon, this couldn't be if I didn't respect and love the essence of the True Light."

"Then I join you together as one, to be forever united in love. Harpreet, you will train Gela in the manner you trained Lon and then set her on the path of discovery that she may become at one with the crystal."

"As you wish, holy one."

"No, Harpreet. I am not to be known as holy or divine. Nor do I wish to be worshipped. There are to be no temples or houses dedicated to me, no portraits or effigies of my person of any kind," Oletha said firmly but with compassion. "If you allow people to hold me above themselves they will forever be looking to me to solve their difficulties. Every spirit upon all the realms of existence was given the gift of free will. They are responsible for their own lives and what happens to them. Is that understood?"

"Yes, Oletha."

"You, my chosen ones, know this. You must never interfere with free will. Lon is the foundation upon which my disciples shall learn. I entrust him with my essence of life. Harpreet, are you ready to be one of my disciples?"

"I am, Oletha."

"Then hold forth the crystal wolf that Lon made for you."

Harpreet extended her arm with the sapphire sitting in her palm, whereupon Oletha placed her hand upon it. A glow of light escaped from between their fingers and warmth travelled throughout Harpreet's body. When Oletha had finished, Harpreet was holding a golden chain in the design of growing vines and a wolf head looking out from a forest in the form of a pendant that hung from the chain. It was identical in design to the rings.

"Know this, that when you put this on, it cannot be removed."

"I wear it with honour, Oletha."

"Lon, this is your last member of the Order of the Phelan."

"Thank you, Oletha." Lon bowed politely.

Oletha shimmered and then vanished, leaving a bewildered populace behind her.

CHAPTER ELEVEN

Andy arrived bright and early at the old abandoned sawmill. The machinery was rusted and the buildings still standing were unsafe. Rows of timber stacked twenty feet high were badly weathered and buckled with age, unclaimed by anyone. He sat quietly in a small office at the back of the cutting shed going over in his mind what he was going to say to Joe.

He wasn't looking forward to this meeting. He had known Joe longer than the others and the thought of him being a turncoat was distressing. Hearing someone coming, he pulled his thoughts together and walked from the shed. He stood between the stacks of wood and waited. Mick was the first to arrive; his face lit up at seeing Andy.

"Andy, are ya the only one here yet?"

"Yeah Mick, just me."

"I got somethin' ta tell ya and ya gotta listen," Mick said urgently.

"Okay, pal, what is it?" Andy asked.

"Ever since we was last together, I've had this feelin' that Joe's up ta somethin'," Mick started. "It took me almost two days ta work out how he chooses the safe houses; every one of them has an animal figurine on the roof. Not only that, they're all from the cat family."

"That would be Joe, all right; he has a thing for totems. So what's the problem?" Andy prompted, remembering how an old woman had introduced Joe to totem animals.

"I just bet the next house don't have one," Mick grimly stated. "I don't trust him anymore and I ain't goin' ta no house that he chooses."

"That's all right, Mick. I wasn't planning ta go ta it anyway, so don't worry," Andy told him.

"Good, and just so ya know, Terry ain't Terry no more either," continued Mick, fear registering on his face as he recalled the look Terry had given him at the coffee shop.

"What are you talkin' about?" Andy queried, puzzlement showing on his face.

"He went real crazy like and wanted ta be alone." Mick felt uncomfortable at the memory. "Then the next time I'd seed him, he said his name wasn't Terry but Enoch and I'd better call 'im that or else. Just thought ya oughtta know."

"Yeah, thanks Mick." Bewilderment showed on Andy's face, *"I wonder what's got up his nose,"* he thought.

A short time later Terry arrived.

"Hi Terry, how's it been?" asked Andy cheerfully.

Terry fixed Andy with a stare that could turn water to ice. Andy returned his gaze with equal intensity and with a slow deliberate movement took a step towards him.

"You want ta head off on your own, Terry, then go!" Andy delivered the order with chilly finality. "But don't you ever challenge me again," he stated, pointing a finger at him. "I'm the boss of this gang, not you!"

Terry recognised Slegna's mark and knew that Andy also belonged to him. His smile was cold and unfeeling. "So, we both have the same master. I'm ta be called Enoch. Where's that snivelling little coward, Joe?"

"He hasn't arrived yet. He still has time," Andy replied, not wanting his information about Joe to be correct.

Joe had been hiding, listening to the whole conversation. Earlier that morning, Detective Dunstan had called in to give Joe a tracking device, which he stuck to the underside of his trouser belt. She also gave him the smallest microphone he had ever seen. This he inserted into the totem animal, which hung on a chain around his neck. Joe waited calming his nerves until Andy, Terry and Mick were in a normal conversation before he walked out from behind some logs with a wave.

"Hi all," he called.

"Where's the safe house, Joe?" Andy asked, moving calmly towards him.

"Sorry Andy, it was compromised at the last minute."

"So you're saying we don't have a safe house?"

"We have several, just no new ones. We could return ta the one in the Downs, your choice," Joe replied as Mick and Andy looked at each other knowingly.

Andy became angry thinking that maybe Joe was the turncoat he had been told about. "Why that one and not one of the others?" he said abruptly.

"Look Andy," Joe said snappily, "ya can go ta any bloody house ya want. I don't give a shit!"

"What's got up your nose?" Andy remarked, surprised at his response.

"I want out," Joe spat angrily while looking him in the eye. "I don't wanna know where ya goin' or what ya doin'. I've just enough money saved ta get me ta another province. Y'know I've been talkin' about leavin', Andy," Joe finished calmly.

"Yeah, I know, but why now, Joe?" Andy said, throwing his arms in the air in frustration.

"I hate the way the gang is headin' with all the violence and the way ya let Terry grab all those women is wrong."

"Listen, ya little poonce, how would ya like me ta rearrange your stupid face?" Terry yelled.

Joe was about eight inches shorter than Terry and carried less weight; he also had a shorter reach. He was counting on Terry to lose his temper, thus giving him an advantage.

"Terry, yer nothin' but a scrawny yellow-bellied piece of shit who has to hit women to feel good about himself," Joe taunted, hoping Terry would take the bait.

Andy had never seen Joe like this before; he was deliberately baiting Terry. He decided to let the situation run its course and see what happened.

Terry eyed him carefully; Joe had never challenged him before and he never would again. Terry blindly lunged. Joe's punch landed perfectly on the side of Terry's face. The force of the blow spun him around, knocking him to the ground.

Regaining his feet, he sent a kick towards Joe, who grabbed his leg and returned a hard kick of his own into Terry's inner thigh. Terry was screaming mad and attacked again. Hobbling on one leg, he threw a succession of punches at Joe, who was calmly blocking and returning an array of successful blows to Terry's face and body.

Andy and Mick were taken completely off guard as they watched in stunned amazement as Joe continued to pulverise Terry. Terry backed away to compose himself, filling himself up with Slegna's power. Joe could sense that something unnatural was happening and decided to attack.

Terry was caught off guard at Joe's unexpected aggression. Joe laid into Terry with boots, fists and head butts. The realisation that Joe was beating the crap out of Terry suddenly sank in. Andy signalled to Mick and they joined the fight.

Joe sent a kick into Terry's gut that doubled him over. Mick grabbed Joe from behind. Joe whacked his head back, breaking Mick's nose knocking him out cold. Joe swung around angrily; twenty years of dormant emotions for the death of his parents and the wanton violence of the gang was unleashed as he grabbed Andy and tossed him aside like a piece of meat.

"Keep out of this, Andy. This is between that gutless turd Terry and me," Joe said in a chilling voice.

Terry hit Joe with piece of timber when he wasn't looking. Joe completely lost control as all his suppressed anger was powerfully released onto Terry who could no longer see out of his eyes. His face was a mass of cuts, awash with blood. Andy came at Joe again, only to meet a punch that sent him sprawling on his rear end in the dirt.

Joe turned his aggression onto Terry once again, pinning him against some logs, beating him until he couldn't stand. The last thing Joe remembered was picking Terry up and throwing him at Andy, who was coming at him once more. Then everything went dark.

* * *

When Joe regained consciousness, he found himself hanging from a chain by his arms and stripped to the waist. He was in an old steel mill. His head hurt and it felt like a swarm of bees were buzzing around inside.

"He's awake."

Andy and Mick slowly walked up to Joe. It was obvious that Mick's nose was broken because of the heavy bruising around his eyes. Behind them came Terry, limping and bloodied. His face looked like someone had attacked it with an iron bar, his eyes could barely open and his mouth was swollen and cut. When he spoke, his voice was barely audible.

"You don't know who you're fuckin' dealin' with, but ya will."

Terry allowed Slegna's energy to build within him. Joe watched in astonishment as Terry's body totally repaired itself before his eyes. He was horrified at the chilling malevolence emanating from Terry.

"My name is Enoch. I am the chosen disciple of Slegna, ruler of all the realms of the Unbalanced. He is The Mystery of the One Truth and you're nothin' before his disciple. By the time I'm finished with ya, you'll be begging ta die."

Mick's face paled at Enoch's words as he looked at Andy. Joe, however, didn't seem to care.

"I've already beaten the shit out of ya, Terry," Joe snarled, feeling for the first time in his life he had stood up and been the man his father would have liked him to have been.

"Ya'll call me Enoch."

"I'll call ya whatever I want!" Joe said bravely. "Why did ya get between me and Terry, Andy? It weren't your fight and what have ya got me strung up like this for?"

"You're a turncoat, Joe."

"If I wanted ta turn ya in, I could have done that and then vanished. Ya would never have found me," Joe said in a level voice. "But it don't matter what I say 'cause y'ain't goin' ta believe me. Y'all nothin' but yellow-bellied cowards, like the one who hit me from behind at the sawmill. You're a pile of gutless turds."

Andy shrugged and walked off leaving Enoch to his pleasures. The sound of the rubber hose hitting Joe's body echoed through the empty factory. When Andy returned thirty minutes later, Joe was hanging limply from the chain.

"He better not be dead, Enoch, I have questions for him."

"He ain't dead, just out cold. I can bring him round." Enoch placed his hand on Joe's body, allowing the healing energy from Slegna to revive him. Joe's body twitched several times and then his eyes opened.

"Feel like talking yet, Joe?" Andy commented, while idly

swinging the rubber hose Enoch had just been using. Joe felt as if his body had been violated from the inside. A dirty unclean sensation was surging through him, making his body respond unnaturally. Joe, regaining his senses, spat in Andy's face.

"You'll be sorry ya did that. All right, Enoch, stop being nice."

A smile of pure evil appeared on Enoch's face. Joe knew he would die and welcomed it. Better death than the vile feelings moving through his body. Enoch enjoyed the brutality that followed. Joe eventually came to his senses from a bucket of water being thrown in his face. Pain showed on his face and he wished for death – he couldn't understand why he wasn't dead already with the torment his mind and body were feeling.

"So Joe, are you ready to talk?"

Joe stared at Andy and didn't say a word; nothing he could say would make a difference. Andy looked at Enoch and walked off. Enoch put on a pair of chainmail gloves and started in on Joe once more. Joe's involuntary screams echoed throughout the factory.

When Enoch had finished the gloves were soaked in blood. There was hardly a piece of undamaged flesh left on Joe's body. Enoch had used his power to make sure Joe couldn't pass out. Then Andy returned with Mick to ask some questions.

"As ya can see, Joe," Andy's commanding voice explained. "Enoch can keep ya conscious the whole time. That way ya can appreciate his skill in causing pain. So why don't ya just tell us what we want ta know? Mick and I don't like ta see you like this." His voice now sounded compassionate. "Who've ya been talking to and how much have ya told them?"

Joe didn't say a word. His shoulders were burning from having to support the full weight of his body and the chain tied around his ankles. His eyes were almost completely closed and, with the amount of blood in them, seeing was painful and blurry. His jaw felt broken and blood was pouring from his mouth. He had at least four broken ribs and his insides felt raw with pain. Joe was unable to talk, so Enoch used his power again, healing Joe just enough so he could speak.

Joe figured he had one good kick in him and he was saving that for Andy. If he whispered, Andy would have to come close to hear and then he would kick the prick hard enough to put him on his arse. Unfortunately, Joe's vision wasn't good. Mick and Andy were together when he spoke and the kick meant for Andy skinned the side of his head hitting Mick full force. It knocked him backwards onto a metal rod that was sticking out of the floor, running him through. Mick screamed in agony for a long time before he eventually died.

"You'll die for this!" Andy shouted, wiping the blood off the side of his face where the chain from Joe's ankles had cut him.

Joe was horrified that he had actually killed someone. He had only wanted to knock Andy to the floor, not hurt Mick. He started calling to the Mystery of the True Light for forgiveness. So strong was his conviction and remorse for the life he had taken, he was sobbing. Everyone thought it was out of fear of what Enoch would do to him.

Slegna had been watching the whole time, enjoying the emotions that were being released. Enoch truly was a demonic fiend in its truest form and he started once again to pummel Joe. Slegna knew they would never break Joe because Joe was mortified about taking a life and believed he deserved what was now happening to him. Oletha appeared next to Slegna and watched.

"Enoch is not letting Joe pass into unconsciousness, Slegna; that is your doing. Release the hold Enoch has on him now."

Slegna was totally unconcerned at Oletha's command as he allowed Joe to sink into oblivion. Oletha had heard Joe's plea for forgiveness and knew there was nothing to forgive. She also knew that Joe would never follow the path of the Unbalanced.

"Slegna, you say that this world has sunk so far into the depths of despair that it's yours. This is your first chance to prove it. Joe, like everyone else on this world, has free will. He has been brought up to endure the horror of your kind. I will bring him before us that he may choose between the Balanced and Unbalanced."

Joe sank into blissful oblivion, free from all the pain and suffering. He became aware of a warming glow and found that he was standing in a beautiful garden feeling the warmth of the sun on his face.

Walking towards him was a woman in her mid-thirties. Her appearance was ethereal and she was stunning beyond belief. She wore a white gown that covered her head, shoulders and arms. It clung to the curvature of her body; a golden cord encircled her waist twice before being tied in a knot. The remaining length of cord dangled from her left hip to just above her knees. Her outer garment was a blue cape, which descended over her head, shoulders and across her arms to travel the full length of her body to the ground beneath.

Beside her was a male. He had a well-defined body, dark hair and beautiful soft brown eyes and was wearing a white body shirt under a tailored dark blue sports jacket and trousers; he was striking in his appearance. Neither of them wore any shoes.

As they came closer Joe noticed they each had a flawless complexion and graceful hand movements. They were both smiling warmly as they approached. The man spoke first.

"Hello, young man, you seem to have fallen on hard times." He had a gentle voice.

"Yeah, sir," Joe responded.

"We have come to offer you a choice."

"Am I dead?"

"No, you're not dead, but depending on the choice you make, you could be," the man replied.

"Who are you?"

"We are the choice," the man responded.

"If I'm not dead, where am I?" Joe asked.

"You're in a place of our choosing," the woman answered.

"I don't understand."

"It's very simple, Joe," she replied. "Your body is back on Telluric, while your spirit is here with us."

"Are ya gods?" Joe responded in awe.

"No, Joe. Your soul, like everyone's, was born out of the creative consciousness of compassion. Your soul then created your spirit and infused it with all its knowledge. People were created autonomous, Joe, so in essence, each person is his or her own god. Do you understand?"

"Sort of."

"Why don't you explain to me what you think I just said?" she asked him.

"Our soul is part of the Mystery of the True Light and the spirit is what the soul made."

"Well put, Joe."

"How'd ya know me name?"

"We know all about you. Every time you make a decision in your life, you are choosing between one of us," commented the gentleman.

"What are your names?" Joe asked, looking at the woman.

"I will tell you after you have made your choice."

"How will I know which one ta choose?"

"The gentleman stepped forward, getting Joe's attention. "Let us look at your life, Joe. At the moment you're in an unhealthy position."

"Yeah, I'm goin' ta die," he said sadly, looking at his feet.

"What would you say if I told you I could arrange for you

to keep living and extract revenge upon the ones causing you pain?"

Joe looked from the man to the woman. *"What are these two up ta,"* he wondered. Looking at the woman whilst he pointed at the man, he asked, "Could he do that?"

"Yes, Joe, he could." she responded calmly.

Joe was suspicious and eyed them both closely. *"I wonder what she ain't sayin',"* he thought. "Would you do that?" he asked her pointedly.

"No, Joe, I wouldn't."

Joe looked at them questioningly. There was something going on he wasn't aware of and he wasn't about to make a decision without knowing all the facts.

"Why would he give me life, when you wouldn't?" Joe asked her.

"What is life, Joe?"

"I dunno; I haven't given it much thought before. You say I'm not dead. The last thing I remember is hangin' from a chain all beat up. Now I'm standin' here talkin' to ya in this here garden and ya say this is me spirit. So where's me body?"

The woman gently waved her hand. There beneath Joe's feet was the steel mill where his body was hanging from a chain, with Enoch still beating into it. Oletha didn't say a word as Slegna spoke.

"You know, Joe, I can stop all this from happening. I can have the police find you and arrest everyone involved. You could have your new life in another province. I would even see to it you were financially rewarded."

Joe wasn't fooled; he knew there was more going on than this bloke was saying and the lady was being real cagey too.

"Ya know, mister, you have a real silver tongue. But there's somethin' I just don't trust about ya. I mightn't speak right, but I ain't stupid." Joe turned to face the woman. "Also lady, what ain't you sayin'?"

Smiling, Oletha looked at Slegna and then at Joe. "You're correct, Joe. There are many things we haven't said. Everyone has free will that can be influenced by others. We wished to give you an unbiased opportunity to choose the direction in life you wish to travel."

"That's why you asked me what life was?"

"Yes, Joe, that's why," she said knowingly.

"Well, I dunno, but it's got ta be more than what I've had. I mean, what would be the point of livin' if when ya die that's all there is. There has ta be more, or I wouldn't be here," Joe remarked, looking about. "You tells me you're a choice I has to make, well what if I don't make one, what then?" Joe demanded.

Slegna looked at Oletha questioningly but Oletha simply smiled.

"Anyway," Joe continued. "I'm already dead or will be, 'cause I ain't buyin' what he's sellin', and I'm not too sure what you're sellin' either, so I ain't choosin' either of ya."

"Your actions will automatically determine which one of us you choose," the woman informed him.

Joe wasn't happy as he looked at her. "So ya sayin' no matter what I does, I will be choosin' one of ya anyway?"

"Yes, Joe, that's correct," was the compassionate response.

Joe eyed her closely; she had gentleness about her while this bloke didn't. In fact, he didn't seem to have any true emotions at all. Joe turned to face him. "What do ya think I should do?"

"Live your life in another province after you get even with those who are hurting you," he answered simply and unemotionally.

"Really," Joe responded, surprised at the answer. "What do ya think I should do?" Joe questioned the woman.

"Whatever's in your heart, Joe." she sympathetically replied.

Oletha and Slegna watched as Joe walked off deep in thought. *"This bloke only acts like he cares, while the lady shows genuine signs of caring. If this lady weren't here it would be easy to think this bloke was for real. I would rather have someone who cares than someone who don't."* Joe turned and looked at the woman. "All right, lady. I'm with ya." Joe said finally.

The man moved towards him. "Are you saying that you're choosing to die in agony, as opposed to the life I can offer you, Joe?" he said in his most beguiling way.

"Look pal, ya seem false to me and I just don't trust ya, okay?" Joe stated firmly.

"Please, Joe, she'll let you die," he pleaded reaching for his hand. "I'm trying to save your life, my friend."

"Friend!" Joe screamed, pulling away from him. "Ya wouldn't know the meanin' of the word," Joe said, shaking his head. "Ya remind me of a bloke who's tryin' real hard to sell something. But ya don't really care about the person ya sellin' to. Now shove off!"

"By saying all that, Joe, am I to understand you are choosing to be with me?" Oletha enquired.

"Yeah, I guess I am."

"The choice is made."

"So who are you, lady?"

"I am Oletha, The Mystery of the True Light."

Joe dropped to his knees. "Oletha, please forgive me for causin' the death of me mate Mick. It were an accident. I only meant to kick Andy in the face, not kill anyone," Joe begged.

"There's nothing to forgive, Joe. What happened wasn't done with vindictiveness or vengeance. You tried to cause Andy embarrassment in front of his friends. There was no malice in your heart, as there is none now." Oletha leaned down and raised Joe to his feet.

"Thank you, Oletha." Joe stood and looked intently at the man. "Who are you, pal?

"I'm Slegna, the Mystery of the One Truth."

"Slegna! You're Slegna! You're a cruel sadistic son of a bitch. You're got Terry beatin' me to death."

"I have nothing to do with that, Joe; that's all Enoch's doing."

"You're nothin' but a bloody liar, 'cause ya could have stopped Terry by not givin' him your power! Ya knew what he was doin', ya heartless prick!" Joe blurted out angrily.

"You're correct, Joe. He is heartless and lacks compassion,

because that is what many people are like. Terry, for instance, thrives on cruelty; he couldn't live in a world without it. It's food for his spirit. Slegna can't make people malicious, Joe; they do that all by themselves. If you lie, cheat, steal, or are unkind, then you're travelling Slegna's path of the Unbalanced."

Slegna moved off, leaving Oletha and Joe talking.

"If you're compassionate and forgiving, then you're walking my path of the Balanced. You chose not to follow Slegna's path, which makes me your choice."

"So you're saying Slegna's not a bad guy but a good guy?" Joe asked, bewildered.

"There is no good or bad. There is only what you know and what you are learning. Take you for instance; your life was one of repayment from previous lifetimes."

"What do ya mean previous lifetimes?"

"Joe, the life you're presently living is only one of countless lives you've already had. Life has nothing to do with the body. It's about the soul achieving true understanding of creation by way of the spirit.

You may choose to incarnate several lifetimes to complete a single task. One of your tasks this life was to resist the temptation of the Unbalanced and to offer care and assistance to the women Terry abducted. Your compassion helped them to overcome the trauma of their captivity."

"Then why am I bein' beaten to death?" he asked, trembling slightly.

"Do you believe you are responsible for your actions, Joe?"

"Yeah, of course."

"This is the life you chose to reimburse previous karmic obligations," Oletha told him.

"What's karmic mean?"

"Karmic or karma is the record that is kept of all you have ever done," she continued. "All your deeds have been recorded as well as any new ones you may have created. Remember Joe, for every action there is an opposite and equal reaction. What you do in one lifetime will return in another. This is the law of Balance and Harmony."

"It seems to me that you can never repay what ya owe, 'cause you're always gettin' into more debt," Joe said sadly.

"Each time you reincarnate, a measure of karma is balanced with the schooling you wish to undertake. In this way your karma will never outweigh your responsibility to the body you inhabit. As your psychic awareness matures through many life experiences, you are more capable of reimbursing your obligations almost immediately."

"Ya mean if ya steal somethin', then somethin' will be stole from ya?"

"Yes, Joe, much of your karma is returned to you in the life you're presently living.

"Well, how do ya know what ya should be doin' then?" Joe asked, concerned.

"It is the simplest thing of all to be honest and true to yourself, to recognise that which will create Unbalanced karma and refrain from doing it."

"Oletha, what happens to me now?"

"You have two choices, Joe. You have repaid a considerable amount of your karmic obligations, so you are free to move on to the Astral Plane where you can recover your strength before reincarnating once more. Or, you can return and clear your obligations completely before going to the Astral Plane."

"If I go back I'm not goin' ta get free of them blokes, are I?"

"No, Joe, you're not."

"So there's somethin' I'm supposed ta do, right?"

"Yes, Joe."

"You ain't goin' ta tell me, are ya?"

"No."

"Can I have a look at what's happenin' ta me at the moment?"

Oletha waved her hand and Joe saw his limp, bloodied body hanging from the chain.

"Cripes, I look a mess. Do ya know Oletha, I feel real sorry for them buggers down there. I actually pity them." Oletha gave a knowing smile as Joe continued. "What are all them black lines snakin' around Andy, Terry and that other feller?"

"They're the Unbalanced choices in life they've made."

"Do I have any of them black things on me?" Joe looked at her with a grief-stricken face.

"Yes, Joe, a couple."

"I want them gone, Oletha."

"Then you must return to remove them."

"How do I do that, remove them black things, I mean?" Joe asked anxiously.

"I know what you mean, Joe. All I can tell you is to follow your heart."

"I ain't lookin' forward ta this, 'cause that looks like it's gunna hurt real bad."

"You understand that your body will die, don't you, Joe?" Oletha said gently.

"Yeah, I just hope it ain't too painful, that's all. You better send me back now, before I change me mind."

"I will ease your passing, Joe, and escort you to the Astral Plane when the time comes."

"Oletha?"

"Yes, Joe?"

"Nothin'."

Oletha knew his feelings and with a loving thought in his mind she returned him to his body.

* * *

Laura and her team had heard everything and knew the house was compromised. She also knew Joe needed help and called for backup from uniformed police so as not to blow his cover. That sounded like one heck of a fight and it seemed as if Joe was winning.

Then everything went quiet; something was wrong. There was a fifth person giving orders and from what he was saying, Joe was unconscious. One of the squad members advised Laura that Joe was on the move and fast. If they didn't hurry they would lose contact. He was already out of range for the microphone to pick anything up. As she ran to her car, she was informed that they had just lost contact. She organised her team into four squads, giving each one an area in the last known vicinity of Joe's signal.

They wasted no time. Team two was the first to call in; they had picked up a faint signal heading south. The other three teams fanned out in a southerly direction hoping to intercept Joe's signal. Team one also received a signal but it was heading in a south-easterly direction towards the old industrial area. Laura advised all teams to focus their efforts on the abandoned factories.

It had taken two hours from the time they lost Joe's signal to identifying his location. They were now close enough to be able to pick up voices from Joe's hidden microphone.

"Well, Enoch, is he dead?" a voice said.

"No, Andy, he's a tough bastard."

"Can he talk?"

"Yeah, he'll talk."

Laura was recording the conversation as her people were surrounding the old steel mill. A groan of pain escaping Joe's lips as he regained consciousness was ample proof that the assault upon his body had taken its toll. His breathing was ragged and shallow, he was awash with blood and his eyes were so swollen they no longer opened. A bucket of water washed over his face.

"Joe, can you hear me? Joe, answer, can you hear me? Enoch do that healing thing you do. I want him revived enough to talk." Enoch placed his hand on Joe's bloodied body, sending waves of healing energy surging through it.

Slegna was pleased at his use of Joe's betrayal; if all went to plan, Enoch would be arrested and put into jail. There he could recruit the people he needed to do his bidding. He would see to it that Andy and the crooked cop Maleko escaped.

Laura was pushing everyone as fast as she could, the steel mill was now completely surrounded and she gave the order to move in.

"Joe," Andy called. "Can you hear me?"

"Yeah," Joe answered weakly.

"Who was the person you spoke to?"

"I'm sorry about Mick, Andy. I was just tryin' to knock ya on your arse."

"How could you betray me, Joe?" commented Andy.

"You're the one who betrayed me, Andy, you and Terry."

"I told ya ta call me Enoch!" Enoch screamed waving his fist at him.

"If that unfeeling arsehole Slegna couldn't get me ta do what he wanted, what makes you think you can?"

"What do ya mean?" screamed Enoch.

"I met Slegna and Oletha; she is the Mystery of the True Light. I was given a choice and I chose Oletha, 'cause she ain't cruel and unfeelin' like Slegna." With his head hung low, Joe struggled to explain. "I pity you and Andy, 'cause I seed what's around ya." Emanations of malevolence surrounded Enoch, Andy and Maleko as Slegna let them know the truth of Joe's words.

"Come on, Joe, tell me who ya been speaking ta and I'll have Enoch kill ya quick," Andy pleaded.

"I forgive ya both for what you done ta me. I deserve it after what happened ta Mick."

A voice Joe didn't know spoke close by. "He's not going to talk, kill him and be done with it." Joe was praying for death; he wanted to be with Oletha again free from his pain and suffering. A squealing sound had Maleko grabbing his two-way radio. He heard Laura giving commands to her team to enter the factory and arrest everyone.

"Enoch," Maleko screamed, "kill the traitor quick and get out of here. Andy, you come with me."

Maleko grabbed Andy and raced up the stairs leading to the roof. Hiding behind a collapsed chimneystack on the roof, Laura's squad didn't see them as they raced past in a bid to enter the factory. They had made good their escape.

Laura and her squad entered the factory as Enoch was swinging at Joe with an iron bar. A dozen voices all called, "Police, drop your weapon!"

Enoch froze in mid-swing; two officers threw Enoch bodily to the floor while reading him his rights. Laura raced over to Joe and, with help from Peter, gently lowered him to the floor.

"It would be quicker to take Joe to the hospital than to wait for an ambulance," Laura told Peter. Laura was aghast at Joe's condition. They carefully put him in a squad car and with sirens blaring drove to the closest hospital.

Laura had called ahead on her radio. An emergency team

met them as they pulled up at the entrance. Joe was placed on a trolley and quickly taken into one of the cubicles where the doctors examined him. While Laura was waiting outside the examination room she was going over in her mind the events that had taken place. She wished she had some idea who that other person was. Suddenly the doctor came from the room and looked at Laura.

"He's asking to see you, if you're Detective Laura?"

"I am," Laura acknowledged, realising she was becoming emotional. "How are his chances, Doc?"

"Poor at best. I've never seen anyone beaten so badly before. I don't know why he's still alive. We're transferring him to surgery right away," said the doctor.

Laura entered the cubicle to find Joe being attended by two nurses and another doctor. They were working to stem the flow of blood and pack his wounds till they could transfer him to surgery. Joe was constantly calling out for Laura.

"I'm here, Joe," she said, steadying her voice.

His arm reached out to find her. Taking his hand in hers she held it firmly.

"I want ya ta have me totem. It's been lucky for me, and me money's ta go ta the beat-up lady. Tell her I tried ta help."

"Come on, Joe. The doctors will pull you through," Laura choked out somehow.

"I got somethin' ta tell ya." Joe relayed his experience with Oletha and Slegna.

"So ya see it's time for me ta go now, 'cause Oletha's waitin' for me and I'm real tired. Thank ya for all ya done for me."

Joe slipped from life, freeing himself from his physical agony. Oletha was there and escorted him to the Astral Plane in a state of peace.

Laura stood holding Joe's hand until a nurse caringly removed it from hers. She escorted her from the cubicle, sitting her on a chair at the nurse's station. She was surprised when the nurse handed her a tissue. Tears were streaming down her face. Wiping her face and clearing her throat, she nodded to the nurse and left the hospital wondering about Joe's explanation of Oletha and Slegna.

* * *

The day was bright and sunny after the dramatic encounter involving Kyros and Slegna. Kyros, Harpreet, Barbette and the chosen ones were asked to attend a meeting of the elders to discuss the future likelihood of such a disaster happening again.

Kyros was up bright and early checking on Nathanial's condition. On his return to the guesthouse he found everyone sitting around a large table talking.

"Harpreet, may I have a look at your pendant, please?"

"Of course, Renae, although I'm unable to remove it, as you are aware."

Renae gently ran her fingers down the chain and over the pendant admiring its beauty.

"It's exquisite," she observed.

"The interesting thing is, when I bend forward it stays in place," Harpreet told them.

"Oh, by the way, Harpreet, welcome to the Order of the Phelan," remarked Renae.

"Yes, Harpreet, welcome," Lon acknowledged.

"Kyros! I thought you would still be sleeping after last night's drama?"

"No, I had to check on Nathanial and my name is Lon to my friends and family, Harpreet."

Lon approached Janelle and presented her with a pair of moccasins that seemed to appear from nowhere. "I believe you will find these comfortable and they will protect your feet."

"Why Lon, that's kind of you, but you know I don't like wearing footwear?" she said, surprised.

"They're not like normal footwear, Janelle. Please try them on. If you don't like them, then you don't have to wear them."

Janelle made herself comfortable and placed the moccasins on her feet. She then walked around the room. "Oh Lon, these are wonderful; it's as if I'm still barefoot. How can I ever thank you?"

"The joy on your face is enough," he replied.

Gela came up and put her arms around Lon. "Well, my little Phelan, how are you this morning?" he asked.

"Very well, husband mine," Gela responded.

Everyone in the room burst out laughing at Lon's expression.

"Had you forgotten that Oletha married us last night, my love?"

"She's right, you know, Lon," Lomasi commented. "You're

an old married man now. Oletha's exact words were: 'I join you together as one, to be forever united in love'. How romantic, and to have Oletha to reign over your wedding. You're married big-time now, mister, or you will have to answer to Oletha," Lomasi finished.

"Lon, are you all right?" Harpreet asked as she untangled Gela from around his waist and sat him down.

"I think he's in shock," Renae responded for him.

A slow smile spread across Lon's face as he looked at Gela.

"If we're married, then that means, I mean we can, we're allowed to..."

"Lon! I think you've said quite enough," Gela replied, blushing.

"Would you all excuse my wife and me while we become acquainted about certain arrangements?" he said, as he caught Gela in an embrace and vanished in a flash of light leaving everyone in stunned silence.

"I didn't know he could disappear like that, did you, Fala?"

"No, Gabbryel, I didn't."

"I wonder where they went and if they're enjoying getting into mischief."

"Janelle!" Gabbryel answered, shocked.

"What? Oh, come on, they're not children."

"Well, wherever they are, I hope they remember we have a meeting with the elders this morning."

"Don't worry, Harpreet, they're both responsible adults."

"Come on Renae, would you be responsible if you were either one of them at the moment?" asked Harpreet, smiling.

CHAPTER TWELVE

Lon and Gela appeared on a world of such beauty that Gela could barely speak. "Oh my," she whispered. "Where are we, Lon?"

"This is the world of the Phelan; the weather here is quite clement all year round. Oletha asked me to attend to someone who is unwell and I thought you would like to celebrate our marriage in an atmosphere of peace."

The look on Lon's face informed her there was something he wasn't saying. "All right, husband, out with it," she admonished.

Lon took her hand in his and smiling, asked. "Does nudity bother you?"

"What are you up to, husband?" Gela moved uneasily.

"Nothing like that," Lon said, laughing. "It's just that the Phelan don't wear clothes; their bodies are covered with exceptionally fine hair so clothes aren't necessary. They're a beautiful species."

Lon held Gela's hand as they walked along a path that wound through the forest. The sounds of wildlife filled the air and the flora dazzled the senses. Hauntingly beautiful songs with unfamiliar words drifted on the breeze creating sensations of joy that gently moved throughout Gela's being.

Without realising, she started singing. Her voice was pure and the songs she sang were from the operas she had attended with her foster parents. She had been trained in singing from childhood. However, since the time when her family died in an accident on the way to see her perform, she had lost the heart for singing and had forgotten how much it had meant to her.

Tears were streaming down Gela's cheeks as she recalled her parents' pride and joy in her singing achievements. Now, she sang with a full heart, expressing the joy of love she felt for Lon. She moved from one song to another, using all the nuances of sound to articulate the songwriter's words to perfection.

They had stopped in a small glade not long after Gela started singing. She turned to face Lon as she sang and his eyes filled with tears for the love she was expressing through her songs. When the last note ended, Lon went down on one knee before her and, clearing the emotion from his voice he spoke. "Oh Gela," he began holding her hands in his while gazing into her face through moistened eyes, "I wish I could find the words to express the loveliness I see before me, for you are more beautiful that you can possibly imagine." Tears of joy were running down his cheeks as he continued. "I humbly request the honour of being your husband and ask that you accept my proposal of love. I promise to be as supportive as I know how and share all that I am with you."

Gela kneeled down to join her husband. "Oh Lon," she replied, tears filling her eyes. "I would be proud to be your wife and share my life with you and I promise to be as supportive as I know how and share all that I am with you too, my darling."

Silence filled their small glade as they became aware that the Phelan surrounded them. Gela observed the Phelan carefully; they had the same human form as Lon and she had. There was no mistaking male from female as it was quite obvious. Their appearance was striking as the sun's rays glinted on the fine golden hair that covered their bodies.

Some of the Phelan wore coloured bands around their heads, while others had strings of beads around their necks, wrists and ankles. A well-built man with a beaded neck choker stepped forward. Lon and Gela stood and walked towards him, bowing slightly. Lon spoke. "This is my wife Gela and I am Kyros. We're disciples of Oletha come to see to the wellbeing of Larlene."

"I be Seanan, one of the elders and you be welcome," he said, speaking with a lilt to his voice. "Would you be following me to the village to meet the rest of the elders then?"

"We would be honoured."

"Honoured is it? I've never been honoured before. We best be off then; if you be following me, we be on our way. Gela, is it?" Seanan commented looking directly at her. "You be having a fine singing voice there."

"Thank you, Seanan. I haven't had much call to sing for a long time. Your beautiful world and the sound of your voices reawakened my love for singing."

"Would you be giving the clan the pleasure of hearing you sing later?"

"I would be delighted to, Seanan," Gela responded.

The village was only a short walk from the glade. Arriving at the outskirts they saw simple huts made from clay and straw with thatched roofs. Children were playing happily and many of the adults were singing as they worked.

"Seanan, I would like to see Larlene first, please," Kyros informed him.

"To be sure, she be just over there in that hut," he indicated. "You'll be finding her mate with her."

Walking into the hut they found it to be simply a place to keep dry from the rain or to sleep; there were no furnishings. Woven reeds formed mats that served as floor coverings with thick soft leaves six feet long and four feet wide interwoven as a sleeping mattress. This lay along the far wall where Larlene was lying with a man next to her who was wiping her head with a damp cloth.

The pink skin and golden hair that was evident in a healthy Phelan wasn't so in Larlene. Her skin was pale beneath mustard hair and her body trembled with every breath as she tossed from side to side. Seanan walked over to the man and spoke quietly to him and then beckoned for Kyros and Gela to approach.

"This is my wife Gela and I'm Kyros. May I attend your lady?"

"My name be Sim and me wife be Larlene and I be thanking you for caring."

Kyros produced Malachy in the form of a Staff and moved him across Larlene's body and then laid him lengthwise beside her. He placed one hand on her head and the other over her solar plexus while intoning a mantra of healing. Then he walked from the hut.

"Are you going to be telling me how my mate be then?" Sim asked worriedly.

"I detected a poison moving through her body. I want you to have her drink as much water as possible to help flush it out. She will recover, Sim, so don't worry. I will return before nightfall to check on her again."

"I be thanking you for your kindness and will be returning to my mate."

Seanan was waiting outside the hut for Kyros and Gela. Having heard the prognosis he escorted them to the waiting elders, who were sitting in council. The council met in a circle of trees in a clearing close to the village. Upon entering they were shown to their place and the leader for the clan commenced the introductions.

"My name be Derron and I be the spokesperson for the clan. We be welcoming you and thanking you for the healing you be giving to Larlene," he stated, inclining his head towards Kyros.

"I am Kyros, Oletha's disciple, as is Gela my wife and we are glad to be of service to your clan. There is a matter I would like to put before the elders. Would this be an appropriate time?" Lon enquired.

"We be listening to what you be saying."

"I humbly request approval to establish a centre of healing for your clan and my family, upon your world. Your healers would attend classes in the healing arts that my family and I shall conduct. We would be completely autonomous, having no vested interest in the running of your clan or the way in which you conduct your life."

Derron seemed ecstatic at Kyros's request, as did the other council members. "Kyros, Oletha be telling us of your greatness; whatever you be wanting is yours."

"Derron, I am no greater than you and deserve only the respect you elders receive for the knowledge you have gained over time. Do not place me or mine above you, for we are all Oletha's children."

"Aye, that be true. Your words be having much wisdom," agreed Derron. "You and your family be welcome here. Now to the land you be needing for your home of healing; we not be owning it, you see, so I can't be giving it to you. You have to be asking the land herself."

Kyros nodded and brought forward his Staff, planting it firmly before him. Malachy extended his roots deep into the earth, asking permission to construct a house of healing and then reverted to his masculine form. All present sat in stunned silence at Malachy's transformation.

"Kyros, this world calls herself Terrene and she asked that the Phelan call her by her true name," Malachy conveyed. "She advises me that all spiritual essences upon and within her body are in agreement with a healing centre."

"Malachy, inform Terrene that healing is offered to all the

spiritual essences that abide within and upon her gracious beauty." Kyros then addressed the elders. "To you elders, the land is named Terrene and she would like you to call her by her true name when you talk to her."

"Tell her we be honoured and proud to be doing so," Derron announced respectfully.

"She acknowledges your response and requests that your clan observe the construction of your centre of healing," Malachy replied and then returned to his Staff form.

Kyros rose and held his hand out to Gela and they walked in the direction that Malachy had been given. At the far end of the village was a forest so dense that entry was impossible and behind the forest was a mountain range. Holding Malachy, Kyros stood facing the forest. The trees seemed to move forming a canopied pathway four feet wide and one hundred feet long. The pathway emerged onto the outskirts and mid-centre of an enormous open area in the shape of a crescent moon and directly opposite, a thousand paces away, was the mountain face.

Kyros, Gela and the Phelan walked to the base of the mountain where Kyros touched his Staff to the rock face. He then retreated to a safe distance and waited. There was an awed breath from the Phelan as the side of the mountain gave way, sending rocks and soil crashing down. The earth rumbled, heaved and then sank, taking most of the debris from the rockslide with it. An enormous circular cavity was formed. Water started pouring from the top where the rockslide began, forming a waterfall that filled the cavity below, while the overflow descended into an underground stream.

Everyone stood in amazement as the water washed away the loose soil, revealing the crystals beneath. The whole rockslide and the pool beneath were inundated with hundreds of different crystals. Rainbows danced within the mist of the waterfall as the sun's rays shone a warm glow upon all.

"You aren't afraid of heights, are you, dear?" Lon asked Gela.

"No, love, why?" she asked, wondering what he was going to do next.

"Your wedding present, my love," he informed her with a smile and a wink. "A penthouse apartment."

Kyros walked to the centre of the crescent, removed a seed from his Staff and planted it. A tree immediately grew defying all the natural boundaries of nature. With a base that covered half the size of the open area of the crescent and reaching hundreds of feet into the sky, it was magnificent.

Encircling the tree was a covered walkway leading to seven enormous branches above. Amid the branches, limbs grew gracefully in all directions.

Kyros smiled and started climbing the steps, indicating for all to follow. When everyone was standing on the first of the seven main branches he turned to Gela.

"Four rooms do you think, my love?"

"That would depend on whether meals are being prepared on the premises or not," she replied cheekily.

"Four and a half then," Lon confirmed. "One for sleeping with a washroom adjoining it, another for recreation and meals, the forth as a private study and the half as a pantry and preparation area."

Kyros tapped his Staff on the branch and then intoned a mantra. At the centre of the enormous branch, smaller branches formed walls that continued growing to create a domed roof with vines that intertwined throughout the entire structure, creating natural insulation and soundproofing. Lon indicated for Gela to enter and inspect the premises.

"What do you think, love? Are you happy with the design?"

"Yes, dear, it's lovely," she said, as she walked through to each room in awe of its creation. "There is ample space in all the rooms and they're large enough for comfort," Gela explained gently running her hand over the walls.

"Then I will make the next five homes identical."

Kyros began intoning the mantra of making, as each small home appeared upon the following five branches. When he had finished, he took Gela by the hand and started climbing. When they reached the seventh branch he asked Gela what she would like.

"How many rooms can I have?" she asked timidly.

"You can have as many rooms as you will use," Lon replied.

"Then I would like one extra room as a council room for the family and it can double as an extra study."

"Is that all, my love?"

"Yes, any more would be frivolous and wasteful," Gela replied.

Kyros nodded, tapped his Staff and intoned the mantra of making. Their home appeared before their eyes. "Would you like carpet or polished floors, Gela?"

"Carpet in the bedroom, study and council room, polished floors everywhere else, I think," she answered.

Tapping his Staff, vines snaked across all the floors where Gela requested carpet, knitting together so tightly that the joins were invisible. Sap then oozed up from the branch in all the other rooms spreading thinly across the floor until it was covered. Kyros tapped the Staff once more and the sap hardened, leaving a golden shine on the floor.

"It's beautiful and the vines are so soft underfoot, just like carpet. We will need windows and doors, dear."

"If you show me where you wish the windows and what size, I'll arrange it so."

Gela went through the home indicating the size and shape of the windows she wanted. The doors were large leaves that rolled up to open and unrolled to close. Kyros then created furniture to Gela's design throughout their penthouse. Gela hugged her husband before showing the ladies present her new home.

Kyros walked outside, stood in an open area clear of the doorway and drew a circle eight feet across. Tapping his Staff he intoned another mantra. The circle glowed but then dimmed, as transport portals appeared outside the seven homes and at the base of the tree.

Kyros envisaged the rooms required for his centre of healing and what they would be used for. The Phelan were watching in amazement as Kyros then constructed an entire community of rooms in varying shapes and sizes with connecting hallways within the forest that surrounded the area of the crescent. There were suites for the healers, cubicles for the unwell, kitchens, dining rooms and visitors' quarters.

Vines snaked throughout the entire complex, interlacing the walls and roof, as well as forming a durable floor covering. The ground heaved and separated as luminescent crystals appeared in all shapes and sizes to form a pile four feet high. These, Kyros distributed throughout the walkway, hallways and rooms. Pointing his Staff to the ground within the crescent, thick lush green grass grew to cover the entire area.

Kyros climbed down from the tree and walked to one side of the crescent across from the waterfall. There he entered a large room. The wall to the right had ten bamboo poles evenly spaced growing from the ground to the ceiling. Tapping each of them at a height of seven feet with his Staff, Kyros triggered a continual spray of warm water that emanated from a slit in the bamboo. He then took two steps back and touched the vine-covered floor, allowing it to slope downward towards the wall. The water that was spraying from the bamboo ran back into the earth.

Moving to the centre of the room, he extended his Staff and drew an oval on the ground twenty feet long and twelve feet wide. The earth within the oval sank from sight leaving a cavity four feet deep. Rose quartz emerged to line the bottom, sides and two feet around the top of the oval. Hot mineral water bubbled to the surface through small holes to fill the cavity entirely.

"Can I be asking you what that be, Kyros?" Seanan enquired.

"On the far wall is a shower to wash under and the pool is called a spa. You use the shower before entering the spa. It is very therapeutic and most relaxing. Please, Seanan, try it for yourself."

Seanan did as Kyros suggested, showering first and then lowering himself into the spa.

"This be wonderful relaxing. How often would you be using it?"

"Whenever you feel the need. Please, anyone who wishes may join Seanan." Around thirty men, women and children raced to the showers so they could join Seanan in the spa.

While many of the Phelan were enjoying the spa, Kyros went to the next room. This one was altogether different. The door was so small that a person must crawl to enter and directly opposite the door at the back wall was a small well filled with water with a ladle protruding from it. The room was circular with a curved ceiling that was too low for standing and there were no crystal lights.

Six coloured leaves hung from the middle of the roof. Kyros hit the ground with the Staff directly under the coloured leaves and a hollow appeared, holding seven rocks that glowed red from the heat. He leaned across, took a ladle of water and poured it over the rocks. Steam rose, filling the room with a moist heat. He nodded to himself and left, tapping his Staff on the doorframe so that a large leaf appeared as the door.

Seanan was standing outside when he emerged. "What be that room for, Kyros?"

"That is a sweat lodge. It is for the purification of the spirit and mind and it also helps cleanse the body of impurities."

"This be a remarkable place you have built for our clan and your family."

"You're welcome, Seanan. Is your herbalist here?"

"I be getting her for you, Kyros." Seanan walked off, returning moments later with a woman beside him. "This be Norleen."

Before Kyros stood a woman of middle years; knowledge shone brightly in her eyes. Her hands seemed no stranger to work and her body was firm and well disciplined. "Hello, Norleen, I'm Kyros and I would like you to accompany me as I have something for you and your clan."

Kyros, Norleen and Seanan walked to the other side of the crescent to where the forest met the mountain. Kyros then extended his Staff and the forest parted forming another covered walkway leading to a sizeable herb garden with a home on one side.

"This is for you, Norleen. You won't have to forage any longer for the herbs you need; they are all here. I place the care and maintenance of them in your capable hands. That house you see has rooms large enough to accommodate your whole family and there are separate rooms for drying and preparing your herbs. Please feel free to move in."

Norleen looked at Kyros with tear-filled eyes and sank to her knees in gratitude. Kyros raised her to her feet. "It is an honour for me to help a fellow healer."

"You not be knowing the joy in my heart, Kyros. Your gift be beyond repayment."

"Seeing your joy is enough, Norleen. Now, do you know where I left my wife?"

Norleen and Seanan laughed at Kyros's humour as they returned to the tree to find Gela chatting with a group of women.

"Seanan," Kyros asked, "would you mind if I addressed the clan?"

"It be our pleasure, Kyros," he replied.

"All healers will find rooms relating to their specific skills within the surrounding structure. I would like each of you to examine your facilities with your apprentices and let me know if anything more is required. Gela, can you think of anything that could be helpful?"

"I was just saying to Mirna and Laidan that some tables and chairs would come in handy scattered about the grass for study and recreation purposes."

"All right, love, where would you like them and how many?"

Gela conferred with Mirna and Laidan and then pointed to several locations. Kyros tapped his Staff so that tables and chairs appeared where requested. Gela smiled in appreciation. Kyros signalled to Gela and they moved over to the crystal pool that received the waterfall. He removed a sapphire from the pool and then moved to the tree and embedded it into its trunk, after which he addressed the Phelan.

"The tree before you is for my family and me. An energy field surrounds it that won't allow anyone to climb the stairs without an invitation. I have embedded a sapphire crystal into the tree; if you wish to speak to me, simply touch the crystal and talk. I will hear you and answer. The crystal will glow when I'm present. Are there any questions?"

"What you be calling this place you built and what be your clan's name?" enquired Seanan.

"I call this, 'Hospice of Life'. My clan was named after a discussion I had with Oletha. I call them the Order of the Phelan out of respect for your way of life and in dedication to Terrene."

"You honour us, Kyros."

"No, Seanan, it is the other way round. There are many worlds that harbour great unrest. There is a crusade looming against Oletha and by her command my clan and I are her defence. Your world is a sanctuary of peace, living in the grace of Oletha's protection. This is where we will come to rest, regroup and discuss our next move. Oletha has placed seals around your world so no one can ever disturb your way of life. This way you remain protected."

"Are other worlds really that bad, Kyros?" asked an unknown voice.

"This be my mate, Riona," Seanan interjected.

"Pleased to meet you, Riona, and to answer your question, yes. The world I come from is so violent that it is not safe for people to walk alone. Women are not respected for the gift of life they can give. There is no sense of family and even parents molest their children. It's cruel and heartless in places and this is where the campaign against the Unbalanced will be decided."

"It be sounding a wretched and lonely place to live. My heart be saddened for their loss of faith in life and I be weeping for their children," Riona said sorrowfully.

"There are many who love Oletha and would change the situation if they could, but they're afraid," Kyros answered.

"If they be meeting her, how can they be doing those horrible things?"

"No one on my world has ever met her. They think of her as the Mystery of the True Light, something that is out of reach, a myth. Many have no morals; they misinterpret morality as cultural rather than a personal responsibility," Kyros said sadly.

"You and I know that morality is a spiritual state of being. It isn't something you learn – it's in the way that you live. People demonstrate their morality by the love in their hearts. Many are afraid to follow their hearts in case they are laughed at or ridiculed."

"I would be hearing more of this, Kyros, but this be not the time. I be letting you go about your business."

"You are welcome, Riona. We will speak again if you wish."

"I be wishing it," Riona said, while directing Seanan towards their home. "Come on, Seanan, we be letting Kyros have time with his mate."

"We be finished here, Kyros?"

"Yes, Seanan. I am sorry to have held your people from their tasks so long."

"This night you and Gela be attending a celebration in respect of your gift, the Hospice of Life, and the joy of your company, whereupon we be hearing your lovely mate sing."

"It would be our pleasure, thank you," Kyros answered.

Seanan and the other elders hustled the clan to their appointed tasks, leaving Kyros and Gela alone. Lon looked at Gela and smiled. He beckoned her to join him and stepped onto the disc at the base of the tree.

"I have created transport portals throughout the tree and at its base. I want you to think of our new home." Gela did as she was asked; they vanished but then reappeared on the branch outside their front door.

"Each member of the Order of the Phelan has a transport portal outside their front door. When they arrive I will complete their homes and show them their portals. This means that no matter which world they're on, they can return to their own quarters." Kyros enfolded Gela in a warm embrace, kissing her gently on her forehead. "Are you happy with your home, my love?"

"A penthouse apartment!" Gela said, shaking her head. "The views are incredible! Lon," Gela queried, "every now and then I hear someone breathing and I have the impression we're not alone."

"That's because we're not alone. Our home is alive. It has thoughts and feelings because it's part of the One Tree.

The seed came from Malachy, who is of the One Tree of Consciousness, so our thoughts, feelings and actions will be felt by this tree."

"I see; we can't keep calling it 'The Tree'; does it have a name?"

Malachy changed from the Staff to his masculine form and responded to Gela's question. "The name by which she is called is Photinah."

"Photinah, that's an interesting name. Well, Photinah, I wish to thank you for our lovely home and for allowing us to live within your embrace," expressed Gela.

Photinah's leaves shook in response to Gela's courteousness. She then entered their home with Malachy and Lon.

"Lon, I want to learn to meditate like you do so I can go to the crystal world and be at one with the emerald crystal."

"Oletha gave Harpreet that task, my love."

"Please Lon, I feel an urgency about it," Gela stressed.

Lon and Malachy merged together, leaving Lon standing before her. The look Lon gave Gela was stern and unwavering. Finally, he spoke. "As Malachy I recognise your situation and agree."

Lon then explained the origins of Oletha, the birth of Chimera and that Gaia was the spiritual heart of Oletha: "We are all an angelic awareness of Oletha called souls and our eternal spirits were created by the soul to travel throughout the realms of Chimera to learn the consequences of our actions."

"It may sound strange, Lon, but since Oletha empowered us with the True Light, I feel I know all this."

"That's how I was feeling at times when Harpreet was teaching me."

Lon then explained the disc meditation technique and asked if she understood.

"While you're talking I can feel the truth of your words, which makes it easy to follow the philosophy. As for the meditation, I understand the technique."

"Well, my love, I have a house call to make. I will leave you with one piece of advice; allow yourself to do the best you can in this moment in time. Don't try to do your best, because trying is an element of failure. I will leave you here to practise."

"Sweetheart, I do love you. You know, all you needed to say was, don't try, merely allow yourself to succeed," Gela replied, smiling.

Malachy separated from Lon as they walked to the portal and vanished, reappearing at the base of the tree. "She's right, you know, you do tend to lecture instead of teach," Malachy commented.

"Seeing as you're so knowledgeable at the moment, you can convey a message to Terrene, thanking all who have contributed to making the Hospice of Life."

Malachy chuckled and communicated the message. The earth beneath Lon's feet rumbled its acknowledgement. Lon made his way to Larlene's residence to check on her progress. He tapped on the side of the hut before entering. Sim was in the process of giving his mate some water.

"I not be wanting any more water, I be drowning in it."

"I be sorry but you must be drinking it," Sim firmly announced.

"Hello, Larlene. I'm Kyros and this is Malachy. You may not remember us, as you were delirious the last time we saw you. How are you feeling?"

"If this man of mine be stopping pouring water down my throat every time I be opening my mouth I be much better, thank you."

"That is my doing. I asked him to flush the poisons from your body by making you drink as much water as possible. I am pleased he has done just that; otherwise, you would have died. Small price to pay, don't you think?"

"I be not meaning to be disrespectful, but I be about to burst and can't go. If you be understanding my meaning?"

"I understand perfectly and that is why I am here. Sim, we need to take Larlene to the place where you relieve your bodily functions."

Kyros and Malachy helped Larlene to the appropriate place where Kyros placed his hand over her solar plexus and intoned a healing mantra. Larlene's body immediately released all the built-up toxins with such a rush they had to support her from collapsing. Once she was finished they took her to the river to bathe and then returned to their hut.

"Kyros, I not be thanking you and Malachy for all you be doing for me," Larlene said, inclining her head toward them, feeling uncomfortable with her earlier behaviour.

"How may I repay you?"

"Larlene, the only payment I want is to see you well and healthy."

"My mate be right, Kyros. I be mourning my loss if it not be for you," Sim gratefully acknowledged.

"There is a feast this night and I would be pleased if my wife and I could share the meal with you. I would like her to meet you both."

Kyros leaned forward and placed his hand on Larlene's forehead, whereupon her eyes closed and she slept.

"When she awakens she'll be completely recovered and can return to her regular duties."

"I be thanking you. Can I be asking you a question, Kyros?"

"Of course, Sim, what is it?"

"My mate of late, well, she be snappish and unhappy. Would that have been the illness you be thinking?"

"Some of it would have been. I will have my wife speak to her; she is very good in these matters."

Sim nodded and Lon and Malachy walked back to see how Gela was getting on with her meditation. They decided a climb would be good for them and started up the steps. By the time they had arrived home Lon was puffing. Gela was busy doing things in her new home and singing merrily.

"Hello, darling, you're sounding a little out of breath."

"I decided to take the stairs."

"We'll have to get you fitter if you run out of breath walking up a couple of stairs, sweetheart." Malachy burst out laughing.

"A couple of stairs! I'll have you know there are over seven hundred steps to this penthouse of ours," Lon protested.

"Really?" Gela pretended surprise.

"The first floor is a hundred feet from the ground and every floor is a hundred feet above the one below it, and ... and ... you're stirring me, you little minx."

"Yes, I am and you bite so well too. Doesn't he, Malachy?"

"Don't answer that; in fact, back in your bottle, genie." Still laughing Malachy became one with Lon once more.

Lon grabbed Gela and gave her a hug and then stepped back with a look of surprise on his face. "You've done it and you are keeping it perfectly balanced."

"It wasn't that hard, Lon, I just allowed myself to do it."

"Gela, do you know how long it took me to master how to maintain what you're doing so effortlessly?" he said, feeling a little miffed and proud of her achievement all at the same time.

"No, love, and I don't think you're going to tell me."

"You're right, I'm not. If you can continue this from now until we return here this evening, then you can go to the World of Crystal in the morning. I had to volunteer you as a marriage counsellor for Sim and Larlene. She's unhappy about being unable to fall pregnant, but she hasn't told Sim. I felt that if she spoke to you she would feel better."

"There's something you're not saying. What is it?" Gela prompted.

"It's a feeling, nothing more. Come on, it's time for the celebration."

Lon and Gela arrived as the last of the food was being distributed around the common eating area. It was a simple affair of fruits, raw vegetables, water and fruit juices. Everyone wandered about, talking, eating and laughing. It reminded Gela of a gala occasion rather than the evening meals she was used to that were all formal, no fun. During the course of the evening Gela spoke with Larlene and Sim. Once the food had been consumed, the singing started.

Gela stood in the centre of a large circle formed by the Phelan where she entertained them with a variety of songs they had never heard before. They clapped, hooted, howled and slapped the ground for more every time she stopped. Finally the evening drew to a close and everyone retired to their quarters.

"Do you have any idea how enormously proud of you I am, my love?" Lon commented as they snuggled up in bed. "Your musical talent is incredible; I'm surprised you didn't take up singing as a career."

"I was going to until my parents died," came a sad reply. "Anyway," she continued happily, snuggling deeper into his arms, "if I had, I would never have met you."

"I want to thank you for the comforting words you gave Larlene and Sim. It was just what they needed to hear." Lon suddenly rolled over to look into her eyes. "And your ability to successfully maintain the silver discs throughout the evening is quite impressive," he finished proudly.

The night was warm and comfortable as they snuggled

deeper into each other's embrace; no bed coverings were needed as they drifted into a blissful sleep.

The next morning they awoke bright and refreshed. Gela prepared a meal of fruits for breakfast and placed it on the table on the balcony. Having finished their meal and drunk water to clean the palette, it was time for Gela to leave. Looking deeply into his eyes she rested her hand on his.

"Lon, darling, it's time for me to leave."

"Yes, love I know," he replied, feeling nervous for her.

"Any advice would be gratefully received," Gela prompted.

"Love isn't just the greatest force in creation; it is creation."

"That's it?"

"Well, I didn't want to give you a lecture on the morning of your departure," Lon said, smiling.

"I see," Gela replied, unsure how to interpret his remark.

"We have talked about everything Harpreet and I spoke on and how I blended with the crystal, so all that you need is within you. You know where you're going and how to return."

Gela smiled warmly, knowing Lon was concerned for her. They embraced for a moment and then she moved to the transport portal and was gone.

CHAPTER THIRTEEN

Gela appeared on a world completely devoid of plant life, having planned her arrival in the evening at Lon's suggestion. She formed the silver discs about her chakras and started walking in the direction her instincts told her. She had been walking for around two hours through the most exquisite formations of crystals when her awareness tingled so intently she thought something was crawling on her.

Hearing the sound of running water she went towards it and found an emerald river dropping out of sight through a sinkhole. On the bank of the river was an outcrop of emerald crystals six feet high. Walking up to it she admired its beauty and then gave it a hug.

"Oh, how beautiful you are! My name is Gela and I long to be at one with you. Think of all the worlds we could visit together and the love we could share. My husband came here and joined his essence with the Clan Sapphire and I would like to share my essence with you."

Gela was so caught up in her emotional outpouring that she was unaware the ground beneath her feet was giving way. By the time she felt it moving, it was too late and she had plummeted down the embankment into the swirling emerald river and was being dragged towards the sinkhole.

It happened so fast she hardly had time to catch her breath before being pulled under. Panic assaulted her mind as she was sucked down the sinkhole. The river finally exited through an opening in the side of a mountain, as did Gela, to fall twenty feet into the basin below.

Battered, bruised, with cuts all over her body, she finally pulled herself free of the river, spluttering crystal liquid from her mouth. Her chest started to pound and pain assaulted her body in so many ways that her mind was screaming.

She never dreamed it could be like this, even with what Lon had told her. She had to rebalance her thoughts. Ignoring the racking torment her body was going through, she re-established the silver discs around her chakras. Gela remembered Lon's words about love being creation and poured the love of Oletha into her heart chakra.

The silver disc around her heart chakra was turning green, her mind was slipping and something else was taking over. Screaming aloud to maintain control of her mind, she felt herself weakening and realised that to fight was to lose.

Opening herself up completely and allowing the essence to flow through her, while saturating her being with the love of Oletha, was the only hope. She allowed the silver to blend with the emerald that was surging throughout her body. Time had no meaning to her, as every time the emerald would try to override her, she would submerge herself deeper within Oletha's love.

Finally the heart chakra transformed into a beautiful

glistening silver green. The struggle continued until Gela realised that all she need do was fill the heart chakra to overflowing. By doing this, love would automatically flow into all the other chakras. She had poured so much loving energy through the heart chakra that there was no more resistance. Silver energy shot skyward while a shaft of green energy shot earthward as the transformation of the final chakras was completed. Gela came to her senses at the sound of a voice talking to her.

"Hello, Gela, I am Me-i, voice of the crystal. You can open your eyes now as you have blended with the crystal in the way you wanted."

Gela opened her eyes, not believing what she saw. Where once there had been crystal now she could see people, buildings, flowers, shrubs and trees. A whole society was about her.

"Hello, Me-i. You truly have a beautiful world," she said, feeling strangely empowered.

"Thank you. So Lon is your partner. Did he retrieve the Staff at all?"

"Yes," she said, moving closer to Me-i. "They are Malachy, although he is called Kyros."

"How are you feeling?" Me-i asked, while indicating to her staff to organise their equipment.

"A little unusual and slightly disoriented, I think," Gela commented.

"That's to be expected. It's time for you to leave."

"How long have I been here?"

"In our time you've only just arrived, in your time three years."

"What!" Gela exclaimed with a shocked expression. "Lon will be worried out of his mind."

"No, he won't. Didn't he explain how to return?"

"Oh yes, but three years, Me-i. I must have been a slow learner," Gela said worriedly.

"On the contrary, I will walk you to the portal. Let Kyros know you are both invited to watch the next blending."

Arriving at the portal, Gela gave Me-i a hug. Me-i laughed. "Lon did the same thing. Do you also like hugging crystals, Gela?"

"It's something we do to people whom we think of as friends," she explained, smiling.

Gela stepped on the portal and disappeared, reappearing on Photinah's enormous branch outside her home on Terrene.

* * *

Lon was sitting on the edge of the branch with his legs dangling over the sides when Gela appeared.

"Do you know, love, I think I should construct a balustrade around the perimeters of all the homes so no one will fall off. What do you think?"

"Well, hello to you too, my love."

Rising to his feet Lon turned to his wife. He had a smile that lit up his face. "I'm so proud to be your husband, Gela, and I'm proud of you. Please don't take this the wrong way, my love, but you have aged. However, you are more resplendent than ever."

Lon took Gela in his embrace and gently caressed her beautiful face, and then kissed her lips. He reached for Malachy and placed him outside the front door. Lifting her into his arms he carried her into their bedroom.

With slow deliberate moves he silently began undressing her, admiring the form of her body with every delicate caress, as her dress slipped from her shoulders. Loving hands moved down the nape of her neck, over her shoulders to glide down her back, returning to caress her face once more. Running his hands through her golden hair, he tilted her head slightly and kissed her passionately. She returned his embrace with equal passion.

Separating from her, he removed his garments, drawing Gela closer. He released the ties of her undergarments allowing them to fall away. Encircling his arms about her he raised her within his embrace and then moved to their bed, laying her gently upon it. Lon lay on his side, his hand supporting her head while tenderly kissing her lips as his other hand explored the contours of her body. Running his hand caringly over her breast and feeling her body responding, he encircled his lips about her nipple allowing his tongue to lovingly embrace her.

Gela's breath quickened as her body responded to his tenderness. Moving from her breasts his lips caressed down the fullness of her body to linger about her groin. Sliding his hands along her inner thighs he gently separated her legs, allowing his mouth full contact with her lower lips. A quick intake of breath escaped Gela's mouth as his tongue stroked her inner lips. As his fingers adoringly explored her lower body his tongue found her place of pleasure. Her breath hastened and her back arched as his finger found its way inside her to the deeper secret place.

Her hands were reaching for him as she rose in an arc from the bed, wave after wave of pleasure assailing her mind and body. She cried out in blissful delight and as her passion intensified Lon tenderly joined his body to hers.

The feelings were exquisite as she responded to his every move. Her joy was heightened with his loving touch, as each stroke of his body in hers lifted her to greater passion. Their spirits soared and Lon expressed in words his love for her.

Trembling with ecstasy, her body finally reached its peak. Moving his body in harmony with the waves of her passion, Lon allowed her to rise again and again to the pinnacle of elation. When she could take no more, he joined her as they climaxed together in a state of ecstasy.

The rapture they felt transcended anything either of them had ever experienced. As they lay in each other's embrace, Gela felt the truth of Lon's love on all levels. She could never have imagined that love like this was possible. Lon interrupted her thoughts when he spoke.

"Gela, my love, you have the most incredible green eyes."

"Thank you," she replied, looking up from his embrace.

"Did you know that your eyes glisten when you're expressing your feelings?" she remarked gently.

"Is that what you call what we were doing, expressing feelings?" Lon asked.

Their conversation was interrupted by Malachy's laughter.

"What are you laughing at, my friend?" Lon asked him.

"You have obviously forgotten Kyros that we are connected. What you feel, I feel and Oletha infused us of her essence, which means we have the ability to create. Gela may not be able to create life but you can. Photinah is now sentient aware with a spirit all her own. I suggest that you two love birds come see what your lovemaking has brought about."

Gela and Lon headed for the front door to see what Malachy was on about. They both stopped in surprise. The sky was an array of colours and Photinah had blossoms all over her. Malachy couldn't stop laughing for there were flowers everywhere, even the vines were blossoming and the Phelan, who were at the base of the tree, were happily singing amongst the dazzling floral display.

"You two lovers were unaware that the intensity of the sky changed colour as you two were enjoying yourselves. The Phelan found the light show intoxicating and the prevailing energies were so strong that they joined in the celebration of life that you two were sharing. If I'm not mistaken, every eligible woman who has a mate is pregnant and nine months from now you are going to be busy delivering babies."

Lon and Gela looked at each other and then down at the Phelan, surprise and wonderment on their faces.

"I'll have to go down and talk to them."

"No, we will have to go down and talk to them, husband."

Lon, Malachy and Gela appeared at Photinah's base. They were greeted with singing and laughter as they moved through the crowd looking for one of the elders.

"Kyros," a voice called out of the crowd. "Kyros, over here. How can we be thanking you for this gift of life you be bestowing on us?"

"Derron, I'm not sure to what you're referring," Kyros said, not understanding Derron's comment.

"The women of the Phelan be having great difficulty in becoming pregnant; every woman who be mated, now be having a child. Such a gift be beyond our measure to be repaying."

"Derron, my mate and I will never be able to have children," Kyros remarked sadly. "We are honoured that your women have become pregnant through the prevailing energies given off by my wife and I sharing our love."

Riona, Seanan's mate, ran up and hugged Gela, thanking her.

"Oh Gela, Seanan and I be waiting five years for a child. I be thinking this joy would never be befalling me. I see by your look that we both be changed and be the happier for it. Kyros truly be a great man as Oletha be saying, and I be believing he be having a grand mate. The love you two be sharing would be of Creation; Oletha honours her disciples, I be thinking."

After spending the appropriate amount of time with the

Phelan, Lon, Gela and Malachy returned to Photinah and their home.

"Well, that was an unexpected turn of events," Lon remarked with surprise.

"There is one thing I want to know, husband, every time we share affection is the sky going to explode with colour and everyone be making out?"

"No, love, that won't happen again. I'm sorry. I completely forgot that Oletha bestowed her life force of creation upon Malachy and I."

"That's one thing I would like to keep private from now on," Gela declared firmly.

"I agree. How are you handling the nudity?"

"The Phelan are so natural about it that they think we're strange for wearing clothes. A couple of the ladies tried to undress me, saying I was suffocating my body by covering it up. I explained how cold it is on Telluric and they felt sorry for me, saying that while I was here the garments should be removed for my wellbeing."

"There's nothing stopping you from being natural if you want, my love. I certainly wouldn't mind."

"I know how much pleasure it gives you look upon me, darling. But the Phelan aren't truly naked; they have fine hair covering their bodies. There's no mistaking male from female and it's beautiful watching the children playing so openly.

"Do you know there are no lustful thoughts among the Phelan? They love each other for their minds and spiritually.

They mate for life and honour Oletha completely," Gela proclaimed proudly.

Lon looked carefully around the terrace. "I think all the homes could do with a balustrade around the perimeter terrace and a set of table and chairs, don't you, love?"

"It would be a lot safer and set of table and chairs would be lovely. While you're doing that I'll get us something to eat."

Lon and Malachy had Photinah construct a balustrade around the perimeter of all seven branches the homes were on for safety, and added tables and chairs.

Gela brought out a bowl of mixed fruits and drinks and placed them on the table that Photinah had constructed. Over an enjoyable meal they discussed recent events.

"As you know, rock people are the record keepers of our lives, past and present. Your physical makeup has been genetically altered. What runs through your veins is as much liquid crystal as blood and crystal resonates at a different frequency from a human body. This means you will have the qualities of the crystal as part of your makeup. In essence, you won't age and people will think of you as immortal," Lon continued.

Emeralds improve communication skills and promote the truth by inspiring calm within the hearts and minds of others. All your abilities will be enhanced now your essence and the emerald are one."

"It sounds as if I will be learning new things about myself for a while," Gela pondered.

"There is one interesting piece of information you are as

yet unaware of," Lon informed her. "You now have a library and librarian inside your head. The information within that library contains all the records of every incarnated spirit. This means that you can look up the history of any person you so desire. But is it ethical to do so?"

"Do you also have a library in your noggin, my love?" Gela enquired cheekily.

"My noggin holds a great deal more than yours. Because Malachy and I are one, the consciousness of the One Tree that is part of Malachy, is also part of me."

"Isn't it a little crowded in there, husband mine?"

"Oh, you are the comedian today, aren't you?" Lon laughingly replied.

"Is there anything else I need to be aware of, darling?" Gela prompted, smiling.

"Your memory and mental skills will improve along with your psychic insight and your vision will be enhanced. Basically, your general health and quality of life is improved."

"Did those things happen to you?"

"Sapphires are known as crystals of divine favour. They balance the physical, mental and spiritual realms and they also symbolise truth and faithfulness. Add to this Malachy's essence and Oletha's spirit of creation and my understanding of life is profoundly different to anyone else's."

"How do you feel about being transformed?"

"I don't believe that either of us has been altered, Gela. We're simply fulfilling our natural evolution of creation,"

Lon stated, looking at Gela with concern. "Are you feeling as if you were forcibly changed?"

"No. In fact, the exact opposite. It's hard to explain the sensations I'm going through.

"That reminds me," Lon said, suddenly remembering he wanted to apologise to Harpreet. "I need to contact Harpreet, if you will excuse me a moment, love."

Lon concentrated sending his thoughts through Harpreet's pendant. "Harpreet, place your thoughts upon the pendant and speak them to me. I will hear you."

Harpreet was in her study going over what she would present to the council elders when the call from Lon entered her mind. On hearing his voice out of the blue, she dropped the paper work she was holding.

"Lon, I nearly jumped out of my skin you gave me such a start."

"Sorry about that. I have just placed directions to our location within your mind, please come at once. This isn't an emergency and you'll be moving through time so we won't be late for the meeting with your elders."

"On my way."

"Harpreet will be here any moment, love. There she is now," Lon said, getting to his feet to welcome her.

Harpreet appeared outside the front door of Gela and Lon's home, looking stunned. Lon and Gela embraced her and then directed her to the table and chairs.

"Welcome to my home. It's my wedding present from Lon; he decided we should live in a penthouse apartment. Aren't the views breathtaking?"

"Where are we?" Harpreet asked.

"This is Terrene, the world of the Phelan. You are standing upon a branch of a sentient-aware lady called Photinah. Malachy produced a seed that Lon planted and this gorgeous tree grew from it. There are six main branches, one for each member of the Order of the Phelan."

Gela turned to Lon. "Husband, you can't count," she said, a little surprised. "There are eight members in our family," as she started counting them on her fingers. "Renae, Janelle, Lomasi, Gabbryel, Fala, you, me and Harpreet."

"You and I are as one now and will be living together so we will only need one branch for our house between us.

"Then where is the seventh house as that makes seven counting us as one?"

"That's a secret for now, my love," Lon replied, smiling.

Gela gave Lon a questioning look and then turned back to Harpreet.

"Anyway, each member of the family has their own home and transport portal. Photinah is standing in the area called The Crescent. Around the perimeter of The Crescent is a school where classes will be conducted in all the healing arts. There are rooms for visiting students and teachers. Lon named it Hospice of Life. Which branch is Harpreet's, Lon?"

"The one below ours, love. Come on, Harpreet, I think you could do with some exercise, we'll walk down," Lon ventured boldly.

Lon headed down the stairs with Harpreet and Gela following. Harpreet was amazed at the extent of Lon's abilities. When they reached the level below they stopped. "This is your home, Harpreet. If you can tell me where you would like the windows and what floor coverings you'd like I will arrange it."

Harpreet, Gela and Lon wandered slowly through the home. Having been through all the rooms Harpreet walked around the outside, looking at the scenery. She indicated the type of windows she would like and watched in wonder as Lon tapped his Staff on the wall and the window appeared. Having requested carpet in the bedroom and study, Harpreet shook her head in disbelief as vines snaked across the floor forming a thick soft carpet. She was even more astonished as sap thinly spread across the remaining floors and hardened into a beautiful golden finish.

"Lon, what about doors?" Harpreet ventured curiously.

"Sorry, Harpreet," he said, tapping his Staff on each doorframe, producing large rolled-up leaves as doors.

"How do they work?"

"I'll show her, Lon. All you do is touch the leaf and it unrolls to close; touch it again and it rolls up to open."

"Oh Gela, how ingenious! Thank you, Lon, but why all this?" Harpreet said, indicating her surroundings.

"Oletha and Slegna are contesting for the souls on Telluric. There will be many confrontations between the Balanced and Unbalanced. As Oletha's disciples, we represent the realm of the Balanced. Slegna also has disciples whom we will confront in the coming conflict. We will need a sanctuary in which to recover and regroup where Slegna is unable to penetrate. Oletha, in her wisdom, devised an aura deflector which inhibits any Unbalanced souls from seeing the world of the Phelan."

"This brings me to my next question," Harpreet said, looking sternly at Lon. "When did Gela blend with the crystal?"

"This morning, which was actually the last three years, depending on how you wish to view it."

"I see, so why am I here, Lon?" Harpreet asked reservedly.

"Let's all have a seat," Lon said, directing everyone to be seated. "Harpreet, you are an exceptional teacher of spiritual truth. I welcomed you into our special family with open arms," Lon said, complimenting Harpreet. "You graciously accepted to follow both Oletha's request and mine without question. It is my feeling that as Kyros, I have violated the use of my power to influence you into accepting a position as a member of our family. I therefore release you of all obligations pertaining to the Order of the Phelan."

"Lon, what are you saying?' Gela said, shocked. "I don't want Harpreet to leave."

"It's all right, Gela. Lon isn't kicking me out; he's allowing me to freely choose my path in life," Harpreet replied, thinking of everything that had happened since Lon had entered her life. It was obvious by his actions he wanted her to stay and she was most appreciative of his candour.

"You will say yes, won't you?" Gela entreated.

"Gela, Harpreet may have commitments she is obligated

to fulfil. Also, she might wish to change her physical appearance as she learns. Life is eternal, but the body isn't. Because we blended with the crystal our physical form will remain the same indefinitely; it will appear to others that we are immortal. Oletha gave us a choice to blend with the crystal, Harpreet wasn't given the same courtesy," explained Lon before continuing.

"In every incarnation, a person adopts the physical structure best suited for their karmic responsibilities and lessons. The fact that the body dies gives the illusion that our present life is all there is. However, bodies are nothing more than clothing for our spirit; we change them depending on the circumstances of our environment. I am simply asking Harpreet to exercise her right of freewill."

"Your powers of persuasion are quite formidable, Lon, and your presence daunting," Harpreet acknowledged. "I compliment you on your ability to recognise the effect you have on the people around you. Oletha has already conveyed a similar decree and suggested that you would do likewise when you stopped to think about the circumstances of my enlistment into the Order of the Phelan."

"Oletha is one extraordinary essence of being."

"Yes, Lon, she is," she replied, gently rubbing her pendant.

"What are you going to do?" Gela queried of Harpreet.

"I have given the matter a great deal of thought, Gela. My greatest pleasure in life is enlightening people about their infinite potential for self-love. To love oneself is to love Oletha, for they are one and the same. Reuniting someone to his or her true self and Oletha is magical," Harpreet intoned lovingly.

"My life is rewarding and heart-warming. There isn't anything I wish for as I already live a full and satisfying life. So the question of long life is irrelevant because as Lon has already said, life is eternal and only the body dies." Harpreet thought for a while before continuing.

"My next incarnation would be to a higher realm of learning. The question that needs to be answered is, will my advancement continue if I remain within this body? The answer of course is yes, providing I allow it. By remaining within the Order, I will have the opportunity to visit all the realms of enlightenment," Harpreet replied excitedly. "So to answer your question, Gela, yes, I'm remaining. Having said that, my next course of action is to journey to the realm of crystal, which I believe is why Lon brought me here."

"Gela and I have been invited to see how the blending with the crystal takes place and as you're the next to join your essence with the crystal ..."

"You decided you would tag along." Harpreet said, smiling.

Everyone laughed as Lon tried to look innocent.

"Okay, Lon, there's no time like the present," Harpreet said, standing.

Lon, Gela and Harpreet stepped onto the portal and vanished, reappearing on the world of crystal. Harpreet saw a world of untold beauty constructed entirely of crystals. Lon and Gela saw a complete society with a populace busy about their tasks.

"Harpreet, each one of us has to locate the crystal that resonates with our psyche. You will need to follow your instincts. What you see about you are solid crystals, whereas Gela and I see a functioning civilisation. So when I start to communicate to the crystal before me, I am actually talking to a person."

"So Gela isn't really hugging a crystal then?"

"No, that's Me-i, the voice of the crystal. We'll go with her while you locate your crystal and blend with it."

Harpreet nodded and walked in the direction her instincts told her, while Lon spoke to Me-i. "Hello, Me-i, do I get a hug as well?"

"Is this something your species does often, Lon?" Me-i asked laughingly.

"Only to people we care about," Lon replied with equal playfulness.

"What's the woman's name who is wishing to become at one with the crystal, Lon?" Me-i asked.

"Her name is Harpreet and like us, she is a disciple of Oletha. She is the one who taught me how to balance my chakra points, so I could maintain harmony with the crystal."

"What was it like, blending with the crystal?" Me-i asked professionally.

"Very painful," replied Gela.

"Really?" was Me-i's shocked response.

"I'm afraid so, Me-i. It's mind-blowing, wouldn't you say, Gela?"

"When Lon told me how much disorientation and pain

the mind would experience, I thought he was being over-protective. I almost lost control, the pain was so intense."

"I didn't know there was any pain involved, discomfort yes, but not the pain you two are describing. That's not how it's supposed to be." Me-i looked deeply concerned.

"When the crystal enters the bloodstream the heart feels as if it's pumping sludge throughout the entire body. The strain is enormous: the chest feels as if it wants to explode and the mind has difficulty comprehending what the body is going through. You literally have to spiritually maintain your composure or die."

"That's terrible. It can't be allowed. We must hurry; Harpreet is about to be submerged within the crystal. I will have to stop her till I can reconfigure the blending mix."

Lon and Gela followed Me-i as she ran to where Harpreet was to join with the liquid crystal. They saw Harpreet kneeling beside a river of Lapis Lazuli. A solid wall of crystal suddenly appeared before her blocking her entry into the river.

"Harpreet," Lon called. "Sorry, but there's a problem that will delay your blending with the crystal for the moment."

"Did you do that?" asked Harpreet, pointing to the wall before her.

"No, Me-i did. She has just found out the extent of trauma the mind and body goes through for the blending to take place. According to her some discomfort is expected but not what Gela and I went through. She is looking into the blending procedure to see what can be done."

"Then thank her for me, please, Lon," Harpreet said gratefully.

"Here, take my hand."

Harpreet took Lon's hand, a surge of energy moved through her and her vision altered. There before her was Me-i talking with others of her race.

"Lon, this is truly marvellous. Is this what you see once you're joined with the crystal?"

"Yes. As you can see there is a whole civilisation around you. As you're not resonating at their frequency, all you see are varying shapes and sizes of crystals. However, when your essence is harmonised you will be able to communicate with them freely."

A commotion caught Lon's attention; he instantly directed Malachy's attention to a man in his mid-twenties around five feet six whom Me-i was trying to restrain. His light-brown complexion coupled with his resonance indicated he belonged to the Clan Crystal Aragonite. He was rather nondescript in appearance and screamed while encircled in a field of living energy that bound him tighter every time he tried to move.

"Thank you, Kyros," said Me-i, relieved. "We have discovered a traitor in our midst. He has been tampering with my mixtures, hoping to cause your failure. I don't know how he got past our detection. Would you like to deal with him, or shall I take him before our council?"

"Let us take him before your council and see what he has to say for himself," Kyros remarked, wondering on how many worlds the Unbalanced was making their presence felt.

Lon, Gela and Harpreet followed Me-i to a large official-looking structure. Two men flanked the one Lon had bound in energy; as they went to grab him their hands were pushed aside.

"Sorry, gentlemen," Lon said. "I will release him if you like."

"That's quite all right, sir. He can't escape this way. How are you managing to constrain him?"

"He is restrained within a force field," Lon politely replied.

"If it's not a rude question, sir, who are you?"

"I'm Kyros."

There was an audible intake of breath from the men as they continued to escort the prisoner to the Chamber of Justice. This was an impressive structure similar in shape to a circular steeple or cone. Entering through a huge door they crossed a foyer into a large open room with two small conference alcoves either side of the entrance. Seating was arranged around the room for any who wished to view the proceedings. At the far end of the room was a semicircular bench where the adjudicators sat. What had Kyros's attention was that fact that the whole upper structure of the building was one enormous cone-shaped window, which provided all the lighting. Lon advised Harpreet not to let go of his hand or she would become imprisoned within the crystal. Me-i presented her findings to a woman sitting at a small table before the circular bench. Crime was uncommon; consequently it was dealt with immediately.

Lon, Harpreet, Gela and Me-i were seated at the table provided and the prisoner was placed in a witness box. Eight women listened silently to the accusation brought against the man before them. A heavy-set woman spoke. She appeared to be in her late fifties with bright orange hair, piercing brown eyes and a pink complexion.

"Mr Benoit," the judge questioned. "I would hear what you have to say about the charges brought against you."

Benoit moved uncomfortably in the witness box as he answered, "If it's wrong to fight for the things you hold dear, then I'm guilty. We enter a war not of our making," he said, smacking his hand on the rail of the witness box. "Slegna will descend upon us with his wrath if we support these aliens," Benoit proclaimed, waving his hand at Kyros, Gela and Harpreet.

"I see," the judge replied calmly. "You believe that justifies your actions." The judge paused for a moment looking intently into Benoit's eyes before continuing. "Your interference could have taken the lives of not only the aliens as you call them, but our own kind as well. Is that what you intended?"

"Of course not!" Benoit exclaimed.

Gela, who had been watching Benoit closely, whispered to Me-i who looked enquiringly at Gela and she nodded. Me-i then addressed the council.

"If I might indulge a moment of your time, your honour, I have here today a woman who is able to discern the truth of any situation. If it would please your honour, she could save everyone here a great deal of time if she were permitted to question the accused."

"Who is this person of whom you speak?" one of the adjudicators enquired.

"Her name is Gela, Oletha's Lady of Truth and partner to Kyros. She was the second disciple of Oletha to blend her essence with our world," Me-i answered.

"She may address us."

Gela stood facing the woman before her. "Thank you. If the accused is agreeable, I can quickly bring this hearing to a close, for by the grace of Oletha I know the truth of any given situation."

Permission was granted and Gela questioned the accused.

"Mr Benoit, my name is Gela; I'm Oletha's disciple of truth. Would you permit me to ask you some questions?"

Benoit looked at Gela suspiciously for a moment before consenting.

"What was your intention in regard to altering the mixtures Me-i uses?" Gela gently questioned.

"I wanted to make things so uncomfortable that you would decide not to continue with the blending," he answered.

Gela watched his life energies closely as he answered, and then she continued. "Why would you do that?"

"You're a violent race not deserving of a long life," Benoit replied with passion. "I love my world and won't see it become embroiled in a conflict between Slegna and Oletha just for your sake."

Gela sensed there was something more as his life force wavered. "Was it your intent to kill?"

A look of horror crossed Benoit's face. "Most certainly not!" he replied, revulsion filling his voice.

Gela knew the man was misguided in his loyalties and not defiant. "Honoured elders, this man is guilty of tampering with Me-i's mixtures, and admits it freely. He believed that if we failed in our attempt to blend with the crystal, we would simply give up. He was ignorant of the dangers involved. He believes he is fighting a just cause to free his people from entering a conflict not of their making."

"Could you ask him who else is involved in this conspiracy?"

"With all due respect, it's not my position to become involved in the internal politics of your world," Gela answered.

"Well said. Please remove the guilty to a place of care until we can ascertain the extent of his betrayal."

One of the adjudicators observed Harpreet holding Kyros's arm. "Kyros, the young lady on your arm is unable to discern our presence without your help if I'm correct.

"Her name is Harpreet, your honour. She was about to commence her blending when Me-i was forced to delay it."

"Me-i, Harpreet is of the spirit Lapis Lazuli – they will flow beautifully together."

"That's where she was when I forestalled her blending."

"Then please allow her to continue her journey so she may begin her sharing," the adjudicator advised.

Me-i escorted the disciples from the building. Once

outside Lon spoke to Harpreet. "This is where we leave you, Harpreet. When I let go of your hand, the crystal will be as it was when you first arrived. You will need to find your crystal essence again, I'm sorry."

"That's all right, Lon. I look forward to seeing and speaking with you in person, Me-i."

Lon, Gela and Me-i watched Harpreet walk in the direction of the crystal river she'd previously found.

"Can you repair the damage that was done, Me-i?" Gela enquired.

"Actually, the problem wasn't with my mixing of the crystal. It was what was done to it afterward that made things difficult for you and Lon. When I think of what could have happened, I feel terrible," Me-i announced, with dread in her voice.

"No damage was done, Me-i, so it's no good beating yourself up over it."

"You're very forgiving, Gela, but it was my responsibility to see that nothing untoward could happen. You both must be spiritually strong to have withstood what the body went through and not have lost control of your minds."

"It's called allowing the transition to take place, right, Lon?"

"Yes, love," Lon replied, smiling. "Me-i, how do you actually blend the different physical forms into one?"

"We immerse the intended host within the liquid crystal that resonates with their psyche. Then we examine their incarnations and determine if the person is worthy of receiving a crystal host."

"What happens if you decide a person is unworthy?"

"Then they never emerge from the crystal."

"Me-i, you said host, do you mean we are carriers of some sort?" Gela asked, surprised.

"You are sharing your physical form with another spiritual being Gela. You were impregnated with a spiritual symbiotic essence of the Clan Emerald."

"Are you all right, Gela?" Lon asked, seeing the surprised look on her face.

"Yes, it hadn't registered that there are now two spirits within this body."

"Remember what I told you about the librarian."

"Yes, but I hadn't made the connection. I must have a good talk to my new friend," Gela replied with vigor.

"Harpreet is about to be submersed within the liquid crystal. If you follow me we will arrive as she emerges from the river. It would be better for Harpreet if she didn't know you were here."

"Gela and I can change to our crystal form, Me-i; nothing will distract her from what she needs to do."

They arrived to see Harpreet spluttering and coughing as she dragged herself from the river. Once she was free she sat in a meditative state.

Lon and Gela watched as Me-i and her assistant approached. Harpreet seemed completely unaware of their presence. They then removed Harpreet's clothing and placed her on a small portable bed.

Me-i opened a chest that contained seven different-coloured crystal ampoules, whereupon she removed one and poured the contents over Harpreet's heart chakra, explaining: "As all physical forms are of Gaia, it is possible with the adaptation of crystal antibodies to produce a transformation of your basic anatomy. This mutation takes place on a cellular level. Every sentient-aware being has seven spiritual focal points that decipher their spiritual and material environment.

"The centre focal point is the one over the heart; it's from here the other six points are balanced. By administering the appropriate amount of material and spiritual life essence over each of those points, it is possible to bring about a metamorphosis into the next level of evolution."

"What you call spiritual focal points, we call chakra points. Why is it Harpreet is unaware of what you are doing?"

"What was going through your mind at this stage, Lon?"

"My full attention was on balancing my heart chakra and not giving in to the physical discomfort."

"Your immersion within the crystal is twofold. Firstly, the crystal recognises your rhythmic vibration and opens up your book of lives. Your previous incarnations are then balanced against your karmic debts. If you meet Oletha's requirements you move on.

"Secondly, you are utterly absorbed in maintaining balance between the mind and spirit. That's when I administer the appropriate amount of crystal antibodies, creating a symbiosis of essence. When that occurs you go through another change as the spirit of the crystal adapts to your body. Can either of you recall what that change is?"

"Yes, that's when the disc emanating from the heart chakra starts to change colour. Maintaining synchronicity between the prevailing spiritual energies so as to have a uniform collaboration is quite a battle."

"Is the encounter really that intense?"

"Believe me, Me-i," Gela explained, "if you lose concentration for a moment, the other spirit will take control of your body and you cease to exist."

"I didn't know that. So at the moment Harpreet would be fighting for control?"

"No, Me-i. That doesn't work either. It has to be a blending of spirits, a harmonising of wellbeing in the grace of Oletha. Otherwise neither can survive."

"This is truly fascinating," observed Me-i. "Nothing like this has ever been done before so the more I know, the easier I can make it for your family, although, I don't think I can help with the blending of spirits. Once the heart's spiritual focal point has been harmonised, I then administer equally to the points above and below the heart until all are as one. At that moment both you and your symbiotic partner release your full power, the spirit of the crystal connects to Gaia and your spirit joins with Oletha."

Lon and Gela watched as Harpreet wrestled with the crystal spirit. Me-i and her assistants massaged Harpreet's body with special oils, helping the organic part of her body to adapt to the mineral transformation taking place. The cuts and abrasions Harpreet had acquired whilst in the river were all healed.

"Me-i, is it all right if I ask questions while you work?"

"Of course, Lon, what is it?"

"You mentioned that your time is different to our time. Gela and I are dimensionally aligned to the crystal awareness of your world, thus making us invisible to Harpreet. This would mean our perception of time and our movement through it is the same as yours. Those cuts on Harpreet's body have already healed, yet we've only been here a couple of minutes. My question to you is this, when Gela and I see and talk to you and your people, are we in your time frame or ours?"

"Both, they work simultaneously. However, because you are blended with the crystal you have the ability to differentiate between the two, thus moving from one time frame to another. Harpreet has been undergoing her metamorphosis now for a little over three of your years and her transmutation is almost completed."

Lon and Gela watched as Me-i's assistants re-dressed Harpreet and returned her to her meditative position. Then a shaft of silver shot towards the heavens as a shaft of blue gold travelled to Gaia. The sharing was completed. Me-i kneeled by Harpreet's side and spoke quietly.

"Harpreet, you can open your eyes now. You have successfully blended with your crystal. How do you feel?"

"A little disoriented, I think. How long did the blending take?"

Me-i laughed. "That is the first question each of you asks. How long does it feel?"

"I have no perception of time; that's why I asked."

"In your time, a little over three years; in my time, only minutes."

Harpreet looked around as Me-i helped her to her feet. Seeing Lon and Gela she spoke. "Have you two been here long?"

"From the beginning," answered Lon.

"You were watching for three years?" Harpreet said, surprised.

"No, only a few minutes," Lon said, moving to embrace her. "It was truly fascinating watching the procedure from Me-i's point of view."

"All right, Lon, what's with that smirk on your face?" Harpreet asked suspiciously.

"Let me just say that we have both seen each other in our natural form."

Harpreet looked down at her clothing and then at Gela and Me-i, who were both smiling.

"Well, it's nothing you haven't seen many times before Kyros."

The use of Lon's title made him laugh and he gave Harpreet a warm embrace.

"True and it's something I would like you to experience. The body's metamorphosis is remarkable."

"Of course, Lon, is it really that enthralling?" Harpreet said questioningly.

"More than you can imagine. The body actually crystallises, replacing your organic structure as it moves back and forth.

You can see the discs you formed around the chakra points changing as your spirit and the crystal spirit contend for control. Then when the blending takes place the structure of your body completely changes. You must see it," Lon said, full of wonderment for what had just taken place. "It's creation in the making."

"He really is Kyros, isn't he, Gela?"

"Yes, Harpreet, he is; I don't think he even noticed the loveliness of your body."

"I'm not dead, my love, her body does have beauty. However, it holds no more interest to me than anyone else's. Now if you would like to remove your clothing ..."

"That's quite enough, husband," Gela said, blushing.

Harpreet and Me-i burst out laughing at Gela as she encircled her arm in Lon's while they all made their way to the transport portal. On arrival, Lon produced his Staff and turned to Me-i.

"Me-i, Malachy and I have a gift for you."

Lon removed another seed from his Staff. However, this one was different from the one he'd planted on the world of the Phelan.

"If it is acceptable to your elders, I would like you to plant this seed in a place of your keeping. It will be the only organic tree upon your world and a means to contact our family. All you need do is place your hand upon it and speak the name of the person you wish to talk to and they will hear you and answer."

"Lon, this is a precious gift. I don't believe the elders will have any objections as they will see it as a great honour," Me-i replied with respect. "I will enjoy meeting the rest of your family. I must be going now for I have classes to teach. Goodbye, Gela. Harpreet, please visit. You are most welcome."

Me-i turned to face Malachy and gently placed her hand upon the Staff. The surprise on Me-i's face was priceless when Malachy took his masculine form and spoke.

"You are a unique individual, Me-i, and are a welcomed addition to our extended family. Don't be a stranger, call as often as you like and that includes me."

"I will, Malachy, I promise," answered Me-i with a smile.

Lon, Malachy, Gela and Harpreet stepped upon the transport portal and disappeared, reappearing in front of Gela's new home. They went inside and collected platters of fruits and decanters of juice, which they placed on the table outside.

"How are you feeling, Harpreet?" Lon asked, watching her aura changing colour.

"Not bad, Lon; why?" Harpreet asked carefully.

"As I explained to Gela, you now have a library and librarian within your mind. When you have a quiet moment I suggest you two become acquainted. There is a wealth of information at your fingertips; the ethical use of the information is yours alone. After we have refreshed ourselves, Gela and I will introduce you to the Phelan."

"I have noticed some interesting changes already," Harpreet acknowledged. "How long does it take before I am fully aware of all the benefits that joining with the crystal provides?"

"That's a good question. I'm still learning, what about you, Lon?"

"I suggest that you read as much as you can about your crystal. That should give you an indication of the enhancements you will receive. Lapis Lazuli harmonises soul, spirit, mind and body, stimulating your higher thought patterns and encouraging attunement.

"Your spiritual visions will be more accurate and contacting spiritual guardians will be easier. You'll also be aware of psychic attack. The list will go on as you become more attuned with each other."

"I see I have a lot to look forward to," she replied, a little overwhelmed.

"I think it's time to meet the Phelan," Lon commented.

"Very well, let's be off."

Lon, Gela and Harpreet stepped on the transport portal and appeared at Photinah's base. Gela insisted on showing Harpreet the Hospice of Life. She was amazed and kept remarking on its construction. She thought the showers and spa were incredible. The sweat lodge had her intrigued and she asked about the different-coloured leaves.

Lon indicated the first leaf as he explained: "East is the colour yellow, the place where Eagle flies; this is a male energy. Eagle represents a time to heal old wounds or remove negative thoughts, allowing illumination and clarity to enter your life. So fly with the spirit of Eagle and allow enlightenment to enhance your being.

"West is the colour black, the home of Bear, which is a female energy. Bear asks you to join her in the silence of her cave that you may face your fears. She reminds you that it is the beginning of all tomorrows. Bear offers you inner strength and power to face anything that is before you."

Harpreet looked puzzled, asking. "Why is a male represented as an Eagle with the colour yellow and a female as a Bear, which is black?"

"Eagle flies in the heavens of the Great Spirit Oletha and the rhythmic vibration of illumination is yellow. Bear seeks the solace of a cave deep within the heart of Gaia. When Bear emerges from Gaia's womb, it is born into a different world. The rhythmic vibration for the solace of nurturing and rebirth of ideas is black."

"Fascinating, sorry, please continue."

"South is the colour red. This is the playground of Coyote, the heart of a child. Coyote is a jester and trickster. He will give you the time of your life, teaching you how to balance work with play. He will have you laughing and crying all at the same time, encouraging you to reconnect to the innocence, regaining the faith and trust of the child within.

North is the colour white, the habitat of Buffalo and the realm of the native elders. They teach you how to express gratitude and experience the natural order of the universe, turning knowledge into understanding and understanding into wisdom."

"I like the sound of that." Harpreet was deeply interested.

"The elders instruct that honouring such wisdom completes the circle of the Sacred Hoop of life, thus also honouring your true heart and the universe from whence you came."

"The other two leaves?" Harpreet looked at Lon.

"Blue is the colour for Father Sky, the Great Star Nation and all things above. This represents the home of Great Mystery and the Thunder Beings' spirits, the Original Source of all Creation, the Eternal Mystery that is Oletha. It shows us that all we ever need is within, as we are created in the image of existence and are co-creators of our own life.

"Green is for all things green and growing; this is Gaia's domain. She embodies all things material, the Stone People, Standing People, all Two-Legged, Four-Legged, Nature Sprites and the Winged and Insect World. She communes with the Thunder Beings who replenish her lifeblood and restore energy to her as she needs it. Their embrace is often quite spectacular. She is in a constant state of rebirth."

"Is there a reason the entrance is so small?"

"That is to remind us that we are no better than any other living being and it teaches humility. The lodge is dome-shaped and circular in order to create even heat dispersal; you must always move from left to right whilst within the lodge.

The women sit on the masculine side, which is the left side of the lodge when entering. The men sit on the feminine side, which is the right side and the shaman separates them. A Door Keeper sits opposite the shaman in front of the door.

When the door is closed prayers are given and the shaman adds water to the hot rocks as directed by spirit. The steam then cleanses the body, mind and spirit allowing the rust of life to drop away."

"Oh Lon, that sounds fantastic. This would help me tremendously in coming to terms with my new abilities. When can we do it?"

"Well, I haven't given it much thought, Harpreet. Let me introduce you to the Phelan and I will see what I can organise."

As they were walking from the Hospice of Life they spotted Seanan and Riona walking towards them. Lon and Gela greeted them and introduced Harpreet.

"You be a disciple of Oletha, Harpreet?"

"Yes, Seanan, I am."

"I see by your eyes you be not normal, like Gela and Kyros?"

Smiling at the remark Harpreet answered, "No, Riona, I'm not normal."

"What be your gift from Oletha then Harpreet?"

Harpreet smiled warmly at Riona and gently rested her hand on her arm. "I'm a teacher of truth."

"That be good. I be coming to your classes then," Riona said, also affectionately touching Harpreet. "When you be running them?"

"I haven't organised a time yet, Riona. When I do I will let you know."

"My mate be most inquisitive, Harpreet. You not be minding, I hope?"

"Not at all, Seanan. Will I have the pleasure of your company as well?"

"Pleasure, is it? Well now, I be thinking about that. Kyros, the elders be meeting at the moment if you be wanting to introduce Harpreet."

"Thank you, Seanan, I will do just that."

"Do you be wanting me to be there?"

"Actually, yes. You and your lovely mate, if that's all right?"

"Well, then we be escorting you," Seanan replied.

Gela, Harpreet and Riona had their heads together talking the whole time they walked to the meeting. The introductions were made, Harpreet's skills were discussed and she was asked to conduct a class as soon as possible.

Kyros informed the elders that he was conducting a sweat lodge and that seven of their clan were welcome to attend. On their way back from the meeting Harpreet thumped Lon on the shoulder.

"What was that for?" Lon asked, feigning surprise.

"For not warning me the Phelan don't believe in wearing clothes."

"I thought you would like the surprise," Lon laughingly answered.

"You can laugh, Gela. I'll get you both for this."

"Why Harpreet, I didn't know you were a prude."

"I'm not, though a little warning wouldn't have hurt. I'm not used to seeing a whole society walking around naked. One of the ladies tried undressing me, saying I was suffocating my body."

"They did the same to me the first time as well. Lon hasn't had that problem."

"That's because I'm Kyros," Lon said, laughing. "Well, you have your sweat lodge, Harpreet. Are you happy?"

"Yes, thank you, I'm really looking forward to it."

The three continued walking back to Photinah. When they arrived Lon explained the transport portal and asked Harpreet if she wished to be alone for a while.

"I think so, Lon. The lodge isn't till late evening, although I would appreciate company for dinner if I might join you?"

"Of course. I'll come and get you," Lon replied.

"Thanks, Lon, see you both then."

Harpreet stepped onto the portal and disappeared. Lon and Gela did likewise. Dinnertime arrived and Lon went to fetch Harpreet while Gela prepared the meal. Gela was wondering where they were when she heard them coming up the steps.

"I decided Harpreet needed to tone her legs. After seeing her lying naked on that bed, I'm sure I saw some loose muscles," Lon cheekily told Gela.

"When, may I ask, have you ever seen me lying naked on a bed?" Harpreet looked shocked at the thought.

"Why, when Me-i and her assistants undressed you and put you on one, of course," Lon advised her.

"He's joking, isn't he Gela?"

"I'm afraid not," Gela said, smiling. "They were very gentle with you."

"Just how close was he?"

"Right beside you being shown how the transformation takes place. He was more interested in what Me-i was doing than your nakedness, I can assure you," Gela responded matter-of-factly.

"We must have a serious talk, my lad," Harpreet said, shaking her head.

"I'm sorry, Harpreet, but I'm in love with Gela. Please don't do anything drastic," Lon implored.

"You're impossible. Gela, what do you do with him?"

"That's simple, I ignore him," she said, continuing with her preparation for dinner.

The dinner went well with Harpreet and Lon stirring each other outrageously. Gela looked on in amusement. After the meal was finished and everything cleaned away they made their way towards the sweat lodge.

"Lon what do we wear in the lodge?" Harpreet asked.

"Something loose."

"What are the Phelan wearing?"

"What they always wear, why?" Lon queried.

"You said it's dark inside the lodge, correct?" Harpreet pressed.

"Yes, except for the dim glow of the rocks."

"Well, I don't think it would be good manners for us to be dressed while they're not," Harpreet suggested.

"Does that mean you're going native the whole time you're on Terrene?"

"Oh, I see your point," Harpreet answered. "But I don't have anything loose to wear."

"Go in your undergarments if you like."

"Gela, your husband is unreal. Here I am offering to go in my altogether and he's trying to talk me out of it. What are you going to do?"

"I will probably go natural, that way I can drive Lon crazy. Besides, it will make the Phelan happy."

"Gela, you're as big a stirrer as Lon. I'll join you." Harpreet commented smiling.

Twelve Phelan were at the lodge when they arrived. Three males and three females, as well as Seanan, had been chosen to enter. Kyros explained that the lodge would run for approximately two hours. Each half hour the door would open so they could quench their thirst and freshen the air. Seanan's mate Riona and the others there would provide the refreshments.

The meanings of the leaves were explained and how to acknowledge the rock people when water was poured upon them. When they were ready to enter, Harpreet, Gela and Lon removed their clothing. The women of the Phelan danced around Harpreet and Gela with joy while Kyros and Seanan looked at each other and shrugged.

The men entered the lodge first and moved to their positions. Then Kyros entered, followed by the ladies. Seanan was offered the office of Doorman, which he accepted with pride. He was the last to enter. Once he was inside Kyros nodded to him and the door was closed. Kyros intoned a prayer for opening the lodge.

"Oh Mystery of the True Light, we ask for your blessings

and guidance. We invite the four directions into this lodge and ask they grant us their enlightenment."

Lon then poured water over the rock people, everyone intoned, "Ho!" as steam filled the lodge.

CHAPTER FOURTEEN

Enoch sat in the holding cell with seven other detainees; he looked upon them with pure hatred as the snivelling cowards huddled up the opposite end of their cell. They had acted tough when he'd first arrived. With the power Slegna had given him he knew they were a mean lot, their attitude emphasised by their tattoos, body piercing, long hair, rough appearance and belligerent manner. However, when they tried to put their hands on him, Enoch dropped two of them so fast they didn't know what had hit them. Then he turned his attention on the remaining five, slamming them against the bars with such force their screams of agony had the police rushing to check on the problem. By the time the police arrived Enoch was sitting quietly on his own at the opposite side of the cell with the other detainees picking themselves off the floor and cradling their wounds. Absolute terror was written on their faces.

Enoch had refused to wash the blood off his face from the cut he received when the police threw him to the ground and handcuffed him. He knew Andy would be organising something and wanted whoever visited him to see how brutal the cops had been.

A policeman unlocked the cell and Enoch was transferred

to an interrogation room. The arresting detective was there with two other officers.

"My name's Detective Laura Dunstan. You're in quite a fix, Terry; you murdered Joe by beating him to death. We found Mick's body impaled on an iron rod and your cowardly leader, Andy, ran off leaving you to take the rap. We know all about the gang, the women you abducted and violated and your contacts for all the jobs you pulled. Your cohorts have all been arrested and will be spending a long time behind bars."

Laura stared at Terry, remembering Joe hanging from the chain. She shut the painful image from her mind and in a cold calculating voice announced: "As it stands, you won't have the luxury of serving a prison term. You're being charged with first-degree murder that holds a mandatory death sentence. However, if you give us the name of the other person at the steel mill we might be able to alter the charge to manslaughter."

"It's Enoch, not Terry, and I ain't speakin' till me lawyer gets here, bitch!" was the retort Enoch shot back.

After that comment Enoch didn't say another word. Laura had him returned to the holding cell and reported to her captain.

"Hi Cap, that little prick won't talk. He's real mean," she told him.

"A few days in the slammer will change his mind."

"No, Cap it won't," she said with finality, remembering the joy she saw on Terry's face as he was about to beat Joe to death. "He thrives on violence and cruelty; prison will only make him worse. This is the first time I believe in the death sentence. If there's such a thing as pure evil it's this Enoch."

"Who's Enoch?"

"That's what Terry calls himself." The captain's phone rang.

"Terry's lawyer has just arrived demanding to speak to his client," the captain informed her.

"Damn, Cap, that was quick," she said, surprise showing on her face. "Well, I had better introduce them."

Laura left the captain's office and headed for the holding cells. Terry was on his own sitting up the far end of the cell. Sinister emotions were emanating from him. The other detainees looked fearful as they crowded together in silence at the opposite end.

"All right, Terry," Laura stated firmly. "Your lawyer's here, let's go." She indicated the cell door.

Enoch looked at Laura with contempt.

"Move your arse. I haven't got all day," Laura snapped out sharply.

Enoch slowly walked towards the door with a smirk on his face. Just as he reached it, Laura slammed it closed and locked it.

"When I ask you to move, punk, do it!" she barked at him and then turned around and walked out of the room, leaving Enoch standing in the middle of the cell.

"What was that all about?" asked the captain, who had followed her.

"He pissed me off. I won't give that piece of shit the satisfaction of knowing he makes me uneasy. Did you see the looks on the faces of the other detainees? They were terrified of him."

"He certainly has a presence about him for one so young, that's for sure. What are you going to do now?"

"Go speak to his lawyer; maybe he can control his client."

Laura walked through police headquarters and found Terry's counsel. She introduced herself and escorted him to the holding cells. She wondered how a twenty year old could afford a lawyer from one of the most prestigious law firms in the city. The emotional distress and malevolence emanating from within the holding cell as they entered the room visibly shook Enoch's lawyer.

"Are you ready to do as you're asked, or would you like to remain where you are?" Laura asked.

Terry walked towards the door without saying a word and waited. Laura opened it and escorted both the lawyer and Terry into the interview room and then left. Terry looked at the man before him. Short, dumpy, balding and dressed in a suit that appeared to have been thoroughly slept in. However, what caught his attention were his eyes; they were as sharp as tacks.

"My name is Jaegar. I'm your legal counsel sent by Andy. I already know you're guilty of murder and I don't care. When I ask you a question you will answer truthfully – that way I can tell you what to say. Do you understand?"

"Yeah," Enoch said. He was more than willing to talk now.

"What happened to your face?"

"The cops did this when they arrested me."

"Did you resist arrest?"

"No."

"Good, I will file charges of assault against the arresting officers," Jaegar informed Enoch. "As I understand it, you were arrested while in the act of beating Joe and the police maintain his death was caused by your mistreatment of him. It is also my understanding that Joe killed Mick by kicking him onto a steel rod that was sticking out of the floor. Are these facts correct?"

"Yeah."

"You will talk to no one without me being present. Is that understood?"

"Yeah, they already tried ta badger me inta dobbin' me pals in by offerin' a manslaughter charge instead of first-degree murder. They said they had all our gang's contacts in the clink. Is that right?"

"Yes. I'll file a harassment charge for today's little encounter. That will stop them from talking to you without my being there. Now you listen very carefully. You will act as if sheepish, even fearful whenever the police come near you and you won't give them any reason to bring further charges against you. Is that understood?"

"Yeah," Enoch replied, not liking the idea.

"One more thing. I've been told you're Slegna's disciple, so whatever you're doing in that holding cell, stop it!" Jaegar said angrily. "I want you submissive and repentant, not smart and cocky. You'll curb your tongue and use your manners; there are many ways in which to manipulate people. This is my field of battle," Jaegar stated firmly. "And like you, I'm good at what I do, so let me do my job by doing exactly what I say. Got it?"

"Yeah, I got it." Enoch found he was warming to this bloke; he was devious and smart, his kind of person.

Jaegar walked to the door and knocked. When it opened he advised the officer they were finished and Enoch was escorted back to the cell. Enoch's hearing was set for the next day. Jaegar had one of his staff arrange for a suit to be delivered to Enoch and a doctor to bandage his head.

Enoch's was the third case for the day and Jaegar had used the time to coach him. Laura entered the court with the people's prosecutor and walked along to their appropriate seats. Enoch was in the detainees' box looking small and timid with two large officers of the court flanking him. The bandage around his head made him seem like a victim and the emanating energies had changed from malevolent to inoffensive and blameless. With a look of childlike innocence on his face, no one would ever believe that he was capable of such cruelty.

The adjudicator called the next case. "The hearing for the people versus Terry Dawson is now in session. Counsel for the prosecution, you may present your case."

The prosecutor advised the court that Terry was charged with first-degree murder for brutally beating to death Joe Mosley. In addition there were charges of kidnapping and assault of five women as well as numerous accounts of breaking and entering and theft. Having finished his summation, the judge asked the lawyer for the defendant to enter his plea.

Terry's counsel told the court it was the first time his client had ever been in trouble with the law and that there were mitigating circumstances in relation to the arrest. He also stated that the arresting officers assaulted Terry before detaining him and at police headquarters he was interrogated and threatened without the benefit of counsel.

When all summations were completed the judge addressed Terry.

"I find enough evidence to warrant a trial. You will appear before this court three months from today where you will present your case. A jury of twelve good people will decide your guilt or innocence. Given the nature of the crimes against you, you are to be remanded without bail in a maximum-security facility. This court is dismissed."

Terry was escorted from the court to a vehicle and he was taken to a maximum-security prison to await his trial. On arrival at the prison he decided he didn't want any more incidences as had occurred previously in the holding cell so he projected an aura with such malevolence it caused a commotion among the other prisoners. The guards, unsure of what to do, placed him in solitary confinement until they could confer with the warden.

Enoch sat in a cell barely big enough to swing a cat wondering why his master had allowed him to become imprisoned, when Slegna suddenly materialised. Enoch was stunned for Slegna was nothing like he'd imagined.

An aura of power gently pulsated about his well-defined body that stood six foot tall. He had a soft face with a warm complexion, dark hair, brown eyes and a voice that was calm but firm.

"Are you questioning my methods, Enoch?"

"Sorry, master. I was wondering how I could serve ya being imprisoned like this," Enoch answered, throwing himself to the floor.

"I know your thoughts, disciple Enoch. Stand before me," Slegna said, gesturing to him.

Enoch did as he was bidden.

"I compete with Oletha for the subjugation of the souls on the world of Telluric. This world is ripe for the taking and I have chosen you to be my ambassador. She will also have her emissary, so you will need to be vigilant at all times. I will confer not only the ability of transportation upon you, but transformation as well. You are now the most powerful person upon this world, disciple Enoch. Raise me an army to convert the people of this world to the Unbalanced."

"Yer will, master," Enoch responded happily. He revelled in the thought of being the instigator of his master's plans; he could feel the power surging through him. What he needed now was to recruit people for his master's new army and he was in the right place to do that. It was clever of Slegna to have him arrested; he would never again doubt his master's methods.

"There is a person within these walls called Roja," Slegna began. "He was a high-ranking soldier in the army from where he was dishonourably discharged for arms dealing. Seek him out and recruit him for my army."

"Yes, master, what does he look like?"

"Six feet tall, thick black curly hair, heavy-set bull of a man with a deep voice, large hands and a gentle way with people," Slegna described, laughing coldly before vanishing.

Enoch visualised himself standing in Roja's cell and promptly disappeared from his cell to reappear before Roja, who fell backward in fright.

"I have a proposition for ya, Roja."

"Who the fuck are you and how did you get in here?"

"I'm Enoch, disciple of Slegna, and walls ain't no problem ta me."

"So, you're the one they're talking about. That's a neat trick," Roja said, looking about nervously.

"Are ya interested in hearing me proposition or shall I leave?"

"You have my attention." Roja was all ears.

"Good, but I think we'll talk elsewhere."

Enoch made a slight movement with his hand and they disappeared. Roja was stunned as they reappeared outside a café he used to frequent. It was just at closing time. Enoch made himself comfortable at one of the tables that as yet had not been put away for the night, indicating for Roja to do likewise. When the waiter returned to remove the other table Enoch ordered two coffees with such finality the waiter obliged.

"I'm building Slegna an army of the new order and I thought ya might like ta join up."

"Who's Slegna?"

"He's what we call the Mystery of the One Truth and believe me, he's real. I warn ya, if ya cross me, ya cross him and not even death will stop his vengeance."

The waiter arrived with the coffee. As he placed them on the table he nearly tripped over when he recognised Roja sitting there.

"I thought you were in the slammer," he said in a frightened voice.

"I am," Roja said, smiling. "Just popped out for a coffee."

The waiter moved off quickly.

"A friend of yours?" indicated Enoch.

"No, I'm pretty certain he was the one who snitched on me, but I can't prove it."

"Really? As a token of my good intentions..." Roja looked on in horror as a hideous beast appeared. Enoch sent it after the waiter. A scream of terror echoed from inside the café, followed by the waiter running from the premises with the hound hard on his heels. The other staff watched the fleeing waiter in stunned silence, as they couldn't see the hound.

"How come they can't see those things?" Roja asked uncomfortably, while hiking his thumb in the staff's direction.

"Only the ones I want ta see 'em can," Enoch replied, a cold smile crossing his face. "Those are some of Slegna's pets. They can be yer worst nightmare, or yer best friends, depending which side yer on."

"Okay, you've made your point!" Roja whispered. "If I'm with you, you're the boss."

"I might only be in me twenties, but Slegna gave me his powers! I know what yer thinking and what ya want and I can tell where people are. I just want ya ta know where ya stand if ya join up," Enoch told him.

"What's in it for me," Roja demanded, "if I join your new age army?" He didn't want Enoch to know he had unnerved him.

"I will make ya a general and give ya all the rewards and power that goes with it. I will also give ya some of Slegna's pet hounds ta help do yer bidding. One of yer tasks is ta recruit mercenaries ta fill the ranks of his army. Ya will be the hammer, and me crime syndicates are the anvil upon which ya will break any organisation that refuses ta join Slegna's new order.

"If ya have any ideas ya think might help, we talk before ya act. Yer the brawn and the syndicates are the brain. Ya will never do nothin' without first getting orders from a bloke called Andy. All your personal contacts will become part of the new order as will every other organisation we bring inta our family."

"What are you calling this new family of yours?"

"It's Slegna's family and it will be called Concurrence Resolutions Pty Ltd. All the crime families will join or face extinction at the hands of the army of the new order."

"That's where I come in?" Roja asked.

"Correct. Ya will need people that ain't particular about

who they kill 'cause there will be at least two families that will resist."

"You know this, how?" queried Roja.

"Like I said, I know what people are thinkin'," Enoch replied scornfully.

"When you said extinction, do you mean every man, woman and child belonging to the family?"

"I want no one left alive who can ever make claim ta belonging ta that family ever again," Enoch said with disdain.

"What about the families that have never had anything to do with the business? Some of them live in different provinces; I wouldn't even know who they are."

"Everyone!" Enoch reiterated sneeringly. "Slegna wants everybody upon Telluric indoctrinated inta his family!" Enoch's voice was filled with malice as he stared at Roja. "Don't worry about where they are. I'll tell ya."

Roja wanted to know just what Enoch was capable of and figured he had nothing to lose by pushing his questions. "What makes you think you can pull off this coup?"

"I already have several high-ranking families involved and more will follow."

"So you say," Roja commented disbelievingly. "But I need more proof than a few tricks that may dissipate over time."

"Tricks are what magicians do. I'm Slegna's disciple!" Enoch proudly announced.

"Okay, disciple of Slegna," Roja mockingly remarked, "what now?"

Enoch knew Roja was purposely baiting him to see if he was strong enough to carry through with his threats. "Back to prison," Enoch said, laughing.

Roja and Enoch vanished from the café, reappearing in Roja's cell from which Enoch promptly vanished, leaving Roja wondering if he had imagined the whole thing. Enoch materialised in a first-class hotel room where Andy was getting dressed, scaring the wits out of him.

"Calm down, Andy; I haven't broken out of the joint. I need ta talk ta ya. I want ya ta arrange a meeting with the heads of all the families yer in business with," Enoch stated as he walked around Andy's penthouse apartment. "Slegna has a proposition for them they can't refuse. There's no need ta contact me about the time of the meeting, 'cause I'll know."

Having given Andy the message, he left. Andy stood open-mouthed in shock. The crooked cop, Maleko from the steel mill, walked into the room to see Andy standing still in disbelief.

"You okay, Andy? Who you talking to?" he asked, puzzled.

"Enoch was just here. He said he wants me to arrange a meeting with the heads of all the families. Apparently Slegna has something to offer that Enoch said we couldn't refuse."

"I don't like the sound of that offer. How are you to contact him with the time and place of the meeting?"

"He said he would know," Andy replied, still in a state of shock. "How does he come and go like that?" Andy looked mystified.

"He's Slegna's disciple and I'm not about to disobey Slegna's request for a meeting," Maleko responded nervously. "I'll get on it straight away."

Enoch reappeared in his cell and lay on his cot to rest. His powers were continually growing. He could listen in on anyone's thoughts, knew their strengths and weaknesses and how to manipulate them. He didn't want everyone becoming hardened criminals, just devious enough to cross over to the realms of the Unbalanced.

Slegna was calling in all his markers and any who reneged would suffer the consequences. People in high places needed reminding about whom they worked for and Enoch, disciple of Slegna, was going to do just that. With a cold, calculating, nefarious smile, Enoch rolled over and slept.

He became aware that he was floating above his body. At first he thought he was dead but then he noticed a cord connecting him to the body on the cot below. The knowledge that Slegna had given him had awakened his dormant abilities. This was called astral travelling; he could go anywhere he wished. A visit to Andy might be fun. Within moments he was soaring through the Astral Plane at great speed, arriving in Andy's room once more.

Andy was enjoying the fruits of his labours with a sexy young brunette who was doing all she could to please him. So Enoch decided to visit Maleko, who was on the phone arranging the meeting Slegna wanted. There seemed to be some resistance to the idea so Enoch removed the reluctant parties from Maleko's mind and sent a hound of despair to each. The person on the other end of the phone suddenly had a change of heart and agreed to the meeting.

No sooner had Maleko hung up the phone than it rang. When he answered it, the voice on the other end also agreed to the meeting. This continued until all the heads of the families who had originally refused, agreed to attend. Maleko seemed confused with their change of heart but didn't say a word. Enoch chuckled to himself, instructing the hounds to remain with their victims. Returning to his body, he settled in for a good night's sleep.

The next day could have been sunny for all Enoch knew; being in solitary confinement meant he didn't get to see the outside. Breakfast wasn't what you would call great fare but it was tolerable. He ate it and returned the plate and utensils in the slot provided. No one would disturb him now for some time, so he was free to attend the meeting.

He appeared in a boardroom at the top of one of the most modern and prestigious buildings in the city, surprising everyone in the room. All the families were sitting silently around a large table with the hounds of despair beside the reluctant members.

"Well, gentlemen, I'm glad y'all decided ta accept Slegna's invitation. I'm Enoch, Slegna's disciple. He has asked me ta instruct ya on how things are ta run from now on." Enoch knew they didn't take him seriously. "Don't let the fact I don't speak refined like you gentlemen lessen his message.

"Now to business," Enoch said, slowly walking around the room. "Slegna is the one youse been gettin' yer messages from all these years and he wants a new company formed called Concurrence Resolutions Pty Ltd. Each family is ta sign over fifty percent of their profits from last year's income ta help start the company. No family member known ta the cops is ta work in the company and no one in the company is ta know who put up the finance."

Everyone in the room looked uncertain as Enoch continued.

"The company is ta be offshore with branches in all provinces. It will cover all importin' and exportin' of goods from all walks of life and will infiltrate all financial institutions. For all intents and purposes Concurrence Resolutions Pty Ltd. will be legitimate. However, it will be a front for all organised crime and the family's activities.

"Now, in case yer thinkin' ya don't want no part of this, I'm ta tell yer that your profits will triple over the next two years and that your hidden non-taxable income will quadruple if ya follow Slegna's advice. Each of yer will still run your own families," Enoch paused before continuing, "However, Slegna is the head of all the families," Enoch emphasised.

A ripple of discontent ran through the room.

"And if yer wonderin' why some of ya have hounds with ya and some don't, the ones with the hounds was reluctant ta attend. Slegna knows, as do I, who will try to weasel out, so I give ya this warning." Enoch looked round the room. "Any family that don't join Slegna's new order will be exterminated ta the last known family member!" His last statement was scathingly delivered.

"Slegna will be the head and you gentlemen will be the body, all movin' together for the common good. I'll leave now so youse gentlemen can discuss amongst yerselves what yer'll do. But remember Slegna's warning! When I return, I will have yer answer."

Enoch vanished, leaving the heads of eight major crime families angry and terrified about the ultimatum that had been put to them. The hounds sat quietly as the conversation between the families became more heated. Emotions escalated as they tried to discuss the position they had been placed in. Two families refused outright to go along with Slegna's new order. Standing, they pulled their revolvers from their holsters and emptied a full magazine into the hounds that were beside them and then left.

Enoch materialised not long after they had left with Roja by his side. "So I see two of ya have decided to ignore Slegna's offer." Enoch walked to where the hounds lay and waved his hand. They immediately got to their feet and vanished. "I sent them ta keep an unseen eye on things. They can't die ya know, but you can," Enoch commented, laughing.

"This here is Roja. He is the general of Slegna's new order army and yer going ta help provide the finances for it. There is ta be no more fightin' among the families or Slegna will have me settle things. Youse'll run yer families just as ya have been doing with one exception. No one will offer any assistance ta the two families that have left Slegna's employ." Enoch eyeballed one of the family heads. "Now there is another family here who thinks they will be the eyes and ears for the two that left. I know who y'are! Be warned, this ain't no game.

"I will only give everyone one warning, then either Roja's marauders or I will settle matters and there ain't goin' ta be no reprieve. Each one of ya has unseen eyes watchin' ya, so stop wastin' time tryin' to outsmart Slegna, 'cause it won't work. Now watch and learn."

Enoch placed his hand over a bowl of walnuts that were on the table. An audible intake of breath escaped everyone's lips as the walnuts transformed into balls of solid gold.

"Each of ya can have a couple of these for your trouble. Andy, Slegna wants ya ta coordinate with Roja all the financial aspects of his army and direct the operations. With the money youse gentlemen put in and what gold's left there will be enough to establish Slegna's new order army and start Concurrence Resolutions Pty Ltd. As ya can see gentlemen, Slegna ain't greedy; he'll give generously ta those who serve him. Are there any questions?"

"Yeah, thanks for your vote of confidence, Enoch," Andy replied, stunned. "But I know nothing about organising an army."

"That's all right, Andy. Once the corporation is organised, Roja will contact ya on how ta go about buildin' Slegna's army. I want Concurrence Resolutions up and running by the end of the week. I leave it up ta youse gentlemen ta arrange that. Remember, no one who is known ta the cops is ta have anythin' ta do with the running or organisation of the company. Roja and I have ta be goin'; however, we will be in touch."

Roja and Enoch vanished, leaving the families to organise the business at hand. Back in Roja's cell, Enoch instructed Roja. "I want ya to request me as your cell mate."

"What makes you think the warden will listen to me?" Roja asked with contempt.

"I'll put the suggestion in his head."

"I'll do my best." Roja shrugged as Enoch disappeared.

The prison warden was reviewing Enoch's case, trying to work out where to place him after his staff had suggested he was too violent to mix with the other prisoners. He decided to find out for himself. Enoch was quietly resting when the door to his cell opened and two burly guards and the warden entered. Enoch had resumed his non-aggressive manner.

"I'm Warden Nibaw, Enoch. You caused quite a disturbance among the inmates when you first arrived."

"Yeah, sorry about that. I was kinda scared when I first got here with all them blokes yellin' and shoutin' at me."

"That's not quite the way I heard it," Nibaw said firmly. "You did your own amount of threatening as well."

"Of course I did," Enoch replied, pretending to act scared. "I didn't want them ta think I was their new bed fella. I heard all the rumours about prison life."

"Yes, well I can't say that sort of thing doesn't go on. However, I stop it wherever I can." The warden indicated Enoch's surroundings. "How are you enjoying your lodgings?"

"I ain't got nothin' ta say about it. I do as I'm told, warden, sir."

"We don't have single cells here, Enoch, everybody shares.

If they don't, they end up here, or in the hole; the choice is theirs. There are rules even here and the consequences are dire if you break them. I don't stand for any nonsense. If you can behave, I will return all your privileges and move you to another cell."

"I'll do as I'm told, warden, sir."

"Warden Nibaw, not sir, we're not in the army here. All right, I'll see what I can organise. Enoch, this is the only warning you will get!" Warden Nibaw emphasised strongly and Enoch knew Nibaw would back up everything he said.

As soon as the warden had left Enoch concentrated on him, giving him the idea that Roja would be the perfect cell partner to keep Enoch in line. It was late evening when Enoch was removed from solitary confinement and escorted to Roja's cell.

"Roja, this is Enoch, your new cellmate. It's his first time behind bars. You can have the pleasure of easing him into the routine of prison life."

"Why thank you, Warden Nibaw, I feel so honoured," was Roja's sarcastic remark.

"Okay, Roja, that's enough. I want Enoch to understand that I have no tolerance for misbehaviour; he will abide by all the rules. Speaking of rules, you were late again to your workstation. Do that one more time and a couple of days in the hole might remind you that this isn't a luxury resort for your holidaying pleasure."

"Gee, and I was going to ask the maid for some peppermints with my clean sheets today too," Roja drawled.

"I'll leave you two to get acquainted."

The cell door closed with a finality that challenged anyone to try to escape.

"You don't seem so malevolent today, Enoch, what's up?" Roja enquired.

"Submissive is the order of business while I'm in the joint," Enoch replied. "I intend ta be an exemplary prisoner, so let all them cronies know it's hands off; otherwise, they will be visited with the mother of all nightmares. I want no incidents ta go on me record. When I return ta court I want everybody thinkin' they was wrong about me.

We're both got ta be about Slegna's business, so I'm goin' ta give ya the ability ta transport yourself wherever ya want. I don't care how ya use it, so long as ya carry out yer assignments. I will also give ya the ability ta know when the guards will be checkin' on ya. Ya must return for all them checks, 'cause this prison is our alibi. Ya could blow someone away in front of twenty witnesses and ya couldn't be charged with nothin' because you're safe behind bars."

"Very clever, Enoch. Very clever."

"Now sit down and I will transfer some of Slegna's abilities."

Enoch placed his hand on his cellmate's forehead and mumbled some strange words and Roja felt energy entering his head. When the transfer was finished Roja looked at Enoch strangely.

"I feel real weird, Enoch. Like there's something else inside my head with me."

"There is. Part of Slegna's power is now inside ya. That is

what yer'll use when ya move from place ta place. It'll also keep ya informed of when the guards will do their head checks."

"It almost feels like I've been violated," Roja alleged, disturbed. "I don't know if I like that although the power is intoxicating. I think I will sleep on it. If I want you to remove it, can you?"

"Of course. Let's get some sleep. Ya can see how y'are in the mornin'."

Slegna smiled knowingly; he knew what Enoch had done. He had shared some of his powers but had also placed a control on Roja's mind. That was something only the advanced demonic fiends could do. Enoch's natural talents were developing quickly.

While Roja slept, Enoch subtly entered his mind stimulating Roja's thirst for power and the ability to use his new gifts through his devotion to Slegna. By the time morning arrived, Roja was totally devoted to Slegna's cause. Enoch explained how the transportation and mind awareness ability worked, reinforcing his previous night's suggestions. Roja's newfound abilities came to him as naturally as breathing.

He then explained that the code name he had given Slegna's unification of Telluric was 'The Gathering' because they were gathering all the Unbalanced on the planet into one family under Slegna. Then they were going to convert everyone else to their cause by undermining the people's faith in the governments and public officials.

The day-to-day doldrums of prison life continued

unabated for Enoch as he and Roja went about Slegna's work between their prison duties.

* * *

Steam rose from the hot rocks until it reach the domed roof where it curled upon itself like a thick fog, descending down the walls to engulf the entire lodge in a dense moist heat. An audible hiss was heard as another dipper of water was poured upon the rocks.

"Ho!"

The "Ho" that followed wasn't as loud as the first as all within the lodge struggled with the sudden overpowering clammy heat. Steam assaulted the body and mind alike as people gasped for breath in the darkness. Another hiss was heard followed by "Ho!" Then Kyros spoke.

"Remember to breathe gently through your nose; this will filter the heat from your lungs. If you're finding the heat oppressive, lower your head towards the coolness of the earth. The lodge isn't an endurance of strength, but a cleansing of the mind and spirit. Allow yourselves to flow with the prevailing spiritual energies and release whatever material hardship you think you're going through. Recognise that you are a spiritual being in a mortal form."

There was another hiss and all intoned "Ho!" as steam filled the lodge once more. The laboured breathing subsided as all present became accustomed to their surroundings and time passed.

"Ho!" This round is at an end, Doorkeeper, open the door," intoned Kyros.

"May the prayers on the steam be going to The Mystery of the True Light. The door be opening," Seanan responded.

As the door opened, steam escaped allowing fresh air to circulate within the lodge. Riona, Seanan's mate, kneeled in the doorway and handed around drinks to everyone to quench their thirst and replace the electrolytes that had been sweated out.

"Everyone be having a drink, Kyros?"

"Yes, thank you, Riona. Anyone who would like a refill is welcome. I don't want anybody becoming dehydrated."

"Kyros, I not be thinking I can be staying in the lodge. I be finding it very difficult to be breathing and focus my mind," commented one of the girls.

"Saoirse, isn't it?"

"Yes."

"What was the reason you wished to be part of the lodge?" Kyros asked.

"I be having trouble organising my thoughts and be thinking this would be a good way to be disciplining myself."

"I see. What are you most skilled at, Saoirse?"

"I be a carer of the old ones, Kyros."

"Would you say this is easy work to do?" Kyros enquired.

"It not be difficult if you be understanding that they be feeling embarrassed when their mind and body not be doing what they ask of it."

"What do you call this understanding, Saoirse?"

"I not be knowing what you mean, Kyros," Saoirse said, sounding confused.

"It's a simple question: what is the understanding you use?"

Saoirse felt as if all eyes were upon her; she hated being the centre of attention.

"Saoirse, you're looking for a complicated answer to something that is simple. I will give you a hint – look within," Kyros prompted.

It was obvious that Saoirse was putting herself under a great deal of pressure. Harpreet sat quietly, knowing what Kyros was referring to. She felt for the girl but couldn't say anything, when Kyros spoke.

"It's not easy remaining quiet when you wish to help, is it, Harpreet?"

Harpreet commended Kyros's move to divert attention away from the girl to her.

"No, Kyros, it's not. I believe she has the answer inside her. She just thinks it's too simple to be correct," Harpreet said, hoping it would prompt Saoirse.

Saoirse's face went through several changes as she pieced together what she was hearing and feeling. If it was simple then she should know it. No it couldn't be, not that, surely not.

"Kyros, would you be talking about compassion?"

"Yes, Saoirse, I would. Compassion, or love and kindness, is the foundation for all growth. The same depth of love and kindness you give to others, you need to give to yourself. You judge yourself too harshly, when in fact, you shouldn't judge yourself at all. Just be aware of your actions and do your best to make every decision in an aura of compassion."

"You be saying I not be liking me?"

"I'm saying that life was meant to be simple and simply enjoyed. You're putting yourself under pressure by placing unfair expectations upon yourself. With the amount of knowledge, experience and understanding of life you have at this moment in time, there is only one path you are able to walk. It's the same for everyone," Kyros stated, looking around the lodge. "Knowledge is gained from moment to moment through life experiences and as each moment is different from the one before it, so we continually learn."

"I be hearing what you be saying, but I should be knowing better, for I know what I should be able to do."

"It's time to recommence the lodge. I would like you to remain, Saoirse. However, I will not insist if you truly feel you are unable to continue."

"I be feeling refreshed, Kyros, so I be trying again."

"Good, except don't try, *allow* yourself to succeed; trying is an element of failure. Doorkeeper, close the door," Kyros intoned.

As Seanan closed the door Kyros chanted and a couple of the rocks started glowing red-hot once more. A moment later a hiss was heard and everyone intoned "Ho!" Then Kyros spoke.

"Saoirse, in her wisdom, has raised an interesting question that I feel needs an explanation. I would like each of you to allow your logical mind to listen instead of analysing, allowing your eternal spirit to feel the rhythmic vibrations of my words. The foundation for all learning is love.

"Love is a harmonic resonance of divine being called faith, The Mystery of the True Light, Oletha. It's beyond our mind's understanding to comprehend how Oletha brought herself into being from the spiritual essence of love that is creation. From that faith she created our soul and gave us the gift of free will, infusing within us the ability to recreate from the substance of life, our eternal spirit. We in turn, infused our eternal spirit with the knowledge it requires to function on whatever realm of Chimera we wish to incarnate into.

"Faith accepts without a hesitation of doubt that we are the embodiment of divine love that is creation and this I call the spiritual heart. It's the spiritual heart that gives the impression that the mind and body are in love."

Kyros poured more water over the rocks and everyone intoned "Ho!"

"The Mystery of the True Light isn't outside us, but a part of us. Love isn't something we have to find for we are love. A lack of faith allows the convictions of others to prevail over our own. When this happens we start to doubt ourselves." Kyros was silent for a moment, allowing everyone to absorb his words before he continued.

"Love is not good or bad, right or wrong: it simply is. By merely allowing ourselves to move through life in a harmonious manner, all that is required to fulfil our needs will be provided. When we undertake a new venture, what we are actually doing is sharing in another aspect of love."

More water was poured over the rocks and with the hiss of steam "Ho!" reverberated throughout the lodge.

"From the rising and setting of the sun, to the expanse of the universe, or the manifestation of Gaia's numerous faces, all are the way of love. I would like all of you to recognise that you and The Mystery of the True Light are one. Find the faith that brought you into being and fully embrace it, allowing your spirit the freedom to move beyond the boundaries of your material form."

Steam rose as Kyros poured three ladles of water over the hot rocks, cocooning everybody within a dense moist hot cloud of steam. "Ho!" Time seemed suspended as all meditated upon the task at hand.

Kyros's words resounded in the darkness. "This round is at an end, Doorkeeper open the door."

An exhausted Seanan replied. "This round be ended, the door be opening. May the prayers on the steam be going to The Mystery of the True Light."

The door rolled open to the relief of all. Cool air slowly circulated throughout the lodge; people sat with their heads in their laps. Riona started passing around drinks, which were gratefully received. Feeling refreshed after the drink, Gela spoke.

"Is it always as difficult as that, love?"

Chuckling to himself, Kyros answered. "It's as difficult as you make it. Was there anything in particular that you found demanding?"

"Clearing my mind while being blanketed in a hot fog that

was so oppressive it took all my concentration not to scream to be let out. Even when I blended with the crystal I didn't feel as helpless. I felt helpless! Why would I feel helpless?"

"I can answer that for you, my love. However, it's better if you can discern that piece of information for yourself."

"No, darling, it was rhetorical. Leave it with me."

"Kyros."

Kyros turned to the boy who'd spoken. "Yes, Naal?"

"You be saying the lodge be like returning to the womb of your mother, be that correct?"

"Yes, it can also refer to returning to the womb of Gaia, thereby being reborn."

"I be sensing myself turning into a bear, it be frightening me at first. I be walking down a path that be leading deep within the earth. It be opening up into a cave where I be lying down to sleep. I be waking up when you be closing the round; then I be walking out from the earth and into the lodge. I be wondering if this be normal?"

"What's normal for some is abnormal for others, Naal. People are unique in their development, each one moving along their own path of enlightenment. To become a bear you must be at one with Gaia," Kyros explained.

"Bear enters the womb-cave of Gaia to hibernate through the cold death of winter. It's there that Bear moves into dreamtime, entering the Great Void to gain understanding of the year's experiences and re-emerging into a new life in the spring.

"Bear, being female energy, resides in the West, the

intuitive side of the brain, the right side. All who seek wisdom will walk this path of silence, calming their inner thoughts to receive their rite of passage."

"So I be doing right then?" Naal asked.

"There is no right or wrong, only what you think you know and what you are allowing yourself to understand," Kyros answered.

"Kyros, I be seeing a woman of great beauty, her body be strangely coloured. She be smiling at me but then she be vanishing like a wisp of smoke. What that be meaning?"

"That was the spirit of Gaia, you saw, Keara."

"Oh my," Keara said with awe.

"It's time for the next round, Doorkeeper, close the door."

Seanan closed the door while Kyros heated three rocks for the next round. As water was poured over the rocks "Ho!" resounded around the lodge and Kyros spoke: "Mystery of the True light, we look to the Northern spirits seeking white buffalo wisdom from the grandfathers and invite them into our lodge. Ho!"

Kyros poured more water over the rocks and everyone intoned "Ho!" Silence hung in the air like the steam that rose from the rock people, broken only by "Ho!" as more water was poured upon them. Then a deep, rich voice interrupted the silence.

"My name is Cloud Dancing, shaman and guide to Seanan, my medium. Am I permitted to speak?"

"You are, Cloud Dancing and welcome," responded Kyros.

"By the Mystery of the True Light, a sacred pipe is to be

made for prayer. The pipe is to be fashioned from your red rock and its stem from your softwood tree. My medium has the design within him. The bowl of the pipe will represent the feminine and the stem the masculine. The stem of the pipe will slide into the base of the bowl of the pipe; this represents the male's fertilisation of the female, the seed of life.

"Have your herbalist blend a mix of herbs containing both male and female components; they are to be crushed not ground. This you will call tobacco. As you fill the bowl with tobacco, honour all creation by asking their essence to enter the pipe and share in the prayer of life. The smoke from the pipe is the visual prayer and it is to be held sacred.

"Before one enters the lodge, the pipe will be lit, honouring the seven directions, North, South, East, West, the Great Star Nation, Gaia and the Spirit within. Have the herbalist also make up a roll of herbs of a cleansing nature; these will be called smudge sticks. A person wishing to enter the lodge will have their aura blanketed by the cleansing smoke from the smudge stick, thereby removing any Unbalanced spiritual attachment and equalising all within the lodge. The lodge is to be held sacred for it honours the abundance of life and the wisdom within the spoken word. My words are at an end."

Kyros thanked Cloud Dancing for his instruction and everyone was hushed while absorbing what had just transpired. Seanan came out of his meditation thinking he had been asleep. Kyros, aware of his return, spoke.

"This round is at an end, Doorkeeper open the door."

Seanan responded. "This round be at an end, may the prayers on the steam be going to The Mystery of the True Light, the door be opening."

Riona handed out drinks as soon as the door opened. Seanan was looking uncomfortable and finally spoke. "Kyros, I be asking your forgiveness."

"For what?"

"I be falling asleep in the lodge. I be most embarrassed about it, I be sorry."

"Asleep, were you? Did you have any nice dreams while you were sleeping by any chance?"

"You be making fun of me and rightfully so," Seanan commented.

"Actually I'm very serious."

"Well, you be thinking me daft if I be telling you."

"I see," Kyros remarked, realising Seanan didn't know what had really taken place. "That strange-looking house you went into is called a teepee and it's made out of animal hides. The markings on the outside indicate that it belongs to a shaman of great power. The inside of his lodge was covered with herbs of varying types and the braves sitting around the fire in the middle of the lodge were beating drums and chanting. They were unable to see you but they knew you were there. They showed you how to make a prayer pipe, tobacco and smudge sticks. The shaman and you seemed to be one person. Then you were back in the sweat lodge, correct?"

"How you be knowing this?" Seanan asked, mystified.

"The place you went to was an Indian encampment. They are a tribe that lives close to the earth as you do. They believe that the Earth Mother is their protector and they call the creator of all things 'Great Mystery'. You didn't go to sleep, Seanan; you are a trance-medium. You channelled your guide by allowing him to speak. Can you remember his name?"

Seanan looked shocked, as the realisation of his experience filled his mind.

"His name be Cloud Dancing."

"Correct, Seanan, and I know this because I am in reality Malachy," he said, smiling. "You are to be trained as a shaman of your clan. You and your family are to live within the Hospice of Life to run sweat lodges. Your words will contain great wisdom."

Riona, who had been listening, beamed with pride for her mate while he sat quietly pondering Kyros's words.

"Does anyone have anything they would like to say?"

One of the young lads spoke up.

"Seanan be one of the wisest among us already, Kyros. There be no living with him now."

Everyone broke into laughter at Seanan's expense.

"I be remembering your comment, young Rayan, when it be time to be choosing someone to be travelling to the high country to be picking the special herbs for Norleen."

"That be all right, Seanan. Norleen be having all the herbs in her garden that Kyros provided."

"The ignorance of youth be sweet sometimes," Seanan said with mischief in his voice. "That particular herb be only growing in the high mountains and thanks to Kyros we not be hunting all over the mountain to be finding it. However, the mountain still be needed to be climbed just the same."

There was an audible groan from Rayan and all burst into laughter once more. When the laughter subsided, Kyros called them to order in readiness for the final round.

"Doorkeeper, close the door."

"The door be closing."

"This is the final round of the lodge. I remind everyone that what happens in the lodge stays in the lodge. Wisdom you can share with all, whatever emotions transpire remain the secret of the lodge and in the hearts of the sitters."

Kyros then heated two rocks and poured water over them. 'Ho!' resounded throughout the lodge, firm and clear.

"This being the last round, we ask a blessing from spirit as the final cleansing takes place."

" Ho!"

Steam filled the lodge as more water was poured over the rocks. Spirit elders and guides added their blessings and the heat rose significantly and several groans were heard. They sat in silence for some time and then finally Kyros spoke.

"Oh Mystery of the True Light, we thank you for your gift of knowledge and ask that we all be granted the understanding to use what has been shown to us wisely."

"Ho!"

"This lodge is now ended. May the blessing of all the spirits be bestowed upon us. Doorkeeper, open the door.

"The first lodge of the Phelan be ended. May the prayers on the steam be going to The Mystery of the True Light, Oletha. May she be granting us the gift of Bear, as we be leaving the womb of her care to be birthed into a new life."

"Ho!"

"The door be opening."

The door opened and all within the lodge sat quietly enjoying the freshness of the night air as it circulated throughout the lodge. Not a word was spoken as Riona handed around drinks. Finally one of the girls spoke.

"Kyros, I wish to be thanking you for your gift of the lodge. It be truly soul-searching and a cleansing for the spirit. I be not having much happen like the others, but I be feeling clean on the inside and at peace, if you be understanding my words."

"By your comments, Maygan, you have shown you received a far greater gift, for you have connected with your spiritual heart."

Everyone started discussing what he or she had experienced within the lodge. Finally Kyros suggested that it was time to leave and enjoy refreshments of food and drink. One by one they wearily emerged to stand under a night sky filled with stars.

Riona and the other ladies had prepared a meal and placed it upon the tables that were scattered about the grounds. Everyone moved off in small groups or on their own, finding the place most comfortable for them.

CHAPTER FIFTEEN

Kalareena lingered by Nathanial's bedside making sure he was cared for. Mesmerised, she watched Kyros draw the spiritual essence of creation into being to repair his lacerated spirit. At the same time the surgeons manipulated matter, reconstructing damaged lungs, kidneys, liver, bone tissue and muscle.

After the surgery Nathanial was transferred to a private room where a nurse was assigned to monitor his recovery. Unlike the hospitals on Telluric, machines weren't used to check his vital signs. The nurses were connected to their patients through a spiritual bond and were therefore able to accurately perceive each one's experience. The nurse, who wore a plain white uniform, smiled warmly at Kalareena, saying, "You'll be able to speak to him in the morning; he will have a full recovery."

As reassuring as that was, Kalareena wasn't about to leave him. She watched his steady recovery and when his spirit was rested enough she communicated with him.

"Nathanial, can you hear me?"

"Yes, my love. Where am I?"

"Your body is on Terraqueous in the medical recovery ward. I am speaking directly to your spirit."

"My spirit feels raw, as does my mind and body. Will I recover all right?" he asked, remembering his ordeal.

"Yes, love. You went through some major surgery so you will need to rest. I just wanted you to know you weren't alone."

"Kalareena?"

"Yes?"

"I'm sorry I caused you so much grief by not listening to you." He felt overwhelmed, his emotional and physical weakness bringing tears to his eyes.

Resting her hand on his, Kalareena responded. "It doesn't matter now, love, you just rest. I'll be here."

Kalareena looked up from her conversation to see the nurse looking intently at her.

"Are you going to tell me how he feels?" she asked politely but firmly.

"Sorry, he said he feels raw in spirit, mind and body," responded Kalareena.

"Thank you. I can give him something that will help his mind and body feel better. Unfortunately, Kyros is the only one who can help his spirit and he's no longer on Terraqueous. He left with Gela, followed by Harpreet, two hours ago."

Kalareena wondered what he was up to and when he would return.

* * *

Everyone from the sweat lodge was happily eating and drinking while discussing their experiences among themselves. Gela realised that her difficulty in the lodge stemmed from unresolved trauma from her parents' death. Harpreet and her crystal entity were in complete harmony now and Kyros was having an in-depth conversation with Seanan.

"So you be saying my guide Cloud Dancing be speaking through me all the time now?"

"Like any partnership you must have guidelines that you both adhere to. Your guide doesn't have the right to control your life. You aren't at his beck and call any more than he is at yours. It's a joining for the common good. Remember, he needs you as much as you need him. Get to know each other, become friends. That way your working relationship will be harmonious."

"I be understanding you, Kyros."

"I'll leave you with this one simple truth, Seanan. Like attracts like."

Kyros left Seanan and moved over to his wife.

"I think an early night is in order, love."

"I agree. I didn't realise just how much energy the lodge can take out of you."

"It only feels that way if you have issues that need dealing with, otherwise you feel refreshed. We will be returning to Terraqueous tomorrow. I need to check on Nathanial and we have that meeting with the council elders. I had better let Harpreet know."

Kyros, Gela and Harpreet said their goodbyes. Kyros reminded Seanan that he could contact him through the crystals if needed. Everyone drifted off to their homes as Oletha's disciples returned to Photinah and their beds. The next day Harpreet joined Lon and Gela for their morning meal. It was a beautiful day and everyone would be sad to leave.

"How long will you be gone?" a soft female voice asked.

Everyone turned to look at who was talking, but there was no one to be seen. Malachy started laughing at the expressions on their faces.

"How long will you be gone?" the voice repeated.

"Photinah, is that you speaking?" Lon asked.

"Of course it is. Who did you think it was?"

"I'm sorry, Photinah, I didn't realise you could speak, although I should have."

"My father Malachy can speak, as can my grandfather Zaki, so why not me?" Harpreet and Gela were just as stunned as Lon to hear Photinah speaking.

"Forgive my rudeness, Photinah," Lon said, feeling slightly embarrassed. "We aren't too sure when we'll be returning, why?"

"I enjoy your company. I take it from your conversations and the homes I built, that more of you will be coming to live with me?"

"Yes, there will be eight of us altogether."

"Is there a limit to the size I'm permitted to grow?" Photinah enquired.

"I thought you were fully grown."

"I'm barely a sapling. You can blame yourself for that with all that creative energy you and Gela were creating and sharing."

"Just how large will you become?" Lon asked, surprised.

"Oh, about quarter the size of Zaki, I should think."

"I don't wish to restrict your maturity, Photinah. However, you're not in the best location to grow to your full potential here. Would it be possible for you to send your root system out to a more appropriate place that you may grow to your full potential?"

"I could transverse the planet if I wish, Kyros."

"Then why don't you talk with Terrene and together decide where the most suitable location would be that would benefit you both."

Photinah was quiet for a moment while she communed with the planet.

"Terrene said she has been waiting for me and that a place has already been prepared. I am to populate the far side of her world. Oletha wishes a forest to flourish about my largest offspring. Each tree will become an element of truth so all who walk within my forest will know themselves. Many will visit my forest of truth but none will be able to venture beyond it. My true whereabouts will be denied to any who seek me as I'm to remain here within the Hospice of Life amongst Oletha's chosen ones."

"Then, my friend, be fruitful and multiply with all our blessings," Kyros warmly responded.

Gela and Harpreet spoke with Photinah at some length until Lon advised that it was time to leave.

"Photinah, you are truly a remarkable being and I am proud to know you. I look forward to many hours of philosophical conversation with you. We must be leaving now," Harpreet stated.

"How do I address you all?"

"You are family, Photinah; you call us by our first names."

"Thank you, Lon. I will see you all on your return."

Gela and Harpreet had cleared the table while Lon was talking to Photinah. Upon their return they all stepped onto the portal and vanished; they reappeared on Terraqueous, Harpreet's home world. Kyros transported them from the portal to the guesthouse gardens. Lomasi was the first to spot them.

"The lovebirds have returned, everybody, and Harpreet is with them."

Gabbryel, Fala, Renae, Janelle and Barbette came in from another room to join Lomasi as they watched the three walking up the steps to the verandah. Their eyes were transfixed on Gela and Harpreet.

"You have both joined with the crystal," remarked Barbette.

"You ladies can discuss that while I check on Nathanial – that is if you still wish to visit him."

"His master's voice has spoken," Barbette said with a grin.

Lon fixed Barbette with a stare that she returned with equal intensity. A slow deliberate smile crossed his face as he walked up to her, catching her in an embrace.

"I see you've been missing me."

"Gela, control this man of yours before I spank him," was Barbette's playful rejoinder.

Lon burst out laughing as Gela shook her head and walked past the two to be caught in an embrace from Lomasi.

"I'm going to abscond with this lovely lady," Lon said with his arms around Barbette. "Harpreet will bring our little family to see Nathanial when they've finished gasbagging. We have a meeting with the council elders in a little over two hours, remember," Lon told her.

Harpreet glared at him as he smiled and disappeared with Barbette. As if she would forget! They materialised in Nathanial's room, startling the nurse who was attending to his comfort. Lon looked at Kalareena and reasoned she wouldn't have left Nathanial's side.

"I hope you're not too heartbroken that I'm married to Gela, Kalareena?" Lon jested.

Kalareena just stared at him, saying to Barbette, "Is he ever serious?"

"I don't think he will ever change, dear."

"You wouldn't think Lon and Kyros were the same person," Kalareena mused. "I watched him draw the creative spiritual essence of being into reality and blend it with Nathanial's torn spirit until I was unable to see that it had ever been damaged. Then he showed the surgeons how to refine their techniques in matter manipulation, explaining that once you understand the ebb and flow of the essence of life, anything could be repaired.

"The surgeons were flabbergasted at the ease with which Kyros could reconstruct matter. He instructed each surgeon in their technique, refining their skills until they had mastered the process and not once did they feel inadequate or stupid. Such is his skill, demonstrating why he is Kyros and he asks me if I'm heartbroken that he married Gela!"

"Well, are you?" Lon joked. "After all I'm handsome, good-looking, sexy, cute, adorable, and modest and they are just my physical attributes."

The look on Kalareena's face was priceless.

"Stop stirring the girl, Lon, and do what you came here for," Barbette admonished.

"Yes, Mother," Lon replied, smiling. Suddenly Lon's pose became officially Kyros as he walked over to the nurse, who had been trying to remain inconspicuous.

"You are showing concern for your patient?"

"Yes," she said, apprehension in her voice. "He should have come around by now but there is no sign that he's even trying to wake up. This isn't normal."

"No, it's not. I put a sleep block over his mind to keep him resting until I returned."

Kyros placed his hand gently on Nathanial's forehead and intoned a mantra to free his mind. Nathanial stirred and the nurse immediately started checking his vital signs. His eyes flickered open. Kalareena's was the first face he saw. He tried to talk but his throat was dry. Kalareena gently lifted his head and held a beaker of water to his lips. After a couple of sips he tried again.

"Thank you. My angel, you are here."

Kalareena's aura brightened so much she had a glow emanating around her body. Turning towards Lon she said, "I hope you won't be too heartbroken, but I'm in love with Nathanial and we are to become one."

Lon burst into laughter, as did Barbette and the nurse who had been privy to their conversation. Nathanial was smiling as Kalareena placed her hand upon his.

"Barbette, it's good to see you. Lon, you have changed a great deal since I saw you last. I feel I'm in your debt."

"Not at all, Nathanial." Kyros turned to the nurse. "I don't know your protocol but I want Nathanial up and about; I am satisfied with his recovery. There's no need for him to remain in hospital. He has some friends visiting shortly and he can leave with them. Can you organise this for me?"

"There won't be a problem, Kyros. The surgeons advised the staff to do as you asked."

Kyros waited as he knew there was something else the nurse wanted to say.

"Barbette, would you help Nathanial get dressed if he's forgotten how? I want to have a talk with the nurse for a moment."

"Of course, Kyros," she answered cheekily.

"I can dress myself, thank you; just show me some clothes."

While Barbette and Nathanial were discussing the different types of garments he could wear, Kyros placed his hand on the nurse's arm and transported them to the garden at the guesthouse. On arrival, Harpreet walked up to them.

"You called, Kyros?"

"Thank you for coming, Harpreet. Do you two know each other?"

"Not formally. Jelena is a wonderful nurse and an exceptional healer. What seems to be the problem?" Harpreet wanted to know.

"You have our attention, Jelena, how can we help?" Kyros prompted.

"I wish no disrespect to the University of Healing or the hospital, that's to be fully understood before I continue."

"We understand," Kyros and Harpreet said in unison.

"Kyros, there is an order within the two foundations I mentioned, to have you banned from Terraqueous, along with all your friends. I'm sorry to say that includes you too, Harpreet," Jelena commented, looking at Harpreet.

Harpreet frowned. "When did this faction make known their intentions?"

"The moment you introduced Kyros. A stranger from one of the outer cities is the leader of the group. He has a way with words that appear to make sense. He has managed to become part of the council that you will meet with shortly. I just thought you should know." Jelena looked worried.

"How much danger have you placed yourself in by revealing this to us, Jelena?" Kyros asked, concerned for her safety.

"I could lose my position and be disbarred. Everyone who is aware of the plan has been threatened in some way, Kyros."

"Jelena, you have a unique healing quality that is being

wasted as a general nurse. Would you consider becoming apprenticed to me to train as a psychic rejuvenation physician?"

"Oh, Kyros, are you serious?" Jelena said, not believing her good fortune.

"I joke about many things, Jelena, but not healing."

"You're not doing this because of what I've told you, are you?" asked Jelena, suddenly thinking it was repayment.

"No, I am asking in spite of what you have told me. If you didn't have the potential then I wouldn't have asked," Kyros replied firmly.

"I accept with all my heart," Jelena beamed. "Thank you, Kyros."

"Nathanial's up and about now, Harpreet, so everyone can visit. We'll speak before the meeting. I'd better return Jelena before she's missed."

Kyros and Jelena materialised in Nathanial's room along with Harpreet. A small, overweight, balding man, dressed in rumpled clothing entered the room just after Kyros and Jelena had materialised.

"For you who don't know the nurse by my side, her name is Jelena. I have just finished interviewing her for an internship as a psychic rejuvenation physician and she has accepted."

Everyone in the room congratulated her on her new profession. The man in rumpled clothing, however, was not impressed and rudely interrupted the congratulations.

"So you have accepted a new position without my recommendation or approval?" he said curtly. "Need I remind you that I'm the head of this department and no one can accept any appointment without my permission?"

Lon turned to face the person who had spoken. Assuming his most formidable Kyros persona he confronted the man. "Are you questioning my authority?"

"You don't frighten me with all your so-called power, Kyros," he sneered. "Who do you think you are coming here lording it over everybody? You're nothing but..."

A flash of light filled the room as Malachy suddenly stepped out from Kyros. "We are Malachy," he intoned. "Oletha's chosen. Are you challenging our right?"

The stunned department official stood dumbfounded at the sight of Malachy and Kyros standing together, his mouth opening and closing with no coherent syllable passing his lips. All in the room were silent as Kyros slowly walked around the man and then stopped beside Malachy. Power emanated with such intensity that all in the room were forced to cover their eyes. When the light dimmed, Malachy, Kyros and the official were gone. Kalareena was the first to speak.

"I think Malachy was a trifle miffed. I wonder where they went."

"Oh my," said Nathanial. "Things have really developed while I've been indisposed."

Jelena looked at Barbette, Nathanial and Kalareena, saying, "Kyros comes across as so plain and unassuming that it's hard to credit the depth of his potential. I had heard that he was the Supreme Healer of all the realms and that his power was unquestionable," she said in awe. "I'm wondering what I've found myself in by becoming his student," she finished, apprehension showing on her face.

"Are you afraid of his power, dear?"

"Oh no, Barbette, not that. I'm afraid I might let him down," she replied anxiously.

Everyone jumped when Kyros spoke. "Not a chance, Jelena. Your abilities come from numerous incarnations of schooling; all I'll do is encourage you to allow them free expression."

Harpreet looked questioningly at Kyros, who simply smiled and continued on as if nothing untoward had just happened. "Nathanial, you have visitors."

Walking to the door, Lon opened it allowing Nathanial's staff to enter. They crowded around Nathanial giving him their best and he asked Renae to fill him in on what had been happening. As best she could, with numerous interruptions from willing helpers, Nathanial was given a full picture of what had transpired while he was going through his ordeal. Disbelief and wonderment crossed his face several times throughout the narration.

Finally he regained his composure enough to ask: "So let me see these rings that Lon and Gair made for you."

Renae, Gabbryel, Gela, Fala, Janelle and Lomasi all extended their hands so Nathanial could see their rings.

"They're exquisite, the workmanship is unbelievable and you say the gold thread is wound through your fingers?"

Renae took hold of her ring with her other hand and

slowly moved it about her finger. The gold thread could be seen disappearing into her finger and coming out the other side to form the ring.

"Doesn't that hurt?" Nathanial asked, concerned.

"I don't even notice I'm wearing it," Renae laughed.

"Incredible," Nathanial remarked.

"If you're feeling well enough, Nathanial, we all have a meeting to attend," Lon queried.

"I feel great, Lon, or should I be calling you Kyros?"

"The same rules apply to you, as they do for me, when it comes to addressing you."

"Rightfully so too, let's be off then. By the way Lon, what's the meeting about?"

"Watch and enjoy, Professor Belmont!" was Lon's cheeky response.

They all slowly walked from the hospital to the council chambers. The chamber was a large circular room with a domed ceiling. On entering through a pair of ornamental doors, the first thing they noticed was an ornate circular table that ran the perimeter of the room. Behind the table were seats ten tiers high that also circled the room; these were filled with members of the populace who wanted to view the proceedings. In the middle of the room was a stand similar to a courtroom witness box and located about the box were tables and chairs. A representative from each quadrant on Terraqueous was seated behind the circular table.

Harpreet, Barbette, Nathanial, Kyros and his family

were escorted to the chamber floor and shown their seats. A member of the council then began the formalities.

"This special meeting of the council is called to order. The subject before the council is the continued safety and wellbeing of its residents. I call councilman Faas to give testimony." A six feet tall, solidly built man in his mid to late thirties strode arrogantly across the council room floor to stand in the box, where he addressed all present.

"Ladies, gentlemen and honoured guests. The other night our gentle world was witness to an extraordinary event. For the first time in living history, our spiritual beliefs were spread bare before us. The existence of The Mystery of the True Light, Oletha and The Mystery of the One Truth, Slegna, appeared before our very eyes," observed Faas.

"Why, you may ask, were we granted the honour of their visit? Was it to enrich our lives with love and harmony? No, indeed, in fact it was just the opposite. It was to wage *war* on our beautiful Terraqueous, thus threatening and frightening our families," Fass intoned with passion.

"Many residents were forced to leave their homes due to the level of violent spiritual energy that was being released between Kyros and Slegna. Undeniably our entire world was engulfed within a sphere of raw energy that tore at our planet's surface, causing disruption and hardship for millions and creating emotional trauma worldwide." Faas looked intently at the council members before continuing.

"This sort of thing cannot be allowed to go on and as responsible members of this council I say it is our duty to see that nothing like this can ever happen again." Faas paused dramatically before continuing. "I therefore request that Kyros and all his followers be denied admittance to our world." Faas went on in his most beguiling voice, "After all, ladies and gentlemen, they weren't born here. Let them bring havoc to their own world and leave ours in peace."

Faas stepped down from the speaker's box to the cheers of some of the people. Order was called for and silence restored. The councilman announced the next speaker.

"Ladies and gentlemen, our next speaker is councilman Tou."

A slim man in his late fifties slowly walked out onto the council floor with the ease and grace of someone used to being in the public eye. He stepped up into the speaker's box. Standing quietly, looking around the room, he surveyed all present before speaking.

"Ladies and gentlemen of Terraqueous, honoured guests and councilmen, my fellow newly appointed councilman, Faas, has given you an in-depth account of his version of what he wants you to believe happened. Now there is no denying that the violent event of the other night was truly spectacular. I personally witnessed the proceedings along with many other concerned citizens. However, I didn't let my emotions become entangled with what was transpiring."

"No, and you never do, you cold bastard," shouted someone from the audience.

"There will be order in this chamber or everyone will be removed," called the council Speaker.

"I see my reputation for truth and fairness precedes me," stated Tou. "I arrived at Professor Harpreet's residence as she and her guests were leaving. I enquired about the matter at hand, whereupon she escorted me through the premises that I may see for myself what was transpiring. I ask you now to forgive my poor rendition of what I saw. Kyros was defending Professor Harpreet and her guests from an unprovoked attack by Slegna."

"How do you know it was unprovoked if you got there after the battle had started?"

"Would the good gentleman who rudely interrupted kindly refrain from doing so, or I will have him removed from the chambers. However, I will answer that offensive remark. Professor Harpreet spiritually showed me the truth of the encounter."

"Yeah, I bet – her truth more likely," an audience member burst out, unable to contain himself.

"Neither Professor Harpreet nor myself are given to untruthful or misleading statements. To suggest otherwise is highly insulting. However, this question can be easily resolved. We have in our chambers today 'the Lady of Truth', Oletha's disciple, who knows the honesty within the spoken word. The professor and I are more than happy to submit to her interrogation. I only ask that all who speak here today do likewise."

"That won't be necessary, Mr Tou; please continue," Faas interjected.

"Why thank you, Mr Faas, that's most generous of you.

However, I would be glad to submit to interrogation by one of Oletha's disciples, along with yourself and your rude cohort," Tou said, while pointing towards the person in question.

"I have already said that won't be necessary, Mr Tou; your reputation precedes you."

"I must confess that I'm more than a little surprised, my fellow council members," Tou remarked, sounding stunned, "that the honourable gentleman refuses to submit to Oletha's disciple. One wonders if it's Slegna he follows," Tou said skilfully.

"I object to such a blatant misleading of these proceedings. He is trying to confuse this chamber with false accusation."

"Order, Mr Faas! You've had your uninterrupted say, now this can be settled very easily. Oletha's disciple is in this chamber. Simply submit to her questioning and the truth of your words will be verified."

"Please, honourable councilmen, if Mr Faas morally feels that speaking to Oletha's disciple would cause him embarrassment, then let it be," Tou stated.

"This council will tolerate no more interruptions, is that clear? Please, Mr Tou, continue."

Renae turned to Lon. "He's very good, isn't he?" Lon nodded.

"On walking out onto the verandah, I saw Kyros extending a hand of friendship towards Slegna as reams of spiritual energy were being discharged from Slegna in frightening succession. Kyros seemed to absorb the energy and change it into a healing aura of love that he directed towards Gaia. It seemed to me that the expended spiritual energy was becoming physically destructive, so Kyros redirected Slegna's energy to the universe where it could be dispersed safely," Tou explained before continuing.

"Night had turned to day as the surrounding area was lit with bolts of energy that exploded in an array of astounding colours and ear-splitting sounds. So intense was the combat that the world was engulfed in an aura of powerful glowing energy as the struggle intensified with every volley Slegna expended.

"I was unable to remain in the house any longer as the onslaught was horrific. The surrounding countryside was slowly being engulfed within the prevailing spiritual outbursts. Harpreet, Oletha's disciples and I had moved some distance from the house where the conflict had started and all that could be seen were intense flashes of light that exploded on impact. Many people had been knocked to the ground with the explosions. Great eruptions of energy burst skyward illuminating the entire night sky." Tou's narration of the events had everybody riveted.

"I wondered over the fate of Kyros and how long he could hold his own. Then an explosion came from the middle of the conflict, the intensity so immense that no one within a radius of five miles was left standing. I think we all feared the worst." Silence filled the chamber as Tou lowered his voice. "But the hostilities began again. Then the voice of Oletha was heard as she called out, 'Be still'. The silence that followed was deafening as it blanketed everything in stillness.

Oletha materialised physically and informed Slegna that this was forbidden and he left. Oletha then restored everything back the way it was and sent healing throughout the world. I don't know what transpired between Oletha and her disciples, but after she spoke to them she left.

As you can see, honourable gentlemen of the council, there will be no more conflict as Oletha has forbidden Slegna's return," Tou stated matter-of-factly. "However, that doesn't mean Slegna's minions aren't among us, as proven today by Mr Faas and his cohorts refusing to submit to Oletha's justice," Tou suddenly declared loudly to all.

Mr Faas looked around the chamber nervously as Mr Tou went on unremittingly.

"On information received from Kyros," continued Tou. "I made some discreet enquiries and found that Slegna's underlings had infiltrated many high governmental positions, including the university and the hospital system. Several members of the hospital staff have been threatened with dismissal, personal injury and disbarment from the Healing Fraternity." Tou mentioned these facts with disgust. Then his manner changed.

A murmur travelled around the chamber as Mr Tou, now in full voice drove his point home. "I have acquired a full set of records called 'Power of the New Order', implicating Mr Faas as the leader of an organisation whose sole purpose is to overthrow this government!" Mr Tou exclaimed while pointing at Mr Faas.

"These documents name other high-ranking members

within the government as well as businesses that supported the move. We also have the names of all its members. You will find a full account of the method they intend using to undermine our trust in our political system." Tou stood proudly as he continued.

There was a commotion in the chambers as Mr Faas and his confederates tried to leave. The authorities quickly apprehended them.

"It is obvious from these records," Mr Tou continued, "that the unrest we have been experiencing throughout our world stems from the members of Mr Faas' 'Power of the New Order'. They were the ones poisoning this council against Oletha's disciples as well as the population.

"Slegna's cronies are ever amongst us and vigilance is always required. I submit a copy of these records as evidence to this council. The originals are in the hands of the prosecuting attorney. It's my belief this concludes the matter before these chambers, gentlemen."

"Mr Tou, we thank you for your concise report and will hand over the perpetrators of this horrendous crime to the appropriate authorities," said the council member in charge of proceedings. "As to the matter of Oletha's disciples remaining on Terraqueous, this council finds no evidence suggesting their presence here exhibits any threat to our continual wellbeing. This meeting is adjourned."

* * *

"How did Mr Tou acquire the information about the Power of the New Order?"

"That was my doing, Harpreet," Lon replied. "Malachy retrieved the information from the official's mind and then I presented him with it as if it was a fact known by all. After that he caved in and gave me the whole story. I knew Mr Tou was an honest man and made him aware of the information. He then made a deal to withhold the informant's name providing he was given all the documentation pertaining to the organisation's transactions. Being the sole administrator for the 'Power of the New Order' he had all the books and accounts from its conception. Simple, really," Lon replied smugly.

"Now that's out of the way, I want to know how Gela and Harpreet came to be joined with the crystal."

"Actually, Lon, before you answer Barbette's question, Oletha gave me the task of training Gela. What happened?" Harpreet interjected.

"I can answer that, Harpreet. My life was at an end unless I joined with the crystal. I could see no future, it was a horrible feeling," Gela told her.

"How long did it take you to understand the meditation technique?" asked Harpreet.

"Around six hours."

"I think you misunderstand me, Gela," Harpreet said, uncertain of her answer.

"You're talking about forming the discs and holding them in place, aren't you?" Gela questioned.

"Yes," Harpreet replied.

"It only took you six hours to master that technique?" was Harpreet's surprised response.

"Approximately. Why?" Gela asked, puzzled.

"What can I say, Harpreet? My wife has a natural talent," Lon proudly announced.

"How long does it normally take to master?" Gabbryel asked.

"On average, around four to five years," Harpreet answered, looking at Gela with respect.

"How long did you take, husband?"

"A little longer than you, my love." Everyone laughed at Lon's remark. The conversation drifted back and forth about the different methods that each one went through to become one with the crystal. Harpreet explained that her blending was easy compared with Gela and Lon's experience and that from now on it would be much safer.

Nathanial sat with his mouth open in amazement at what he was hearing. He could see the differences in Gela and Lon and had watched Lon perform some remarkable feats, so he knew that what they were saying was true. Kalareena, seeing the emotions playing across his face, finally spoke.

"How are you handling what you're hearing, Professor Belmont?" The sound of Kalareena using his title was just the medicine he needed.

"Well, my dear, the scientific observations of some of Lon's actions have been a little hard to evaluate and I'm a little taken aback at his spiritual abilities."

"I think it's time we all returned to Telluric and the bookshop. We all need familiar surroundings about us at the moment," Lon suggested.

"Speak for yourself. Except for Nathanial being badly hurt, I'm loving all this travel and excitement," Lomasi commented.

"When can we all join with the crystal, Lon?"

"That is Harpreet and Barbette's call, Gabbryel, not mine. They are responsible for your training from now on and you had all better listen to them. There are no shortcuts to knowledge," Lon affirmed. "We will say our goodbyes for now, Harpreet. You and Barbette can work out between you the schooling that your students require and who will join with the crystal."

Nathanial and his staff circled Lon. Harpreet watched as they disappeared from view, leaving her and Barbette alone.

CHAPTER SIXTEEN

Kalareena, Nathanial and his staff materialised at the base of the staircase inside Enigma Books.

"I have some things to attend to, Nathanial. You'll be safe with Kyros until I return. I'll say my goodbyes to everyone now." Kalareena nodded to all present and then vanished. Nathanial stood mystified; after all he had gone through, how could she just leave? Renae spoke to Lon, interrupting his thoughts.

"What day is it, Lon?" she asked, suddenly remembering the business of running the bookshop.

"It's the following day from Kalareena's unexpected visit, Renae. The shop will be opening in an hour's time."

Everybody went about their duties, readying the bookshop for reopening. It seemed a little strange after all that had transpired. Promptly at nine Lon opened the front doors. Around midday a letter appeared at the base of the stairs addressed to Nathanial. Gabbryel was the first to spot it and immediately buzzed Nathanial on the intercom.

"It's Gabbryel, we have another one of those messages for you," she nervously announced.

"Don't touch it!" Nathanial responded. "I'll be right down." Leaving his office, he put his head around Renae's office door, interrupting her paperwork. "Renae, another one of those messages has shown up." Renae was out from behind her desk in a flash, causing papers to rustle to the floor. Concern showed on both their faces. By the time they reached the letter Lon had it in his hands.

"Don't panic it's quite safe," Lon said, handing the letter to Nathanial.

Nathanial carefully opened it, reading it quietly to himself before he made an announcement.

"I would like a meeting after closing time on the mezzanine with everyone, please. Until then, work as normal." He returned to his office having indicated for Renae and Lon to follow; once they were inside he closed the door.

"What I have here is a message from Kalareena. Lon, have you heard of someone called Enoch?"

"No, why?" Lon queried.

"Kalareena believes he's a disciple of Slegna and the one who sent the hounds of despair after me and tricked me into the trap box."

"Interesting," Lon said, running his hands through his hair. "Of course that mightn't be his real name. I've heard that Slegna sometimes likes to change the names of his disciples."

"Does Kalareena say anything else?" Renae asked, staring at the letter in Nathaniel's hand.

A smile crossed his face. "Nothing relating to the situation at hand."

"What do you want to do?" she asked.

"Nothing for the moment," he replied, looking intently

at the letter in hand. "I'll talk to the staff as planned after work. Kalareena is unable to return as she believes she is being followed; she asks that Lon keep a sharp eye out for anything unusual."

"That goes without saying, Nathanial," he replied.

"That's about it," concluded Nathanial. "I just wanted to know if either of you had come across this Enoch, that's all."

Renae and Lon returned to work and the day progressed normally. After the store was closed, all the staff assembled on the mezzanine where a worried Nathanial addressed them.

"Kalareena has discovered that the person who tricked me into the trap box is called Enoch. If anyone hears this name mentioned under any circumstance, you must tell Lon before doing anything. Is that understood?"

"Who is this Enoch, does anyone know?"

"Not yet Fala, but I have the feeling we will know sooner than we wish. I don't want any of you drawing attention to yourselves by doing anything out of the ordinary. Go about your lives as if nothing has happened; you mustn't draw suspicion," Nathanial looked each employee in the eye. "When this Enoch finds out I'm free of his trap, he's likely to come looking for me. If he thinks you are nothing but my employees, he might just leave you alone." Gathering his thoughts he continued. "Now, from what I understand, you've all become disciples of Oletha." Everyone present nodded in agreement. "This means you have important work to do. Part of that work is to study hard and complete the necessary training required. Are there any questions?"

"When do we start our training?" asked Fala with keen interest.

"Right about now. You will be coming with me," said a new voice. Standing five feet and impeccably dressed and with a winning smile, silver hair and trim figure Mrs Philips had stood to one side of the group, unnoticed until she spoke.

"Barbette!" Fala exclaimed. "When did you arrive?"

"Lon contacted me earlier. I've spoken to Harpreet and you're to commence your training immediately. If you could follow me, dear, I'll send you on your way."

"What do you mean, send me on my way?" Fala queried.

"I'm sending you to a special classroom, dear, where you can't be disturbed. You will meet Harpreet there. Come along now."

Barbette walked to the portal with Fala and they both vanished. A moment later Barbette returned.

"How long will she be gone, Barbette?" Gabbryel anxiously enquired.

"Don't worry, she'll be fine," Barbette advised her with finality.

"That wasn't an answer," Gabbryel persisted.

"No, dear. I think it's time to call it a day."

"Barbette's correct. I will see you all bright and early tomorrow everyone and don't forget what Nathanial said." Everyone did as Renae instructed, grabbing their belongings and headed out the door.

* * *

Fala found herself in a place that was composed of various shades of white. It was like being in a thick fog without the dampness or discomfort. However, it was disorienting.

"Harpreet, are you here?"

A voice emanated from out of the mist above her. "Yes, Fala, you're not alone."

"Why can't I see you and why is everything white? It's very disorientating."

"This is a special classroom; you will see when you've mastered your lessons."

As she had with Lon, Harpreet explained that all life forms are derived from the same spiritual essence. Her lessons focused on the soul's unique rhythmic frequencies that are the embodiment of the True Light.

"Having been endowed with the True Light, Harpreet, I know that the True Light is not outside of us, but a part of us and that love isn't something we have to find, for we are love," Fala clarified.

"Very good. Do you know the position of the seven chakra points within the body?" Harpreet questioned.

"Yes."

"Good, I want you to meditate on your heart chakra, creating a state of peace throughout the mind and body. Once that has been achieved, create a silver disc emanating from your heart chakra outward from the body to the fingertip if your arms were outstretched. It must be of the purest silver, without any imperfection."

Fala's mind was filled with a vision as Harpreet spoke.

She knew what was required of her and started meditating on the vision she had been given. Every time she faltered, Harpreet's words would fill her mind.

"You are of the True Light, not the mere thought of mind. Start over."

Fala could master all the chakra points as far as the third-eye chakra but then all would misalign. Instead of silver a gold disc would form and then Harpreet's voice would enter her mind. She was becoming rather irritated with Harpreet's continual comment.

"You are of the True Light, not the mere thought of mind. Start over."

"No, Harpreet, I don't believe this is right," Fala stated firmly, trying to keep the anger out of her voice. "Something deep inside me is unhappy with what you are asking me to do."

"Each one of us is unique, Fala. I suggest you follow your heart and see what happens," Harpreet encouraged.

Fala started her meditation once more. This time she created gold discs about her chakra points instead of the silver. The effect was instantaneous as gold discs immediately formed about her, sending a shaft of gold to the Universe and one to Gaia. As soon as the last two chakra points were completed the totally white room suddenly became visible, and before Fala stood Harpreet, indicating for her to stand and follow her. Moving out of the room and down a corridor they entered a small garden; on the far side were sleeping quarters for the students. While heading for the guest quarters, they spoke.

"You have done well, Fala. You are the first person who has ever formed golden discs instead of the silver. I would say that's rather significant of your gift."

"I was beginning to become frustrated until I remembered we are of the True Light, not just part of it. I realised that I could do anything because Oletha and I are one."

"It takes some people many years to accept that simple truth," Harpreet informed her.

"How long was I in that room for?" Fala asked, while looking around at the guest room they had just entered. It was far more luxurious than she was used to.

"Not long at all – about eighteen months."

"It didn't seem that long," Fala remarked, before looking at Harpreet questionably. "I don't remember eating or drinking. What did I live on?"

"Spiritual energy," Harpreet said, smiling at Fala's bewildered expression. "I will answer your questions tomorrow," Harpreet said, forestalling any more queries.

While Harpreet was settling Fala into her quarters, a woman walked in carrying a tray of food that she placed on the table.

"I want you to eat your fill and then rest. There's a lovely garden outside through the sliding doors. No one will bother you. If you need me, use that intercom on the wall; it will reach me wherever I am," Harpreet informed her.

"Thank you for being such a patient teacher, Harpreet," Fala said timidly. "I know I'm a slow learner."

"Actually, Fala, you are anything but slow," Harpreet

asserted. "It took Lon two years to master that technique. Now rest."

Harpreet left Fala to her thoughts and returned to her other tasks. The next morning she found Fala walking the paths that wound round the abundance of flora and the meditation places the garden provided.

"Good morning, Fala, have you rested well?" she enquired.

"Yes, thank you, Harpreet, it's very peaceful here," she commented, looking around.

"That's the idea," Harpreet remarked as she joined Fala in her stroll. "Do you have any questions for me?"

"Not about the meditation. Something is changing in me and I'm not too sure how to deal with it."

"Can you explain what you're feeling?" Harpreet asked.

"It's as if my gift is greater than me, as if I'm secondary to it," Fala remarked, fidgeting slightly.

"There has never been a true Oracle before," Harpreet explained. "To become what you can be, you will have to sacrifice something precious to you. An Oracle is a state of being, not a spiritual ability," Harpreet stated, looking intently at Fala. "Do you understand what I am saying?"

"I think so," she replied uneasily. "You're saying I won't ever be normal again."

"It's more than that, dear. To become the Oracle you must cease to be Fala."

Fala was quiet for some time, mulling that over, before she spoke. "Is it like Lon is not really Lon anymore, but Kyros, and Kyros is really Malachy?"

"That's a very good analysis. You will be so changed that the person you once were will no longer exist. However, as you can see, Malachy takes the guise of Kyros, who keeps the persona of Lon about him so people can identify and communicate with him. You will simply do the same."

"Although I will be forever changed," Fala answered passionately.

"Yes, Fala, you will," Harpreet replied sympathetically.

"There's also one other thing," Fala announced sadly. "I will be totally alone, whereas Lon isn't."

"What makes you think you will be alone?"

"I will become Oracle. That's a singular solitary status."

"All I can suggest is that you fill yourself up with the love of Oletha. Remember, Fala, you have chosen this path for yourself in life, so embrace it with a full heart or not at all."

Smiling from her heart Fala turned and embraced Harpreet, deciding to fully accept her fate. "So now I'm off to the crystal world, correct?"

"Correct," Harpreet replied. "I will walk with you to the portal. Keep in mind, Fala, that you and Oletha are one. Good luck."

"This will be the adventure of my life and I intend to own it!" Fala announced bravely.

"Good for you!" Harpreet congratulated her.

Fala stepped onto the portal and vanished, reappearing in the realm of the crystal. It was late afternoon so the light wasn't bright. She had heard the stories about Lon's, Gela's and Harpreet's blending, so she knew she was to find the liquid crystal that resonated to her rhythmic vibration. She went in the direction that she felt pulled towards. The landscape really was as lovely as she had heard. Eventually, after trekking to near exhaustion, she found a relatively comfortable position and slept.

Me-i, the voice of the crystal, had been following Fala since her arrival. She had travelled far beyond the boundaries of the crystal cities and deep into crystal forests. It was Me-i's responsibility to know where all the rivers of crystal were. The only one this far from civilisation was Phenacite, which was an extremely rare crystal that ran as a river only once a year.

Fala awoke to a bright new day and covered her eyes with a cloth she had brought with her. With purpose in her step, she continued walking for another twelve hours before she settled down again to sleep. She continued this way for a better part of a month, living off the spiritual energy that surrounded her. Fala was beginning to wonder if she had missed her crystal altogether and decided to give it one more day before contacting Lon through her ring to ask his advice.

Me-i admired Fala's resilience and wondered how long she would go on before giving up. The river she was looking for never travelled the same path twice, so for her to find it would be providential.

The following morning, Fala suddenly turned up a steep incline. On reaching the top, she found below her an oasis of liquid crystal nestled between the mountains. She started down the embankment in easy steps until she stood beside a colourless crystal pool. Kneeling beside the pool Fala gently ran her fingers through a warm soft texture that was unlike anything she had ever felt. It seemed alive to her touch and appeared to caress her hand as the crystal liquid ran through her fingers to return to its source.

"Well, my friend," she said, addressing the crystal, "you took a bit of finding. My name is Fala and at the moment I'm a reasonable visionary. However, if we were to join together, my physical form would change forever and I would no longer be me. Also, you would no longer be you. I have already decided that I wish my next step on the evolutionary scale to continue; you need to do the same. I will wait until tomorrow and if you are still here then we will become as one."

Fala removed her hand from the crystal and retreated further up the bank, settling herself down to wait. Me-i contacted her staff with her communicating device, advising them of her position and that Fala was waiting until morning to blend with the crystal. She was amazed that Fala had located the crystal. She must have an affinity with the Crystal Clan Phenacite to find them at all as it kept moving in order to check her resolve. Me-i only hoped Fala had extraordinary abilities or the blending wouldn't take place. The morning sun woke Fala bright and early. She wandered down to the crystal's edge and spoke once more.

"Good morning, I see you haven't gone. I take it you are willing for us to blend together as one to serve Oletha. I'm not sure how to actually begin the process so I will meditate until the answer presents."

Me-i had been listening to the whole conversation and smiled to herself. Fala didn't know that it was her helpers who would join her with the crystal. They had arrived late last night with all the apparatus required for helping with the transformation. Fala had been meditating for an hour while Me-i checked that everything was how it should be. Then she asked her assistants to immerse Fala within the crystal.

Fala felt the crystal sands collapsing beneath her. Before her body had time to react it was too late. She grabbed a mouthful of air just before she went under. Fighting her way to the surface, she sucked another mouthful of air into her bursting lungs before she went under again. Her head was spinning, as she was pulled down and out into a river that flowed through the mountains. She was buffeted and dragged from the bottom to the sides of the river. When she finally surfaced her lungs were near bursting. Gulping in mouthfuls of air she used the last of her strength to swim to a bank of crystal sand where she collapsed exhausted.

Me-i and her helpers had watched as Fala had fought her way to the surface and then they dragged her under again. They found the river's flow and sent her down it, following her every move. When she finally crawled from the crystal river onto the bank, they removed her clothes so Me-i could treat her.

Fala was completely unaware of this procedure; she was in

a world of her own fighting to maintain balance throughout her chakra points. She was doing all right until the crystal reached the third-eye chakra. Pain then seared her eyes with such intensity she almost passed out. Her mind reeled as the crystal and the material body fought the changes taking place. With all her strength Fala sent wave after wave of Oletha's love throughout her body.

Me-i became aware that something was different when the crystalline formation around Fala's eyes started to change. A metamorphosis was taking place that was restructuring Fala's eyes into something different. This had never happened with the others. Me-i administered the appropriate soothing tinctures that eased the physical discomfort.

Fala had filled her mind with Oletha's gentle smile and soothing words, remembering her from Terraqueous, and felt the pain subside. Finally the third-eye chakra was complete and she moved on to the last two chakras, completing them without incident. A streak of silver shot skywards as gold travelled earthward joining with the crystal planet. The blending was complete.

"Fala, my name is Me-i. I am the voice of the crystal. You can open your eyes now."

Fala opened her eyes, but she could see nothing. "Are my eyes open?"

"Yes, can you see me?" Me-i answered her.

"No, I can't see anything. Wait, yes I can, but it's different somehow," Fala said, confused.

"Fala, can you see my finger?"

"Yes, although it's a little blurry at the moment."

"I want you to follow it," Me-i instructed.

Me-i moved her hand in front of Fala's face, but her eyes didn't move.

"What's the problem?" Fala asked.

"You say you can see my finger but your eyes didn't follow its movement."

"Yes, I did see it. You moved it from your right to left and then back again."

"What am I doing now?" Me-i asked, examining Fala.

"You're looking at my eyes with a sort of instrument. Now you're putting it down and talking to three other people."

"You were correct with everything you said. How is your sight now?" Me-i questioned.

"It's becoming much clearer," Fala paused for a moment. "In fact, it seems to have more detail than before," she said, her voice strangely distant. "What I'm seeing seems alive somehow."

"That's great. Let's get you back to my place where you can rest up before it's time to leave."

The trip back was much easier as they had a form of hover transport vehicle instead of having to walk.

Settling Fala into her spare room, Me-i went out to the tree Malachy had given her. Placing her hand upon it, she called Kyros.

"Kyros, come quickly. We have had some complications with Fala's transition. I will be waiting at the portal."

Lon was busy serving in the bookshop and his heart jumped when Me-i's call came through. He politely passed the consumer over to Lomasi and walked into Renae's office, nodded to her and then disappeared. He arrived at the portal to find Me-i pacing up and down.

"What's the problem, Me-i?" he asked, concerned.

"Fala blended with one of the rarest and strongest crystals in spiritual energy. Her eyes have changed. They are now multifaceted and colourless. She's blind, Kyros."

"Where is she now?"

"Resting at my place." Me-i paused before continuing. "Kyros, she doesn't know she's seeing spiritually, or that she's physically blind." Me-i and Kyros went to where Fala was supposed to be resting. When they entered the room, Fala was up and about.

"Hello, Lon, what are you doing here?"

"I needed to talk to Me-i. You've blended with your crystal, I see," he said, looking intently at her eyes and wondering how much she could see.

"I feel so different and things look strange; it will take some getting used to," she said, picking things up and feeling them before putting them down.

"Explain to me, if you can, how things look strange," Lon requested.

"Well, the colours seem to have greater depth and they shimmer," said Fala, as she struggled to voice her thoughts. "When you came into the room, you flowed in rather than walked. There is much more detail to everything now."

"Make yourself comfortable," Lon said, smiling, while indicating for Fala to sit. "I'm going to be Kyros for a moment."

Once, Fala had been a young seventeen-year-old girl with brown curly hair, olive skin and deep brown eyes. She was now a woman in her thirties. Her brown hair was now honey coloured and fell in graceful ringlets to her shoulders; her olive complexion had a golden tinge that enhanced her maturity. But the most noticeable change was her eyes. They were now the most incredibly deep, multifaceted, colourless eyes that had the minutest tints of yellow, red, and brown throughout their structure.

Fala sat and waited for Kyros to talk.

"As yet, you are unaware of your physical changes. I'm sorry to be the one to tell you but you're no longer seventeen; you are around thirty years old. However, you will never become any older and you're very beautiful, so you haven't really lost anything."

"I'm thirty!" Fala exclaimed. "You mean I've lost thirteen years of flirting with boys, going out on dates and parties and all that fun stuff?"

"I'm afraid so, although I wouldn't worry about not attracting men. You're rather gorgeous actually."

"Watch it, mister, you're a married man," Fala said, smiling. "Am I really attractive?"

Me-i laughed. "Yes, Fala, you really are a very lovely woman."

"Ah well, I've gained more than I've lost. What colour are my eyes now?"

"That's the next thing I was about to tell you when you got caught up with boys," Kyros replied.

"Well, that was important stuff you know, so tell me, what colour are they?"

"Your sight is incredible and can only improve. Your vision, on the other hand, is different."

Fala was confused. "What do you mean my sight, isn't that the same as my vision?"

"Not at all, sight refers to your spiritual ability to see with the third eye, vision refers to how you see through your physical eyes."

"What are you saying, Lon?"

"I'm saying you have excellent sight that will serve you better than your normal eyesight."

"So I'm not seeing through my eyes?"

"No, Fala, you're not. You're using your spiritual sight to see the world around you. Your eyes are incredibly deep, colourless and multifaceted with minutest tints of yellow, red, pink, and brown throughout their structure. But, you're physically blind."

"Blind!" Fala's face was full of panic.

"Don't go down that road, young lady," Lon firmly announced. "You have perfect sight, better than it was. So don't start doubting your abilities or you will lose them."

"I don't intend to lose the sight I have, Lon. Sorry, Kyros."

"Call me Lon," he said lovingly, placing his hand upon hers. "I said I was Kyros so you would know I was serious."

"There must be a reason my eyes are like this. Oletha

isn't cruel or vindictive. Let me think for a moment." Fala quietly mulled over her experience with the crystal and what Harpreet had said.

"Lon, there's something I want to try; I think I know how my eyes are to be used." Fala allowed her eyelids to close and then meditated. After a while she opened them and saw only what an Oracle could see, the differing intersecting timelines throughout the realms of Chimera.

"My eyes are the means by which I observe the future," she said, looking at Me-i and Lon. "The best way to describe it would be to liken the realms of Chimera to a large book. All I need to do is to look up the index of any situation or person to foresee the most likely outcome. For instance," Fala went on excitedly, "when the book opened, I saw a vision of you and me, visiting Zaki and then Photinah, before returning to the bookshop on Telluric," she explained knowingly.

Lon and Me-i looked at each other in wonderment at Fala's abilities.

"In that case, oh wise and beautiful Oracle, your wish is my command," Lon said, standing. "Are you well enough to travel?" he asked gently.

Rising to her feet Fala smiled and held her hand out to him. "Shall we be off?"

They all walked back to the portal, with Fala and Me-i arm in arm. On their arrival Fala said gratefully, "Me-i, I want to thank you for all you have done. I wouldn't have made a successful transition without you and your assistants.

As Oracle, I see a beautiful life ahead of you with the man you've always wanted."

"Why Fala, what a lovely thing to say." Me-i was delighted.

Then Fala and Kyros disappeared, reappearing upon the world of the One Tree. Fala stood in amazement at the sheer size of Zaki.

"Impressive, isn't he?" Lon commented.

"I know you said he was enormous, but this blows the mind. We have to go to his trunk."

"Lead the way, Oracle." Fala looked at Lon and smiled, appreciating the respect and trust he gave her. They walked for about an hour, finally reaching Zaki's trunk. When they arrived Zaki addressed them.

"Oracle, I have awaited your arrival, I have something for you to give to my granddaughter Photinah. Please cup your hand against my trunk." Fala did as she was asked and a large ball of sap filled her palm.

"Please give this to Photinah. Kyros, you and Malachy have Oletha's work to do. Heed the words of the Oracle and use her insight wisely. She is to be kept separate and in Photinah's care for the moment."

"Is it safe for her to return to the bookshop now?"

"For a short time only, then she must return to the care of Photinah," Zaki confirmed.

"It shall be as you say, my friend, and now we will take our leave of you," Lon said with respect.

Fala and Lon returned to the portal and transported to the world of the Phelan. They appeared outside Gela and

Lon's home. Fala walked to Photinah's trunk and spoke to her.

"Photinah, my name is Fala. I'm now Oracle and I have just come from Zaki, who asked me to give you this." Fala held out her hand with the sap in it and waited.

"Hello, Fala, please place the sap against my trunk." Fala did as she was asked and the sap disappeared into the trunk. Photinah's trunk and branches started to change, growing thicker and wider as the tree expanded another ten feet in every direction around her base. Remarkably, everything moved in proportion to Photinah's growth. Then a discolouration appeared, the size of a doorway within the trunk, fading until it could barely be seen.

"Fala, please enter your new home; just walk up to my trunk and the door will open for you. You may like to show Lon around," Photinah suggested.

Fala was amazed as she and Lon walked through the door and into the trunk of the tree. They walked up a flight of stairs into a lounge room area with table, chairs, shelves and sideboards. To one side was a small kitchenette. The stairs continued upward into a bedroom with a washroom adjoining it. Continuing further up the stairs they walked out from the trunk onto a large branch that had a balustrade all around the edge and a table and chairs to one side.

"Oh Photinah, this is magnificent. How can I ever repay such an incredible gift?"

"You have lovely manners; it will be my pleasure to have you here under my protection. I know how you people like to see the view, so let me know where you would like windows and I will arrange it for you. Kyros can organise the carpets or polished floors for you. Whatever you want, Oracle, just ask and it is yours."

"Photinah, why is my home different to the others?"

"This is your sanctuary, Fala. Only Oletha can enter your home without permission. You may have visitors if you desire, but none can enter if you aren't here or without your permission. None may know where you live but your fellow disciples. This is for your protection. Do you understand?"

"Yes, Photinah, I understand and will honour your instructions," Fala responded. "Lon, can I have carpet in the lounge and bedroom, please, and polished floorboards everywhere else?"

"Your wish is my command," he said, producing his Staff and placing Malachy before him. He began to intone a mantra. Halfway through, Lon stood on a chair and then he asked Fala to do likewise. He then recommenced the mantra, causing sap to flow out from the doorway and across their branch where it hardened.

"Let us see if it meets with your approval." Fala and Lon walked back the way they had come. Fala was awestruck at the depth of colour in the floors and stairs. The carpets were thick and soft underfoot. The bed had a mattress of vines that was supportive and comfortable.

Fala then requested that Photinah create windows in such a way that anyone looking at the tree would be unable to detect them. Photinah chuckled and said that no one would be able to see them from the ground so not to worry. Fala indicated where she would like the windows to be and then watched in amazement as they appeared before her. Once that was finished, Fala and Lon returned to the front door where a walking stick made from one of Photinah's small branches leaned against it.

"This is for you, Fala. To the outside world, you will appear to be blind. This cane will be your guide and can communicate with Nature wherever you may be. It will also give you a direct link to me and return you home anytime you wish."

"This is lovely, Photinah. I will keep it with me at all times," Fala said, thanking her.

"Remember, you are blind to all but your fellow disciples!"

"I'll remember Photinah, thank you."

"It is time you met some of the Phelan, Fala." Lon transported them to the base of the tree and then they went to find Seanan and Riona.

"Kyros," Riona called as he and Fala walked towards her. "Who be this beautiful woman by your side?"

"This is Fala. Fala, this is Riona." Fala held out her hand as if she didn't know where Riona was. Riona took it and looked sadly at Kyros.

"You be unable to see, Fala. That be a shame, because you be missing the most beautiful thing your eyes be ever seeing."

"What would that be, Riona?"

"Why, that be you, of course!" Riona held Fala in an embrace, which was returned in equal measure.

"You're very kind to say so; Kyros is the only one to tell me that, Fala said to her. "But we're family so it doesn't count."

"Who be this charming woman you be embracing, my love?" came a gruff voice from behind her.

"Seanan, this be Fala. She be one of Kyros's family."

"I be very pleased to be meeting you, Oracle."

"Her name be Fala, you great dolt," Riona admonished.

"It may be, my love, but she be Oracle. That be why her eyes be as they are. You be welcome, Fala. I be Seanan, newly appointed shaman, thanks to Kyros."

"Yes, he has a habit of doing things like that I've noticed," smiled Fala.

Seanan and Fala laughed as he placed his arm about her and walked far enough away from Lon and Riona so they couldn't be overheard.

"My guide, Cloud Dancing, be telling me of your coming and that you be seeing spiritually, better than most people's physical sight. He be warning me to be reminding you that no one be suspecting that you be having The Sight and that your whereabouts be kept a secret. If you be requiring anything I be at your disposal."

"You are most kind, Seanan; I know I can trust your discretion. From what I perceive, we will become good friends and have many hours of philosophical conversation."

"All right, you two. Seanan, I'm surprised at you flirting with another woman with your wife watching," Kyros jested.

"Ah, that be the trick, she be never suspecting me of misdoings in plain sight," Seanan laughingly responded.

They walked back to Riona and Kyros where Seanan embraced his wife with such love that she snuggled into his arms.

"It's time for Fala and me to leave. We will return at a later date to introduce Fala to the whole clan. I just wanted you two to meet her first."

"That be most gracious of you, Kyros," Riona and Seanan answered.

Kyros took Fala's hand, intoned a mantra and vanished.

* * *

Enoch and Roja were sitting in their cell reviewing the various types of mercenaries required for the different operations Enoch had planned.

"I want ya ta assemble an elite group of individuals ta train as assassins," Enoch said, continuing his strategic operation. "Don't pick nobody known ta any government organisation. I want them ta be invisible and highly skilled in the art of making the assassination look like the person died of natural causes."

"Where do you want them based?" Roja asked.

"Pick an overseas country with jungle we can hide in and an economy that is fragile," Enoch replied. "Have a subsidiary of Concurrence Resolutions invest in local businesses. Then through the government, establish investment houses and an import and export business that will bolster their economy. This will make it impossible for the government ta remove us without destabilisin' their financial system. Next, I want ordinary mercenaries based in every capital throughout the world."

"That's a tall order, Enoch; you won't have enough people to fill the ranks," Roja objected.

"Pull all the bullyboys and ruffians off the streets and train 'em. If they object, eliminate 'em. Oh, and that includes the bitches as well."

"Just how am I supposed to pull off that little feat of magic?" Roja asked, annoyed.

"I'll have Concurrence Resolutions set up a worldwide youth organisation with hostels ta support the underprivileged. That will be our cover. We will even employ genuine government community workers while we do our recruitin'. We'll have two types of youth camps, one more regimented than the other," Enoch replied.

"That's brilliant, Enoch," Roja remarked, amazed at how devious Enoch's mind was. Standing, he walked round the cell deep in thought. Stopping, he turned to Enoch and smiled. "I know just the person to help set the ball rolling," he said.

"I also want hardened military types for Slegna's regular army, with a full range of armaments ta complement their ranks. For the elimination jobs, I want the cold cruel bastards who have no morals. Them I want assembled first, and Roja, if one of 'em puts so much as one toe out of place, they're dead!" was Enoch's cold-blooded statement. "I think that just about covers it. Can ya think of anythin'?"

"If I do, I'll let you know. As soon as the guards do their final check I'll be off."

After the final check for the night, Enoch and Roja went about their individual tasks. Enoch visited the crime family's solicitors to enquire how the new corporation was coming along. Things were better than he thought. The company had already been set up and many of the crime lords had dissolved some of their businesses, giving the opportunity for Concurrence Resolutions to legally purchase them.

With the gold Enoch had provided, plus the contributions from the families, the company was quite solvent. Enoch was advised that the business world had welcomed a fresh competitor into the market and their enterprise was growing faster than they could have imagined. They were already making a steady profit.

Enoch mentioned to the solicitor his idea of forming a worldwide youth organisation with hostels. He was advised that most governments would provide some of the funds and workers if the company provided the rest. They could also set up a donation fund to help support the underprivileged. Enoch asked the solicitor to have their new company start the ball rolling. His next visit was to Andy at his penthouse apartment. He was in the middle of getting dressed when Enoch spoke.

"Hi Andy, how's it hangin', pal?"

Andy dropped the clothes he was holding. "Shit, Enoch, you scared the crap out of me," he said, trying to catch his breath. "Do you think you could give a person warning before you come barging in?" he finished angrily.

Enoch laughed. "Yeah, I suppose I could, but I like the look on ya face. It's priceless."

"Understand something, Enoch, Slegna's power or not, you need me and the rest of us to make this coup d'état of yours work. So stop being such a smart arse and flinging all your power around and use your brains. That's still the best tool you've got!" Andy stated heatedly while retrieving his clothes from the floor and finishing getting dressed.

"I seem ta remember ya telling me that before; ya were right then and you're probably right now. Truce." Enoch slowly walked toward Andy.

Andy's face softened slightly. "Truce it is then. What can I do for you?"

"Has Roja arrived yet?"

"Been and gone, that's one busy man," Andy confirmed.

"Yeah, I gave him a bit to do. I'll be off then."

Enoch return to his cell to think on what Andy had said. Andy was never a smart arse and the gang had come a long way with him running things. Maybe a bit of diplomacy was in order.

* * *

Fala and Lon materialised in Renae's office, scaring the wits out of her. "Could you please make some sort of a noise before you appear like that?" Renae admonished.

"Sorry, Renae. I brought a guest with me. Allow me to introduce ..."

"Fala!" Renae was astounded at Fala's transformation.

"Oracle," explained Lon.

Renae came out from behind her desk to embrace her, but stopped when she noticed Fala's eyes were white and she was holding a cane.

"We came back at closing time so as not to cause a commotion in the shop. I wish to introduce Oracle into our family. Is Nathanial in his office?"

Renae eyes looked upward. "Where else would he be?" she replied.

"Good, I'll go speak to him after which I will contact Barbette and Harpreet to meet us here. Would you be kind enough to organise the rest of the family for a meeting?"

While Lon was in Nathanial's office, Renae arranged for everyone to assemble on the mezzanine floor. Barbette and Harpreet arrived as Lon and Nathanial walked out of the office.

"Everybody's here, Lon." Renae advised him.

"Thank you, Renae, I appreciate that over the last couple of days you've all had a lot to contend with. In essence, our lives have been turned upside-down. Each one of us has unique abilities beyond this world's capability to understand. We have chosen to become Oletha's disciples. This means that in some way, each one of us will move through changes beyond our current understanding.

"My own metamorphosis has been an interesting learning curve and I believe the same can be said for Gela and Harpreet's transition. My disappearance today was in answer to a call for help from Me-i. The nature of that call was about Fala's blending with the crystal."

"She's not dead, is she?" squealed Gabbryel, nervous for her friend.

"No, Gabbryel. Fala's metamorphosis has matured her body beyond her years, causing considerable changes to her physical and spiritual perception of life. She is no longer the shy little girl you all remember."

Lon entered Renae's office and walked out with a beautiful woman on his arm holding a cane. Everyone looked on in amazement; they could barely recognise the young girl that had once been Fala. Her brown curly hair was now honey coloured and fell gracefully to her shoulders; her olive complexion had a golden lustre that enhanced her maturity. But the most noticeable change besides her age, were her eyes.

"I have the honour of introducing you all to Oracle," he said with pride.

When Fala spoke it was with a rich musical voice. "Thank you for such an eloquent introduction, Lon." Harpreet and Barbette were by her side the moment Lon moved away.

"You have paid a hard price for your gift, dear," Barbette commented.

"Actually, Barbette, I don't have a gift. As Lon became Malachy, I have become Oracle," she remarked sedately.

"What do you mean she paid a hard price?" Gabbryel stated. "She looks great and can see into the future, right?"

"Gabbryel, why do you always let your mouth run away

with your brain?" Renae scolded her. "Can't you see the cane she is holding and her eyes are white? She's blind."

Gabbryel drew in a sharp breath and ran from the room sobbing.

"I'm sorry, Fala. She didn't mean anything by it."

"That's quite all right, Renae, I'm not offended; please bring her back," Fala replied compassionately.

Harpreet had been observing Fala from the moment she'd walked into the room. Something didn't seem correct to her way of thinking and Lon was just too smug about something.

"Fala, you can see?" Harpreet announced.

"Yes, but not through my eyes."

"What do you mean not through your eyes? How else would you see?" Janelle asked.

"How did I see Nathanial's predicament?"

"Yeah, but you have spiritual sight. Oh, of course. Don't mind me Lomasi, my brains are on holiday. Sorry Fala."

"That's all right, Janelle. It's natural to think in the material and forget the spiritual. However, to the outside world I appear to be blind."

Renae had walked back onto the mezzanine with Gabbryel.

"Did you hear that, Gabbryel?" Fala enquired.

"Yes, Fala, to everyone else you're blind," she answered hesitantly while wiping her eyes.

"Please, no one forget. Fala no longer exists; there is only Oracle. I'm already seeing numerous future events, being amongst you all like this, which is why an Oracle's life is a solitary existence. I have a home prepared in a secluded location safe from those who would do me harm," Fala informed everyone.

"As Oracle, I will share my vision of the forthcoming events and then I will be leaving. You will not see me again unless I so desire it. I hope you can all understand why it must be so."

Nathanial walked up to Fala and enfolded her within a loving embrace. "My heart is sad for the loss of Fala. However, my spiritual heart sings with pride and joy for what you've allowed yourself to become. I am forever here for you."

Fala returned Nathanial's embrace and as they parted he kissed her on the forehead. One by one everyone embraced her and wished her well. Fala gathered everyone around her and bid them to listen.

"I see a great storm coming that will encompass the world. The leader of this tempest is called Enoch and he is your mortal enemy. He is Slegna's chosen one, his disciple. Transmutation and transportation are just two of the powers Slegna has bestowed upon him. His range of abilities almost equals Malachy's. Don't underestimate him for he is devious beyond reckoning and can never be trusted.

"Slegna commanded him to form a corporation called Concurrence Resolutions Pty Ltd that is based offshore with connections in all the provinces. This will be the front for a newly appointed world crime syndicate. Enoch is gathering every crime lord, bullyboy, gang and ruffian on Telluric under his wing; any who refuse Slegna's offer will die. I see mass murders and civil unrest to the point of martial law.

Governments worldwide will falter and the economy will plummet as the people's faith crumbles.

"A prophet shall walk the land preaching the Mystery of the True Light in the face of the Mystery of the One Truth. Many will try to pull him down as he gives hope to those weak of spirit. Thus ends my telling. It is time for me to leave." Oracle tapped her cane and vanished, leaving everyone in awe.

"Well," said Nathanial, "that was certainly a bleak future she painted."

"Yes, and it puts us in the middle of it," commented Janelle.

"What do we do now, Lon?" asked Gabbryel.

"Well, I don't know about the rest of you, but I'm going home with my lovely wife and will have something to eat," he said, enfolding Gela in an embrace. "Then it's an early night for me as I'm tired."

"That reminds me, where are you two staying?" Lomasi asked.

"Oh, didn't I tell you?" Gela said, moving out from Lon's embrace. "Lon gave me a penthouse apartment for our wedding present; we'll be going there."

"This I've got to see, considering he's never had two coins to rub together," Lomasi said disbelievingly.

"It's true, I've seen it. In fact, I live on the floor below theirs."

"Come on, Harpreet, you can't be serious!" Lomasi said in astonishment.

Harpreet and Gela laughed as Lon looked at them both and shook his head.

"Actually, Lon, being the gentleman, has acquired rooms for all of you. Believe me, the views are breathtaking and I can literally say they're out of this world!" Harpreet continued.

"Harpreet, you are as big a stirrer as Gela," Lon chuckled.

"Barbette, my one and only, would you give Gela, Harpreet and me the pleasure of your company tonight? There is something I need to discuss," Lon enquired.

"I wish Fala was here, I'd grab that cane of hers and hit you with it," remarked a feisty Barbette.

"Why Barbette, I thought you loved me," Lon teased.

"I'll give you 'my one and only', Boyo!" Barbette said, pretending to be offended.

"Okay, let's call it a night. I will see you all bright and early tomorrow," Renae called.

As everyone departed, Gela, Harpreet, Barbette and Lon walked to the portal and vanished, reappearing outside Gela's penthouse apartment.

"I would like to introduce you to Photinah. Photinah this is Barbette," Gela said, pointing to the tree.

"Pleased to make your acquaintance, Barbette," Photinah responded.

"Well, I'll be! What an absolute pleasure it is to meet you, Photinah, and what a beautifully rich feminine voice you have. I take it you are female?"

"Yes, Barbette, I'm female," Photinah laughingly replied.

"I love trees, but I've never had the honour of having one talk to me before," Barbette announced.

"I like her, is she family Lon?"

"Yes, Photinah, she's family; but watch her, she's a flirt."

Barbette shook her head at him with a sigh. Just then there was a rustling sound and everyone turned around to see Oracle standing behind them.

"I take it, Lon, nobody knows where I am?"

"As Oracle you already know that answer, so why ask it?" he answered.

"Thank you for bringing the people I requested. I think we will talk at my place. I contacted Seanan and he supplied me with food and drink. He is such a gentleman; Riona is most fortunate to have a mate like him. I have given him permission to enter my quarters at any time."

Oracle turned and seemed to walk into Photinah; Lon smiled and indicated that they all should do the same. As each one touched Photinah's bark they found themselves being absorbed within her trunk, reappearing before a staircase that led up to a lounge room.

"Where are we?" Gela asked.

"We're inside Photinah. She takes her protection of me quite seriously," Fala informed all present. "No one can enter without Photinah's express permission; she is my faithful protector. As you can see, this is the lounge room and over there is a kitchenette; the bedroom is the next floor up with a washroom adjoining it, followed by a beautiful terrace with a table and chairs.

"You're welcome to look around. Food and drink have been prepared on the terrace." Everyone expressed their admiration for the design and loveliness of Oracle's home as they made themselves comfortable on the terrace.

"So, husband mine, the mysterious seventh house."

"Sorry I couldn't tell you, love, it was for Oracle to decide," he said apologetically.

"At least you know the secret now, Gela," Harpreet commented.

Barbette enquired about Harpreet's mysterious statement and was informed that Gela thought Lon had miscounted the members of their family. He only requested Photinah to grow seven large branches where he could construct homes for his family. Oracle chuckled and pointed to the refreshments. "Please, help yourselves to the food. I asked Lon if he would arrange for us to meet in private. My identity must be kept secret from everyone outside the family. No one is to even talk about an Oracle. The Unbalanced will be looking for me very shortly and they will stop at nothing to find me. For that reason no other family members are to know my location," Fala emphasised.

"Each one of us was brought to Telluric from different worlds by Oletha's disciple, Barbette," Oracle remarked, indicating Barbette. "This was done without our knowledge so Slegna would never suspect that the representatives of the Mystery of the True Light were already present when he made his move to turn the people from Oletha.

"This means we are to preside over Telluric and create stability wherever we encounter Slegna's forces of the Unbalanced. However, we don't have the right to interfere with a person's free will. As for this Enoch, Malachy is the only one strong enough to face him and hopefully win."

"When you say Malachy, do you mean just Lon's Staff?" asked Gela.

"Lon, Kyros and the Staff are Malachy, you cannot separate them. Lon simply refers to himself as Kyros, because that's what people call him. In reality he is Malachy. The same as I am Oracle. We didn't develop our gifts, we metamorphosed into what we are now."

"Are you saying that if Lon goes up against Enoch, he could lose?" Gela persisted.

"There is a war coming that will encompass not only the materialistic world of Telluric, but its spiritual aspect as well," Oracle predicted. "I'm unable to see the outcome, only the factions within the battle. These I will advise you on as the flow of energy permits.

"Each one in our family has a particular spiritual gift pertaining to the world we came from, along with specific character traits inherent to that world. This unfortunately presents us with a problem." Fala's voice showed signs of anxiety.

"Gabbryel's character is true to form for her species, wherein she is unable to keep secrets until she reaches her maturity. Unfortunately that's not for another four years. This then makes her the weak link in the chain. Gabbryel's ability to interpret the rhythmic frequencies left behind by others will make her brilliant at psychometry. We just have to get her through the next four years."

"I think it might be best if Gabbryel were removed from Telluric and taken to my home on Terraqueous," Harpreet suggested. "I can instigate a training program that will cover the time necessary. It has always been my impression that she would need a firm hand; she's a little too smart for her own good. The discipline will be excellent for her training."

"Are you sure, Harpreet? She can be quite a handful," Lon asked.

"Don't worry, Lon, that little minx won't get the better of me. You forget Terraqueous is a highly developed world spiritually, having many students who think they know everything. I'll put her in a class with students who think they're just as smart as she is and then knock them all down to size," Harpreet stated.

Everyone laughed at Harpreet's comment.

"This is all well and good, but we're leaving the bookshop short of staff. Renae won't be happy. She's devoted to Nathanial and the store," Lon commented.

"I'm sure she will understand," Barbette said.

"She might, but that won't change the fact that she will have lost two staff members."

"I have two students in my advanced class that are due to go off-planet," Harpreet explained. "The bookshop would be perfect, if you think Renae wouldn't mind?"

"I could put them up at my place, Lon," Barbette interjected.

"Well, if Renae is in agreement, I don't see a problem. What do you think, Gela?"

"Harpreet, your students would need to understand that

Telluric is, for all intents and purposes, spiritually blind. They couldn't use their abilities there like they would on Terraqueous."

"That wouldn't be a problem," Harpreet reassured her.

"Fala, do you have something to add?" asked Barbette.

"It is as I have foreseen," Fala replied calmly.

"Then why didn't you just tell us what to do then?" Gela blurted out.

"Everyone has free will. What I saw had several possible outcomes. That was merely one of them."

"Well, was it the right one?"

"There is no right or wrong Gela, only the choices you make," Fala affirmed.

"Harpreet, what age are the students, and are they boys or girls?"

"Two very polite sixteen-year-old young ladies. I believe you will find them delightful company, Barbette."

The conversation swung back and forth to different subjects until it was time to call it a night. Barbette was offered accommodation but decided to return home, as did Harpreet. They both had things to do. Fala bid everyone goodnight and they left. Lon and Gela went to their home. They awoke to a bright sunny day full of promise and after an enjoyable breakfast, transported themselves to the bookshop.

CHAPTER SEVENTEEN

Renae entered the bookshop to the sound of her staff happily joking and singing to themselves. Lon had asked for a meeting at 10am with herself and Harpreet if it was convenient and she had agreed. Nathanial was busying himself with research into something that had caught his attention and Kalareena hadn't been seen. Renae decided to catch up on the never-ending paperwork that goes hand in hand with running a bookshop. It seemed she had only just sat down when Lon politely tapped on the door.

Renae absentmindedly called "Enter."

Lon put his head around the corner of her door. "Is this not a good time?" he asked her politely.

"Is it that time already?" Renae commented looking up from her paperwork. "Come on in."

Lon opened the door fully. Standing to one side he allowed Harpreet to enter first. Renae indicated they be seated around her coffee table. Lon pulled a seat for Harpreet who made herself comfortable.

"Renae, I'd like to say I'm sorry for all the inconvenience you've been put through lately," he said apologetically, while pulling a chair out for her. "My life has gone through some major changes and you've been such a sport about everything that I just wanted to say thank you."

"You're welcome, Lon," Renae said with a smirk on her face. "So what are you buttering me up for this time?"

"No, I really wanted to say thank you," he said, taking the seat opposite her. "It's just that this is the first time I've stood still long enough in one place to be able to say it."

"Your life has been completely turned upside-down, hasn't it?" Renae said. "How does it feel to be Malachy, Lon?"

"You're the first one to refer to me by my true title. It's strange having so much knowledge at my fingertips and the power can be intoxicating. You have to continually remind yourself you're not one of those gods from a children's fairy tale," he said, shaking his head. "Do you know that if I want riches all I have to do is this?" Lon picked up an apple from the fruit bowl on the coffee table and ran his hand around it, transforming the apple into pure gold. He then picked up some nuts from another bowl, smiling he blew on them and scattered a mixture of precious gems across the desktop. Harpreet and Renae looked on in disbelief.

"It puts a different perspective on wealth. You very soon realise the greatest gift in all creation is love," he affirmed.

"Well, I guess you're not here to ask for a pay increase. So what can I do for the both of you?" Renae asked wearily.

Lon informed Renae of Oracle's concerns about Gabbryel and the possibility of sending her off-world for training under Harpreet's capable hands.

445

"Lon, before we continue, could you do something about that?" Renae commented, calling his attention to the untold wealth sitting on her table.

"Oh, sorry." Lon waved his hand, returning the fruit and nuts to their original form.

"The decision should be Gabbryel's," Renae said, concerned. "I understand your concerns though. What would her training entail, Harpreet?"

"I would start her off on the rudimentary concepts of spirituality throughout the different planetary systems, including her home world. Then establish a foundation of truth from which all spiritual knowledge is based and the interpretation of that truth upon her field of expertise."

"I'm sorry, Harpreet. I didn't mean to doubt your abilities," Renae remarked, realising she had inadvertently questioned Harpreet's qualifications.

"If we leave it up to Gabbryel, she will remain here. I know her," Lon interjected.

"You're probably right. We would have to make it sound like the opportunity of a lifetime that only a fool would reject," observed Renae.

"Harpreet, did you bring that article I requested?" Lon enquired.

Harpreet reached into her pocket and withdrew the object. "Yes, I have it here."

"Good, could you please place it on the table?" he requested.

"What are you up to?"

"Watch and learn, Renae, watch and learn," he said, as a

mischievous grin crossed his face. "Could you please call Gabbryel to your office?"

Renae called Gabbryel on the intercom, asking her to come to her office. Not long after, there was a polite knock at the door and Renae bid her enter.

"Ah Gabbryel, there's something I think only you can resolve for us," Lon said. "You see that item on table?"

"This one?" she asked politely, picking it up.

"Yes, that's the one. I need you to interpret what you feel from it."

Harpreet understood what Lon was up to and winked at Renae, who gave a slight nod in return.

"Lon, that's not fair on the girl, she's had no training. Putting her on the spot like that isn't right."

"I must agree with Harpreet, Lon. I think you're asking too much from her," Renae played along.

Gabbryel looked from Renae to Harpreet and then back to Lon. She was becoming angry that they were talking about her in the third person and she spoke out. "If Lon thinks I can help, I would like to try," she insisted.

"Very well, Gabbryel, if you insist," Renae replied.

"Don't worry, Renae. I know what I'm doing." Gabbryel slowly turned the object around in her hands while she moved about the Renae's office. Her face went through several delightful expressions before she spoke. "I'm sensing an enormous amount of joy and laughter. There is also some very serious instruction taking place and the rewards are truly breathtaking. I'm seeing a beautiful landscape with rolling hills and lakes. There is a building close to the lake used for teaching."

Harpreet was looking at Lon as Gabbryel was describing what she was sensing. This girl had real raw talent. "I know all that, Gabbryel," Lon said, disappointment showing in his voice. "There was a specific thing I was after. Maybe Harpreet and Renae were right and I'm asking too much of you," Lon suggested.

"Then give me a direction and I will see if I can find the information you're seeking," Gabbryel entreated.

Lon pretended to think for a moment. "Very well then, it's something that was partly lost."

While Gabbryel allowed her spirituality to extend beyond her immediate range, Harpreet was tuning in on her skills. She was very impressed. The strength of Gabbryel's latent power would be a force to be reckoned with, once fully developed.

"The thing you seek is within; it was never lost, just forgotten," Gabbryel informed Lon. "Return to your youth and you will discover it. That's all I can receive, Lon. I hope that has been of help."

"Did that answer your questions, Harpreet?" Lon asked.

"Yes, it did. Gabbryel, would you like to fully develop your abilities of psychometry?"

"Now just one moment, Harpreet, Gabbryel could learn that here with Barbette," Renae commented. Harpreet, Renae and Lon started discussing Gabbryel's training between them as if she had no say in her future. Finally she had heard enough.

"Excuse me," Gabbryel said, annoyed. "But this is my life and I say where I will and will not go. Harpreet is a professor of some renown on her world. In fact, if my information is correct, she's considered the best in her field. I don't wish to be disrespectful to Barbette, however, I believe Harpreet would be the more qualified teacher."

"You understand, don't you, Gabbryel, that if you go with Harpreet you will remain there until your studies are finished?" Renae queried.

Gabbryel nodded. "I don't mean to be bad-mannered, but I'm no fool."

"Are you absolutely sure about this, Gabbryel?" asked Lon, rising from his seat.

"Yes, if Harpreet will have me."

Harpreet rose to address her. "I would be pleased to be your teacher, Gabbryel."

"That's settled then. You had better run home and pack what is needed. When you return you can say your goodbyes and leave for your training," instructed Renae.

Gabbryel squealed with delight and left Renae's office.

"I feel like a cad doing that to her," Lon remarked.

"I know how you feel, Lon, but it's for the best. Harpreet, how accurate was she with her interpretation?" Renae questioned.

"She was spot on," Harpreet remarked thoughtfully. "She has real talent. Unfortunately she knows she is good at what she does," Harpreet turned to look at Lon and Renae. "What have I let myself in for?"

"So, I have to ask," Renae said, standing next to Harpreet, "what was partly lost?"

Harpreet laughed at Renae's question. "What is it we often wished we still had now we're adults?"

Renae thought carefully on Harpreet's question; suddenly her face lit up. "Our childlike innocence of life," she ventured.

"Very good, Renae," Harpreet replied.

"I'm now down two staff members with Fala and Gabbryel gone."

"I can help you with that, Renae," Harpreet interjected. "I have two graduate students looking for work experience off-world. I was hoping you would accept them as your replacements; they are fine workers who know their way around a bookshop. If you are agreeable, Barbette is happy to have them live with her. What do you say?"

"Are they handy?" Renae was quick to see if the students could be interviewed.

"Why yes, they're very good..."

"No, are they with you?" Renae asked.

"Yes, they have been getting acquainted with the store."

"Trot them in then," Renae said in a businesslike manner.

Harpreet's face showed surprise. "She means show them in, Harpreet," Lon explained.

"You do have an interesting phraseology." Harpreet concentrated for a moment. "They're on their way up."

Renae looked questioningly at Harpreet. "Sorry, Renae, we use mind projection on Terraqueous to communicate with our students."

Harpreet walked to the door and opened it just as the girls arrived. She ushered them into the office to stand before Renae's desk. Renae nodded to Lon, who took Harpreet by the hand and led her from the room. It was obvious she would rather have stayed in the office with the girls.

"The girls will be fine Harpreet. Renae won't eat them," Lon advised her.

"I've tutored those girls since they were little tots," she said, looking at the closed door. "I guess I'm a little protective."

Lon smiled knowingly as he escorted Harpreet to the kitchenette for refreshments. About twenty minutes later the girls came down the stairs laughing and joking among themselves. Harpreet walked up to them and they immediately became silent.

"Leave it be, Harpreet. I take it you two lovely ladies are now working here?" Lon queried.

"Yes, sir, we are," they answered together.

"Good, my name is Lon, not sir. Have you met everyone in the bookshop?"

The two girls looked at Harpreet and then Lon before answering.

"Yes, sir."

Lon looked at Harpreet, who shook her head and walked up to Renae's office.

"Harpreet is no longer your tutor. We are now your family away from home. Please give us the courtesy of being yourselves, not some prim and proper makeover you were told to be. Now what are your names?"

The taller of the two girls addressed Lon first. She was a common-looking lass with no particular distinguishing features. She wore a plain-white fitted blouse and a light-brown skirt and shoes. She stood five foot nine, her dark hair was tied into a bun at the top of her head and she wore no makeup. Her voice was firm but quiet. "Thank you, Lon. I am Jacinda."

"Pleased to make your acquaintance, Jacinda," Lon said, smiling, and then turned toward the other lass.

"My name is Keisha. Thank you for your cordial welcome."

Keisha stood five four with auburn hair that fell to her shoulders. She wore a red twinset over black slacks and shoes. She didn't wear makeup either; her voice was rich and, like Jacinda's, quite firm. "Is Gabbryel going to our home world to learn under Professor Harpreet?" she asked.

"That she is."

"Please don't misunderstand; we love the professor very much ..."

"But she can be a real stickler for protocol," finished Lon.

"Yes. If Gabbryel can overlook that side of her she will learn a great deal."

"Maybe you could discreetly mention that to her. It might help ease her way. I'd best be going." Lon walked back up to Renae's office to overhear her and Harpreet talking about protocol and discipline. This was the first time Harpreet had actually dealt with Renae on a professional level when it came to her staff. She wasn't making any headway whatsoever.

"Could you two ladies refrain from all this aggression? After all this is Telluric not Terraqueous. The lifestyle here is different," Lon interrupted.

Renae and Harpreet looked at each other and then started laughing. Everything was turning out the way Oracle wished it. Gabbryel returned with all her belongings and said her goodbyes after which she departed with Harpreet.

Around a fortnight later Nathanial walked into Renae's office with Kalareena.

"Excuse me, Renae, do you have a moment?"

"Of course, Nathanial," she replied, observing them both. "What can I do for you?"

Indicating Kalareena, he replied. "Kalareena and I are heading off so she can help me reawaken my latent spiritual talents."

"That sounds interesting," Renae said, grinning. "How long do you think you'll be gone?"

"Let's just say I wouldn't wait up for me," he replied laughingly.

"Okay, Nathanial," she answered. "But I want regular communication from you so I know you're alive and well."

"Yes, Mummy," he answered as he and Kalareena headed for the door. When they reached it Kalareena turned. "I'll see to it he keeps you informed Renae," she advised her while cuddling Nathanial's arm.

* * *

Enoch's trial had taken place and the jury had reduced the charge of first-degree murder to manslaughter. He was given twenty years for the manslaughter charge, another ten for the abduction of five women and the rape of four, and another five for theft. In all, he had to serve at least thirty years before being eligible for parole. Enoch rather liked the idea as it gave him the perfect alibi for all his activities.

Over the following months Concurrence Resolutions Pty Ltd had become the fastest growing company in history. Its conglomerate was worldwide and had infiltrated most financial organisations and government facilities, plus it controlled nearly all the import and export trade.

The families that refused to join Slegna's New Order were being progressively squeezed out of business. Enoch's military forces were steadily growing and his special assassins and elimination squads were complete.

Enoch had successfully enticed, threatened and bullied almost every crime family around the world to join Slegna's New Order. Now it was time to eliminate the rest. This would be a deterrent against those who might be having second thoughts. The first elimination squad made an example so all would know that what Enoch said must be obeyed.

The newspapers boldly reported the carnage of a known major crime family who had been butchered to the last man, woman and child. Not even their distant relatives who had no connection with the family's criminal activities were spared. The television stations displayed vivid pictures of hundreds of bodies strewn about for the whole world to see.

Before the shock of the first horror was over, it was followed by another massacre that numbered in the thousands. Every continent on Telluric was experiencing mass murders as three more times the slaughter took place in different places around the globe. The public outcry worldwide was deafening for the authorities to do something to stop the horrendous bloodbath.

Those families that had originally declined Enoch's invitation now wanted to join. In his malevolence he allowed them into the fold and then had the head of each family killed, the remaining family members split up and their assets transferred to Concurrence Resolutions Pty Ltd. Things were going well for Slegna's New Order. Enoch had succeeded in accomplishing what no one had ever done before. He had gathered the entire Unbalanced worldwide under his control for the single purpose of converting everyone to Slegna's rule. Now was the time to strike! The violence on the planet suddenly escalated, resulting in martial law being enforced in four different countries.

* * *

Jacinda and Lon were rearranging one of the bookshelves in the shop when suddenly a call came out of nowhere.

"Kyros, come quick!" echoed through Lon's mind, resulting in him dropping the books he was carrying.

"Kyros, come quick!"

Jacinda looked at Lon in surprise. "If the call is for you how come I heard it?" she asked, puzzled.

"You heard that?" Lon asked, baffled.

"Yes, it was very clear, but with no direction."

"That's very well put, young lady," Lon remarked. "It could be the call is an open-mind projection and that's why you're receiving it."

"Kyros, come quick!" the voice was gradually receding.

Lon settled himself down to listen with all his senses and waited.

"Kyros ..." once more the cry came.

"I have it, Jacinda. Let Gela know I'm off to an emergency." Lon disappeared along the spiritual lifeline to answer the call. He appeared at the base of a mountain high in the hills that surrounded one of the cities on Snakeisles. This he hadn't expected.

"So you're the great and masterful Kyros, are ya? I've heard a lot about ya."

Kyros was immediately on the defensive. Producing Malachy, he stared at the figure of a person pulsating with red and orange energy.

"That must be Wood," stated a malevolent voice.

This could only be Enoch, Slegna's disciple, for that's what he'd told Slegna he called Malachy.

"So how is that one-sided master of yours, Enoch?" Kyros asked calmly.

Enoch was surprised Kyros knew who he was. "Better than the bitch ya follow."

Enoch was trying to bait him, was he? "Everyone is entitled to his or her opinion. Are you unwell that you call me?"

"I don't need your help if I'm sick, 'cause I don't get sick," Enoch spat back.

"Please don't waste my time, Enoch. If you've got something to say then do so."

The attack came with such force it knocked Kyros off his feet. He was barely standing when the next energy blast hit him. Enoch's power was formidable and not to be underestimated. Kyros directed the following attacks skyward where no harm could come from them. The following succession of assaults seemed more as diversionary attempts than to do him harm.

"Ya havin' fun yet, Kyros?"

Kyros held the next couple of volleys Enoch fired in check and returned the energy to its source. Enoch was thrown hundreds of feet in the air, landing hard enough to knock the wind out of him. Kyros encircled Enoch in a force field that pinned him to the ground, walked up and stood over him.

"You having fun yet, Enoch?"

Enoch smiled. Kyros felt a rumbling and knew he had walked right into Enoch's trap. A wave of orange energy exploded all about him freeing Enoch. Kyros was momentarily taken off guard and then Enoch did the unexpected; he physically punched Kyros in the face sending his senses reeling. Kyros recovered just in time to block another punch coming his way but received one in his abdomen for his trouble. Every punch Enoch threw had Slegna's power behind it.

Backing away to regain some form of defence, served to no avail. Enoch was relentless and his combinations were skilfully delivered. Kyros wasn't a boxer and knew nothing about defence; the few hits he landed were making no headway against Enoch's onslaught. He was losing and he knew it. He tried putting up a barrier but Enoch crumbled it before he could complete it, so he transported himself to the base of a mountain far from Enoch.

Beaten, bleeding with his head spinning and his eyes almost swollen closed, he gasped for breath. A rumble behind him had him turning to face a new threat. Unfortunately his mind was numb and all he could think of was to take on his crystal form as the mountain behind him collapsed. Thousands of tonnes of earth descended upon him encasing him in a rocky prison, and the only sound he could hear was Enoch's sadistic laugh echoing within his mind.

Author Profile

Born into an underprivileged, struggling family in the slums of Melbourne, Australia, young Carl Read found life a battle. Poorly educated and having to fight roving gangs in the streets, Carl lived a hard life. His spiritual sensitivity made him aware of the flaws in society and its rules. Carl was able to intuitively perceive the reality of people; noticing how they constantly misrepresented the truth gave him a pessimistic view of life.

On reaching adulthood he moved from one job to another trying to better his position as well as live a spiritual life. He suffered great unhappiness after a bitter divorce. His spirituality grew steadily and he became an exceptional clairvoyant, healer and trance medium.

His second wife taught him to read, patiently showing him the process of formulating words into a coherent story. She introduced him to the world of fantasy novels; this transformed his life, allowing him to escape reality for a while.

After a lifetime of hard work he became a skilled natural therapist, counsellor and clinical hypnotherapist, specialising in painless childbirth. When his second marriage ended, Carl followed the directions of his mentor and guide Big Eagle who inspired him to travel to Canada to live with the First Nations American Indians for a time. The shaman of the tribe recognised a fellow shaman and trained Carl in the running of ceremonial sweat lodges.

Returning from Canada he worked hard at rebuilding his life, but struggled to survive as well as support his son from his second marriage. He was always searching in his mind for the answers to life's questions. Why life? Why are we here?

Big Eagle encouraged him to travel once more, this time to Spain, where he walked the legendary Camino trail.

With the help of a spirit animal guide called Mother Wolf, along with some highly enlightened beings, he worked through the pain and torment of his life to become a teacher of the greater path. On his return from Spain he took on the role of carer for his mother and eleven years later, at the age of ninety-five, she passed into spirit.

At age sixty-seven Carl happily lives a solitary life in the hills surrounded by nature and genuine friends. His son has grown into a beautiful man and they are the best of mates.

He still occasionally conducts ceremonial sweat lodges for his friends where he imparts knowledge of the greater path. Carl has travelled extensively throughout the spiritual realms with his guide Big Eagle acquiring philosophy and wisdom. The adventures they shared and the situations they found themselves facing have seemed unbelievable. Encouraged by his friends to share his exploits he has shaped his experiences into stories that he hopes will encourage people to walk a more balanced existence upon the good red road of life.